THE KING'S FAVORITE

BOOK 1 DAUGHTERS OF AVALON

TANYA ANNE CROSBY

OLIVER HEBER BOOKS

All rights reserved.

No part of this publication may be sold, copied, distributed, reproduced or transmitted in any form or by any means, mechanical or digital, including photocopying and recording or by any information storage and retrieval system without the prior written permission of both the publisher, Oliver Heber Books and the author, Tanya Anne Crosby, except in the case of brief quotations embodied in critical articles and reviews.

This eBook may not be re-sold or given away to other people. If you would like to share this book with another person, please purchase an additional copy for each recipient. If you're reading this book and did not purchase it or borrow it, or it was not purchased for your use only, then please return it and purchase your own copy. Thank you for respecting the hard work of the author.

PUBLISHER'S NOTE: This is a work of fiction. Names, characters, places, and incidents either are the product of the author's imagination or are used fictitiously. Any resemblance to actual persons, living or dead, business establishments, events, or locales is entirely coincidental.

Published by Oliver-Heber Books

The King's Favorite Copyright © 2018 Tanya Anne Crosby

Cover art Gene Mollica Studios

0 9 8 7 6 5 4 3 2 1

❦ Created with Vellum

SERIES BIBLIOGRAPHY
A BRAND-NEW SERIES

DAUGHTERS OF AVALON

The King's Favorite

The Holly & the Ivy

A Winter's Rose

Fire Song

Rhiannon

PRAISE FOR TANYA ANNE CROSBY

"Crosby's characters keep readers engaged..."

— Publishers Weekly

"Tanya Anne Crosby sets out to show us a good time and accomplishes that with humor, a fast-paced story and just the right amount of romance."

— The Oakland Press

"Romance filled with charm, passion and intrigue..."

— Affaire de Coeur

"Ms. Crosby mixes just the right amount of humor... Fantastic, tantalizing!"

— Rendezvous

"Tanya Anne Crosby pens a tale that touches your soul and lives forever in your heart."

— SHERRILYN KENYON #1 NYT BESTSELLING AUTHOR

MAP OF MEDIEVAL ENGLAND & WALES

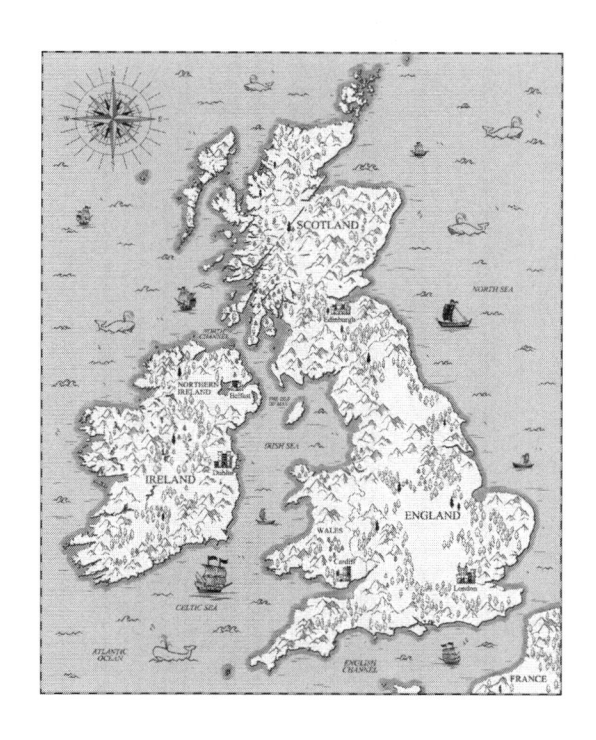

"Watch with glittering eyes the whole world around you... the greatest secrets are always hidden in the most unlikely places. Those who don't believe in magic will never find it."

— Roald Dahl

PROLOGUE

ALDERGH CASTLE, NORTHERN ENGLAND 1137

Two long years Malcom had prepared for this day, all the while kings and queens battled over a dimpled crown. Henry of England was two-years dead, leaving his Empress daughter to succeed him and even as the breath left the old king's body, those who would not follow a woman had turned their eyes toward Stephen of Blois. Now, Britain was at war—brother against brother, brother against sister, cousin against cousin. But, at long last, Aldergh was his, little thanks to the Scots King—little thanks to anyone, save his lady mother and the sweat from his own brow.

He'd learned the hard way how fickle kings could be. Shortly upon hearing the news of Stephen's usurpation, David of Scotia had swept down into the border lands, laying claim to all he could seize, promising Aldergh to Malcom, only to rescind that promise. Face to face with Stephen, the Scot's king returned much of what he'd taken in a treatise at Durham, keeping Carlisle and Newcastle for himself and relinquishing Aldergh to Stephen, thereby forcing Malcom to bend the knee to England for the return of his lands. And so he had, much to his father's dismay.

At long last, he had the legal right to call himself Aldergh's lord. Come what may, he was prepared to fight for what should be his. He might not be flesh and blood to Fitz-Simon, but his step-mother was the dead lord's only living heir and Malcom was her son by law.

Besides, if he didn't accept her behest, these lands would return to the English crown, unclaimed, and there was no one else to hold them in her father's name—never a woman, obvious by the way the barons received Matilda, and certainly not her Scots husband, the infamous chieftain of a Highland clan. He sidled his mount closer to his mother, giving her a glance, acutely aware of the elder man at her side, and settled his gaze on the prize.

A ghost from his past looming large, Aldergh appeared much as he recalled it—a sprawling monstrosity, with soaring corner towers and a twenty-foot thick curtain wall, built with old Roman ingenuity and stone. Sizable enough to house an entire village, it was designed to withstand a siege, but the castellan was no lord trained in the art of war. With a bit of luck, the man would yield the castel without a fight. Up on the ramparts, armed men scurried between machicolations, the silver in their armor winking defiantly. But, of course, that was to be expected with an army at the gates.

Eager to prove himself as a worthy commander, Malcom dispatched his messenger, handing the man a copy of the writ from Stephen, and then he himself rode to the front of the line, hoisting the flag with the dead-lord's sigil—a two-headed falcon on a blood-red field, with one minor alteration: a silver-threaded thistle in one of the falcon's beaks. It was a nod to his Scot's brethren, and yet, absent, by design, were the colors of his father's clan, the intent being, to send a clear message—that Malcom Ceann Ràs had not arrived here this day as a warden from the north, wearing his father's cloak, but as the new and rightful lord of Aldergh, unfettered by obligations to his kin. He was ready, willing and able to serve a new sovereign... if that's what it took to keep his lands.

Careful to remain outside missile range, but moving close enough to read banners, he anticipated the castellan's response, waiting until the suspense grew thick enough to cut with a blade. If tensions turned to hostilities, his father would rush his mother from the field. But so long as there was a chance for a peaceful transition, she'd insisted upon remaining.

Never daring a glance at his father, he thrust the standard higher, watching as the messenger spoke to the ramparts, tossing the weighted parchment over the wall.

The gates did not open at once, but neither did they fire upon the man, and after what seemed an eternity, the messenger turned and trotted back.

Even before he returned to the fold, a single, warbling horn-blast trumpeted across the landscape and the heavy portcullis began to rise, straining against ancient chains and groaning like a tired old man. The hairs on Malcom's nape stood on end as the moment of truth arrived.

Now, at long last, he cast a glance toward his brooding father... *hoping for what?*

Seated atop his warhorse, Iain MacKinnon cut a daunting figure, even at his advanced age. The silver in his hair glinted more fiercely than did the steel in his scabbard, and his displeasure was evident in the set of his shoulders and the lock of his jaw, but he said not a word as his wife proceeded to tug her father's signet ring from her finger. Once removed, she placed the heirloom into the palm of her hand, offering it up for Malcom to take—and this was the one concession she'd made to his father: that Malcom must knowingly and wittingly accept all that came with her father's legacy. "Put it on your small finger, Malcom. And remember... what happens from the moment you ride through those gates determines how they will receive you. You are Aldergh's new lord now."

Beside her, his father averted his gaze, his jaw clenching with barely suppressed fury. If it were up to him, he would have tossed FitzSimon's ring into a bog as readily as he had embraced his Sassenach bride. Time and again, he had beseeched Malcom to stay and bide his time. But Malcom had refused, soured by the prospect of waiting for his father to die before beginning a new life. Far better to take what was offered now and pray his old man lived to raise more sons. But his father did not see the world through Malcom's eyes, and while he lent his sword to this cause—for his wife —he would not lend his heart.

So be it.

Resolved, Malcom plucked up the sigil ring from his step-mother's palm and slid the golden two-headed falcon onto his small finger, then hesitated but a moment, thinking about the last time he and his father had stood here together... on this field before FitzSimon's castel... thirteen years ago... a boy of six, unashamed to weep in his father's arms.

His mother must have misunderstood his hesitation because she said, "You have the writ from King Stephen and my father's ring. It will be enough."

The gates were open now... waiting... still he lingered. In truth, the best of all scenarios had occurred, and still, somehow, inexplicably, he felt a surge of loss in his heart.

Had he hoped to fight today, if only to prove himself?

Had he wanted his father to say, 'Good show, son'?

Perhaps, after all, he had but longed for a clap on the back, and a bit of reassurance that all was not lost?

By God, he was old enough to choose his own path. He didn't need his father's approval, and so it seemed he wasn't going to get it...

"Art certain, mother? he asked—one last time. If she had a mind to, now would be the time to change her mind. Once he took possession of Aldergh, nothing would be the same.

"You *are* my son," she reassured, mistaking his question.

With a steel glint in his eyes, his father said, "Let us be done."

Malcom straightened his spine, raising his banner. "Aye," he said. "Let us be done." And then, without a word, he spurred his mount forward, hardening his heart.

Dressed in his grandfather's cloak, and wearing a dead man's sigil, he surged ahead of the troops, looking like a king in his own right and carrying with him all the fury of the north.

1

LLANTHONY PRIORY, WALES, JULY 1148

Elspeth reread her mother's letter, her breath catching painfully.

So, it seemed, for abetting a usurper, the prize should be an Earldom and King Henry's favorite daughter... *Elspeth*.

"Married," her sisters said in unison.

Elspeth nodded affirmation. "Married." To the new lord of Blackwood. In her boundless greed, their mother had betrayed their grandmother, and in the process, forsook their rights to Blackwood. And for his prowess in battle, that legendary fortress now belonged to an assassin. The estate would return to their family by virtue of marriage, but though the marriage would grant Elspeth the title of lady, it was still her mother d'Lucy was bound to.

Sacred cauldron! It wasn't enough that Morwen forsook them all these years past. Offered the chance to profit from her daughters, she meant to take it—and make no mistake, while she'd called it a wedding, Elspeth knew very well that she would be naught more than a prisoner changing hands from one gaoler to another.

How sorely she missed the ivy-tangled courtyard and the

view of the sea from Blackwood's tower window, but as much as she relished the notion of returning to the home she'd shared with her grandmamau, she could never bear the thought of lying beneath a vassal of the Usurper. The thought made her feel wretched and filthy.

"Lady of Blackwood," said Arwyn with a note of wonder. "What I wouldn't give to see our ancestral home, if only but once."

Rhiannon's amber eyes glinted by the firelight as she turned to address the eldest twin. "And would you put our sister at the mercy of an assassin only to appease your curiosity?"

"Of course not," said Arwyn, defensively. "I was but saying—"

"I know what you were saying," Rhiannon snapped. "Elspeth needs no more reason to accept this unholy alliance. I, too, would love to see Blackwood, but I will never step foot there if it means forsaking my flesh and blood."

"Sisters, please! Let us not fight," Seren pleaded. "We all knew this time would come. We must steel our hearts and minds."

At twenty, Seren was the peacemaker. She was the middle child, possessed of their father's rufous coloring, but with skin so pale and smooth it made the moon and stars weep with joy.

At Nineteen, Rosalynde was the youngest of the living twins, only minutes younger than Arwyn.

Rhiannon was the second eldest, only two years younger than Elspeth. Her amber eyes narrowed. "The granddaughter of a witch is still a witch, *even* if she has no knowledge of the Craft. Have you forgotten what they do to witches, Seren? Would you truly wish Elspeth in the hands of a man such as that?"

As always, Rose defended Arwyn and Seren. "There's no reason for anyone to believe we are aught but good little servants of the realm. For all anyone knows, the *sins* of Avalon have passed away with our Grandmamau. Why would anyone accuse Elspeth?"

"Sins of Avalon?" Rhiannon asked, incensed. "Do not speak such rubbish to me again! And do you truly believe they do not suspect Morwen?"

"That is my point, precisely," argued Seren. "Mother seems to have weathered suspicion well enough." Elspeth understood that she was only trying to make the inevitable more palatable. "Elspeth," she entreated, "For all we know, d'Lucy could be a gentle man. But you might never know it lest you give him a chance."

"He's an assassin, Seren!" Rhiannon exploded. "How gentle a man could he possibly be? You needn't suffer this fate," Rhiannon pleaded with Elspeth. "You can still leave. *Tonight.* We have the means and know the words."

Understanding intuitively what Rhiannon was saying, the sisters all exchanged nervous glances, then peered at the door.

Tonight, as always, the guards had been called to vespers, but as soon as prayers were over, they would return, and in this day and age, when so many feared the Old Ways, the Craft must remain a closely guarded secret. Even the act of referring to sorcery put them all at risk.

Elspeth shook her head, refusing to consider it.

It wasn't the first time Rhiannon had proposed such a plan. Last time, she'd tried to get them all to leave together, but words or nay, it wasn't likely all five sisters together would ever succeed in slipping past the guards. And even should they manage to escape, with no one left to delay them, it wouldn't be long before their presence was missed, and they wouldn't get very far. Therefore, Rose had steadfastly refused, deathly afraid of what the chaplain would do to them if they were caught.

However, far more of a deterrent to Elspeth, was this: The "words" Rhiannon spoke of were rites of *magik,* never to be uttered lightly. While she would like to believe they could evoke them without consequence, it simply wasn't true. Here, in the dominion of men, there was no leave to change the will of gods without altering the warp and woof of life. There could be no denying the Law of Three—which was to say, that any *magik,* good or bad, once unleashed into the world must return to the summoner threefold. And nevertheless, she deliberated, flicking a thumbnail across the frayed edge of the parchment, wishing things could be different.

If only Matilda could win herself the throne...

"Why should we care who wears father's crown? It will *never* be Matilda." Rhiannon said, clearly intruding on Elspeth's thoughts. "You are too beguiled by our father and his *politiks*. Say what you will about Morwen. At least she knows who she is."

"*I* know who we are," countered Elspeth.

Rhiannon lifted her chin. "*I* know who we are as well, Elspeth. We are Daughters of Avalon, and if we but join together, we can do what no other woman can do—including Matilda, for all our *sister's* bold, brave words. In truth, she has never given any of us a passing thought—not even you, despite that you seem to enjoy defending her."

Elspeth overlooked Rhiannon's bitter tone, realizing that her sister had just cause to feel aggrieved. "She's had her hands full trying to unseat a usurper," Elspeth reminded. "What wouldst you have an Empress do? Come have tea in our little hovel?"

Rhiannon said, "Why not? At least then she wouldst know how we live. She never acknowledged me, perhaps, but she knew you well enough. It would seem to me that if she cared at all, she would wish to see how you fared."

Elspeth sighed, wearied by that particular discussion. It wasn't always so easy to defend Matilda, because it was true: Matilda had only once ever bothered to come to Llanthony, and even then, she'd never bothered to see her sisters. She'd come to remind Ersinius of his oath to support her. But, of course, that was fruitless. As had so many who'd knelt before Matilda whilst Henry still lived, Llanthony's illustrious chaplain, like most of Stephen's barons, would never abide a woman on England's throne.

"Elspeth? Please... you *must* trust me. I have a plan."

"What plan?"

"Trust me," Rhiannon said, her eyes revealing her desperation as the first rays of twilight crept in through their window.

The Golden Hour was swiftly approaching—that hour between times, when the veil between worlds was at its thinnest and the *hud* was at its strongest.

Elspeth said, her eyes glinting with unshed tears, "I do trust you, Rhiannon, but what you propose may have consequences beyond our imagining. Remember the White Ship?"

"Precisely," Rhiannon argued. "And for that meddling, what price has Morwen paid? If you ask me, she has profited greatly, and to this day, I have never once seen any evidence that our mother suffered a single day."

Elspeth held her composure. "We know not what price she'll pay, but I cannot be made responsible for the burden this could heap upon your shoulders. You are my sisters," she said. "I love you dearly. Can you not understand? I would never forgive myself if aught should happen to any of you because of me. Let us say no more. I'll wed that man, come what may."

Silence met her declaration, and no one spoke another word. The weight of her decision sat like an anvil on each of their breasts, pressing the life and breath from their lungs. And nevertheless, to wed this man seemed Elspeth's only legitimate choice.

Fat tears shone in Rhiannon's eyes. "I cannot bear it," she said. "Come tomorrow evening, you would trade yourself like an old goat and a sack of meal."

"Nor I, in truth," admitted Elspeth, and she rolled up the parchment and rose from her chair, leaving her sisters to stare helplessly at one another, while she tried to salvage her composure. She made her way to the window, tears spilling into her lashes. For these past thirteen years they'd been trapped in this godforsaken priory, waiting and waiting... *but for what?*

For this?

Sweet Goddess, nay...

She peered out the window, searching for the guards, some little part of her perhaps still considering Rhiannon's plan, reckless as it might be.

Despite the tumult in her heart, the evening seemed perfectly tranquil, with a blushing sky that brushed the rooftops with warm vestal light. Their crude little cottage lay at the back of the priory on the highest point of the hill, like a tower prison without a tower. And nevertheless, from this vantage, Elspeth could spy the entire vale of Ewyas.

At this hour, the west-facing windows on the chapel glinted unevenly against a well-spent sun. The rare and expensive forest glass was smashed three *sennights* past—a keen reminder that so long as the Welsh had breath to resist, so they would.

Mayhap her sisters could not remember, but Elspeth could never forget: This land was once hallowed land—not blessed by the dictums of the Holy Church or the men who sought to profit through her favor, but by the spirit of the Welsh, and the divinity of the land itself.

It was changing now... more every day, but it still bore a trace of that wild, untamed country, where *faeries* whispered through swaying branches, and the wind blew sweet over mortal's brows. The chapel of their hearts had been constructed of arches, but unlike those forged by men and scarred by chisels, these were built by the Goddess herself, whose loving hands had bowed the ancient heads of trees to create a magical place beneath.

Now, like a cancer, the priory had grown and grown, stretching like a greedy lover in the middle of a verdant bed, unfurling farther and farther into Welsh territory. What had begun as little more than a prison to hold the king's "witchy daughters," had become a strategic center of power for the Usurper. Llanthony was now the richest, most well-endowed priory in all of Britain, completely self-sufficient, despite its remoteness. There was even a new hatchery and once a week, wrapped in damp rushes, fresh fish were brought all the way from Llangorse. Likewise, from the newly consecrated Abbey Dore, came huge casks of ale. Ten years ago, at her mother's direction, they'd built an aviary unlike any that graced the king's land, filled with pigeons and white-necked ravens that could speak the king's tongue. Both birds were bred for correspondence. But, unlike the messenger pigeons, which naturally returned to where they were born, the ravens were drawn to only one place—wherever Morwen should be, making her indispensable to her king.

Alas, for all that these monks were "servants of God," they were naught but conspirators with her mother and so long as Elspeth lived, she would never, never abet them... and yet, here she was... about to wed a man her mother ordained.

The light in the cottage grew fragile now, as dust motes danced in the sun's fading rays. The golden hour was here. If, in truth, Elspeth meant to change her mind, she must do so *now*. Once the sun had set, it would be too late...

Rhiannon must have sensed her wavering. "Elspeth, please... you *must* go."

"I cannot, Rhiannon. I have sworn to protect you."

Rhiannon pressed her. "And how will you do such a thing after you have gone? One way or another, you *will* go. Only think better of it, please! If you do not leave tonight, you *will* be forced to leave on the morrow. And how will you help us then?"

It was true. One way or another—with or without her sisters—Elspeth would be forced to leave the priory... and still she hesitated. Even *white magik* could be treacherous, though only their mother had ever dabbled in the *hud du* —*black magic* as the English were wont to call it.

Before she was born Morwen had conjured a mist like the one Rhiannon would have them summon tonight. It lured the White Ship over the rocks, sinking the fated vessel, and carrying their father's only legitimate male heir to the cold, black depths of the sea. That single conjuring changed the fate of nations and claimed two hundred and fifty innocent lives. So, then, it was not the intent that dictated consequences. Rather, it was the nature of the harm inflicted. And there was no way to foresee such a thing.

Black *hud* or white, there was a price to be paid. Finally, Rhiannon offered the only argument that could possibly sway her. "A man such as d'Lucy might use your skills against Matilda—or worse..."

All five sisters understood instinctively what the worst might be: If he were a godly man, like Ersinius, he could beat Elspeth until she bled. As her lawful husband, no one would have any right to stop him—not even Morwen. He could call her a witch and pythoness and mistreat her for what he did not understand... or... he could put her to the pyre, like they did to their grandmother. But, if she left...

"If I go," Elspeth said, reasoning, "he will simply wed the next of you. Tis not as though he bears me any love."

"Aye, but let's speak true, Elspeth. I am next. He would never have me," argued Rhiannon, and her sisters' gazes all turned in her direction, looking abashed. "Well," she said with perfect conviction, turning up a hand in resignation. "Tis true. He would never wed an afflicted daughter with a disagreeable temper." She lifted the hand up, silencing them, when they opened their mouths to console her. "Regardless, Morwen is greedy. She would never allow him or anyone else to take Seren—her prized jewel—whilst I remain unwed. Therefore, it buys us time."

It was true. If Morwen didn't insist upon Rhiannon being next, all hope of profiting from her second eldest would be lost. And, unless he were forced to, Stephen would never saddle any of his barons with a cross-eyed *Welsh* witch —more's the pity, because Rhiannon was as inherently lovely as she was loyal—even if she did tend to make men cross themselves at a glance.

Sounding more hopeful now, Arwyn added, "'Tis true, Elspeth... Morwen will be steadfast... how many times has she said her daughters must each wed according to their turn. I do not believe Stephen will test her. Remember, when his wife insisted Morwen be removed from their apartments? He would not even remove mother to satisfy his lady—and that woman scares me more than mother."

The sisters all laughed nervously, but it wasn't precisely true. No one was more frightening than Morwen. And still, the king's wife was no wilting flower. They'd only chanced to meet her on a single occasion, when Morwen first settled into her quarters in the White Tower, and the girls were summoned to meet Henry's successor. As petite as the queen might be, she was like a mastiff. She'd marched into Morwen's quarters and told their vicious mother in no uncertain terms to be discreet, lest she defy her lord king and feed Morwen's eyeballs to her precious ravens.

Elspeth contemplated out loud. "So, then... if I leave? What then? Eventually, Stephen will tire of waiting and he'll endeavor to convince Morwen to offer Seren. But regardless of who is next, if I leave tonight, it only buys you time."

Sensing victory, Rhiannon's smile unfurled. "Oh, dear sister, you of all must realize there is so much a witch can do given a little time."

Elspeth blinked, enthralled by the twinkle in her sister's gold-flecked eyes. And then suddenly, as though everyone were singing the same chorus, Arwyn said, thinking aloud, "Tomorrow is the day they bring ale from Abbey Dore."

"There will be comings and goings," agreed Seren. "We could say Elspeth remained abed with some malaise. Nobody would be any wiser until the envoy arrives."

"She'll need a disguise," said Rose. "I have one."

The sisters all turned toward their youngest sibling in surprise.

"If, indeed, I cannot dissuade you, I would give you the tunic and breeches I use on occasion to steal into the woods and look for herbs—and before you lecture me," she added defiantly, "remember that had I not done so, we'd not have the mugwort we need for tonight."

Rhiannon's smile widened. She swept a hand before them. "You see," she said. "The Goddess has preordained this." She turned again to Elspeth. "I do have a plan, Elspeth. And if you leave tonight," she promised, "we'll soon follow."

Elspeth bit at her lip, pressing the tender skin between her teeth with a trembling finger. "Art certain?"

Rhiannon nodded enthusiastically, and Elspeth considered the logistics a bit more soberly. If she left tonight, she would have naught but the clothes on her back—or rather, whatever clothes Rose had stolen from the guards. They had no money, and unless she pilfered something from the chapel, she would have naught to trade, not even for food or a horse for travel.

And yet, she did not have the blood of cowards in her veins, nor was she without her wiles. She knew well enough how to forage for food, and she knew how to make her way using the talents her grandmamau taught her. "Very well, then," Elspeth relented. "I'll go."

Rhiannon clapped.

"'Tis settled," Seren said, suddenly excited, bouncing up from her chair to meet Elspeth halfway across the room. She took Elspeth by the shoulders, and said gently, "If Rhiannon says there's a will and way, there's a will and way." And then, smiling, she hugged Elspeth and moved past her toward the bed, digging beneath the mattress for the herb pouch she'd hidden there.

Knowing their time was short, the rest of her sisters all rose from their chairs to gather around the hearth. Elspeth moved to bar the door, swallowing the lump of fear that rose to choke her. And once the door was barred and the shutters closed against prying eyes, she joined her sisters by the cauldron, knowing intuitively what they were about to do.

The cauldron in their hearth was not unlike the ancestral cauldron in the quadrangle at Blackwood, only that one was large and black, licked by a hundred thousand smoky tongues. This one was small and squat and smelled like cabbage stew.

Unlacing the small pouch that contained the necessary herbs, Seren placed two fingers inside to remove a pinch, then tossed the mixture into the cauldron. Her words were breathy and low, as she sang, "Our song arises from the cauldron, unrestrained be our tongues."

Rhiannon stepped forward to pass a hand over the bubbling water, and then plucked a strand of her own dark hair, tossing it into the pot. Then, one by one, each sister offered a benign sacrifice of her person—a strand of hair, a bitten fingernail, an eyelash, plucked.

Beneath the cauldron's black belly, the fire quivered, then leapt, reborn. Flames in the shapes of fiery hands moved to cradle the pot in much the same way a woman might stroke a pregnant belly. And then, after each of the sisters had given of her essence, they joined hands, and Elspeth said with a lump in her throat, "Mother Goddess hear us calling..."

"We are your daughters," continued Rhiannon.

And Seren added, "Wherever we may roam."

"Sister Moon hear us calling," said Arwyn.

And the youngest rejoined, if only reluctantly, with tears brimming in her wide blue eyes. "In your light we are never alone..."

Outside, the last ray of sunlight stretched thin, quivering

as though the incantation had forced it to linger against its will.

Altogether the sisters whispered low, "Breath of life, powers lend. We hail the sky your mist to send. By all on high and law of three, it is my will, so may it be."

In answer, a thin, cold mist crept out from the cauldron, sliding down the dull black belly and spilling onto the dirt floor. Slowly, it coalesced about the sisters' feet, and then after swallowing the dirt floor of the hovel, it crept out beneath the door...

2

THE BLACK MOUNTAINS, WALES

Neither king nor church held sway in such a time-forgotten place. It was a country unfurling with mists, overgrown with brambles and painted in copious shades of green.

Malcom Scott, first of his name, Earl of Aldergh, vassal to Stephen of Blois, made his way past wizened old yews with twisted, broken backs and white-skinned aspens that shivered as he passed—and perhaps it was the sight of him that made them tremble, for at thirty, Malcom bore the scars of too many battles. His hair, like his sire's, was heavily brushed with silver, and his shoulders, once lean with youth, were wide enough to bear the weight of worlds.

By now, he had managed to betray both kith and kin—and for what? An ill-begotten piece of land in the hinterlands of England? Thirteen years ago, he slew his own kinsman, and what he'd won for this effort was a castel in the border lands and a rising silence from the north that left him cold by night and longing for simpler days. Scowling over a memory of that day so long past—in woodlands distinctly different from these—he peered down at the sigil on his finger, given to him by his mother, the daughter of Aldergh's first lord.

Altium, citius, fortius.

It was Malcolm's maxim now.

Swifter, higher, stronger.

And this he was: swifter than his sire, taller and stronger. But as for the noble dictum his maxim proclaimed, Malcolm feared he was more the spirit of his grandsire, for in the name of avarice—what else could it be?—he'd committed grievous sins.

Alas, though, if his mother regretted the bestowal, Malcolm couldn't say. He'd not spoken to either of his parents in more than ten years and he had a ten-year-old brother that, to this day, he'd never laid eyes upon. But at least his father had an heir. However, having received word of the MacKinnon's failing health, neither king, nor duty could prevent him from traveling north.

Cursing softly beneath his breath, he made his way through brambles, wincing as thorns pricked at his back. At one point, the mist grew so thick he was forced to dismount, and taking the lead rope, he guided Merry Bells, testing every step before the horse. Even then, like bent auld hags with claws for fists, the brambles tore at his *sherte* and picked at his *coif*. He'd left the headgear on, as much to protect him from the thorns as he had from Welshmen's arrows.

Behind him, the horse snorted in protest as a branch snapped backward after catching his *sherte*, and he frowned. By damn, once they were done here, they would be a sore sight for his armorer, who scarce had time to mend his accouterments before Stephen called him back to war. This time the man had his work cut out for him because Malcolm took an arrow to the shoulder and there was a gaping hole in his armor where the arrowhead had pierced him. The damage to his flesh was minimal, and fortunately, he'd managed not to succumb to a fever, but at some point, it would behoove him to stop and tend to the wound. He counted it his good fortune that these Welshmen had but intended to frighten them. Otherwise, his body would be rotting at the bottom of a ravine by now. Certainly Daw would never have made it ten steps in his flight and he cursed yet again over the loss of his squire. That lad took to his heels the instant the Welsh fell from the trees and Malcom was pretty certain he'd seen the last of his squire—a young man he'd trained for nigh on two years. Sure, he'd rather Daw be gone and still breathing than dead, but it troubled him how fickle these soldiers had become over the course of Stephen's reign. There was hardly any consequence for waffling when Stephen rewarded his own cousins for treason.

He rolled his eyes over that nonsense. Last year, at the tender age of fourteen, whilst his mother was working her own manner of treason, Henry Fitz Empress had launched himself a coup, waging a petty war that, in the end cost Stephen plenty—not the least of which was his credibility. The Empress's upstart landed at Wiltshire with an expensive army, meant to put Stephen off the throne, and then, once the battle was lost, Stephen paid the lad's debts and sent him home to his mama, with but a slap on the wrist, little more.

Considering that, why shouldn't Daw run? And thank God for Malcom that he hadn't needed the lad. Never in his life had he witnessed men so skilled with bows. These Welsh were masters at melding with their environs, suspending themselves from trees, and leaping down like spiders from webs. As he made his way through the woods in this pea-soup fog, he was painfully aware of the fact that it would be impossible to ascertain whether someone was hovering overhead. Even now, he could have longbows trained at his head...

"We'll be east-side afore ye know it," he assured Merry Bells, and hoped to God he wasn't about to lose another horse. *Bloody hell.* He'd named her Merry Bells in honor of a good friend's dog—God love the sweet beast. She'd served her master well and Malcom should be so fortunate if his mare had an ounce of Merry Bells' canny and devotion.

Alas, his first Merry Bells didn't live up to the name. She'd been a temperamental animal who'd unseated him during the battle of the Standard. She nearly broke his neck. Unfortunately, she'd died there as well, and so did Malcom's heart, for that was the first time he'd been forced to choose between his Scots' brethren and the oath he gave to Stephen. For his services, of course, Stephen lifted him to Earldom, but that was also the last time he'd spoken to his sire. To this day, he would never forget facing his Da across the field at Cowton Moor and the disappointment and fury in his eyes as Malcom felled a man wearing Scot's livery. It didn't matter that they didn't trade blows that day; it was enough that Malcom had opposed him, and he never saw him again.

The second Merry Bells had given Malcom more hope, but she, too, met her fate on a field of battle, only rather than die as her predecessor died, in the midst of warfare, she'd broken her leg on a patch of ice during a winter siege. With his heart in his hand, Malcom himself took her life, putting the sweet girl out of her misery, but it haunted him still that Stephen's men had butchered her for dinner and gobbled her to her bones. One thing he'd learned; in the midst of a long, hard siege, men themselves became little more than beasts.

This particular Merry Bells seemed more attuned to him, but she was young as yet, and betimes too skittish. The last time he gave her shoes, he'd performed the task himself, and she nearly clipped a slice from his head. Now, again, she snorted in protest over a nasty bramble and Malcom spoke to her gently. "Bear with it, lass. We'll be free of this wet, black hole afore ye ken."

Thankfully, once they emerged from these spiteful woods, they would immediately descend into England and make their way north through far more civilized country. In the meantime, the hairs on his nape stood on end, and he felt eyes on his back...

WHAT HOUR WAS IT? Had the envoy arrived? Elspeth had a growing sense that any minute now they would come searching for her.

Come sunrise, she'd climbed into this tree to find a safe place to rest and, somehow, she'd fallen asleep in the crook of the elm. Here she sat now, with too little distance between herself and the priory and a pang in her heart that wouldn't diminish. She missed her sisters terribly, and with every ten steps she took, she took two more back, growing confused and enervated. Of course, she blamed it on the long night traipsing about these woods, but she supposed it must also be a consequence of that aether spell. But she couldn't remain here. The veil they'd conjured would soon fade, and no doubt by now Ersinius had loosed his minions.

It was her greatest hope that, whilst she sought herself a safe haven to await her sisters, d'Lucy would find himself another match—preferably one not of her blood. And, in the meantime, she hoped Rhiannon would find a way to extricate herself and the rest of her sisters from the priory, although she hadn't a clue how Rhiannon intended to do it.

I have a plan, she'd said. But what if she was wrong? What if Morwen did, indeed, allow Seren to wed out of turn? What if all this came to naught? What if d'Lucy decided that marrying Rhiannon was worth the price of his Earldom?

More and more, Elspeth was beginning to doubt the wisdom in leaving, and considering these things, and more, she longed to close her eyes and sleep—even now, perched in this tree like one of Morwen's eerie little birds. Holding tight to the branch overhead, she battled her way through the drowsiness, considering Rose's thievery. How was it that her sister could feel so self-assured to hunt these woods without permission, yet so adamantly refuse to leave the priory? She would risk Ersinius' wrath for berries, but not for freedom? How much sense did that make?

And nevertheless, Elspeth was grateful for her disguise despite that the breeches were too snug. Unlike her crude gown, it provided much more freedom to move and climb about, and most importantly, it kept her legs snug and warm in this bone-dampening weather.

Sweet fates. Wasn't it July already? It felt like December! Shivering from the cold, she squinted to peer through the mist and considered scrambling down to get on her way, but then, suddenly, she sensed she was not alone... She *felt* the presence before she saw him, and braced herself for the worst, trying to gauge how many were coming in her direction. *One? Two?*

Stay with me," she begged the fog, inching down to spy between branches.

Presently she saw a dark figure lumbering through the

woods and her heart leapt at the sight. Only after an instant she could better see that it was a big black horse being led by a man—a tall, strapping man, wearing a Norman-styled hauberk and coif, with leggings and boots as inky black as his horse. Unfortunately, Elspeth slipped from her perch, pinching her fingers on the bark, and whispered an oath. The man must have heard her, because he froze. Panicking, Elspeth whispered a spell she knew by rote:

> Spirit of vision, Spirit of night. Cast me a
> shadow to shield me from mortal sight.

But it didn't work. He was still searching, unfazed by her feeble spell. But, of course, no spell could ever make her disappear. It merely dimmed her presence to the sight and sense of others. But it wasn't working. She was out of practice. Or she must have gotten something wrong.

What to do now?
Take an example from Rose; steal his horse
Yes, of course!

The voice in her head was Rhiannon's and Elspeth smiled, grateful not to be alone—at least, not yet. Fortunately for her—unfortunately for the man—she'd never met a beast who didn't adore her. That man's horse should be little different. She concentrated, bidding the animal nearer, recognizing the instant she connected with the beast, because the beautiful mare shimmied inside her skin, like a cat with pleasure over the stroke of a hand. And then, naturally, she sought Elspeth's gaze. "That's it, sweet girl," Elspeth whispered. "Come closer..."

She wiggled a finger at the mare.

3

"Who's there?"

Malcom clutched Merry Bells' reins, ready to mount, but hesitated. The last thing he wished was for the horse to break a leg in this foul weather. Not only would it pain him to put the girl down, but it was a long, long walk back to Aldergh. But neither was he in any mood to spend a minute longer than was necessary in this ill-begotten territory.

"Who's there?" he asked again, acknowledging the absurdity of his question. If, indeed, he had arrows trained on his head, he was unlikely to know it until he became a pin pillow.

"Come closer."

Soft and whispery, the voice slid through him, like a summer breeze shimmying through birch leaves... but it was strange. It sounded far away, and yet still close, like the memory of a whisper breathed at his ear. Was somebody speaking to him?

Searching the woodlands, like Merry, he scrutinized the environs, peering this way and that, but still he spied no one. But rather than press closer to him, as was her usual response to danger, Merry Bells shifted away, twitching her black ears and lifting her head to peer into a canopy of green.

"What is it, lass?" Malcom asked, following her gaze—and caught sight of a figure swooping down from the trees, a boy, intent on landing in his saddle.

With every nerve in his body prepared for battle, Malcom reacted swiftly, taking the youth by the scruff of the tunic as he landed astride his saddle, then jerking him down, and launching himself into the saddle after him. It was a fluid maneuver, perhaps one to be expected from a man with expertise in mounting on the run, but betimes Malcom underestimated his own strength.

The boy landed face up in the bracken, and then he lay there, stunned, peering up at Malcom with dazed violet eyes. Malcom furrowed his brow.

"Ye dinna believe ye'd get awa' wi' such a thing, di' ye?"

The would-be thief—a skinny, lanky boy—placed a hand to the back of his head, wincing, as he said without remorse, "Nay, but it was worth a try." And then he sat up and groaned, loudly as he freed a ratty knot at the back of his head, and, in the process, released a rich cascade of red-gold curls. The sight of those tresses startled Malcom, so he forgot his ire, and even his question.

It wasn't a boy.

"What in damnation are you doing here, lass?"

The girl's voice was curt. "Must I remind you, sir, that you put me down in the weeds." And then she rose, brushing bits of leaves and twigs from her clothes.

Blinking in disbelief, Malcom watched her with a growing sense of wonder as she peered up at him with almond shaped eyes, completely unafraid, and perhaps even daring him to defy her.

He wondered if she could be Welsh—a scout perhaps? He wouldn't put it past those bastards to employ women in such a fashion. But her clothes were not those of a Welsh dissenter, which was to say, they were not battle-weary rags. As much as his own kinsmen had once been, these people were greatly oppressed. But rather, she was dressed in a courtly fashion, with well-stitched leather breaches and a tunic that bore the standard of the Holy Church—a red cross extending across the entirety of her tunic, with four small, identical crosses beneath each arm of the crucifix. He scratched the back of his head. Fortunately for his sense of modesty, the tunic was overlarge, covering her long, lean legs, else he would have found himself stupid and tongue-tied as well. So then, she must have come from Llanthony. Or perhaps from Abbey Dore and lost her way.

"You may shut your gob now," the girl said. "The look doesn't suit you."

Malcom snapped his mouth shut. He didn't bother asking *what look*; he suspected he already knew. He was, indeed, gobsmacked by the sight of her.

"Impious little thief," he said.

"Aye, well..." She cast him a mean glance under long dark lashes. "Better I should be an impious little thief than a minion of the Usurper."

And she shied away, giving herself space between them, as though she suddenly feared Malcom might get the gumption to seize her. He found that fact inordinately amusing—particularly so, considering the fact that it was she who'd assaulted him. He would have been perfectly content to walk on by.

She narrowed those shrewd violet eyes. "In any case,

what I am doing here is no concern of yours," she said baldly. "The question seems to me: what is a reaving Scot doing in the south of Wales?" Malcom lifted his brows, though he scarce had time to process what she'd said, before she added, "Do your kinsmen not have enough to quibble over scrapping after each other's bones?"

Bloody impudent wench.

Despite that fact, Malcom couldn't help himself. For the first time in a long damn time, he burst into laughter.

He would laugh?

Elspeth screwed her face, feeling a sudden overwhelming urge to rush forward and punch the fool in the shin. His chortling—at her expense—was jovial enough to enrage her.

Sweet fates. She was hardly any shrew, but she welcomed the fury to distract her from her sorrow. In truth, she might have expected ire, or condemnation—or even lechery—but not this.

At the moment, she was so unsettled by his laughter that she could scarcely bear to look at the man. Mother Goddess, how could any man that size move so swiftly?

If only he'd not kept such a tight hold on his reins, or if he'd moved a little slower, she might be on her way by now. Instead, she was standing here like a ninny, trading quips, though not by choice, with a man large enough to comprise two of Llanthony's chaplains.

And yet, make no mistake, the fellow was far from fat. Every bit of flesh Ersinius possessed in his belly would have to be shoved up, forcibly, into his man breasts and then mindfully sculpted in order to be half the size this man was.

At long last, the stranger overcame his hilarity and bothered to ask, "Art hurt, lass?"

Daring to meet his sea-green eyes, Elspeth found him leaning in his saddle, the evidence of his mirth still clinging to the corners of his lips. "I'm unharmed," she confessed. "No thanks to you."

"If I recall aright," he said, his eyes gleaming, "I was strolling by, minding my own affairs. *You* assailed *me*."

His Scots accent was subtle, but Elspeth recognized it all the same. He had the diction of one who'd been away from his country overlong, but that did nothing to settle her ire. She had *no* love for Scots—and even less for reavers. Why should she feel guilty over stealing a thief's horse? "You were not riding her," Elspeth said, unreasonably.

"No," he agreed. "I was not. For a good reason."

Elspeth hitched her chin. "What good reason, prithee?"

"Not that I should owe you explanations for why I dinna ride my own horse, but I dinna wish to have Merry Bells harm herself in this foul weather."

Merry Bells?

Elspeth blinked, then frowned, chastened, though he couldn't possibly have understood why. Naturally, she had already known there would be consequences for the aether spell, but she hadn't taken much time to consider all the many possibilities. That horse's life was no less valuable to the Goddess than her own, and now she worried even more about the Rule of Three, mostly for sisters' sakes, because she had selfishly allowed them to abet her in this failed escape—failed because, only now that she was caught, she realized there was so much more they should have considered. And, of course, with the recent vandalisms, Stephen would send reinforcements. From the beginning, this was doomed. And yet, surely, the Goddess had something better to offer a humble servant than this? The very thought of being trussed over this man's horse and returned to Ersinius like some sack of meal, disheartened her. And then would he hand her over to the Bishop to be made an example of—like her grandmamau? It wasn't inconceivable. No matter that they couldn't prove that mist wasn't an act of God, they would consider Elspeth a poor example to her sisters. If they didn't escort her by blade-point to Blackwood, they might still wish to be rid of her and what better way than to burn her at the stake?

Calm yourself, Elspeth.

I am calm, she lied. *I'm calm, Rhiannon!*

But in the meantime, the Scotsman continued to berate her. She didn't hear half of what he said, but she focused on his words now.

"The fact that *my* arse was not planted in *my* saddle was not an invitation for thievery."

Elspeth would like to have forgotten he was there, but he gave her a thorough once over, and added, "Then again... judging by the fit of your clothes, this wasn't your first thievery. Di' ye burgle some *puir* sentry too deep in his cups to notice you were nicking his breeches?"

A warm flush crept into Elspeth's cheeks. "Are you through being amused?"

"Not quite," he said, "though I assure you my amusement is far more pleasant than the alternative."

Elspeth arched a dubious brow. He couldn't possibly be such an ogre if he loved his "Merry Bells" so much. And anyway, what sort of name was Merry Bells for a warrior's horse? *Merry Bells?*

If she weren't so furious, she would have returned the favor by laughing—heartily—rolling over the ground with a hand to her belly.

Indeed, Elspeth wished to do so, but considering how angry and heartsore she was, laughter wasn't forthcoming—unlike this fool, who seemed incapable of wiping the infuriating smirk from his lips, even whilst he berated her.

But then something occurred to her—something remarkable. He appeared wholly unaware of who she was, which meant... he wasn't sent to fetch her.

Relief vied with irritation. For all that he rankled her, Elspeth desperately needed help, and as much as she loathed to acknowledge the truth, she sensed a certain virtue in his aura—and this, after all, was her greatest skill: reading people. Whilst Rhiannon could read actual thoughts, so long as Elspeth remained in proximity, she could read emotions—betimes like an aura, filled with colors.

This man's air was lit pale orange, with just the tiniest hint of blue, like the shades of a low-burning flame. It was perhaps for that reason she'd felt so emboldened to provoke him.

But here, now, they were at a standoff, unless Elspeth relented—which was to say that if she wished to engage his help, she realized she was going to have to be nicer. "So, then..." She swiped primly at her tunic. "You did not say *why* you are here?"

"Aside from dodging pretty little thieves?"

Elspeth flushed, ignoring the backhanded compliment. It didn't matter to her that he thought her pretty, but her cheeks burned nonetheless.

"I was sent by *your* king."

Insulted, she pressed a hand to her breast. "*My king?*"

He showed his straight, white teeth. "Mine, too, whether we like it or nay."

Elspeth blinked, reconsidering the man. So, then, he was

a reluctant warrior, serving a king he did not love? Perhaps, indeed, they could be allies after all? But just to be sure, she asked, "Which king?" Naturally, she presumed the most obvious. "The Scots' king, David?"

"Nay."

Her brows collided. "Rhys ap Hywel?"

"Nay"

"Owain Gwynedd?"

"Nay.

"Rhys ap Gruffydd."

"Nay."

"Madog ap Maredudd?"

He chortled again, only this time, it was a deep-throated chuckle that gave Elspeth a discernible shiver. "Nay, lass," he said. "Though I commend you on your knowledge of dissenters."

Elspeth bristled. "Dissenters, sir? You are in *Wales*. No matter that the Usurper would endeavor to deny it, these men are *all* kings, chosen properly by their people." The implication was not lost to him—unlike, Stephen, the Usurper. "Every last one with more right to be here than you—but, very well, if not them, *who*?"

"The only king you've yet to mention," he said, his lips twitching at the corners. "The one who actually rules these lands."

"Humph!" said Elspeth, her hands going to her hips. "Stephen of Blois will *never* rule these lands!"

He leaned forward in his saddle, as though preparing to confide in her, and said low, "Perhaps, *my lady*, but my sword is pledged to him nonetheless. And *never* is a very long time."

Lady? Elspeth suspected the courtesy was but a taunt, meant to needle her. He no more believed her a fine lady than he had any true consideration for his horse. He didn't wish to break his own neck was all. "*My fath*—Henry would turn in his grave to hear you say such a thing," she said, studying the man with narrowed eyes. It wasn't unheard of for a Scotsman to bend the knee to an English sovereign, but he was not dressed as she might have expected for a vassal of Stephen's to be dressed—completely without regard for his liege. And, if, indeed, he served her despicable cousin, he must be one of those feckless idiots who'd forsworn an oath to her father. Incensed, she clapped her hands together, ridding herself of imaginary dirt. "Anyway," she said sourly, "I thought *your* king supported *my*—Matilda—who, by the by, happens to be *our* rightful queen."

"So, he does."

Elspeth poked a finger at him. "Aha! He *is* your king!"

"Who?"

"David!"

"Nay, lass." The Scotsman frowned. But he peered down his nose at Elspeth with far less mirth, and Elspeth considered his diminished good humor a small, but decisive victory. "I have pledged my sword to Stephen and I always honor my vows," he said. And that was all. He gave no further explanation.

"You mean to say, you honor your vows when it suits you?" There was probably a good reason his armor wasn't blazoned; that way he could choose his side according to his mood. "I understand," she said, and watched his aura deepen to an angry orange, and despite that, Elspeth couldn't hold her tongue.

"What is it ye ken, lass?"

"You're a reaver!"

. . .

MALCOM'S LIPS THINNED. His previously unanticipated good humor vanished.

Reaver?

Were all Scots considered little more than thieves? By God, she was a lovely little termagant, but a termagant nonetheless. But he hadn't any time or patience for this. Already, the girl had waylaid him long enough. He appreciated the fleeting instant of mirth, but he had a long, long way to go, and an ailing father to see to. Tugging Merry's reins, he said, "Aye, well... tis been lovely, lass. Much as I would love to remain and continue this fascinating discourse, I'm afraid I must take my leave now. Good day," he said.

Wide eyed, and looking suddenly very contrite, the girl stepped in front of his horse, startling Malcom, but Merry Bells didn't protest the hand in front of her nose.

"Wait!" she said. "Where will you go?"

"Home," Malcom answered, and once again peered into the tree-tops, suspicious. Could it be she was waylaying him so her fellow brigands could come relieve him of his valuables? Whilst he kept little silver in his bags, his armor and horse were indispensable. As it was, he'd put far too much time into working with Merry Bells to start over again. The thought of losing her soured his belly. Not quite trusting the girl, he kept the grip on his reins, preparing to bolt, but, for some odd reason, despite his pique, there was something in the girl's stark violet gaze that held him transfixed. Once more, he scanned the tree-tops, looking for compatriots.

Please, please don't go.

That voice... it was the very same voice he'd heard moments ago, like a silky whisper carried by the wind... *Was it her?* But he never saw her lips move.

Who was she? Despite having pounced on him from the

trees, he didn't believe she could be a scout. Her hubris told him she was highborn. But even if she had perfected the haughty demeanor, she lacked the refinement he'd so often encountered in the women from Stephen's court. In fact, there was something about the lass that reminded him quite a bit of his stepmother. Left to her own devices, Page Fitz-Simon had been a waif with a viper tongue. This girl, dressed in the manner of men, was equally as impudent as his stepmother had been, only with a wit twice as sharp. Yes, indeed, she was exactly like his stepmother, with that stinging pride she wore like a suit of armor, all the while she was frightened and alone. But that wasn't all they had in common... there was something else... something about the tumult in her gaze... a sad, sad depth of despair that called to Malcom's soul.

"Which way are you traveling?"

"North," he said.

Her brows lifted. "Wonderful!" she said with false bravado. "It just so happens to be the way I am traveling as well."

Malcom arched a brow. "What you mean to say is... north is the way you intended to travel *after* stealing my horse?"

"Aye," she said, with a bit of a blush, and Malcom meant to press her further. In fact, he wanted to ask her if she even knew which way was north because she appeared as lost as any soul had ever appeared. He opened his mouth to goad her—mostly because she deserved it—but then came a sudden chorus of barking hounds, and the girl stiffened, looking for the first time frightened out of her wits. Wild eyed, she peered up into the treetops from whence she'd come, and for an instant seemed to consider scrambling back up, but she met Malcom's gaze. With eyes as wide as saucers and moisture brimming over thick, dark lashes, she begged, "Please."

Confused, he asked, "Please what?"

"Please sir, we are going the same way..."

"Elspeth!" a man's voice called, near enough to be understood. And then another shout. "Elspeth!" The hounds were closing in now, barking in a frenzied refrain.

Gone was any pretense at pride. "Please, please, help me!" she begged. "Please!"

4

It was the look of desperation in her eyes that convinced him. "Can you ride astride?" Malcom asked.

"As well as any man," she answered. "Hurry!"

The hounds were close now. Malcom offered the girl his hand and she seized it without hesitation. He lifted her up into the saddle before him.

"Elspeth!"

Whoever was searching for the girl knew her well enough to use her given name. Malcom lingered only an instant, wondering what manner of quarrel he'd got himself into.

"Please," she begged, urging him to leave before she had even a chance to place her legs astride the pommel. Responding to the fear in her voice, Malcom obeyed.

He snapped Merry Bells' reins, but rather than demand the horse go in any particular direction, he let Merry Bells lead the way, hoping the mare's instinct would serve them better than his own. "God have mercy. You chose a bloody fine day to flee!"

"Don't worry," she said, waving a hand as though she were dismissing the mist. "'Tis clear ahead."

Bolting in a direction he would never have led her—into a thick cloud of fog—Merry Bells hurled over a low-lying bush, and even before Malcom could think to ask how she could possibly know such a thing, they stepped outside the curtain of fog, under a bright spring sky. Stunned though he might be, he knew they hadn't time to waste. The barking grew frenzied as he urged Merry Bells into a full canter.

"Thank you," she said, and Malcom felt her shiver.

Feeling strangely protective over the lass, he slid an arm about her waist.

By damn, like his Da, he must be a bloody fool for a lady in distress because he knew beyond a shadow of doubt, as they flew over brush and bracken, that he wouldn't give the girl up, no matter how many Welshmen's arrows were trained at his back. They could riddle him with holes and he would take his last breath defending her. He wasn't about to leave her to whatever fate those men intended to deliver. Leaving the barking and chorus of shouts in their wake, Merry Bells swallowed the ground that rose to greet them, and soon enough, the woodlands gave way to moorlands, the Welsh countryside vanished before England. All the prideful words that had been spoken between them were cast aside like dust in their wake.

THE CROSSOVER into England occurred uneventfully—no signs of pursuit—and once returned to English soil, Malcom settled Merry Bells into an easy canter.

Whoever had been after 'Elspeth' mustn't have realized how close she'd been. Obviously, the fog had worked to her benefit. And, for all the girl's previous contention, she was silent now, so much so that Malcom might have feared she'd gone mute, save he knew better.

Saucy little vixen.

Better I should be an impious little thief than a minion of the Usurper, she'd said, and the recollection turned his lips yet again. By the stone, he couldn't remember the last time he'd smiled over anything at all, much less a tongue-lashing by a slip of a lass.

These days, he couldn't even find so much pleasure in another manner of tongue lashing, though he certainly found himself daydreaming now over far better uses for 'Elspeth's' tongue.

He rather liked the way she looked, with her thick red-gold hair and that smattering of freckles that made him long to brush a thumb across her cheeks.

Not for the first time, her head lolled back, resting on his shoulder, and Malcom found his grin widened, silly though it might be.

North, she'd said.

But how far north did she intend to go?

Eventually, he might bother to ask, but for now, he was reluctant to break the spell of silence. Far too easily, he'd grown accustomed to the warm curves of her body and the sweet lavender scent that drifted from her hair. God's teeth, there was naught sour about the girl, except her temper.

Elspeth, they'd called her.

He longed to test the sound on his lips.

Elspeth.

For all he knew, he could have stolen some petty king's daughter, and then, in truth, he would have inherited another battle. Considering how well she'd known her rivals

—or rather, King Stephen's rivals—it was a distinct possibility.

My king? she'd asked with such impudence he'd laughed. But, in truth, there was little humor to be found in treason, and now he considered how best to navigate this conundrum. Because, if, indeed, she was an enemy of the realm, he should hand her over to Stephen—and nevertheless, despite that truth, he knew he wouldn't do that.

Snoring loudly, she melted against him like a sleepy lover, and, knowing instinctively that they'd encounter no trouble here, Malcom didn't wake her. For much of their journey, he could tell she was struggling and he surmised that the stress of her flight had wearied her. Adjusting his position so that she could rest more easily, he felt inexplicably contented.

Thankfully, they were traveling through familiar territory, and though he wasn't flying his banners—thanks to his missing squire—there was little need for concern.

Robert of Gloucester was dead. Matilda's rebellion was well and duly thwarted. She'd had no choice but to return to her Angevin husband to lick her wounds, and now that the Empress was gone, Stephen's barons were far too preoccupied making treaties with each other to secure alliances and war gains. Neither the Empress, nor her upstart son, would be returning to England any time soon—unless Stephen should happen to agree to finance yet another of his cousin's campaigns.

Obviously, the king was not so as adept at ruling as Henry was—in part, because he had more honor than the former. However, honor didn't seem to be a trait well-suited to a sovereign, and Stephen made too many concessions. For his unyielding sense of compromise, what had he received in turn? A hollow pledge from erstwhile barons who were all still placing wagers on who should keep Henry's throne—and, aye, these many, many years later, the crown was still said to be Beauclerc's. Stephen of Blois was still called Usurper, most recently by the girl in his arms.

Malcom sighed. For what it was worth, he liked Stephen. He might, indeed, be an ineffectual ruler, but he was an honorable man, who, whether or not he was justified in his succession, had been moved to seize the crown only because he'd believed his rule was best for the realm. It was for this unwavering sense of devotion to England that so many of Henry's own barons had abandoned support for Matilda in order to support him—not because the archbishop finagled it, or because some witch beguiled him. Even now, despite all she'd done to undermine him, the king's loyalty to Matilda was as thick as their blood and, in fact, he'd had plenty of opportunity to take the Empress's head if that's what he'd meant to do.

On the other hand, his predecessor had ruled with an iron fist, with a temper not unlike that of a berserker's, and the older Henry had gotten, the more temperamental he'd become. The man remained full of piss and vinegar until the day he'd died—so much so that Malcom betimes wondered if he were poisoned by his own bile.

Screw the eels. Screw the twisted plots and rumors of witchery. Anger was Henry Beauclerc's bane, and his daughter was just the same, only coupled with an arrogance that left everyone cold.

But, of course, it could be that Malcom was biased. Most notably because, four and twenty years ago, Matilda's father had dared to reach into Scotia and steal a wee boy from his father.

Even so, Malcom wasn't blind to Stephen's weaknesses.

Much of the time their king's ambivalence managed to create a world of strife—take these parklands for example.

Ever since leaving Wales, Malcom had been careful to remain on chartered land, but to either side of the easement, these parklands belonged to Graeham d'Lucy and to William Beauchamp—both men pledged to Stephen, but Malcom trusted d'Lucy far more than he did Beauchamp.

Back in the day, Henry Beauclerc had insisted upon designating certain lands as his royal hunting grounds, to be used only by invitation. But, of course, that did not go well with his barons, and least of all d'Lucy and Beauchamp. So, in exchange for their support and fealty before his coronation, Stephen had promised to reverse Henry's charter.

Regrettably, he'd not counted on the greed of his barons or the willingness of nobles to lie. Whilst, in truth, Beauchamp had lost little land—if any at all—due to Henry's appropriation, it didn't stop him from challenging the return of d'Lucy's parklands. Four years ago, the elder d'Lucy was slain during a scuffle over these parcels, and to date, this had gone unpunished by Stephen.

What was more, whilst d'Lucy continued to support Stephen in all his endeavors and sent his bastard brother to answer all his summonses to war, Beauchamp supported Stephen only in word, never in deed, and remained elsewise engaged in his never-ending feud, entirely without consequence. Unfortunately, Malcom knew much of this because Stephen was keen on a union between Malcom and Dominique Beauchamp, William's young sister—perhaps as a means to ensure Beauchamp's loyalties. And while Malcom was still considering, he was unconvinced Beauchamp would make anyone a suitable ally—his lovely little sister be damned. Dominique was far too meek for his taste. And though she comported herself well enough,

Malcolm supposed he liked his ladies more like the ones he'd left behind in Scotia, whose hearts were ever-faithful, but whose temperaments were true to their minds.

Like the woman in his arms.

At long last, she stirred, waking herself with an indelicate snort.

"Welcome back to the world of the living, lass. Di' ye sleep well?"

5

Elspeth shook herself free of her strange languor. "I... I wasn't... sleeping," she lied. But how odd—how imprudent—to sleep in a stranger's arms! The last thing she wanted was for him to think she would be so compliant as to allow him to do aught that he willed.

"You weren't?" he asked, and his smile returned, because Elspeth heard the note of good humor in his voice. So, too, did her ire.

"I ask only because I thought I heard you snore."

"Nay, my lord. I. Do. *Not*. Snore."

He leaned forward—scandalously close—challenging her. "But how can ye know you don't snore when you're sleeping? Are ye perchance a seer?"

The warmth of his breath—sweet for a man—tickled the back of Elspeth's neck and she lifted her shoulder, shrugging him away. Of course, she was. But she didn't need sight to know whether she snored, although perhaps she should say yes just to see what he would say. "I would not know if I were sleeping, but I was not sleeping."

Elspeth realized he must be teasing her, but she wasn't

in the mood, and the farther she traveled from Wales, the more she fretted about her sisters. And nevertheless, it wasn't as though she wasn't grateful; she was. It was more that now that she was out of immediate danger, she didn't know what to do or where to go. She couldn't very well ask him to put her off right here, could she? Where would she go? She tried to consider possibilities but couldn't think with him whispering at her ear. "Only humor me," he suggested. "How can ye *know* for sure?"

Elspeth huffed a sigh, shrugging him away, again. "Because. If I snored—if I ever snored—my sisters would have told me so."

That answer seemed to mollify him for a second, and then he asked, "Sisters? From the priory?"

"Aye."

"Nuns?"

"Nay."

"Aha," he said now, but did she imagine a note of relief? Silence for a moment, and then he proposed, "So, tell me, Elspeth... how many *sisters* have you?"

The way he spoke her name, so gently, gave Elspeth a quiver, and no matter, she didn't wish to tell him anything more than she must. "Four," she said, because he asked.

"Living?"

"Aye."

"And where are they now?"

"Precisely where we are not," Elspeth returned, and this, once more, inspired a low rumble of laughter from her reluctant champion.

Ye gods, his mirth was unshakable.

As a matter of fact, she'd already acknowledged that she'd left four sisters at the priory. She didn't feel particularly compelled to repeat herself. If he couldn't properly hear, he should clean out his ears. By the cauldron! Was it possible that all Scots could be so annoying?

For most of her years at court, the Scot's king's son had teased her mercilessly. It was only after being warned about the possibility of incurring Morwen's wrath that he'd ever deigned to stop. It was unthinkable now that *that* man should be made the Earl of Northumberland—particularly so, since Elspeth wasn't the only one who didn't trust him. Much like Stephen's son Eustace, he was a petty tyrant with an eye for his father's laurels. As far as she was concerned, with the likes of Eustace so close to her father's throne, England was descending into darkness. And the most infuriating thing of all was this: David of Scotia had once knelt before her sister Matilda. He swore his love and fealty while her father watched, and now he and all his barons paid homage to Stephen instead of Matilda. So, then, did he, or did he not, support Matilda?

And what about this Scotsman at her back? How could he support Stephen, when her sister was the rightful claimant to the throne?

Be nice to him, Elspeth. You need him.

The voice was fainter now, and Elspeth couldn't, in truth, be certain it belonged to Rhiannon. It could well be her own voice of reason. Because it was true; she did need him.

For love of the Goddess, she didn't want to need this man, but she did. And nevertheless, she knew so little about him, save that he mustn't be lowborn. Her first clue was the ring on his finger—the one on his left hand that by now had slipped to her thigh. She'd allowed it to remain there, if only to study the ring. Casting her gaze down again, examining the signet, she studied the golden two-headed falcon and read the maxim: *Altium, citius, fortius.* But she couldn't recall whose standard it could be. She had been gone from court so long now that she didn't know anything about Stephen's new barons. There were hundreds of them, all building adulterine castels her father would have smashed with his fist.

Lulled once more by the lazy trot of his horse, Elspeth found herself leaning back against his sturdy form, and mostly because he didn't protest, she relaxed. After all, it was going to be a long, long journey to wherever they were going.

North, he'd said.

How far north was north?

IT DID NOT ESCAPE Malcom that she'd yet to ask him to put her down... and regardless, it was past time to discover who she was, and more importantly, her destination.

North was not enough to go by, and as much as he was warming to the notion of taking her all the way to Aldergh, it was also past time for Merry Bells to rest. He'd been watching the horse closely for signs of exhaustion. But strangely, he suspected the mare was championing Elspeth as he was, putting as much distance between her and her pursuers as possible. But how much sense did that make? As much as he liked to think Merry his companion and friend, she was only a simple beast who rested when she must, ate when she must, slept when she must. And subsequently, only a cruel master would push her beyond her endurance. Therefore, as much as he relished the notion of spiriting the lass all the way home, it was past time to discover who she was.

He opened his mouth to speak, but she returned her head to his shoulder, and he shut his mouth again, because the gesture inexplicably pleased him.

He couldn't deny that he was drawn to her in ways he hadn't been drawn to any woman in far too long, and yet, he felt an obligation to keep her safe, even from himself.

Was this what his father had felt for Page?

God's truth; he didn't know the girl. How could he feel anything for her at all?

"Elspeth," he prompted, and then, because she didn't seem to hear him, he nudged her awake. "Elspeth?"

She straightened, but didn't respond, and Malcom thought perhaps she must have fallen asleep again, so he gave her a moment to regain her bearings, and said, louder, "Elspeth." Her head bounced off his shoulder, and he tried not to laugh. Reaching up to wipe the smile from his lips, he said, "Now that Wales is behind us, it occurs to me that you should know I mean to ride all the way to Northumbria."

She swiveled to glare at him. "I knew it!" she said. "You *are* a reaver!" And then she leaned forward as far as she dared, so that Malcom couldn't possibly touch her—which was entirely ludicrous, because her arse was nestled sweetly between his thighs.

And nevertheless, her reaction vexed him. Whilst so many of the northern lords were fickle in their loyalties, seizing opportunities where they may, he'd never once even considered raiding north or south. "I am no reaver," he maintained. "I am Malcom Scott, rightful Earl of Aldergh."

"Aye, well," she said stiffly, quite sourly. "I am quite certain you won your title by *honorable* means."

Malcom's good humor came to an abrupt end, for nay, he had not. As far as he knew, it was quite the opposite of honorable to sink a blade into one's kinsman's heart, and despite this fact, that detail was none of her concern— neither was his worth as an Earl. "God's love, woman. Must everything be a quarrel?"

Malcom shook his head, tugging the reins, urging Merry Bells to a halt. He'd had more than enough of the girl's temper. Whatever bond he felt to the lass, she obviously did not share it, and he wasn't a glutton for punishment. She was out of danger now; it was time to put her off.

"What are you doing?"

"Considering the wisdom in leaving an impertinent lass on lands belonging to a man I detest. Perhaps a good, long walk will settle your ire."

She stiffened, and he heard her swallow. "I-uh... I'm sorry," she said. "Tis been a while since I have conversed with anyone save my sisters."

Malcom's tone no longer held any trace of amusement. "You mean the four sisters you left behind at the priory?"

"Aye."

"And did you speak to them so rudely?"

"Nay."

"Well, then, lady, allow me to enlighten you. When one is asked a question, the proper response is not to answer with another question—or worse, with rudeness. The proper response is to answer politely."

She answered now with silence and Malcom sensed she must be warring with her pride—something she had in abundance. No doubt, she longed to gnash her teeth at him, but she couldn't argue with his logic, and neither had he impugned her, save to say she was rude. And, by God, she was. Her chin lifted, but slightly. "So, my Lord Aldergh... what is the proper response if a stranger intends to pry? I was taught it was bad form to ask a lady intrusive questions, and therefore how should *one* answer rudeness but with rudeness?"

Malcom blinked. She was right, of course. Given normal circumstances, he'd never have approached her, even to ask her name, much less more personal questions. And nevertheless, these were not normal circumstances and he couldn't let it go. "*My lady,* I do believe we ceased to be *strange* after hearing you snore."

She stiffened, and despite his pique, Malcom felt the urge to laugh. God's teeth, what was it about the lass that called to his better nature? Certainly not her temper.

"You are the one who is rude," she said, sounding injured, and Malcom felt contrite, though try as he might, he couldn't quite keep the quake from his shoulders, and she turned to cast him another evil-eyed glare.

"Dear lady, I am... not... laughing... at you," he reassured. "I am simply... overcome... by... your... mettle. Where I come from, 'tis precisely the way a woman ought to be—fearless. Only, tell me, despite your attempted thievery of my property, have I yet to treat you dishonorably?"

Her answer was given ruefully. "Nay."

"Why, then, do you persist upon despising me?"

"I do not," she confessed.

"Art certain?"

She hesitated. "Quite."

Malcom didn't budge. He held his ground, urging Merry Bells to stay. Although he was refreshed by her forthright nature, he was also bound and determined to earn not merely her trust, but her good manners and gratitude as well. He waited for an apology.

"Very well," she said, obviously expecting it to be the end of their discourse. She leaned forward, pressing her knees into Merry Bells' withers, but the horse, like her master, remained steadfast. Nibbling at tufts of grass, she, too, stood stubbornly, and after a moment, she urinated where she stood, squatting so that Elspeth was forced to lie back against him.

Malcom smirked. "Very well what?"

The lass sighed louder than she snored, and Malcom suppressed another chuckle.

"Very well! Very well!" she snapped. "If you will not abandon me on this detestable man's land, I will endeavor to be..."

"What?"

"Less rude."

"Thank you, madam," he said, still waiting. "And perhaps even agreeable?"

"*Aye*," she said. "I will."

"Thank you," Malcom said, and clicked the reins, prompting Merry Bells into an easy canter, despite the lack of proper apology. It was enough that she would cease and desist with her temper.

6

Feeling chastised, with good merit, Elspeth lapsed into silence, listening to the *clop, clop* of the horse's hooves —a sound that was slowly, inexorably, lulling her back to sleep.

Sweet fates. What was this terrible languor?

Even now, seated before this stranger, she fought a new wave of sleepiness as her gaze scanned the vaguely familiar landscape—less mountainous now, with light and airy forests.

She had no idea what lay ahead, but she did know what she was leaving behind, and she swallowed her grief like a glob of sticky porridge, her emotions bedeviling her.

It wasn't merely her sisters she was taking leave of. It was Wales itself, and the spirit of the land, which was even now shedding itself from her like a mantle being stripped from her back.

If she was cross, it was because her heart ached, and Malcom seemed far too ready to taunt her. If only he understood how devastating this was. If only he could comprehend what travesty had befallen her the last time she'd arrived in this land—mayhap then he wouldn't tease her so mercilessly. It was more than twenty years later now, but she knew too much as a woman of four and twenty to feel aught but trepidation over returning to England.

She remembered only too well that journey she'd taken to London with her grandmamau. Less than six months later, she was dead.

Remember, Elspeth, never forget...

I will not forget, she promised Rhiannon. *I will never forget.*

And yet, unlike Rhiannon, Elspeth dared not make revenge her *raison d'être*. It was far more honorable to fight her mother by championing all that was good. It was for that reason she must remain Matilda's champion. Like Robert, she would do so until her dying breath. And, if, in truth, Elspeth was more invested in Matilda's cause than her sisters, it was because she believed with all her heart that if Matilda won this untenable war, only then could justice ever be served.

It aggrieved her so much that Rhiannon could not understand and forgive their half-sister. Instead, she huffed and fumed, and the more she did so, the harder grew her heart—and if there was one thing Elspeth feared in this world, it was the thought of Rhiannon following in Morwen's path. It was a terrifying visage. Already, Rhiannon had too much of their mother. In fact, but for the color of her hair and eyes, she was the spitting image of Morwen. Like their grandmother, Rhiannon bore the mark of the Mother—the crossed, amber-lit gaze that distinguished her as the regnant priestess, and the Craft was stronger with her than it ever was with Morwen. But if her sister ever learned to use her gifts with such a bitter heart, Elspeth loathed to think what might become of her.

Of all her living sisters, Rhiannon loathed their mother most, with good reason. Nestled in Morwen's womb, she and a twin had suffered a mother's worst betrayal. Having sensed the bounteous gift their grandmamau had bestowed upon the unborn twins—strong Welsh *magik*, powerful enough for two babes—and realizing she'd been deprived of her birthright, Morwen had concocted a potion to still their beating hearts. Rhiannon lived; the twin did not. And now, Goddess save anyone who came between her sister and her vengeance.

Insomuch as Morwen seemed to defy the tenets of their coven, and as horrible a mother as she was, the Goddess had certainly blessed her womb well enough. She'd born two sets of twins in her lifetime, and she hadn't a nurturing bone in her body. Elspeth hoped with all her heart that Rhiannon would rise above such meanness, but only time would tell.

One thing was certain. Ersinius had better stay out of Rhiannon's way. Contrary to what folks believed about witches, she couldn't turn him into a toad, but she could easily mix a powder to sprinkle in his robes and rot away his manhood, and *that* she would do.

Doddering old man. Annoyed by the stupidity of men and thinking about the way Ersinius used to cross himself every time they chanced to breathe the same air, Elspeth shook her head.

Really, it wasn't as though any of them could raise the dead or bewitch the living. Not even Morwen had that kind of power—then, again, perhaps she did. After all, it was said she'd beguiled Henry, and whatever sway she'd held over Elspeth's father, she now appeared to hold over Stephen as well. In truth, Elspeth didn't know what her mother was capable of. She'd heard rumors of glamour spells and shapeshifting, such as was done by the Death Crone, but she'd never once witnessed any of that manner of *hud du*. When pressed, her grandmamau had said that all knowledge of those dark arts—if ever they'd existed—had passed away with the fall of Avalon. But, in truth, unless Elspeth ever got her hands on her grandmother's *grimoire*, she would never know for sure. Whatever spells she and her sisters knew, they knew by rote, after watching Morwen or her grandmother perform them. But witchcraft was not so much what people supposed. To her own people it was better known as the Craft of the Wise. And, in their native tongue they were known as *dewines*, not witches. Translated more precisely, they were, indeed, enchantresses, but also bards, prophets and seers, and, as with any art, not everyone had the same skills. Certainly not all were dark. Her people held the earth in great esteem and believed all beings were connected—living and otherwise. *Magik* was but another word for transformation, conjuration and creation and life was filled with these things—a butterfly emerging from a cocoon, a child born of a woman, a seedling emerged after a long winter, life born from a drop of water. But people were simply no longer open to miracles, even when proof existed before their eyes. Only now, in this time of persecution, this was their saving grace: People no longer believed in the Old Ways.

Elspeth cast a glance over her shoulder at her dubious savior—a minion of Stephen's. Whatever gratitude she felt toward this man, it was tempered by resentment over his unswerving loyalty to the pea-brain who'd cast their nations into war.

In truth, she was not usually so ill-mannered, but she didn't wish to like this man, even though she needed him. So, aye, it galled her that *he*, of all people, would endeavor to educate her about rudeness—even ruder yet was faithlessness. Whether or not he'd come to his titles after her father's death, and whether or not he'd reneged on his vows, anyone who was an enemy of Matilda's should rightfully be an enemy of Elspeth's.

Forsooth, how could he possibly approve of the way his Scots king had agreed to aid his niece, then so conveniently abandoned his support? Did he have no care at all that Stephen had no right to rule any lands, less Wales? Did it never concern him that "their king" had forced his own brother to deliver him the support of the church? Or that he'd seized the treasury without right?

The bounds of Stephen's treachery infuriated Elspeth to no end. And yet, she felt painfully ambivalent about Malcom, because, aye, she realized he could have easily abandoned her to the mercy of Ersinius' men, and if he had, he might have been justified in doing so. After all, he didn't know her, and she could have been fleeing a rightful persecution. But nevertheless, once the moment arrived, he'd pulled her onto his mount, with nary a hesitation and swept her away, holding her close—so close that she'd dared to feel... safe.

Certainly, it was the last thing she'd expected from a man she'd attempted to rob—or from a professed minion of Stephen's.

Who are you Malcom?

Peering down at the ring on his finger—closer now that his hands were on the reins and no longer resting on her person, she wondered how and when he'd acquired his lands and title. Of course, she didn't know his standard—or his name—so he must have ascended after her father's death—and therefore, he must be one of Stephen's new barons.

Men like Cael d'Lucy...

And once again, she sighed, and, for a moment, allowed herself to consider how things would have been had she stayed with her sisters...

She would have been carted away by now, and soon enough found herself wed to an Earl as well. She would have been sent back to Blackwood, where she could have ruled her own demesne, but at what cost?

But now... above and beyond the spell they'd cast, what cost would her sisters pay for Elspeth's defiance? Surely, Morwen would never suffer this insult lightly, and there was no doubt she would fly at once to the priory. She would want to know precisely what her sisters knew. But did even Rhiannon know where she was going?

With every mile she traveled, Rhiannon's voice grew fainter and fainter... and for better or worse, soon... very soon... not even she would be able to reach her.

Sweet fates. How will I bear it?
Look to your champion, Elspeth.

Champion? Elspeth dared again to peek over her shoulder and found Malcolm's gaze fixed upon the horizon. At the instant, he didn't seem to sense her scrutiny, so she allowed her gaze to linger...

He had a strong jaw with a small cleft in his chin, and his eyes—blue-green—were veiled by thick, dark lashes. His skin was swarthy, as though he spent much of his time in the sun, but it was impossible to say what color his hair might be because it was covered by that coif.

Was it true? Could he be her champion?
Did you send him, Rhiannon?
Silence.

Elspeth's heart wrenched.

Rhiannon, she called again, and again, her answer was silence.

Swallowing the lump that rose in her throat, Elspeth turned as far as she could in the saddle, craning her neck as tears pricked at her eyes.

She knew the instant she passed outside her sisters' reach… because she suffered the void acutely… it was a great sweeping darkness… illumined only by the man riding at her back.

Elspeth peered up at him, tears swimming in her eyes, and prayed that, indeed, the Goddess had sent him to aid her. Without her sisters, she had no one else to trust.

"What is it, Elspeth?"

She turned, giving Malcom her back, and said, "Nothing." And once again, more to convince herself. "All is well."

7

One chair by the small hearth remained conspicuously empty, the seat as cold as the ashes beneath the cauldron. Silence, thick and dismal, became the Ewyas sisters' fifth companion.

"She's... *gone*," said Rhiannon. No two words were ever spoken more woefully.

Swallowing the knot of grief that formed in her throat, Rhiannon rose from her seat to stand before the small cauldron, peering down into the kettle's bottom to see what she could see...

Betimes, a bit of *majik* lingered there, in the last drops of beguiled liquid; but today there was none. The long night had rendered the contents powder dry, leaving only a trace of ash to reveal the herbs they had burned. Alas, she didn't need a scrying stone or spells to know that, for better or worse, today was the day their lives began to diverge.

Holding tight to her emotions, keeping her back to her sisters, Rhiannon was afraid they would glimpse what she loathed to tell them. Life was so much like a spider's web—

so many threads flowing from its center, all leading to destinations unknown and the slightest deviation had the potential to place them at very wide berths.

But her sisters' destinies were not hers, and as similar as they might be, having spent nearly every waking moment together, not a one of them had the same fire burning in their soul.

Rhiannon wanted *nothing* as much as she wanted revenge—for the grandmother she'd never known, and for the twin she'd mourned inside her mother's womb. Elspeth carried a torch for justice. Seren wanted peace. Rose and Arwyn longed for things they might never see. But, at least this was still true: Wherever Elspeth was going now, her future would be her own to choose. The same could not be said for the rest of her siblings. Her careless spell had changed their fates.

And yet, had she known... if she had but suspected the outcome... she would have done it all the same all over again. Rhiannon was wise enough to know that Elspeth's cause was the most noble of them all. Wales itself could be lost if she did not pursue her crusade for their sister Matilda.

Goddess save them if Stephen's son took that throne. Darkness would descend upon this land... a darkness unlike even the one that had dimmed the grace of Avalon.

It was a long, long moment before Arwyn finally breached the silence, inquiring about Elspeth. "Do you know where she is going?"

Too easily, Rhiannon lied with a shake of her head, even as she loathed herself for doing it. By the cauldron, it was said that lies were like steps descending into darkness, and that even when they were well-intentioned, they had the ill effect of spreading gloom.

But this was also true: Of all her siblings—Elspeth included—Rhiannon was the only one who could hope to defeat Morwen. It was safer if her sisters did not know where Elspeth was going. Morwen would too easily read everything their tongues refused to speak. As lovely as her sisters might be, they were equally as guileless.

"Fear not," she said, at last. "Our Goddess sent her a champion."

"Hmm," said Seren, furrowing her brow, but she said nothing more, perhaps guessing at the truth—that Rhiannon had summoned this man herself, not the Goddess, at least not without intervention. Alas, it was impossible to say what might come from wresting the lord of Aldergh away from his chosen path... or whether the effect of it would be good or bad.

Rose worried her hands. "Did you note the direction they were traveling? We'll want to know so we can follow."

"East," lied Rhiannon, though it wasn't entirely a lie, for whilst she did know which direction they were headed, and she also knew the name of the man who was bound to her, Elspeth's true destination was unknown even to Rhiannon. So much now depended on the decisions her sister made. Free will was a gift of the one true God and even her own future was foreseeable only in glimpses. Any new path taken, or any new decision made—like that spider's web— could steal her away to an entirely new destiny.

Yesterday, she'd a very good plan to get her sisters away from this priory. Today, that plan was no more viable than it had been for Elspeth to remain. And yet, Rhiannon had no regrets. This way, at least she knew her sister had a champion to defend her.

"I miss her already," lamented Seren.

"Me too," confessed Rhiannon, as she reached down to

smooth her callused fingertips over the cold, hard rim of the kettle. She had a terrible feeling that she would miss *all* her sisters every day for the rest of her life...

"Does she know... what you did?"

"The sleep spell?" Rhiannon shrugged, and shook her head. "Not yet." Though neither did her sisters realize the full scope of what she had done. All they knew was that Rhiannon had cast a wee spell to settle Elspeth's nerves. But that spell was not the spell that changed their lives. By wresting one man from his chosen path, she had, in truth, changed her own fate entirely, because she had been wrong. The new lord of Blackwood didn't care whatsoever who warmed his bed.

"You did the right thing," reasoned Seren, mistaking Rhiannon's distress.

Arwyn agreed. "It was for her own good, Rhiannon. She's too prone to worry."

"So now what?" asked Seren.

A tear slipped past Rhiannon's lashes as she realized her sisters were looking to her for direction. But, of course they would... as they had once looked to Elspeth.

Alas, though Elspeth's skills were no match for Rhiannon's, Elspeth had something else Rhiannon did not possess, a pure heart, and an unwavering sense of loyalty. That's why, after all these years, her sister could not abandon her crusade for Matilda. Though it was also precisely why she would have been compelled to return. Even now Rhiannon felt a tempest turning inside her. And, Elspeth, her one true anchor, was moving further and further away with every clip-clop of that horse's hooves. No matter that she could no longer hear Elspeth speaking to her, she could still hear that sound, like drums beating in her head.

Clip. Clop. Clip, clop. Clip, clop.

Putting her hands to her ears and glaring down at the long-spent embers below the kettle, she considered the hatred she felt for her lady mother and watched the white coals turn slowly red...

Morwen was a heartless demon, without an ounce of regret for all the horrors she had committed. *Death. Terror. Fear.* These were all the things her mother reveled in, and the worst of her sins were as yet unknown to her sisters. There was nothing of the Maiden or Mother left in Morwen; she was the Death Crone, and her darkness had begun to eat away at her from the inside out.

In order to keep her spell of glamour, she would continue to sacrifice innocents. She'd struck herself a bargain with the Crone, but she was, indeed, worse than Cerridwen ever was, and the fallout from her treachery would be far worse than the vanishing of an Island or its people. She would drag England itself into oblivion... along with Wales and Scotia, and any lands or persons that came under Stephen's rule. And whilst their *king* might respect and even love his portly wife, few ever had the power to resist Morwen's wiles. After all, it was Morwen who'd planted the seed of greed into Stephen's silly little head. She had been using her Craft from the beginning. And once she'd realized Henry had learned to resist her wiles, she moved on to Stephen, turning Stephen's heart against the uncle he'd loved so well, convincing him that he must betray his blood for honor and justice. But he was not lost... not yet... And yet, if Eustace ever rose to power, with Morwen by his side, England as they knew it would be lost... forever. Therefore, Elspeth *must* champion their sister. She must win her champion to her side, and she must find a way to return Matilda to the throne.

As for Rhiannon... she would destroy their mother.

Fueled by so much hatred, and despite the lack of proper kindling, the fire lit beneath the kettle, bursting up and around the course black belly.

Seren gasped, leaping up from her chair. She rushed to grab an armful of kindling. "Rhiannon, nay! You mustn't do such things!"

Far too late... the storm inside her was already raging, dancing on a fateful wind, turning, whirling, gaining strength, like a maelstrom. Thankfully, none of this was notable to her sisters, because, at the instant it raged only inside Rhiannon.

"If anyone should ever see you do such things, not even the king's mercy will stop them from condemning you! The only reason Ersinius puts up with us is because deep down he does not believe we are born to our grandmother's sins."

Merely because their grandmother had been withered by age and the sisters were too lovely to be evil—but hadn't Morwen proven that to be a lie? In her youth, she had been far more beautiful than any of her daughters, but there was little doubt that she was the evilest witch to walk this earth than they had known in quite some time. "Only because he enjoys his gold," Rhiannon said.

"If I had my guess, he would sooner see us burn," argued Seren as she continued picking through the tinder, gathering the best pieces.

It was the wrong thing to say. Rhiannon's fury grew hotter, and the fire below the cauldron burned brighter, hotter. Alas, they had not been allowed to leave since Elspeth was discovered missing, and nobody brought them anymore wood. If Rhiannon guessed correctly, this was not an oversight, for neither had they had anything to eat since early this morn. Once the envoy had arrived and Elspeth was summoned, chaos ensued and the four of them had been ushered into their prison hovel with permanent guards at their door.

With arms laden, Seren rushed back across the room to toss the kindling into the flames, at first piece by piece, and then she dumped them all at once as a knock sounded at the door. "Forsooth!" she exclaimed, peering over her shoulder and meeting Rhiannon's gaze.

Rhiannon was not surprised.

"Who can it be?"

"Ersinius."

Arwyn's eyes widened. "Here?"

Rose asked, "Now?"

As long as they had ever known him, the chaplain had never once missed Vespers. His devotion to the church—at least as it could be measured by others—was unshakeable. Of course, after the envoy's departure, a visit from him was inevitable, but her sisters had not expected to see him again this evening. Rhiannon lifted her hand, bidding Arwyn and Rose to remain seated as she moved to the door. In the meantime, Seren rushed to grab another armful of kindling to prop up the fire as best she could before Ersinius could see it was mostly bare.

Giving her sister time to put down her handful, Rhiannon unlocked the door, and no sooner had she removed the bar, when the door flew wide, revealing the florid face of their illustrious chaplain. "Father," Rhiannon said quietly.

Undaunted—at least by Rhiannon, although he should have been petrified—Ersinius shoved open the door and marched into their meager home. "I have come to inform that your mother's arrival is imminent."

"But, of course," Rhiannon said silkily. Her sisters might be cowed by the man's temper, but she refused to be bullied.

Because she had such a pure heart, Elspeth always believed Ersinius crossed himself for fear of their bloodline; Rhiannon knew better. He crossed himself because he coveted them—all five sisters together. And he loathed himself for the weakness of his flesh. How he longed to punish them for the temptation they offered. And yet, it was his greatest displeasure to have to share his holy house with those less worthy. He despised the fact that he had served Henry's pious wife, only to become no more than a warden to five profane little girls. Regardless of whether they were in fact born to their grandmother's 'evil ways,' he would have preferred to hand them over to be dealt with by the Pope—and more significantly, he'd have preferred to win admiration for his tireless crusade for the church. The chaplain glared at Rhiannon, warning her without words, and she read every thought that crossed his oily brain. He was thinking how much he loathed them—merely because they had menses. And, furthermore, he was thinking how much he wished he'd caught them undressed... so that, later, he could pleasure himself to the image of them naked in a cluster, all writhing with their sweet, tender flesh over his fat, greasy body. For her sisters' sakes, Rhiannon tried to be submissive, but failed miserably, smiling thinly.

"You will not find yourself quite so smug once you face her," he warned Rhiannon. "And you have sorely disappointed your cousin."

"He is not *my* cousin."

Once again, all three sisters looked at Rhiannon, silently begging for her to calm her raging heart. But she was nothing like Elspeth. Filled with righteous fury, Rhiannon held her smile, and after an instant, the chaplain averted his gaze, uncomfortable with the affliction she'd been born with—her crossed eyes. "He is your father's nephew, and therefore he *is* your cousin, despite that you seem so disinclined to offer him the respect due him."

Rhiannon shrugged, and, for her sisters' sakes, she declined to say that, in fact, Stephen was no kin to her at all, even if he was to her sisters. Her father was *not* Henry Beauclerc and she had known this for most of her life. But she held her tongue, because she knew it would never serve her to reveal the truth to anyone who held her fate in their hands—not even her sisters. Let them all think her father was the same man who'd fathered Elspeth, Seren, Arwyn and Rose.

The chaplain's face was purple with rage. "From this moment on," he continued, "until such time as your mother arrives, you will not be allowed to garden. In fact, you will not be allowed outside your cottage at all. *Ever.* You will take your meals in this room. Ungrateful brats!"

Seren blinked. "So... you mean to keep us prisoners?" she asked.

Besides their companionship, the only one thing that had kept them sane throughout these long years was their ability to garden—and to be outdoors.

"We have *always* been prisoners," Rhiannon argued, and the chaplain continued to address her sisters, ignoring Rhiannon as best he could.

"Your mother will determine what best to do with the lot of you, though I suspect your days at Llanthony are numbered—thank God!"

Yes, do thank God, said Rhiannon without speaking, and he turned his gaze partway to peer at her out of the corner of one eye. And then, with a shudder, he glanced away, casting his gaze at the hearth, and there he narrowed his gaze. He spun to examine the wood pile by the door, and, finally, as he must have longed to do from the instant he stepped into their hovel, he crossed himself, only this time, Rhiannon felt inordinately pleased for the startle he must have felt to find their fire burning strong, with so little wood. What skinny bits Seren had placed beneath the cauldron had already burned away to ash, and still the flames burned strong—as strong as Rhiannon's rage.

Only, now, before they left his priory, she wanted Ersinius to know: Aye, she and her sisters bore the blood of the Great Goddess. And they were also descended of the fair-faced druids who'd settled the Sunken Isle, long before Wales was Wales or England was a thought in the minds of men.

At long last, Seren shook herself free of her stupor, rushing forward to settle a hand on the chaplain's arm, placating him. "We are humbled by your presence, Holy Father, and we are sorry for any trouble we may have caused."

"As you should be," Ersinius berated her. He cast a glance at Rose and Arwyn, neither of which had yet to speak a word. "Alas, there's little I can do for you now."

"Of course," said Seren. "We humbly await our just deserts."

With a flourish, the chaplain turned his back to Rhiannon, appeased by her sister's deference. "In the meantime," he said unapologetically, "empty stomachs and a cold bed should give you much to contemplate. Best you'd pray for your sister's soul. She has endangered alliances."

He dared to glance once more over his shoulder at

Rhiannon, and said, before departing, "And you, wicked girl, best you speak your farewells whilst you can."

"Farewells?" asked Seren, confused. But the chaplain closed the door on her question and Rhiannon held herself together until she heard the slam, then crumpled to the floor.

8

It was early yet, but Merry Bells was spent, and barring another two or three hours of travel time—something neither the girl nor his horse could endure—their options were few. Up ahead, there was a small copse where Malcom made camp with his squire on the way south.

"There's an inn nearby," he said, shaking Elspeth to rouse her. "Alas, I would not recommend it to my worst enemy."

After their most recent argument, they had formed a truce of sorts, and perhaps an easy camaraderie, though probably more due to the fact that Elspeth couldn't seem to stay awake. "Really?" she asked drowsily. "So now I am your worst enemy?"

Malcom smiled. Even in slumber she had sass.

"So where are we going?"

"Well, lass... that's what I am trying to determine."

Elspeth rubbed sleepily at her cheek. "Whether I am your worst enemy? Or where you might prefer to deposit me?"

Malcom chuckled low. "Both," he confessed, though, in

truth, he had already begun to settle his heart on taking the lass all the way home to Aldergh. Strange that, but he felt a growing sense of obligation to her, and though he would do precisely as she bade him, he was beginning to loathe the idea of abandoning her to anyone else's care. He had come to think himself her champion.

He sighed and scratched at the back of his neck, irritated by the biting midge.

Best case scenario: They would take a short respite, water the horse, eat perhaps, then nap, and awake early enough to arrive at Drakewich before dawn. Alas, that would mean asking Elspeth to nap on the cold, damp ground, and to persevere when she might not have the fortitude. She had been so weary all day long, and he rather missed her fury, because at least it kept her awake—not that he minded her lying against his shoulder. He could easily grow accustomed to the curves of her body, and he had begun to daydream about what it might be like to have himself a wife—daydreams he'd not ever entertained despite alliances proposed. Hoping for a little persuasion, he told her now, "Well," he explained. "I had hoped to ride as far as d'Lucy's."

She stiffened. "D'Lucy?"

"The Earl of Drakewich," Malcom explained, wondering over her reaction. "But we'll not make it that far this evening. Instead, we could call upon Amdel."

Was it his imagination? Or did the girl seem to relax in his arms.

"Amdel?"

"The seat of William Beauchamp," Malcom explained. "'Tis another thirty minutes northeast." He didn't bother to add that they were still skirting the same man's land—the one he'd claimed to detest. But despite his mild dislike of the man, his reluctance to call upon that demesne had less to do with any personal feelings he might have for its lord, and more because of his sister.

"Is he perhaps loyal to Stephen?"

"Aye, lass, he is."

Elspeth nodded and said, "But, of course."

It was becoming clear to Malcom that she had no love for their king. Nevertheless, she left it at that, and said nothing more. Malcom did not press.

Alas, he wished he did not but could well understand her woes. There were still many people who feared Stephen would never be strong enough, or wise enough, to forge a lasting peace. Already they'd suffered more than a decade of war, and England was little closer to peace. If Robert of Gloucester hadn't died, or if Matilda had more money in her coffers, or even if Duke Henry had won a victory at Wiltshire, they would still be trading blows.

And despite the strides they'd made in the right direction, there could still be war to come, for he'd heard say that Stephen's own brother, the Bishop of Winchester, was busy courting Matilda—a fact that boded no good, because it was the Bishop who'd handed Stephen the treasury and no doubt, he could take it back as well—diminished though it might be after thirteen years of warfare. And perhaps this was as it should be if, indeed, Stephen meant to crown his son. No honorable man under Stephen's banner trusted King Stephen's only son. But that was neither here nor there. Until such time as Stephen abdicated, Malcom was sworn to serve the man.

Alas, for the moment, they could travel no farther. At long last, he hoped he could persuade Elspeth to reveal something of her plans. She must have intended to go somewhere when she fled. He had business in Scotia, but he would try as best he could to see her safely to her destination. "I suppose we should discuss how far *north* you mean to travel... unless you mean to go as far as I will go."

Elspeth frowned over the question.

Sadly, she hadn't any place to go. Blackwood was no longer the refuge of her kinsmen. London was her mother's domain. And the priory was no longer a safe haven—if ever it had been. She wasn't foolish enough to believe she could make it alone in a hostile land, but if she could, she would fly to Matilda.

Only now she realized that perhaps she and her sisters should have thought better of this plan before Elspeth fled the priory, with no more than the clothes on her back—not even her own at that. But if there was one blessing to be found, it was this: Wearing the layers of a man's clothing, she didn't feel so acutely aware of every muscle in Malcom's body. Her thin, undyed wool gown would have spared her little, and, as it was, she was much too aware of every twitch.

Of course, at the time, anything—including death—had seemed better than finding herself wed to Cael d'Lucy. Now, however, her choices seemed limited, and, despite that it may have spared her some embarrassment in such close proximity, her choice of clothing seemed unfortunate, for how could she arrive at Amdel—or any place else—wearing men's attire? Never in her life had she encountered any woman wearing men's garb—not even her sister Matilda, who dared so much. Surely, it would raise suspicion. And what then? What if this lord of Amdel should demand to know from whence she'd come? What would Elspeth say? What would Malcom say?

And then, it occurred to Elspeth that they hadn't ridden

so far since he'd threatened to put her off his mount. "Is this the same lord you claimed to despise?"

He took a while to answer, but said, "Aye."

Why? She wondered. Was he loyal to her sister? Could she dare to hope for such a stroke of good fortune? In such case, no matter how grateful she might be to Malcom for having abetted her escape, she would have to speak up and ask the man for sanctuary. She hoped that would be the case and she was glad now that she hadn't disclosed more of her circumstances to Malcom. In her father's house she'd been protected; under Stephen's reign, she was mostly ignored; now that she was away from the priory, she must be so careful who she allowed too close. It was never far from her mind that women were put to the stake for less than what she and her sisters had done.

And yet, if, indeed, this lord of Amdel was a loyalist for her sister, would Malcom dare consider stopping for the evening? Wouldn't he prefer that inn to an enemy's abode? Or even a campfire out of sight?

Rhiannon, she begged. *Help me, please.*

Silence returned to her—an empty, weighted silence that fell like an anvil pressed against her ribs making it difficult to breathe and making her long to weep.

And sleep.

Why couldn't she shake this languor? She was like a sleepy babe, content to while away the day in her mother's arms, waking only when necessary.

Once again, she tried to read Malcom as her sister might have done, but his thoughts eluded her. It was just as well, because that type of connection could never be made without consequence. As it was, she was terrified he might discover who—and what—she was, and then everything could change with the snap of his fingers. The consequences could be far, far worse than merely being left alone to walk, and perhaps this was why she'd felt most comfortable with her ire?

Still considering his question, she remained tongue-tied —unsure how to respond. After all, what could possibly be her final destination?

After a long, long while—longer yet than she'd spent deliberating—he finally said, "If you wish it, I would give you sanctuary at Aldergh."

Surprised by the offer, Elspeth drew in a breath. She turned in the saddle, attempting to meet Malcom's seagreen eyes. "You would?"

He pulled at the reins, bringing Merry Bells to a halt. "Aye, lass. I can see you're in need of succor and I would give it without question."

Confused by his generosity, Elspeth said nothing. Already, she owed him so much, and she must find a way to repay him if she could.

In the blink of an eye, he slid down his horse, alighting on his feet, releasing the reins as he peered up at Elspeth, and for a long, tense moment, Elspeth was acutely aware that she could so easily fly away and leave him stranded— on this land belonging to that man he detested—just as he had threatened to do to her.

If she dared to do it, she would have his saddlebag for the effort, and no doubt a few coins as well. And perhaps then she would have enough to book passage to Rouen, where she'd heard her sister had gone, but Malcom had done naught to deserve any such treatment. So she could not do it.

But somehow, though she could not read his mind, he must have read hers. His bright green eyes glinted, though not with mirth. And nevertheless, he handed Elspeth the reins to his horse—only daring her to go. And furthermore, he turned his back on her, moving to his satchel.

Hie now, a little demon taunted. *Go, now* whilst you can. But this, too, was not Rhiannon. It was her own little demon clinging to her shoulder, trembling in fear.

Elspeth lapped at her lips gone dry. "You... you have been kind to me. Perhaps you could tell me... Malcom..." She peered down at Merry Bells' reins in her hand. "Why would you embroil yourself in affairs not your own?"

She heard that he opened his satchel and felt his glance on her back as she fiddled with Merry Bells' reins. "Because you asked for help and I would never shun a woman in need —but," he said, in a voice that sounded quite stern, "I would have you ask for succor with your own two lips, rather than assume 'tis what you require." He continued to rummage through his saddlebag and drew out something rather large, then came about and stood before Elspeth with a ruby-red cloak in his hands. "A wise man once told me 'tis wiser to ask than to suppose."

"What man?"

"My Da," he said and offered her the cloak.

For a befuddled instant, Elspeth was torn, still considering snapping the reins and ordering the horse to bolt, but then he thrust the cloak at her, and she dropped the reins and took his offering, only briefly meeting his gaze. "Tis a... fine... cloak," she said, squeezing the material. "Fit for a king." It was, in truth, more splendid than any cloak she'd ever seen, and she wondered if even Matilda, as the widow of a Holy Roman Emperor, had ever owned something so fine.

Ersinius did not, and he lined his coffers with all the gifts he received. So, then, who was this northern lord who could afford such finery?

"It belonged to my grandsire," he said, as though he'd read Elspeth's mind. But she knew he could not, because she would have *felt* him prying—just as Merry Bells had felt her.

"He must have been a wealthy man," she said.

"So he was, but wealth alone is not the full measure of prosperity."

She nodded agreement and smiled. "More wise words from your Da?"

The color in his cheeks heightened. "Nay, lass, those are mine."

Now, it was Elspeth's turn to chuckle, but his next words silenced her.

"Would you ask me for succor, Elspeth?"

He was staring at her now, arms crossed, and a shrewd look in his eyes that made Elspeth think he expected some favor for his "succor." But of course—had any man ever done aught for a woman simply because? She folded her hands into the rich fur of his cloak, warming them against the cool air, reluctant to throw the garment over her shoulders—not until she knew precisely what he would have from her. "And you have conditions, of course?"

"Of course."

Elspeth looked at him crossly, instantly regretting not having taken his horse and fled. "Well?"

Without a word, Malcom reached up, putting both hands into the air in supplication, asking her to willingly dismount. *Trust me,* she thought she heard him say, though his lips never moved. But that was preposterous. There was no way this man—this Scots—could have any knowledge or skill for the *hud.* And yet, wasn't it true that her grandmamau had said *all* men and women had some ability to harness the *hud.* Regardless, much as his horse must have felt when Elspeth summoned her back in the forest in

Wales, his arms held the same ability to coerce her. Hating herself for acquiescing, she fell into Malcom's embrace, allowing him to pull her down and put her feet on the ground. Alas, she didn't expect to find her legs so unsteady, and she wavered, tumbling into his embrace. "I beg pardon," she said.

"You have sea legs," he teased.

Elspeth held on to him, embarrassed. "I have never been to sea," she confessed.

Only once after she was steady, he released her and confessed, "Neither have I." The confession wrangled a smile from Elspeth, although it vanished the instant he reminded her, "As to my condition..." He looked at her soberly. "If I am to put my neck at risk of the gallows, I *must* know from whom you flee."

Without realizing she'd held her breath, Elspeth exhaled in relief and said with surprise, "Is that all?"

"Truth is the only payment I require," he said, lifting a brow. "Unless you have something else of value you wish to trade?"

Elspeth blushed hotly as he released her and moved back again, to his saddlebag, drawing out a smaller length of cloth, and tossing it over his shoulder. He sauntered past, grabbing Merry Bells' reins and started to walk away, leaving Elspeth to follow. "There's a stream nearby," he said. "If 'tis your wish, you may refresh yourself. When you are ready, we'll call upon Amdel. There is a woman there who would give you aught you need."

Woman?

What woman?

Curious now, Elspeth rushed after him, frowning, but this time, it wasn't precisely annoyance that turned her lips. She watched Malcom walk away, and suddenly had a thousand questions rushing to her lips—evidently, quite some more than he had for her, even after having warned her that he expected her candor.

"Be sure to use the cloak," he said. "And when you have a moment, turn the tunic inside out. Or everyone will know you are from Llanthony. I dinna care overmuch though it seems to me you do."

Elspeth stopped in her tracks, startled.

9

"How?" she sputtered. "How did you know I am from Llanthony?"

Malcom didn't turn to look at her, because he was still sore over the fact that she'd considered breaking faith with him—again—even after he'd proven such a willingness to help.

"Ach, lass, it takes no seer to reckon you stole your guard's clothes."

"Though why Llanthony?" she persisted, sounding befuddled—as though the mysteries of life were hers alone to decipher. "'Tis not a women's cloister."

"The cross on your tunic," Malcom explained. "Llanthony happens to be the only monastery for leagues, save for Abbey Dore, but Llanthony is closer. And, since, as you say, 'tis not a women's cloister, it would make an ideal place to hide a woman who's otherwise not meant to be found."

"I see," she said, sounding nonplussed.

Surmising he must be correct, based on the tone of her voice, Malcom continued. "As to the matter of your clothing... I dinna ken too many lassies who don men's attire and perch themselves in trees. Therefore, you must have been hiding. And since you were so ready to risk life and limb to steal my horse, it stood to reason you must be running away. 'Tis but a matter of deduction."

Elspeth fell silent too long, and Malcom glanced over his shoulder to find her standing still, wringing her hands through his grandfather's cloak, her brow furrowed, deep in thought.

"Am I right?" he pressed.

She started after him. "Tis much more complicated than that," she said. "But, aye." She sounded wounded by the next thing she asked. "And would you truly have taken my life merely for stealing your horse?"

Malcom shrugged.

"Even after discovering I am a woman?"

Malcom shrugged again. "I have dismembered wee boys for less," he confessed, though it wasn't entirely true. He'd merely meant to frighten one of his fostered boys after he stole another fellow's dagger. And, having compelled the lad to put a hand on the table so Malcom could exact his "justice," Malcom fully intended to miss, but the boy moved his hand. Alwin lost two fingers that day, but he never again stole from his fellows, and thereafter, he'd learned to swing an axe with far deadlier results than most of Malcom's seasoned men-at-arms. These days, Alwin was far more to him than just a man at arms. He was Malcom's steward, and Malcom trusted him with the keys to his house.

"Why freshen *before* calling?" Elspeth inquired, and the question rankled Malcom more than it should. In truth, it irritated him that she would presume to ask for details when she was so unwilling to provide any of her own. "I should think our host would be pleased enough to provide the courtesy of a bowl of water with *vin aigre*."

Malcom would prefer washing in an ice-cold stream over a bowl laced with soured wine. But he didn't respond, and he kept on walking, the morning's good humor entirely diminished—even despite their recent truce.

And to make matters worse, his shoulder was hurting, and the wound was bound to raise questions. This was the primary reason he preferred to wash himself *before* facing Beauchamp. And yet it was not the only reason, and neither was it any of her concern that merely by virtue of the fact that he would arrive bearing a female guest, he would be forced now to declare one way or another for Beauchamp's sister. Once he denied the girl, Beauchamp was bound to be angered, and he was as shrewd as he was dishonest. If Beauchamp sensed a means to profit from Malcom's misfortune, he would surely do so. Were Malcom alone, as he was meant to be, he would have taken respite here in the woods, and left Beauchamp to wait for an answer. But that was no longer an option. It was either call upon Amdel or take Elspeth to that inn, and Malcom had only stepped into that hellhole but once—and that was one too many times. He'd known more than a few men who'd claimed they'd meant to shelter at Darkwood en route from court, and curiously, knew at least two who were never heard from again—not barons or earls, merely vassals whose horses and purses were fat enough to make them worth the while of burgling, but who might not be so quickly missed.

However, if not Amdel or the inn, Elspeth would be forced to sleep on the hard, cold ground—right next to him, because he hadn't but one blanket. And so much as he believed he could enjoy the last of these options, he was equally certain Elspeth would not. She was no nun, so she claimed, but she was also no camp follower, and there was something about the lass, despite her current manner of dress, that made him feel she was gentle-born.

Nevertheless, after all that was said and done, he was also quite livid she had judged him and found him unworthy of her trust. Malcom was honor-bound to help the girl, but he couldn't help her if she refused to divulge the details of her circumstances. And regardless of his reputation, he had no intention of torturing a woman to compel the truth from her, and so, his only option was to allow her to confide in him, of her own accord, which was proving far easier said than done.

Unfortunately, Malcom had a growing sense that he had embroiled himself in something larger than he'd first supposed, and the longer she kept silent, the greater his foreboding.

And far and above all the day's happenings, he had his own troubles to contend with. Either his sire was ill—near to death, so the missive had said—or he wasn't ill at all, and there was something significant afoot, something portentous enough that they would summon a known king's man from a commission in Wales and put his entire demesne at risk. And this was yet another reason he did not relish the thought of facing Beauchamp: He was a damned poor liar, despite his duties for the king. He was struggling to form a plausible story—and she would thank him for his consideration by stealing his horse. God's blood, he didn't wish to be angry now that he had begun to wrest a few smiles from the lass, but there it was. And here they were.

As they slipped through the brush, Elspeth followed quietly behind him, although Malcom sensed she had a hundred questions perched on the tip of her tongue.

Malcom tossed his towel over a tree branch, then

proceeded to peel off his coif, thereby revealing the damage to his hauberk beneath the shoulder mantle.

Refusing to look at Elspeth, he settled the armor into a dingy pile of ringed metal and inspected the damage to his hauberk.

The blood was mostly gone, with a bit of it crusted here and there. Nevertheless, he was in a good deal more pain now, and he wished he'd seen to the wound sooner, with or without his squire. Indeed, he had meant to stop as soon as he could commit himself to the considerable time and effort it would take to divest himself properly. But he hadn't counted on meeting Elspeth—or her need to escape. He cast her a glance now, and found her watching him with wide, curious eyes.

"You're injured," she said softly, surprised, and Malcom nodded, acknowledging the truth of that matter.

He was grateful now that he'd opted in favor of his old *hauberk*. Much to the armorer's dismay, he'd chosen not to wear the new arming doublet, with the fancy chainmail gussets sewn into the vest and the sigil of his house emblazoned on the front. As handsome as it might be, and easy as it might have been for travel, he would have incurred a far more serious wound had he been wearing the doublet. For all its weight and discomfort, there was something to be said for old-fashioned ingenuity. But the hauberk was ruined now and in need of repairs. His jerkin was also pierced all the way through, attesting to the force and speed of the missile. And the *sherte* itself was rent.

He sighed. As much as it galled him to have been left to defend himself, he was glad for the fact that his squire fled whilst he could. Malcom hoped Daw found himself refuge, and whatever ill humor he'd borne over the man's desertion, he was over it now. The lad was young—perhaps too young to have taken him into battle. And so much for thinking the embattled Welsh would prove to be easier foes. It was inconceivable that Stephen should ever hope to subjugate those people.

He cast another glance at Elspeth. He could manage on his own, if he must, but the *hauberk* was heavy and unwieldy. With a sigh, he moved to lift it up by the hem, finding that his arm ached. "Wouldst ye, please?" he asked her.

"Oh, yes!" she said, and at once, she tossed his grandfather's cloak over the same branch where he'd hung his towel and rushed to aid him.

Gratitude tempered Malcom's ire as he sank to his knees before her, allowing her the height she would need to negotiate the armor.

"I am so sorry," she said.

Malcom arched a brow. "For what, precisely?"

"For the wound..."

His brogue was thicker now that he was weary. "If ye dinna shoot me, lass, ye ha'e naught to be sorry for." What he wanted her to be sorry for was her stubborn silence and her readiness to flee. And then he wondered aloud, "Ye dinna shoot me, di' ye?"

"Oh, nay! I would never... and still..." Her gaze met his briefly, before bearing up the *hauberk*, and Malcom could never have anticipated the thoughts that assailed him as she prepared to undress him. His blood simmered over the look of concern in her bonny blue eyes. God help him. For too damned long he'd yearned for a proper home—a gentle woman who might see to his needs... and more... someone who would greet him with warm spiced mead and sweet, gentle kisses—someone who might soothe his soul, if not his body. Elspeth was *not* his intended, nor was this his bed chamber, but he swallowed convulsively, because, far from leaving him cold, her proximity stirred a fire in his blood that Malcom couldn't deny. She shifted to give herself leverage, gingerly pressing her knee against the side of his chest and the warmth of her thigh made him instantly hard. For but an instant, a vision appeared before his eyes, and he saw they were not surrounded by trees or a gurgling brook, but by a warm, crackling brazier and a fine curtained bed... He saw her face much as it was now, but her lips were bruised by his kisses, and her cheeks were flushed with desire. She was naked and unashamed, her skin lit copper by the fire burning in the brazier, and her breasts were bounteous enough to fill the palms of his hands.

He blinked and saw her straddle him with a smooth-skinned thigh, pushing him down on the bed with a splayed hand, then climb atop him with a siren's smile.

Elspeth gasped, startled—as though she too had shared the vision—and remembering herself, she tugged up the hauberk over Malcom's head, scraping his nose during the process, successfully shifting his focus from one aching appendage to another.

The instant he was free of the *hauberk*, Elspeth stepped back, and Malcom avoided her gaze as he shrugged free of the leather jerkin, and then the long-sleeved cloth *sherte* he wore beneath, inspecting each in turn. All the while, Elspeth stood, watching.

When finally he dared to look at her and her eyes fell on his wound, he watched the play of emotions that crossed her features. Sorrow—*for his injury?* Confusion—*why?* And something else... something Malcom daren't acknowledge. *Desire.* It was as though she too had borne the vision, and it was an excruciating long moment whilst they stood, staring into one another's eyes.

Finally, she said, "Why did you not tell me you were injured?"

Malcom peered through his lashes. "When would have been a good time? Whilst we were fleeing your captors? Or whilst you were sleeping and snoring?"

A rosy flush crept into her cheeks, but she let his jibe pass. "We have long since departed Wales," she said. "And still... you said naught."

He answered peevishly, "I suppose you are not the only one who likes to keep secrets."

She averted her gaze. "But... it was stupid. You could take a fever."

"I am fine," Malcom assured as he rose from his knees to retrieve his washrag.

He went to the brook to dip the cloth, and perhaps realizing what he meant to do, Elspeth rushed forward to take it from his hands. "Sit," she demanded. "I can do it better."

Lifting his brow, Malcom did as she bade him. He found and sat on a nearby log and waited whilst Elspeth dipped the towel into the burn, then wrung it free of excess moisture. Alas, whilst he appreciated the effort, it didn't do much to cool his ardor.

"Who did this to you?"

"I would presume one of your Welsh compatriots." He lifted his brow. "Perhaps Rhys ap Hywel or Owain Gwynedd or mayhap Madog ap Maredudd..."

Elspeth said nothing, but her brows twitched, and Malcom instantly regretted trying to bait her. To make up for it, he meant to set her mind at ease. "I know I offered, lass... but dinna worry... if ye dinna wish to travel all the way to Aldergh, I ken. We are not willing companions and, clearly, ye dinna trust me."

. . .

"But... I *do* trust you," Elspeth said, surprised to discover how much she meant it. And yet, why she should trust *any* man was a mystery as perfect as the Virgin Birth.

Evidently, Malcom would have her reveal everything, but he evidently had no intention of returning the favor. What did she know of him, after all? Naught more than the fact that he was a northern lord, sworn to her cousin. And once again, she'd found him prying.

Naturally, she held her tongue, unwilling to share more than she'd already revealed. Trust went only so far.

It would never serve Elspeth to confess that she was a daughter of the late king.

And it would serve her even less to disclose her relation to Morwen—even if he did not personally know her mother. Of course, Morwen would be discreet, but if anyone had ever spent any good time in Stephen's court, they would certainly have encountered her mother. She was not so easily overlooked. Whether or not she'd ever meant to heed the queen's warning, she would never be so bold—or so stupid—as to make her counsel to the king so widely known. She would, in truth, be discreet, if for no other reason, because she wouldn't wish to remind anyone who she was—a daughter of Avalon.

She realized she must make a decision soon—to seek sanctuary at Amdel or continue on to Aldergh, and if she sought sanctuary with Malcom, she would be forced to confess. But at the moment, she was leaning toward Amdel. Even if Beauchamp was loyal to Stephen, perhaps he could still be a reluctant vassal. Malcom was not. Quite obviously. But there were many, many barons who were. Shortly after her father's death, Stephen had divested his enemies. And now, so many of her father's barons found themselves dispossessed, sheltering amidst Matilda's

Norman holdings and living off the good graces of a Would-be Queen. Elspeth would hardly be surprised to learn that, in order to protect their holdings, many of the old guard were simply biding their time, remaining quietly loyal to her sister, waiting for the opportunity to renounce their vows.

Forsooth, even the king's own brother, the Bishop of Winchester, was waffling. Elspeth knew this only because the Bishop had come to Llanthony a few weeks past, counseling with Ersinius. Elspeth overheard their conversation in the garden.

Elspeth's good sense told her that Malcom might not love his king, per se, but his loyalty would never be in question—and even so, she sensed a darkness in him... an aura of fury that burned hotter when he spoke of his fealty to Stephen. There was something about his vows to Stephen that gave him grief. But, alas, his was a confusing mix of emotions, and Elspeth wished, not for the first time, that she had her sister's skill to read his thoughts. It might give her a clue as to what she should do... beg for help from the lord of Amdel... or trust Malcom to see her through.

Sad to say, she only knew what she wanted to do... and this made too little sense.

In truth, she had begun to think of Malcom as her champion, reluctant or nay. And now, after that vision they'd shared... she feared he could be something more.

Goddess save her, she would never again be able to look at him without seeing the bare-chested image of a man with heavy-lidded eyes leaning back on one elbow, watching her, with smoky blue eyes that glinted by firelight, and sun-kissed hair that curled about his face.

"For what it's worth," he said, his tone less curt, "if you ask it of me, Elspeth, I will speak to the lord of Amdel on your behalf. However... I should impress upon you to consider this very carefully as I mistrust that man."

Elspeth wiped carefully at his wound. "So you have said... but has he done aught to incur your ill-will?"

"Not to me," he said cryptically.

"To someone you care for?"

"Not precisely."

"Why then should you detest the man?"

He eyed her pointedly. "Have you never simply had a feeling? A sense of something you cannot name? You can't see it... you can't smell or touch it... but you know in your heart it simply is?"

Elspeth averted her gaze. Of course she had. She was having one now—with him. This, after all, was the essence of the *hud*, and some people knew how to sense things more deeply. She bit her lip as she cleaned Malcom's wound, considering the "feeling" he had but couldn't name. And in the midst of these thoughts, she had another far more startling thought: She could dare to be happy with a man like Malcom. *Couldn't she?*

Wincing over the torn, raw flesh, she parted the damaged skin to peer closer at the wound, making certain there was no detritus remaining. To his credit, Malcom did not complain, allowing her to do as she would. "We are but hours away from Drakewich," he persisted. "I would warrant d'Lucy would serve you better."

Elspeth studiously avoided his gaze, not wanting him to see how much it discomfited her to hear that name, even despite that she knew this lord of Drakewich was not the same d'Lucy who'd been awarded their beloved estate. She also realized that sharing the same blood did not mean those two men shared the same heart. There were many families torn asunder by Stephen's tumultuous reign—

including her own. At long last, realizing that Malcom must be expecting an answer, she said, "Thank you." But, clearly, that wasn't the answer he sought, and he must have realized she was being evasive. After that, the silence between them lengthened, until it grew uncomfortable.

Leave it be, Elspeth. There were more urgent matters to tend to anyway. His wound was festering, and she marveled that he could have ridden all this way without so much as a complaint.

Considering her own foul temper, all day long, she felt abashed. He'd had far more reason to grouse than she did, and he never did once.

In fact, most of the time he'd answered her own complaining with good humor, and for all his poor judgment in sovereigns, he seemed to be a decent man. Realizing he needed intervention, she stared at his wound, hesitating....

She could heal him now if she chose to... and she did wish to. But the last thing she meant to do was to reveal herself this way. She could see it now—the marvel in his eyes when the wound closed before his eyes, and then afterward, once clarity returned, and the wonder and gratitude subsided, he would revile her, calling her a witch and a devil.

A thousand lifetimes might pass, and Elspeth would *never* forget the way those people had treated her grandmamau, tossing stones to bash her head, even as the flames had engulfed her.

Tears pricked at her eyes, and she pushed the image away, focusing on Malcom's wound. Pressing the blood-soaked cloth against his skin, she considered what Seren might do...

Her sister had a true gift for healing. Elspeth now found

herself lamenting the fact that she'd not learned more of her skills—as well as her temperament. Her middle sister was far more even tempered than she was. Indeed, she could have been their father's favorite, save for the simple fact that she had not yet grown into her wit and beauty before Henry's death. As often as her father had lamented Matilda and Elspeth could not exchange places, he would have found himself bemoaning it all the more with Seren. Matilda was too willful, he'd so often said—and once, when Elspeth was ten, she'd witnessed her father's fury over Matilda's bad temper. Cursing the day his eldest daughter was begot, he'd hurled his crown after her departure.

"Don't be like her," he'd said once she was gone.

But, as was the case with all her sisters, Elspeth found she could not help but admire her eldest, who, by the age of twelve had already wed a holy Roman emperor, and who, at three and twenty, had stood before their haughty sire, unyielding in her resolve. Any lesser woman would never challenge Henry's barons.

And, yet, make no mistake, her father had fully intended to install Matilda on his throne, for inasmuch as he'd loathed the fact that she could be so headstrong, he'd also said she was the only one of his children who was strong enough to keep his peace. As far as Elspeth was concerned, Henry would no more have abdicated his crown to his lying nephew than he would have crowned a bastard son he'd loved so well—not whilst he had a legitimate heir to pass the realm to.

So then, her cousin was a liar. For all those years she'd spent at court, he'd been a boot licker, bowing to every word her father said. *"Yes, your grace, no, your grace."* And then, behind Henry's back, he'd worked his wiles the same way Morwen did. There was little wonder those two were close.

In truth, Elspeth suspected they'd been in cahoots from the beginning, and if that were true, her mother might also be responsible for her father's death. After all, it was Morwen who'd introduced Henry to those eels, and it was she, as his mistress, not his wife, Adeliza of Louvain, who'd been with him on the day he'd died. If it be the last thing Elspeth did, she intended to discover what treachery befell her father... and perhaps not today, or tomorrow, but someday, her sister would return to England, and she would not stop until she wore their father's crown.

In the meantime, Elspeth's loyalties *must* remain absolute. She didn't know how or when, but she fully intended to join her sister's crusade, and considering that—and the fact that she would be remiss to reveal herself and take any chance of failing Matilda—she continued to clean Malcom's wound, wiping away the last traces of blood and grime.

So, nay, she decided. She would not heal him now. First, she would advise him to cauterize it. "You are fortunate," she said, after a while. "The wound is deep, and it festers a bit, but it will heal. I would put a hot blade to it as soon as you can."

He sought her gaze, his blue-green eyes gleaming. "We haven't any fire," he said. "I did not mean to kindle one... not if we intend to call upon Amdel..."

It was a question, Elspeth realized.

Evidently, he was leaving the decision up to her. If she wished for him to seek refuge there, he would do so. She handed him back the towel, but she did not mean to say what she said next. "Kindle a fire. I will help you cauterize your wound."

10

There was a wealth of meaning in the look they shared. Malcom took the blood-soaked rag from Elspeth's hands, grateful for her ministrations. "Art certain, lass?"

She shook her head, but said, "Aye." And despite the mixed message, Malcom wouldn't argue. He no more wished to call upon Amdel than he cared to lick Beauchamp's arse.

"A fire it is," he said. Let it be done. He would build a fire, here on chartered lands, and leave his business with Beauchamp for another day—that suited him fine.

And nevertheless, although he was relieved by Elspeth's choice, some part of him mistrusted her reason why. Already, she'd attempted to steal his horse, not once, but twice; he could but surmise she meant to try again. And regardless, he would take that any day over sharing a cup of gritty *vin* with Beauchamp.

For the sake of modesty, he rose and put on his gambeson, intending to wash the *sherte* in the burn—just in case Elspeth changed her mind. If later he were forced to face

Beauchamp, he'd prefer to be wearing a wet, clean *sherte*, over one stained with his own blood.

"Art hungry?"

"What about your wound?"

"Not now."

She frowned at him, and more than ever, Malcom wanted to ask: Who was she, and why was she so reluctant to confess anything to him? Why now had she decided to avoid Amdel?

However, for the moment, until he knew what she intended, he didn't want her anywhere near his bare flesh with a hot blade. God's truth, no matter his opinion of Beauchamp, he didn't know very many ladies who'd give up the chance for a bath and a change of clothes—particularly since her manner of dress did not suit her. The breeches were far too tight, and the tunic was overlarge, and she'd fidgeted uncomfortably all-day long. Perhaps she'd taken his warning about Beauchamp to heart, but then again, what did he know? She might easily have more to lose than he did by allowing herself to be discovered by someone like Beauchamp. He sighed, and considering the answers to these questions, Malcom chose a spot to construct the fire— a location well concealed from prying eyes. So far, it boded well enough that Beauchamp's men had yet to confront them, and it was growing late enough to hide the smoke from their fire.

Once the flames were burning evenly, he hobbled Merry near the burn, where she could graze and drink freely, and then he left his strange new troupe to hunt for supper.

It didn't take long to find suitable fare. He settled on a small hare, but immediately rued the decision to make camp so close to Amdel. Certainly, it wasn't anything so significant as deer, but it was nevertheless game belonging to the crown. He had been very careful to travel outside Beauchamp's parklands. Strictly speaking, these lands were part of Henry's charter, but Malcom realized very well that it wouldn't prevent Beauchamp from assuming the role of an injured party, as he had with d'Lucy—and he might do so if Malcom were forced to repudiate his sister. As reluctant as the man was to part with his little sister, he seemed greedy for an alliance. But Malcom wouldn't fool himself over the reason why. Beauchamp couldn't give a damn about Malcom per se; he was far more interested in allying with a member of Stephen's Rex Militum—an elite division of the King's guard tasked with securing the king's justice. Any member might have served him well enough, but to his utter displeasure, most of them had far greater influence than Malcom. They would have too many options at their disposal to bother allying with a baron, whose favor remained in question.

But rather fortunately for Malcom, Stephen's heart was not in the enforcement of Henry's charter. It was just that since he'd abandoned his post in Wales, he worried Beauchamp would take the matter to Stephen, and if he did so, Malcom might be forced to answer for far more than poaching. His assignment in Wales was left incomplete, and Stephen might even be annoyed enough to enforce Henry's Forest Law to its fullest degree. He was proving quite good at redirecting his displeasure. What was more, if Stephen should ask why Malcom had left his post... well, he was, indeed, a poor liar. If, in truth, the summons to Scotia was a ruse, Malcom stood to lose everything he'd worked for over the past eleven years. All his many sacrifices would come to naught.

He exhaled wearily, for at times like these, he so much lamented his fealty to England. Life in Scotia had been much simpler. And nevertheless, shoving the past out of his head, he wondered again who might sequester a lovely lass —and four sisters—in a remote priory in the Black Mountains of Wales. And, furthermore, why did she take such a fright every time he mentioned d'Lucy's name?

In truth, Malcom couldn't imagine anyone, save a loyalist to the Empress, who might take offense to the Graeham d'Lucy. Graeham's brother was another matter entirely. Blaec, like his cousin Cael, inspired fear, and Malcom himself wouldn't relish meeting either of those two fellows on a battlefield. However, Blaec was a second son and had nothing to offer a woman of substance. Cael, on the other hand, was in a position to benefit from a well-placed alliance. For his service to Stephen, he was recently awarded a Marcher demesne. But while Cael was hardly a man to be trifled with, Malcom did not believe him so villainous as to merit the fear he sensed in Elspeth.

But the more he thought about it, the more sense it made that Stephen would offer Cael a high-born wife to substantiate his claim so deep in the Marches. So if Elspeth was offered to Blackwood—*why*? Who was she? And more importantly: God save Malcom, because Blackwood was the last man in the realm he would have liked to have had as an enemy.

Brooding over the possibilities, he returned to camp to clean and dress the hare, relieved to find that everyone remained.

Tossing down the cony on a stump near his pit, he sat, drawing the blade from his boot, taking note of what everyone else was doing. Merry Bells was still hobbled by the burn. Elspeth had evidently taken it upon herself to wash his *sherte* and hang it to dry. And, then, having discovered the bedroll behind his saddlebag, she'd untied it and laid it down near the firepit. And furthermore, she'd taken to heart his advice about her tunic. Whilst Malcom was gone, she'd turned the garment inside out. Right now, she sat on his blanket, inspecting the damage to his *hauberk*.

"I don't suppose you have extra rings?" she asked after Malcom was seated, careful not to meet or hold his gaze.

"Nay, lass," he said. "I do not."

And still, she fiddled with the *hauberk*, while Malcom threw himself into the task of cleaning the hare, cutting the skin at the back of the cony's neck, then, holding the carcass by the back of its legs, and gathering the soft skin to tear it off—like his father taught him.

It was at times like these he felt closest to his Da, remembering the times they'd gone hunting and fishing together. He missed those days, more than he cared to admit.

As for Elspeth, he was pleased to see she had skill at tending fires, because the one he'd built was burning stronger now, and was trimmed with fieldstones. Putting lie to his previous summations about her, that was not what he would have anticipated from a highborn lady.

Now, once again, as he watched her fiddle with his hauberk, examining the small links, he suffered the same thoughts he'd had earlier, and an altogether different and more potent heat stirred his loins. *Bedamned.* There was something entirely too intimate about their time here together, putting thoughts into his head he shouldn't be having. For the moment, she was his ward, but that would change the instant she decided to open her mouth and tell him what he needed to know.

"It can be repaired," she said, offhand, and the sight of her trying to mend his accoutrements hardened him fully for the second time in the span of a single day—a state of arousal he'd enjoyed less and less over the past years. Lifting a leg to hide the evidence, Malcom leaned an arm atop his knee, and settled into the task of skinning the cony, hoping it would cool his ardor.

"Easier said than done," he said, trying not to notice the provocative way her tunic rode up her thighs, revealing her too-tight breeches.

Bluidy hell. He might armor elsewhere, if she should happen to notice he'd formed a tent in his breeches. Sighing again, he tugged at the skin of the cony, trying not to notice the delicate way she was fingering the small loops of his mail. And, perhaps, he took out some of his frustrations on the cony, lopping off the animal's feet, and then its head. He proceeded to gut it, the task effectively cooling his ardor. And nevertheless, whilst he worked, he came very aware that Elspeth had stopped what she was doing and now she was watching him intently. Glancing up to find her mouth twisted with disgust, he lifted the bare-bodied cony. "Hungry?" he teased.

She shook her head, but Malcom knew it to be a lie. Her stomach gurgled nearly as loudly as the brook, and he chuckled. "I presume you've never killed or cleaned your own dinner before?"

Casting the *hauberk* aside, she abandoned the puzzle of his *sherte*, and said, "Nay."

"I promise it will look more appetizing after I'm done."

Her hand went to her belly. "I might never forget the sight of it now."

Malcom worked quickly, realizing the process unsettled her.

"My sisters and I… we… I… never… well… what I mean to say is we were more familiar with gruel than we ever were with… *that.*"

"Cony?"

"Aye."

"More's the pity," Malcom said with a wink, thinking about the stews auld Glenna had prepared for him back home. Like his mother, she could whip up a fine kettle with anything she was given.

OF COURSE, it wasn't as though Elspeth hadn't sometimes wished to kill a hare or two—particularly when they munched on her garden. But *that* was disgusting.

Up until now, they'd traveled over much of the day without ever stopping for respite, and she realized only belatedly how hungry and thirsty she was. But, to be sure, she thought his choice of food rather crude. Whilst she and her sisters ate whatever was put in front of them at the priory, their meals had rarely consisted of animal flesh. If there be one true sin, it would be the unnecessary taking of a life, and therefore, where it concerned a body's sustenance, it was well enough to harvest what could be wrought from the earth—mostly tended by their own hands.

Betimes they'd foraged for berries, ate bread and cheese, and rarely a bit of fish. After all, some flesh could not be avoided with the monks in such a proud state over their new hatchery. They'd also kept hens, and these were mostly raised for eggs, and goats for milk. But whilst Elspeth was no stranger to the butchering of animals for sustenance, this was not something she had ever become familiar with until she'd spent time in her father's court.

Her father's tables had been replete with flesh—great sows still bearing sad heads, pheasants posed as though they could still take flight. Long stretches of intestines were filled with crushed organs, betimes blood staining the trenchers they ate from. It always made Elspeth sad to see all that carnage, but that's where Morwen probably developed her taste for blood.

But, indeed, she was hungry. And since Elspeth was not the one who'd killed the poor beast, she wouldn't turn it away, and neither should it go to waste. It was one thing to be the one to kill it, another thing to eat it, she supposed. And neither was it a sin to kill sparingly for food—so long as one gave atonement and thanks and took no more than was necessary. After all, theirs was not a religion, and contrary to what folks might believe, neither did they worship demons.

In fact, her grandmamau had taught her that *all* gods were *one* god, born of the same Great Mother, from whose womb sprung the world itself.

For that matter, Taliesin's works had been well aligned with Holy church, and, in his day, his counsel had been sought after by the Holy Roman Emperor himself.

Their priests and priestesses were not unlike Christian priests, who in their hearts and minds were merely closer to God. Indeed, Elspeth might even call herself a Christian, save for the way they'd treated her and her sisters at the priory. And yet, despite this, she followed many of the tenets of Holy Church, because the teachings were scarcely different from the teachings of the Goddess—and the one most profound was: Do good, harm none.

The darker arts were something else entirely. In the performance of *hud du,* some of those spells were cast with sacrificial magic, which in itself was a blasphemy to the Goddess—and perhaps this was why the eating of flesh was discouraged.

She watched Malcom pull off the cony's fur and averted

her gaze, unable to stomach so much blood, and feeling flush, she lifted the back of her hand to her cheek.

So much for worrying that Malcom would take a fever; she was the one who was warm! And not for the least of reasons, he was seated there before her, despite the cool evening, wearing only a sleeveless *gambeson* over a tight pair of breeches. For all that she could see, he might as well be nude.

She tried not to notice, but his muscles were wickedly sinuous, tightening and twitching all the while he worked his ornate little dagger over the hare. Merely the sight of it was enough to leave her face burning as hot as the coals in his pit—and perspiring despite the coolness of the air.

Much as it had been this morn, his aura was a pale orange, with hints of silver. All living, and even non-living entities, radiated colors that revealed more than words alone could say. Whilst the most prominent color in Malcom's aura remained orange, and this revealed a generally kind-heart and honest nature, it could also mean that betimes he was quick to lose his temper. He could be passionate in all things, and whatever he set his heart to, that's where it would remain unto death.

Fortunately, Elspeth hadn't noticed any trace of black in his aura, and, no doubt, this was why she'd felt so at ease to goad him. Everyone had a thin, dark vein now and again, but she knew to be wary if it was present all the time. Ersinius' was perpetually black, though she didn't need to read auras to know that to be the case. His actions spoke for themselves.

As she sat watching Malcom work, she was chagrined to see that a deep red began to rise. This was the color of desire. *He desires me,* she realized. And more to the point: She desired him. How this was possible after such a short time, Elspeth didn't know, because she had never in her life experienced any such connection. And yet whatever it was that called to her—perhaps their shared vision—she felt a stirring in her belly like the fluttering of butterfly wings and a prick in her nipples that made her long to suckle his babes. Thankfully, he could not read her as she could read him.

Her gaze moved to his lips, and she flushed, averting her gaze. "So... how far is Aldergh?" she asked casually, hoping to occupy her mind with something other than desire and form.

"Far," he replied. "I would not blame you if you chose not to come."

Elspeth nodded, casting him a quick glance. At the moment, he wasn't even looking at her, and for some reason, his quickness to dismiss her as a traveling companion, pricked at her self-esteem. Mayhap, in truth, he did not desire her after all?

"In case you've not noticed, *my lord,* I've no need of coddling. I am quite capable of traveling over long distances. And, indeed, were I so opposed to privation, I would have insisted we call upon Amdel." Her tone very clearly revealed her displeasure.

"Fair enough," he said, peering up from the naked hare he was skewering on a long, sharp stick. "So... what you're saying is... you prefer the long trek to Aldergh... with more fare like this..." He lifted his hare. "Rather than seek refuge with d'Lucy?"

"Well..." Elspeth frowned. Put like *that*, it didn't sound so appealing. However, far less appealing was the possibility of discovering herself at the mercy of another of Stephen's minions—not that they should be any worse than Malcom, though she suspected they were. "Aye," she confessed. "I suppose that would be true."

He nodded, then winked, and Elspeth's heart fluttered yet again, and her face burned hotter. Thankfully, he didn't seem to notice.

He set down his butchered hare, turning his attention to the construction of a simple roaster, burying two sturdy, but straight little saplings on either side of his pit. Once those were firmly planted, he hung the skewered rabbit onto the newly formed spit, and once the rabbit began to cook, she found the scent of roasting meat made her mouth water. Her belly grumbled as well, and she settled it with a touch as Malcom leaned back on an elbow to watch his fire burn. Every once in a while, he reached over to turn the spit. And by the by, he had yet to even thank her for trimming his fire, as all responsible people should do—unless, of course, it was his intent to burn down these sacred woodlands. "So, won't you tell me... how came a Scots man to be an English earl?"

He flicked her a glance, and once more reached over to turn his poor little scorched beast. "Aldergh belonged to my grandsire," he said. "It passed to me once he died."

"Oh," she said. But now she was curious. "How did he die?"

"How do most dishonorable men meet their end?"

"Oh," she said again, nonplussed by the answer. "I am sorry." Thereafter, the silence grew thick between them, until the crackling of the fire sounded too loud. She heard insects chirping, and even the distant gurgling of the brook. "I take it he had no sons?" Elspeth pressed after a while.

Malcom shook his head. "Only a daughter... my mother."

Elspeth furrowed her brow. "She did not want her bequest?"

Malcom shrugged.

"I see," she said. Of course, it only figured that they would pass over the daughter and give the estate to a grandson. *Sweet fates.* It brought to mind her own sister's plight, and it galled her so much that this sort of thing could be done. But she realized it wasn't any of her concern.

For his part, her father had been generous to *all* his children, whether they be legitimate or nay. And despite not having access to her settlement, she and her sisters each had a dowry rich enough to put a gleam in any man's eye—including Rhiannon. Of course, they had no means to take it without the king's approval. By the letter of the law, like Blackwood, she and her sisters had become wards of Stephen, but obviously Morwen had something to say over the matter.

It seemed to Elspeth that so much strife had come to pass only to keep what rightfully should belong to a woman. And for this alone, she was committed to helping Matilda. For love of the Goddess, even if they were not blood relation, being a woman, Matilda was so much a beacon of hope, for not since the time of Hywel's Law had any woman outside Wales benefited from a good King's rule. It used to be that women had rights—perhaps not in England, but certainly they did in Wales. If a man and lady wed, even after seven-years' time, it was a woman's right to divorce him, and if she chose to do such a thing for whatever cause, there were laws in place to provide for her keeping. For example, she had the right to take a goodly portion of the estate, because she'd earned it. There was none of this wardship by men. In her own country she would have been free to choose her own mate, but then... would she have chosen a man like Malcom?

Once again, her cheeks warmed. "So... your mother was English?"

"Nay," he said, casting her a pointed glance. "If you must know, my birth mother leapt from a tower window on the day I was born." He said it with so little emotion that it sent a frisson of horror down Elspeth's spine. "Page is my father's lady wife, and aye, she is English." He turned to look at her. "You remind me of her."

"Your mother... or Page?"

"Page."

She scrunched her nose. "Page? What sort of name is that for a lady?" As far as Elspeth knew, page was not a name—it was a manner of service for a boy to a lord. After a certain age, most sons of noble families were sent to receive instruction from greater houses, serving the liege by running errands, cleaning laundry, dressing the lord and learning the basics of combat—but none of these tasks were remotely suitable for a woman. She had a terrible vision of a nameless girl running about a castel, dirty and dressed in rags, being ordered about by her lord. *Page—get this, get that, clean this, clean that.* And she shuddered.

"Tis no name at all," agreed Malcom, though he did not elaborate, and Elspeth regretted having brought up the matter at all, because she'd never heard such woeful tales.

Even her own story wasn't quite so dramatic, although she tried to imagine what life might have been like had only Morwen leapt from a tower window. Morwen had never been a proper mother—not to Elspeth, nor to her sisters. *Hateful, hateful woman.* She'd traded her own mother's life for a price—a dear lady whose sole purpose on this earth was to make the world a better place.

At least Henry had been a doting father—as much as he could manage. Unlike her sister Rhiannon, she had only good memories of their father. And, in their father's defense, he'd never known what to do with a child such as Rhiannon.

"You recall me to someone, too," she confessed to Malcom. "You remind me of my brother." She studied him in profile as he poked a small stick into the licking flames. Until his death, Robert of Gloucester had been one of the richest barons in all of England. He had been as noble a man as any who'd ever lived, and their father had loved him well.

Now that Malcom's coif was gone, and his hair was dry, Elspeth could see that his hair was fair as flax, and thick and wavy, though perhaps too long. But he did, in truth, remind her of Robert, with those bright blue-green eyes—the color of the sea from the highest perch at Blackwood. There was something else about him as well... something she couldn't put her finger on, but she suspected that it had less to do with the way he looked, and more to do with his underlying sense of nobility—a fierce determination to do what was right, no matter the cost.

Seated by the fire, his face was bronzed by the flames. The sinew in his arms was unmistakable by firelight, sculpted by copper light and shadows. His face itself seemed chiseled as though of stone, with sharp contours and a tiny cleft in his chin. His hair, light as it was, seemed to sparkle with silver, and she saw now that he had a long, thin scar on his temple. However, rather than mar his beautiful face, it somehow gave him more character...

She realized only belatedly that she was staring. By the cauldron, she sorely wished she didn't find him so appealing. Could that be this was why she'd asked him not to call upon Amdel? Because she didn't want to leave him? But, nay, such a thing would be preposterous. She would never make decisions about life and death—or her sisters—simply because of a man's pretty face. And even so, for some reason, the thought of parting ways held no appeal.

But, of course, he would ask, "Who is your brother?"

"No one of import," Elspeth answered quickly, hoping Malcom wouldn't press. There was hardly any chance Malcom wouldn't know who he was, and if she named Robert as her brother, it was short guesswork to determine exactly who she was.

His lashes lifted, and once again, he met her gaze—those sea-green eyes glittering by the firelight—but, thankfully, he said nothing more. He rested his head back on the stump behind him and closed his eyes. "Thank you for washing my *sherte*," he said after a moment.

"It was my pleasure," Elspeth assured.

"And thank you for tending the fire."

"Also, my pleasure." She rose to her knees now, then to her feet. "I will return," she said, and a blush warmed her cheeks as her gaze followed the length of his body. Much as she would like to ignore it, it was time to do the necessary—and give herself a break from this man who confused her.

"Dinna wander far," he said, his Scots brogue thicker now that he was resting. But he did not open his eyes. And despite that, Elspeth had every impression that, whilst he pretended not to see her, he was acutely aware of every step she took.

Just to be sure, she turned to see if he was watching, and found that he'd turned his ear toward the sound of her footfalls. But he didn't open his eyes, and neither did he rise to follow so Elspeth turned her back on him and tried not to think of their overly familiar conversation.

Only this time, as she passed by his sweet mare, grazing so placidly by the brook, she realized that if she wished to, she could still take Merry Bells and flee...

Thinking about the particulars of that, she stood for a while, and then, after a moment, she moved closer to Merry Bells to stroke the animal's fine mane.

"Thank you," she said to the mare. "I appreciate your willingness to help, and you were so good to fly away so quickly. I do not know what I would have done elsewise."

The animal snorted—perchance to acknowledge Elspeth's thanks, or perchance to remind her that she had not done so alone. Stroking her lovingly, Elspeth spoke to her in another language—one that needed fewer words. *I mean you no harm, my friend...*

MALCOM LAY UNMOVING, listening to the sound of Elspeth's retreating steps.

When she stopped in the vicinity of Merry Bells, it took every ounce of his self-control not to leap from his repose and fly after her.

Presumably, she'd stopped to see Merry Bells.

The woman was famished; he knew that much. Despite her look of abject horror over the cony, he could hear her stomach grumbling. But regardless, where would she go? He had already removed his saddlebags and laid them aside, so she couldn't get far without his money.

Besides, he'd already assured her that he would take her wheresoever she pleased. Why should she feel the need to go? Inexplicably, he'd placed himself at her disposal, despite his own pressing affairs—the summons to his father. He was committed to doing whatever was required of him.

Come what may, she was not a stupid woman, so he let

her be, allowing her the time and space she needed to deliberate her choices. Mostly, because he wanted to see what she would do.

Certainly, Malcom didn't wish to lose another Merry Bells, but so much as he loathed the prospect of seeing Beauchamp again, he was close enough to Amdel that he could easily impress upon the man to sell a horse. The inn was even closer, and he could pick off any one of their stabled mounts and probably do it without compunction, since all of those animals were likely stolen in the first place. Darkwood was a den of thieves, with the occasional dupe to be found.

At long last, Elspeth left off her chat with Merry Bells, and Malcom exhaled a long sigh when she did. Trust was a fragile thing, but this, at last could be a start...

11

They ate quickly. Elspeth ate sparsely—barely enough to settle her raging belly. And, then, whilst Malcom prepared a pallet for their slumber, she took the opportunity to dry his *sherte* by the fire. Once that was done, she went foraging for wild *fenyl* to settle her belly. She found none, but she did happen upon lovage and *Alchemilla*, and she harvested a bit of those herbs to begin a new medicinal supply. And then, when she thought she'd discovered all there was to find, she also discovered a bit of coltsfoot as well, which pleased her immensely. She could use it to *see* with. And it could be used one of two ways, either by sprinkling the herb into a fire, or by infusing it in a tea.

The second way was more effective, but it was also less healthful—particularly since the side effects of a seizure could be the straight edge of an axe or a burning at the stake.

Unfortunately, her grandmother discovered this the hard way.

As for the *Alchemilla*, it would serve Malcom's wound well enough, though she wished she had betony instead.

That herb grew aplenty around Llanthony—not just in their garden—mainly, because Seren once happened to mention to Ersinius that it could be useful in protecting against witches. Elspeth rolled her eyes over that nonsense, because it grew everywhere now—under windows, beside doors, in small pots in the vestibule. Of course, Seren had been jesting with him, but Elspeth had this to say to Ersinius: Witches were *not* spirits to be vanquished. They were flesh and blood men and women and bled like everyone else.

Annoyed, Elspeth turned onto her side, listening to night sounds: Crickets chirping, Merry Bells snorting. Some distance away, a fox cackled.

Malcom had said he'd hoped to rest and rise early, but now she couldn't sleep. And considering how long she'd fought off that strange, annoying languor all day long, she found it rather curious.

On the other hand, Malcom himself appeared to be fast asleep, and she wondered how he could sleep so peacefully when his wound was festering so terribly.

Of course, he'd had some help from her herbs, and now she wished she'd drunk some herself. Huffing a sigh, she turned to stare at him in profile—his strong chin and aquiline nose.

Look to your champion, her sister had said.

Aye, well, she was looking, wasn't she?

Can you hear me, Rhiannon?

Silence.

Rhiannon...

Silence.

Elspeth frowned. As far as she knew, the ability to communicate outside proximity simply did not exist for any witch from time immemorial. But it *was* possible to consult a scrying stone, and for that reason, no one was ever truly out of Morwen's reach.

A few times, Elspeth had awakened to catch Rhiannon creating shapes out of mist, but what came so easily to her sister, did not come so easily to Elspeth.

Rhiannon? She tried again, even despite that she knew it to be useless.

But why? Why was it useless? If the Goddess could hear them wherever she might be, and, indeed, the entirety of the world was connected, why couldn't she speak to her sisters wherever she might be? Why was this so different from the sight, which could be invoked over great distances?

She studied the contours of Malcom's face.

Betimes she had the strangest feeling he could hear her. She thought about his demeanor this morning... in the woods... when she'd beguiled Merry Bells. His body had gone taut, and he'd looked about the same as Merry Bells—searching the tree tops for Elspeth. In fact, Elspeth had only pounced when she had because she'd feared being discovered.

Was it possible Malcom could hear her?

Her grandmamau claimed all living beings had inherent knowledge of the *hud,* but they didn't know how to use it. Perhaps tomorrow she would test this theory.

For a long, long while, she tossed and turned under the heavy cloak he'd given her, shivering and thinking how best to engage him—but more importantly, whether she dared.

And, finally, when her teeth began to chatter, she moved closer to Malcom, and gave him a bit of her cloak, not caring overmuch about propriety. What good was modesty if the poor man froze to death? Where would she be then? And then she worried: He was lying so very still.

Looking closer, searching for signs of life, she worried

even more when she couldn't hear him breathing. *Oh, no!* Now that she had convinced him not to call upon Amdel, he would die here and leave her and Merry Bells all alone!

It was just like a man to think himself invulnerable. The fool had refused to allow her to cauterize his wound, but she'd tried. And now, fearful of what she might discover, Elspeth placed a hand before his nostrils, exhaling in relief when a light stream of warmth blew against her hand.

She could heal him... now... But what would he do when he awoke to find himself healed? Would he suspect her?

She had put a poultice on his wound, but if he'd ever suffered a wound of any kind, he would know very well that it wouldn't heal overnight, with or without any poultice.

And yet, he couldn't possibly suspect witchcraft after a single occasion, could he? People simply did not believe in the Craft any longer. They would rather believe in coincidence and miracles. And regardless, how could she allow any man to continue suffering, when she had the means to help him? *Do good, harm none*, she reminded herself. It was the one golden rule.

And anyway, wasn't she honor-bound to use her talents for the good of men? What was he, but a man? A handsome one at that—far too handsome for Elspeth's peace of mind. But what did that matter? And he was fast asleep. Whatever he thought, or didn't think, he could never prove it one way or the other. So, now that she could focus without his scrutiny, she placed her hand atop his shoulder, hovering close to his wound—as close as she dared without touching him.

When finally she could feel heat emanating from the affected area, she cupped her palm to catch it escaping, taking a moment to harness her own healing power before whispering...

> Goddess, we are one, take his pain, make
> there none.

The words were adequate, but, possibly, not quite enough. Elspeth wished not only to ease his pain, but to rest assured his wound would mend. What was the point of exerting herself only to do it halfway? Once again, very gently, she lowered her palm over the wound, gasping softly as it fell to meet hard, muscled chest, and then, for a befuddled instant, she forgot what she was supposed to do, so entranced was she with the gentle rise and fall of his breath.

His skin was hot where she laid it. *Fever. Raging.* It was more than enough impetus to remind her of her purpose. Concentrating on lending him her own energy, little enough as there seemed to be, despite her restlessness, she used her third eye—the one peering inward to her heart—and envisioned the small moon that was the essence of her soul. Little by little, she made it swell, until she could feel it as potent as a tiny sun. Then, she traveled the palm-sized sphere of light down her arm, all the way to her hand, watching the faint glow as it passed through her palm to Malcom's abused flesh. In the utter darkness, the place where she touched him exploded like a thousand twinkling stars. And then, once she was ready, she whispered again.

> Healing wight lend your light. Spirit mend,
> sickness end.

And once the words were spoken, she was utterly spent. Her limbs felt like porridge and her mind turned to mush. She was so weary that she forgot to take away her hand from his chest, and her last waking thought was for her sister Rhiannon...

Her sister was wrong... The only reason Morwen hadn't sequestered them sooner was because of Henry, no matter what Rhiannon believed.

It was merely that Rhiannon had been such a willful child, howling and wailing from the instant she was born. She'd come into this world full of rage. And later, once she'd got older, she was so often discomforted by the presence of people. She would rock and wail, rock and wail, with her sweet little hands pressed to her ears and Henry hadn't known what to do with her.

Naturally, since he had a nation to tend to, an odd little daughter was too easily forgotten. And nevertheless... Elspeth remembered the disconcerted look on her father's face when the midwife was commanded to carry Rhiannon away from his hall.

If only Rhiannon would settle the fire in her heart and try to remember...

THE DREAM ARRIVED LIKE A BREEZE...

Rhiannon was sobbing. She was three years old and weeping inconsolably because she hadn't the words to tell anyone what was wrong. All about her, servants hustled, some carrying platters, others bearing ewers. And still others prepared the trestle tables and moved long, noisy benches.

Her sister had to carry her, but Rhiannon was far too heavy, and Elspeth set her down amidst the rushes, patting a hand atop her head, and saying words Rhiannon couldn't comprehend, though she certainly understood the love. Only now Rhiannon refused to look at her, because not even Elspeth seemed to understand Rhiannon. There were too many thoughts flying about her head—pictures without words. Her dress was too tight in places, and her head felt like bugs crawled inside her skull. Squealing with displeasure, she slapped her ears vengefully, trying to get out the bugs, and then, when she couldn't seem to do it, she shrieked at the top of her lungs—so loudly that the servants all stopped to stare. She curled into a ball, precisely the way she'd lain in her mother's womb—but even then, there hadn't been any reassurance. Her twin sister was dying—dying! Once again, Rhiannon felt the waning heartbeat, the light in her soul going dim. She hadn't even a name, but there in the womb, floating in water, she had reached out to tangle her fingers into the fine threads of her twin's hair.

Don't die! She bade her, don't die! But even as she tried desperately to share her own life force, the light grew dimmer, and dimmer, and dimmer... until finally, it guttered and extinguished.

"God's teeth, girl! Where's your mother?" Henry was shouting at Elspeth as Rhiannon tucked her knees to her chest, rocking back and forth.

"I... don't... know."

"Christ! She left you with no one to care for you?"

"Aye," said Elspeth. "But, don't worry, she said she would return anon."

"Where is Seren?"

"In her crib."

"By the bloody saints, the dinner hour is no time for children to flounce about the hall. What in God's name ails your sister?"

Elspeth shook her head, her blue eyes filling with tears. "I think she's hungry."

"Stay here," her father demanded, but then he lifted up Rhiannon and marched across the hall, shouting at the top of his lungs. "Someone, for the love of God, please see to this child!"

Rhiannon awoke, blinking away an image of a pair of desperate brown eyes peering into her face. The eyes were narrowed, but not angry. For a disconcerting instant, she was light enough to be wafted into the air, and momentarily disoriented as the memory vanished, dissipating into thin air.

This is now; that was then.

She lay in the bed she shared with her sisters at Llanthony, not in London. Elspeth was not four, and she was not two. Her twin sister—the first set of twins her mother carried—was twenty-two years dead, her life force extinguished long before she'd taken a single breath. Sadness enveloped her, and a loneliness that not even her living sisters could assuage.

And nevertheless, just like that time, once again, Morwen had been summoned and soon enough she would arrive like an ill wind.

Sleeping peacefully, her sisters were huddled together, one less than before, and although Rhiannon couldn't see Elspeth, she felt her sister's loneliness as acutely as she felt her own. Instinctively, she knew that her sister must be calling for her, but Rhiannon was powerless to answer. Outside, tonight, there was a waning moon lending its light.

Inside the cottage, it was cold enough to show her chilled breath. She exhaled a puff of frozen air and swirled her finger through the mist, watching quietly as shapes coalesced.

A man and woman... sleeping peacefully on a pallet... under the moonlight.

The smaller form was huddled beneath a mountain of wool and velvet and fur. The man lay beside her, perfectly still... without blankets.

Rhiannon sighed. Alas, she was too far away. She could not speak to Elspeth, nor could she interfere, no matter what transpired. It was some terrible form of torture that would compel her look when she could see all but do nothing. It was for this very reason she had refrained from showing Seren, Rose and Arwyn.

She puffed away the image, and reached up one more time, swirling a finger through the thin veil that had yet to dissipate, and once again, shapes took form, only this time settling into the image of a long and winding road... the king's road from London.

Two dark figures on horseback, one man, dressed in black... and a woman, with a cold wind blowing at her back. This would be Morwen.

Her mother was on the way.

Vengeance is in my heart,
death in my hand,
blood and revenge are hammering in my head.
—William Shakespeare

IT'S NOT ALWAYS *about a man.*

I am Morwen, only-born daughter to the regnant *dewine* priestess, born to be seneschal of Wales. Conceived by the Beltane fires, I should have been preordained, but my own mother gave my legacy to my unborn babes. In truth, for that offense alone, I would have ripped my own belly and dragged them out to strangle them with my bare hands; consider what I would do to a child not my own. In this world, there are no true kings. There were never any kings. And no man ever ruled save by the grace of a woman. And therefore, some may think otherwise, but this has naught to do with Henry or Stephen. It is about a haughty little child by the name of Matilda. It is about her unbridled arrogance and the way she swept through her father's halls, crooking her little finger in defiance. It is about a spoiled child-bride who'd resented her papa's paramour so deeply that she'd determined to undermine him at every turn. And even after Henry banished that little shrew from England, wedding her to a whey-faced emissary of the Church, she grew worse, persecuting me from afar, with greater and greater power, thanks to the greed of her sire and the backing of the Church.

But it isn't enough that I gave my own mother to be judged by these cretins—a sacrifice for their altar. She would tirelessly campaign against a "faith" she so imperiously presumes to be evil, when all the while what she truly desires is to destroy me. Her meddling cost me everything—never mind my own mother and thankless daughters. It cost me the only man I've ever loved... Emrys, dead, by my own hands. And the irony is lost to all, for his druid name meant life immortal.

And now he is gone, and despite that it breaks every tenet I am bound to, I will show that wretched woman the true face of evil.

One day soon, Henry's high and mighty Empress daughter will discover what it means to anger a Daughter of Avalon. That bitch thinks herself better than me, but she has no more than a sharp tongue to defend her, whilst I have the blood of my ancestors and a fury unlike any she will ever encounter. Only once she's spent an adequate amount of time groveling on her knees, and only after she's crawled from baron to baron, begging entry at every once-held fief, only then will I squash her life—but not before she understands her folly, and not until she learns that *I* am the reason her children will never sit on her father's throne. In the end, I give not one whit who wears her father's crown, only that whoever wears it serves me well.

For much of the journey from London, the king's road remains clear of woodlands—mostly to discourage brigands—but as the road begins to narrow, the trees huddle closer and darkness enfolds me. I breathe a lungful of relief.

Tonight, the night air is thick and damp. It is the time of year when the soil holds enough warmth that mist rises naturally from the road, unfurling before me like a lady's veil, teasing the way.

Opting for privacy and making all due haste, I travel light this evening, riding, not sidesaddle as most genteel ladies might feel compelled to do, but legs astride, like the warrior queen of the late Iceni tribe. This is how I see myself, and, this is how others will see me so long as I have breath and life. No matter how wrinkled I may grow beneath my spell of glamour, I will ride tall and proud in my saddle, with my velvet cloak flying at my back like the wings of a vengeful angel.

And can you guess what pleases me most? This: Rather than employ an entourage and carry a portmanteau filled with jewels and gowns and maquillage to maintain my youthful visage—as Matilda must certainly do—I need only carry my scrying stone and my mother's *grimoire*.

Mine now. All mine. Keep a hundred thousand crowns if it be your wish, little darling! None of your gem-studded tiaras will ever come close to the worth of my heirlooms.

Mothers and daughters, daughters and mothers; so much toil and trouble. But whoever said blood is thicker than water is a fool. Not even the simple fact that my five comely brats were wrenched, screaming from my womb, can make me feel aught but fury over them. How it galls me even now to hear the fruit of my own loins described as beauteous! Unparalleled! As though I, myself, am not also gifted with the prophet Taliesin's blood. Like Matilda, my own children are ungrateful brats, and why shouldn't they be? They all share the same blood—save for Rhiannon.

Rhiannon, oh, Rhiannon, you could have filled my heart.

Alas, my dearest daughter, there can be only one high priestess, and it will forever be me.

It has been years now since I last returned to Wales, but I know these woodlands well. Instinctively, I sense that Bran has flown ahead, certain in the knowledge that I do not need him. Still, I cast my head back to peer at the waning moon—a glowing orb that pulses in time to the beat of my own heart. *Ah, yes! It is a lovely night for blood magic...*

The night is still young.

Fueled by vengeance alone, I would sweep through these lands like a black and terrible flame, but tonight I have more pressing matters to contend with before facing my wayward daughters. It is such a costly thing to keep my glamour, and the price of allowing it to fade is too dear. But soon enough, dear ones, you will learn what it means to defy your lady mother—Elspeth most of all.

Like a hound on the hind of a kill, I catch the scent of blood. "Ride ahead," I say to my companion. "I will require immediate sustenance."

"A bath, m'dame?"

"Aye. Fresh, please. I cannot abide the stench of old blood."

"Aye, m'dame," he says, and breaks away, putting his shining silver spurs to his horse's flank, and I think to myself: What a good servant, he is... and why shouldn't he be? He enjoys the benefits of my Craft, and rides so spryly for a man so close to ninety. Alas, should he ever decide to defy me, he would be dead on the morrow, for he is the vessel that harbors my blood sins. His body might be beautiful on the outside, but inside lies a cancerous mass, eating him to his bones. Inhaling deeply, I watch him go, content enough to ride alone for the last mile to Darkwood.

12

"Rouse yourself, scrounger!"

Malcom awoke with a boot to his ribs, rolling over Elspeth, taking her with him. She squealed in surprise when he pulled her up from the pallet, sheltering her behind him. In the same fluid movement, he unsheathed the knife he kept at his boot, only belatedly recognizing the livery of the men who'd assaulted him. He turned his knife so that it cast a glimmer by the moonlight, letting the blade speak for itself and his words came terse. "'Tis nay way to wake a sleeping mon," he told the fools. "And ye're fortunate ye dinna touch *my lady*."

Both were slow to grasp their folly. "Lady? What lady? I see only a camp follower, wearing cast-off clothes. Did you wipe your hairy flute with *your lady's* gown?"

The idiots laughed, amusing themselves, and with every bark of laughter, Malcom's fury burned hotter. He did not think before he said, "She's no camp follower, *eegits*. She's my bride."

Behind him, Elspeth gasped in startle, and he cast her a

quick glance, pulling her close, tightening his hold about her wrist.

"Bride?" they asked in unison, both chortling.

"Aye," he said. "*My* bride. And ye'd do well to show respect," he demanded. "Or, I'll forget I ride beneath Stephen's banner, and you're his liegemen."

Very purposely, Malcom re-sheathed his blade, knowing full well that his reputation would speak for itself. And if they were too stupid to realize their mistake he could retrieve it quickly should he need it. More to the point, he could disarm them faster than they could blink.

"You are met with the lord of Aldergh," he said. "And I would count your blessings I do not cut off a foot for planting your boot where it did not belong." He eyed the man he suspected of the transgression, and silence met his declaration.

The two men stood looking at one another, uncertain what to say, and finally, the taller of the two relented, "Pardon, Lord Aldergh. We saw no banners. We thought—"

"I dinna give a bluidy damn what ye thought," he said. "And now that ye've sae rudely awakened my lady, you may run to your lord and wake him. Inform him he has guests and I am certain he'll appreciate the summons at this late hour. You can be sure I will endeavor to explain the circumstances."

The two men peered at one another again, and Malcom said calmly, "Go," he said. "Now."

"Y-yes, lord!" both men replied, and one after the other hurriedly returned to their mounts. They couldn't depart quickly enough, and Malcom said, "I am sorry, lass. It seems we must dally, after all, thanks to these simpletons." He moved to put out the fire, grateful now that he'd taken time to dismantle the spit and bury the remains of the hare.

. . .

Elspeth blinked.

It did not escape her how swiftly the prowlers had had a change of heart and attitude. And now she wondered: Who was this lord of Aldergh that he had men trembling in their boots with barely a word? By the blessed cauldron, not since her time at court with her father had she ever met a man whose commands were so unequivocally obeyed. For all his unpleasantness, not even Ersinius commanded so much respect, much to his dismay.

Somehow, she'd never imagined this of Malcom—not after having encountered his unfailing good humor. But now, as she watched him work to douse the fire, she realized her mistake.

All the while he was laughing and jesting, she'd pricked and prodded him, appealing only to his anger, but Malcom's anger was the last thing she wished to encounter. "Well," she said, cautiously. "I have never seen anyone move so hastily."

Casting her a glance, he shuffled dirt into the fire pit with a boot, then tamped it down, arching a brow as he considered her. "Betimes 'tis advantageous to be known as a mad Scot."

"I see," she said. Though, in truth, she didn't want to consider how he must have received such an ill-tempered epithet—and dared not ask.

Certainly, it wasn't because he was staid and sensible. But how at odds this was with everything she knew of the warrior who'd dared to name his horse Merry Bells!

And now, after all, they were going to Amdel, and no matter that he'd claimed to detest this lord, there was little in his demeanor that gave Elspeth any impression he feared that man—or for that matter, anyone at all. Not for a moment had he seemed cowed by Beauchamp's men.

Angry, perchance. And, yes, indeed, she had noticed that he'd re-sheathed his knife even before introducing himself, and still unarmed those fools had dared not cross him.

Watching as he made short work of their pallet, Elspeth eyed the swirls of black that settled into his aura—dimmer now that Beauchamp's men were gone, but present nonetheless, and ebony, like the wraith of death.

Having slept fully dressed and still wearing his boots, he wasted little time setting the camp to rights and Elspeth would have gladly helped, though she was still quite stunned over the realizations she'd made. Consequently, she prayed he would not think to look at his wound—not now. Please, no, not now! And that same little demon that kept telling her to flee from him returned to put a needle to her head.

"Now what?" she asked, when he returned the bedroll to Merry Bells' hind quarters.

He gave her a shrug. "Now, *my lovely bride*, we call upon Amdel," he said, his fury finally abating. "I suppose if there is one blessing to be found in all this, we'll lay our heads on a proper pillow tonight."

Elspeth shrank back. "Together?"

He gave her a twisted smile. "Unless ye wish to remain here?"

Elspeth shook her head, unwilling to argue when there would be time enough for that with a proper chaperone at Amdel. And suddenly, she didn't relish any thought of angering Malcom further. As startled as she had been by those men, at the moment, Malcom seemed far more dangerous. And even so, she dared to ask, "Will you reveal the truth once we are arrived?"

"What truth?"

"That we are not betrothed."

"Nay," he said. "And yet you are quite welcome to do so at your own discretion. The decision is yours. But if you choose to let it be, Elspeth, you will do us both a favor."

"Favor?"

"Aye," he said, lifting his cloak from the ground where it lay, brushing it off. He cast her an arched glance over the garment. "If not for you, his sister would be my intended. And if there is aught you can do for me, Elspeth of Llanthony, it would be to save me the unpleasantness of having to repudiate his little sister."

He handed her the cloak. "Wear it, please. I would prefer not to offer more explanations than necessary." And he turned away, leaving Elspeth to consider all he'd said.

He had an intended?

For a moment, Elspeth stood, astounded. Certainly, *that* was nothing she had foreseen! So then, was she losing her ability to sense fates? Evidently, she had not read Malcom properly, nor had she guessed at his true nature. She had ignorantly taken for granted the smiling man she'd encountered in the woods.

"Art ready to ride?"

Sweet fates!

"Elspeth?"

No, no, no, no, no... She *must* go back. This was not right. Something was wrong. Everything was wrong! And she was quite certain her sisters must need her. Elspeth yawned, and her eyes grew heavy and she realized belatedly that her sleepiness had returned.

Rhiannon!

No sooner had the thought occurred to her when her knees buckled, and Malcom rushed forward to sweep her into his arms.

. . .

"Elspeth," he said, gently patting her cheek.

Feeling more protective over the girl than would seem natural, Malcom considered the fact that until yesterday morning, he'd never set eyes on her before. He wasn't at all sure why he'd blurted such a lie—*his bride*? What in God's sweet name had possessed him to say so?

Not only was she *not* his bride, he was beginning to suspect, more and more, that she was meant for someone else. And nevertheless, he had no regrets, despite that he would now have explanations to make. No matter; his heart was not set on a union with Dominique Beauchamp. He'd set out to help Elspeth, but it was equally as likely that he'd spoken the lie for his own self-gain, because, to put it mildly, he didn't care for Dominique at all. And, perhaps, for the first time in all his life, he considered that there might be another woman he could bring himself to love...

"Elspeth," he whispered again, patting her cheek insistently.

Her face was unnaturally pale, and though it was only a moment or two before she reopened her eyes, blinking up at him in confusion, it was the longest moment of his life. He breathed a sigh of relief as she refocused her gaze.

"Elspeth?"

"I-I am fine."

"Art certain, lass?"

She nodded uncertainly, but that was enough to settle his nerves. "You did not eat well enough," he scolded, sounding too much like a mother hen though he didn't care. "Nor did you rest long enough. We shall see to that as soon as we are arrived at Amdel."

And it struck him then how much she'd endured in the space of a single day—and yet despite this, how well she'd fared. For all he knew, she could have been afoot in those woods for days and days, and he'd never even bothered to ask. Like his stepmother, she was too prideful to admit any weakness. And, even now, she was as impenetrable as any fortress made of mortar and stone.

Whether he liked it or nay, Elspeth harbored secrets, and if he wished to know them—or her—it would be at her own discretion.

She pushed his hand away, like a proud little foundling—looking more lost than she'd looked even when he'd discovered her back in the woods in Wales. But now, once again, she shut him out, and it was quite evident that he was only a means to an end.

Her trust would not be forthcoming, and whatever it was that he was beginning to feel for her—if indeed it was real—he suffered those feelings alone.

Nodding to himself, resigned to the unpleasant fact, he took one last look at Elspeth as she rallied, lifting herself up, half-heartedly smacking the dust from her clothes.

He left her alone. "Sit and rest whilst I pack," he said.

"Nay," she snapped. "I am fine. I would like to help." And she bent to pick up his trampled cloak and once again endeavored to brush it off.

13

Elspeth was furious, though not with Malcom.

Evidently, not only had Rhiannon cast some annoying dozing spell to settle her nerves, she'd wrested some poor soul straight from his life, plucking him out of his intended path. That was reprehensible, and completely outside their coven rules. No man should *ever* be used against his will. *Ever.* Not even for good—certainly never for selfish concerns.

Rhiannon! she screamed to herself. *What in the name of the Goddess have you done?*

Of course, Elspeth did not expect an answer. But it was clear to her—so very clear—that Malcom's wishes were never considered.

Not that it should upset her so much to have a man gaze at her with such affection and—*dearest Goddess, was that affection?* But now she understood, perfectly, why his demeanor had changed so drastically. Her sister's enchantment would have been like a love spell. It would, indeed, have made him light-hearted and giddy, even if that wasn't his true nature.

And more! As impressed as Elspeth was that Rhiannon could cast such a complicated spell outside proximity, and that she must have used her sight to find and summon this poor man, whatever now came of the Law of Three, Elspeth was also responsible, because, whatever decisions Malcom made or didn't make, they were in part because of her.

Sweet, sweet Goddess! He was promised to another woman! And now he would break faith with her and her brother because of Elspeth.

And it made Elspeth wonder: What else had Rhiannon taken from him? What business had he been about in Wales? Because surely, he was acting on behalf of his King. He'd said more than once that he rode under Stephen's banner. So he must have been after the King's business— whatever that might entail near Llanthony—and Rhiannon had embroiled Elspeth in this magnificent travesty, because now his life was inexorably tied to hers—*and hers to his!*

Forsooth! So much that she hadn't understood before she understood now, very clearly. And what if he should realize his life had been altered per force? What if he discovered *what* and *who* Elspeth was? *A dewine! A child of the Goddess! A daughter of Avalon!*

Her head reeling with questions, and bewildered over the possible consequences, Elspeth walked about, holding Malcom's cloak, like *y meirw byw*—*the living dead.*

Only once they were ready to ride, she mounted at his behest, then sat stiffly before him in the saddle, whilst Malcom placed his arms about her waist to keep her steady —but how could she allow herself to be comforted? None of this was done by his own free will.

Oh, Rhiannon, Rhiannon... what have you done?
Silence.

But, of course. Now that she had meddled so rudely—so

irrevocably—she'd abandoned Elspeth to this warrior, who evidently felt spellbound to protect her.

And, worse, he was, in truth, her enemy, merely by virtue of his affiliation with her cousin.

And regardless, he held her so gently, pulling her close as though she were in truth his beloved, and Elspeth could feel the heat beneath his palm as surely as she'd felt her own healing light last eventide. It wrenched at her heart in ways she had not known her heart could be wrenched.

They rode in silence, arriving at Amdel as the first blush of dawn arose over the horizon. And, then, sweet fates, as though the morning's revelations weren't enough, the sight of the stronghold left Elspeth breathless.

The fortress rose up from black earth, like a stone effigy, and its aura was black as a moonless night. If it could be possible that an assembly of stone and timber could have a spirit likeness, the edifice was like a sepulcher, and Elspeth felt its sentience like something living but dead. The very sight of it racked her body with shivers.

"This... is Amdel?" she asked, and Malcom pulled the reins to stop, giving her a moment to survey their destination, drawing her back to keep her warm.

"Aye," he said, pulling her close. Alas, though Elspeth sensed he did it by rote, she was perversely grateful for the reminder that, in truth, she wasn't alone.

Unsettled by her own ambivalence, she shivered yet again, and Malcom adjusted his cloak around her shoulders, pinching the garment at her breast.

As a matter of self-preservation, Elspeth's hand fell over his, and for a long, long moment, they sat atop Merry Bells, with her hand covering his.

"Art ready?"

Nay, she was not. Her heart pounded like hammers, but she swallowed and said, "Aye."

And with that single word from her, Malcom spurred Merry Bells into a canter toward the stone bridge. And the closer they got, the blacker the aura that rose from the stone like a glow from a fire, and Elspeth wanted desperately to turn and run.

Fear and Malcom's reassuring embrace kept her silent. As best she could, she sank into his arms and held her breath as they rode into the outer bailey.

At first glance, she could tell that the fortress had been erected on the remnants of an old Roman stronghold. It was easy to see where the old stone left off and the new construction had begun. The outer walls were made from timber and remained half-burnt on the east side. A new stone wall had begun construction on the inside of the motte, encircling the edifice. When it was finished, there would be enough mortared stone to build the entirety of Blackwood.

The lord's standard flew from a half-constructed gatehouse—a bright red hawk with wings spread over a midnight sky. She turned to peer at the charred timber as they passed.

Of course, it was quite possible that this was one of the strongholds besieged by her sister. Matilda's last bastion in England had been Devizes Castle in Wiltshire, not so far as the ravens flew, but she'd been beleaguered enough there, attempting to maintain the stronghold, and in the end, with Robert's death, she'd abandoned it to her son.

But nay, rather, Elspeth had more the sense that work here had been waylaid—perhaps for lack of funds? Or mayhap Stephen finally raised a hand against adulterine castels?

Without a word, the gatehouse sentry waved them forward, and Malcom did not linger to speak to the man as he ventured into the lord's bailey. Elspeth had a keen sense he had been here before, and such would be the case, since he'd already confessed to her that the lady herein was his intended.

Was she beautiful?

Well, even if she was, why should that matter to Elspeth? And nevertheless, it soured her mood—as though it could be sourer.

Art jealous, Elspeth?

Of course not.

Why should she be? She barely knew this man. More importantly, she should be concerned all the more that he would consider fostering an alliance with the lord of this demesne.

And, really, Elspeth, 'tis not as though you are his bride.

None of this was real. It was all but a consequence of the spell her sister had cast. If she'd met Malcom without benefit of the enchantment, he could well have run her through with his sword—because, isn't that what warriors did?

What a travesty this was, but at least now, for the first time since leaving Llanthony, she was far more preoccupied worrying about herself than she was about her sisters.

In the middle of the bailey, Merry Bells came to a halt, and it seemed to her that, like roaches, men suddenly crawled out from beneath their spaces and flew at them from every direction.

A groomsman came to take their horse, but Malcom hesitated, until the donjon doors flew wide and a well-dressed man sauntered out to greet them. Dressed all in black, the man hurried across the lord's bailey, his aura reaching Elspeth long before the man did, and his telling blue eyes gave her a punch to the gut.

"William," said Malcom in greeting.

Their patron nodded. "Malcom."

And yet, despite the use of given names, there was nothing amiable about the exchange. Perhaps after all, Rhiannon's spell had saved Malcom from an unwanted alliance. For all that they seemed familiar, he didn't appear to bear Beauchamp any kindness—but then, again, hadn't he said that he detested the man? Obviously, this was true.

Malcom slid off his horse, and Elspeth daren't follow. Leaving her seated for the moment, Malcom removed his saddlebags, casting the heavy leather satchels over his shoulder.

Instinctively, Elspeth drew his cloak more firmly about her person, pinching it in front of her tunic to hide her Llanthony sigil, despite that she'd already hidden it from view. She wished to God that she could hide her breeches as well.

The lord of Amdel inclined his head toward her, giving Elspeth a long look, veiled with disapproval. "My lady," he said curtly, then quickly dismissed her, returning his attention to Malcom, and offering with a bit of reproach, "I am told good wishes are in order."

Malcom gave the man a curt nod. "They are, indeed," he said, finally reaching up to assist Elspeth. In the brief instant their gazes met, his blue-green eyes beseeched her to remain silent, and Elspeth had no trouble complying. But though she had no desire to dismount, his arms compelled her to do so, and keeping herself covered as best as she could, she once again slid into his embrace. Once she was down, on her feet, Malcom handed the horse's reins to the groomsman, and he took Elspeth by the hand, warning her with a gentle squeeze. In answer, Elspeth squeezed him back and Malcom released her hand, then left her to follow, as he and the lord of Amdel fell into step beside one another, while Elspeth was left to walk behind.

Considering the circumstances, it was perhaps irrational that she might hope for more equitable treatment. Evidently, Scotsmen and Englishmen were not at all like the Welsh. They had not the same sensibilities where women were concerned. But, of course, Beauchamp would expect Malcom to treat her as any Englishman might treat his bride.

But he's not really your husband, you silly fool.

Still, she chafed a bit as the two men spoke so familiarly, despite that Elspeth sensed so little amity between them, and once again, she had the most overwhelming urge to flee.

Even here, in the heart of the demesne, there was a darkness emanating from Amdel... and for a terrible, sinking moment, it seemed to Elspeth as though the door they walked toward could be an open maw, ready to devour them, flesh and bones.

Swallowing for courage, she fell into step behind the two chatting men.

"We had a bit of misfortune," Malcom was saying. "I'm afraid my lady is in need of a new gown, and whatever else your sister might be kind enough to provide."

They climbed the stairs into the donjon, and Elspeth took every step with uncertainty, though she daren't fall behind.

"But, of course. Dominique is too kind to begrudge you aught," the man was saying. "She would gladly welcome the opportunity to make your bride at home."

They walked together in silence for a time, and then Beauchamp said, "I only wish you might have sent word... to apprise us... of your change in *circumstances*."

Elspeth wanted to tell them both that she was still there—that she could hear every word they spoke. But Malcom's silent warning kept her tongue tied.

"It could not be helped," said Malcom, as they entered the great hall. "Consequently, I would beg pardon. We—my Lady and I—" Finally, he turned to check on Elspeth, and she reassured him with a quivering smile. He turned back around as Elspeth's eyes scanned the lord's hall, searching for signs of Amdel's loyalties. His banners were all his own, none of Stephen's. But neither were there any of Matilda's. "Considering the circumstances," he said, "we did not intend to burden you today." Inside the keep, the mood was less that of a vanquished ruin and somewhat more presentable. There were fresh rushes on the floors, and all the tapestries were new, with brightly embroidered thread. However, none of this compensated for the threatening aura that only Elspeth could see.

Following the lord up a stairwell at the back of his hall, she listened quietly to Malcom's apology. "I may have preferred to return from my commission in Wales and send you a formal letter as you were due, but I suppose an explanation *facie ad faciem* is far more suitable. However, I must apologize to Dominique, even as I must thank her for her generosity."

"Of course," said Beauchamp, as they came to a landing and moved into another hall. "But first, we should see to your bed. I am told you were awakened rather rudely, and for this it is I who must seek pardon, Earl Aldergh. We had some wandering guests from Darkwood over the past few days, and we expected—well, my men were tasked with seeing they returned to the road. You know how these wayfarers can be. One can never be too certain these days."

Malcom said nothing.

"And, then of course," Beauchamp said, after a long awkward silence, "My affairs with d'Lucy are as yet unsettled." He sighed wearily. "I have cried peace, time and again, and so far, that infuriating man refuses to reconsider his position. He's as stubborn as his sire."

"At least you must deal with Graeham, not his brother."

Beauchamp made a gesture as though to shudder, but Elspeth did not sense any fear in his actions. It was more, disgust. "God forbid—that black-hearted bastard. Did you know they were born of different fathers?"

"Twins, I supposed?"

"Do they look like twins to you? Nay. I warrant 'tis true: She conceived those sons by different sires. And 'tis no wonder that old fool was so cross with the world."

Elspeth kept pace behind them, listening as the lord continued to ramble, clearly incensed by his troubles, and more than ready to share his woes with any sympathetic ear.

"At any rate," Beauchamp said, continuing, "last I heard, now that the Empress has returned to France, d'Lucy plans to issue a suit over the death of their sire."

Hungry for news of her sister, Elspeth listened intently.

"You must agree; I cannot be faulted for acting in self-defense, and, mind you, that man died here on my lands—in this very room," he said, as they arrived at their intended destination. "With my physician attending him, no less. As you must see, despite that he attacked me, I offered him every due respect, even despite that he persisted with his inventions."

"I understand," Malcom said, nodding, all trace of his Scots accent expertly excised from his diction. At the moment, he sounded as English and cultured as did Beauchamp.

Malcom cast Elspeth a quick glance, and said, "Perhaps

now that the lady Dominique is free to wed, you might consider the benefit of a union between her and Graeham d'Lucy. Despite your quarrels with that family, I know Graeham to be an honorable man, and you can be sure he would treat her well. Whatever child came of that union would settle your feud for all time. Wouldn't it?"

Beauchamp blinked, looking startled by the prospect, as though he'd never considered it. His eyes rolled back into his head as though he were seriously considering Malcom's suggestion. And all the while, Malcom stood patiently, with his hands linked behind his back—like a wise old counselor, adept at manipulation, and finally, he reached for Elspeth, drawing her near.

Elspeth pinched her cloak tighter to keep Beauchamp from noticing the inappropriateness of her dress. "At any rate," he said. "I thank you. And my lady thanks you. And because I ken this must have come as a surprise, I will look forward to a full explanation once we are rested. If you would but send my regards to your sister, I will offer my deepest, sincerest apologies when I see her. I know you must know—and she must know—that these things are no fault of your own."

Beauchamp seemed to be warming to Malcom, his body language far less stiff.

Malcom said, "For all your troubles, perhaps you would allow me to send you a bit of wine from Aquila once I am returned to Aldergh? It's fine wine, acquired after searching the demesne of a traitor to the realm. We confiscated his wine, among other things, and Stephen was kind enough to award it to me. I would love to share."

Beauchamp nodded absently, perhaps still thinking about Malcom's initial proposal. "Spanish wine would be lovely," he said. "But no worries. I shall explain everything to Dominique once she awakens. And in the meantime..." He turned to Elspeth and bowed. "My lady."

"My lord," Elspeth said, proffering a hand from beneath her cloak.

But, of course, there was dirt beneath her fingernails, after tending Malcom's fire, and it did not escape the lord of Amdel's notice. He scrunched his nose, pecking the air before her hand but he did not touch her hand with his lips. "I... ah... trust you will rest well... my lady."

"Thank you," said Elspeth, and she curtsied awkwardly, as best she could remember how to do it. Did one curtsy the same as a child as they did as a lady? She couldn't remember the last lady she'd encountered, aside from her sisters.

It didn't matter; Beauchamp didn't notice. He must still be thinking about Malcom's proposal for his sister, because he couldn't be away quicker. "Malcom," he said, before departing. And Malcom nodded to the man, thanking him again, and once his back was turned, Malcom ushered Elspeth into their room, before she could think to protest.

It wasn't Malcom's first stay in this particular room, though he examined the guest bower with entirely new eyes, altered by the knowledge that d'Lucy's sire had breathed his last here.

He hadn't realized as much—nor had he known they'd brought the wounded man back here to be tended by Beauchamp's physician. Of course, Beauchamp was right; it was hardly a place you would tend your enemy—especially one met in combat. And though he was hardly any sort of man Malcom would like to hold in confidence, perhaps he had been too quick to judge? Perhaps

Beauchamp was but maladroit, and not so much the demagogue so many thought him to be? He was, indeed, an awkward man, this much was true, but annoyed though he might have been over the affront to his sister, he'd leapt at the opportunity for fellowship, filling Malcom's ears.

As they entered the room, Malcom swung his bags onto the bed and turned to Elspeth.

She looked wearied, and for all the world like a frightened doe, her graceful form tense and ready to bolt. She averted her gaze for an instant, picking beneath her fingernails, and then back, as though she suddenly didn't know him—as though he'd not slept the whole night through with her head tucked beneath his arm.

She looked nervous. "Perhaps... perhaps, before explaining to that lord... you might better explain to me?"

Malcom gave her a quick smile, torn between his longing to hold and comfort her and wanting to shake her. Would she dare ask him for more than she was willing to give?

Ignoring her entreaty for the instant, he turned to survey the guest room. It was clean and well kept, and he noted the flagon of *vin* and the copper mugs on a table flanked by chairs.

Thirsty as a tippler after a night with Seana's *uisge*, he made for the *vin*.

Lifting up the flagon for a sniff, and finding it relatively inoffensive, he poured a few fingers in each glass—one for him, one for Elspeth. And then, remembering the *shite* they'd served him last time he'd visited, he lifted up one glass to his lips to taste, before offering it to Elspeth, and then immediately spat it back out, setting down the glass.

Sweet ever-loving mercy—*there*, she had her *vin aigre*,

only instead of lacing their washbowl, they'd offered it to drink.

Damn Beauchamp—just when he was softening toward the man. He smiled with curses between his teeth and gave them soured wine to drink—or maybe he didn't know good *vin* from bad. He certainly drank it himself without discretion. "Drink at your own peril," Malcom suggested, and sighed wearily, considering the discourse with Beauchamp.

Despite everything, it might in fact prove propitious that they'd ended here today, because he would otherwise never have suggested an alliance with d'Lucy, and Beauchamp seemed quite receptive to the notion—so much so that he would bet the man was off and away, already scheming. All the better for Malcom. He had long tried to convince himself to accept this alliance, but there was nothing to his knowledge that would sweeten any alliance with Beauchamp—not even Dominique's kindness or beauty. Her brother was a conundrum, for certain. It was impossible to say whether it was true that he was a miscreant, or just a fool with very poor judgment.

The small table set for them also offered a trencher of bread with two wee pieces of meat and two slivers of cheese —barely enough for one, but it would do. Malcom had had more than enough of the cony, but he couldn't possibly have missed Elspeth's reluctance to eat it, so he left her the cheese as well as the bread and plucked up a slice of meat, shoving it between his lips.

Salted beef, too chewy, over-salted. He swallowed with some difficulty, and made a face, moving to the window. God's love, if the man couldn't put a sword through Malcom's heart for the insult provided, it seemed he would kill them with kindness and vittles.

Elspeth was still waiting for his answer, he supposed,

but Malcom wasn't feeling particularly generous. He moved to the window, pulling the curtains tighter.

Aldergh had no drapes, but he was grateful for these, nonetheless, because he was hardly accustomed to sleeping during the day, like some Black Donald with cloven feet. The entire situation left him ill at ease.

"Malcom?"

He turned to face her now, and she was looking at him expectantly. "What more would ye ken, lass? Stephen has asked I take his sister to wife, but she does not suit me, and I thank you for holding your tongue."

"Of course," she said. "It was the least I could do."

Nay, Malcom thought. The least she could do was speak the truth—all of it. But he resigned himself to her silence.

On a stand across the room, there stood a small basin for bathing. That too, he would leave for Elspeth and he would wash only after she was through. That way she wouldn't be forced to bathe in his filth... although, he might need her help to wash and dress his wound.

"Are you inclined to sleep?" he asked. "Or do you prefer to wash first?" And then he added a bit sourly, "I dinna ken if he laced the basin with *vin aigre*, but he certainly left us plenty to use." He pointed to the cups.

She shook her head at once. "Oh, nay! I could not," she said, straightening. "Not... here... with... you..." And then she wrapped his grandfather's cloak around herself so snugly that she might as well have formed a cocoon. Malcom tried not to chuckle, but failed, despite his pique. And hoping to reassure her, he closed the distance between them, until he stood before her, studying her face, wishing he could read her thoughts. There was a wayward curl that defied her make-do braid, and he wanted nothing more than to reach out and brush it away.

He wondered how she would look in a woman's garb, with her lovely copper tresses plaited and her face scrubbed pink. "Of course, I would leave," he said reassuringly. "But if you are inclined to rest, I would like to shut my eyes." And then he turned and made his way to the chair, and sat, sprawling in the chair as she watched.

Her brows twitched. "You mean to sleep... in that chair?"

"Aye."

"Oh, but nay! You need not do that! If you but leave me to one side of the bed, that should be enough. 'Tis but that... well..." She looked pained by what she was trying to say. "I thought that... because you said... we were... I was..."

He arched a single brow. "My bride?"

She nodded, and Malcom said, "Elspeth, I would never dishonor you. If I seem cross, 'tis only because I have asked for your candor and you refuse to give it."

She said nothing, and he looked at her pleadingly. "Am I to go down there and face that man with no more than what you have already given me?"

14

He sat, staring at her expectantly, and Elspeth flushed so intensely that she was forced to shrug off his grandfather's cloak and lay it down on the bed, suddenly much too warm.

And, then, inexplicably—considering that Beauchamp was already gone, and Malcom had already seen her dressed this way—she felt vulnerable and far too aware of the unflattering way she was dressed, perhaps in part due to the fact that she was now expected to play the role of his lady wife. So, then, as surprised as she had been by his declaration, she trusted there must be a reason.

Betimes people behaved inexplicably, particularly when listening to their gut. She and her sisters betimes behaved irrationally, and it nearly always had to do with a glimpse of the sight, subtle as Malcom's may have been. *Normal* people might not have visions as clearly as a *dewine* might, but they too had instincts that drove them—not that they always listened.

Obviously, he did not like this lord of Amdel, and perhaps not the sister either. And if the sister was anything like her brother, Elspeth could well understand why.

She furrowed her brow. Could they dare fool this lord? What would Malcom tell him? And if anyone should ask how they came to know one another, Elspeth herself would have little to say.

I peered longingly into his sea-green eyes and heard a call from Ersinius' men that made me cast myself into his arms. Pshaw! The very thought brought the faintest smile to her lips, but, of course, she daren't make light of their circumstances. It could all go very, very wrong.

Malcom sat relaxed in the chair, and now that Beauchamp was gone, his aura returned to normal, albeit with tints of green now. Those who bore any shade of the forest in their ambience could be loyal and generous, but they did not suffer fools very gladly. This rang true of Malcom, even despite that she'd known him such a short a time.

And nevertheless, both times, when facing Beauchamp's men and then Beauchamp himself, she'd sensed a darkness in him, and she suspected he could be capable of atrocities just the same as anyone else. The minds of men were often changeable, and the consequences could be disastrous.

Not for the first time, he seemed to guess what was on her mind. "I'll tell him as little as possible," he said. "But how should I say we met?"

Confused, Elspeth sat on the edge of the bed, crossing her arms, considering the consequences of revealing herself to Malcom. She desperately *wanted* to tell him everything but dared not... the words wouldn't come.

She couldn't see her own aura, but she had been told hers was pink and green, which was much to be expected for a *dewine. Dewines* were natural healers, highly intuitive, with a strong affinity for the Craft. Pink was also the color for those who bore the blood of Taliesin. In days of yore, there had been many, many of their ilk, all known to one to another by their colors. Now they were dwindling in numbers. And soon, they, too, would go the way of the faeries—like so much vermin. One after another they were being exterminated. So, now, how could she dare reveal herself to this man? She opened her mouth to speak and swallowed her words.

"Elspeth..." His eyes beseeched her as he rose up from the chair. "Only give me munitions I will need to aid you."

Watching her intently, he came forward, lifting up the cloak she'd discarded on the bed, bringing the garment to his nostrils, and breathing deeply of its scent—her scent, for she'd been the last to wear it. For some strange reason, that simple gesture made Elspeth shiver and it set her heart to pounding. "I... I am sorry," she said, her brows slanting.

Alas, he was right. The lord of Amdel would surely expect their company once they were rested, and if Elspeth allowed Malcom to face that man again without greater knowledge of her predicament, they could easily raise suspicions...

And to that end, she thought perhaps she'd hidden her tunic well enough, though it wasn't very likely Beauchamp had missed her breeches. So much as she might have liked to toss the entire ensemble into his garderobe, she knew that wouldn't serve her. The last thing she meant to do was alert anyone from whence she'd come—and, yes, of course, she understood why Malcom needed to know more, but what could she say now that could come close to appeasing him... and still guard her secrets? "My mother would have me wed a man I cannot abide," she said, at last.

He arched a brow. "D'Lucy?"

Elspeth peered up at him in surprise. "H-how... how did you know?"

He offered a slow smile. "Ach, lass, ye're not sae difficult to read, ye know. I sensed your distress every time I mentioned his name."

Elspeth blew out a sigh, and continued, despite that she meant not to. "'Tis not the lord of Drakewich, but another."

"Cael?"

Elspeth nodded. "Aye."

And now he whistled low, then sat beside her on the bed, allowing a moment for what she'd told him to settle into his bones. "I suspected as much but hoped I could be wrong. So then... your mother would have you wed the new lord of Blackwood?"

Elspeth nodded yet again.

"And your sire?"

There could be little harm in sharing this truth. "My father is dead," Elspeth confessed.

"So," he said, trying to make sense of it all. "Stephen has consented to this marriage to d'Lucy?"

Feeling like a child discovered at foul play, Elspeth nodded yet again.

And once again, Malcom whistled low, then shook his head. "My Da always said I had a bent for trouble," he told her. But then he grinned, as though to reassure her and he pushed his grandfather's cloak behind her, rising from the bed. "Done is done," he said. "Somehow we will make it right."

"Will you leave me here at Amdel?" Elspeth asked, afraid that he meant to wash his hands of her now and abandon her to Beauchamp—and his sister, with whom Malcom was no longer betrothed, thanks to Elspeth.

"Is that what you would have me do?"

Elspeth shook her head, as it was the last thing she could want. She needn't consult any knuckle bones to know that anything having to do with Beauchamp could only lead to disaster. He had that quality about him, and she was still unnerved by the aura of this castel, despite that she didn't feel so overwhelmed now that she was inside the dwelling itself. And nevertheless, this place—this pile of stones—could only be that way if it had long been the receptacle for evil.

"Never fear, then. I would not abandon you."

Elspeth exhaled a breath she hadn't realize she was holding as she watched Malcom return to the table and lift up the glass he'd sipped from only moments before. Only this time, instead of spitting out the contents or setting the glass down with a sour face, he tossed the entirety of it down his gullet, and then poured another and drank that one down as well.

"So, then... what will you tell this lord of Amdel?"

He swallowed a third glass before answering. "I'll know when it comes to mind," he said. "In the meantime, you should get some rest."

Stronger than lover's love is lover's hate.
Incurable, in each, the wounds they make.
—Euripides

NAMED FOR THE SURROUNDING WOODLANDS, Darkwood Inn lives up to its name. The number of its years in existence equal the number of years of Stephen's reign, but it appears

The King's Favorite

far older. The interior pillars are filled with knotholes and greying with age.

The innkeeper here is the third to serve, and he's as discreet as he is loyal, toiling behind his bar, waiting for his cue. If he were not loyal, I would suck the life from his body and leave him for a dried-up carcass, in the same manner a locust discards its shell, only to find itself no more than dust beneath the hammer of a fist.

So I sit here at my favorite table at the back of this familiar tavern, resting, though not ready to choose. Tonight, there are two offerings, both comely, if boring. But then, again, *they* are *all* boring to me—Henry, Stephen, Eustace, every man the same but with a different face.

The last I knew worth his salt was my Emrys, my lover, my dear brother.

So then, which to choose?
Which to save for later?

More to the point, I wonder which of these men might be persuaded to linger, because I fully intend to make another stop on my return to London. Only then, I will be in the company of three of my daughters, excluding Rhiannon.

I fiddle with the ring about my forefinger, the one I always wear. It was my mother's ring, though Morgan preferred to fill hers with coltsfoot, so she could *see* any time she pleased without her scrying stone. I have found another use for the receptacle beneath the obsidian stone. It is rare that I can find time to slip away for a *treatment*, so I must come prepared. This ring contains the most precious of my *grimoire's* recipes—an ingredient for deathlessness, so powerful that a small pinch in my bath will extend my youth. And more than a pinch... well, let us say... I have ideas.

Using this particular recipe, my great, great grandmother lived to be two hundred and twenty years old. She would have lived much longer had she not found herself an enemy to Orkney's King Lot. Three generations of Morgans followed thereafter, none worthy of the name... until me. Pity that my mother's oversight gave me another name... but tis appropriate, don't you think?

Morwen. Maiden.

I smile serenely, in love with myself and pleased with my progress. I will be a *maiden* for all eternity, with skin softer and suppler than my daughter Seren's.

Alas, poor sweet Seren—I smile more deeply—perhaps my most beautiful daughter will discover a bit of irony in wedding a beast... someone beneath her... someone who offers me great riches and power... but hideous to awake to. I will arrange this. *But later.*

Right now, I study my choices: One man wears a doublet, with chainmail gussets sewn into the vest and the sigil of his house emblazoned on the front— a golden two-headed falcon with a maxim that read *Altium, citius, fortius.*

Swifter, higher, stronger...

How swift would he be if I should happen to drop my spell of glamor and show my true self? I laugh inwardly at this... my breasts quaking with amusement, for not even my own daughters could possibly anticipate the truth: I am seventy years old—my mother's age when she died. And, aye, she had me when she was but twenty, and spat my brother out one year later, before letting her womb rot and die.

I did the reverse. I let my womb lie fallow until I grew older... wiser.... I had my first-born child at the age of forty-six—older than my lover, and he never knew it. I bore Elspeth to bind him to me, and then, I was weak, allowing Emrys to get me with child—and oh, how my brother loved this news, even as I lamented an end to my plans. But life gives us choices, does it not?

Alas, my Emrys is gone—his bones resting in a reliquary—and one day, I will hand them to my daughter Rhiannon, because it will please me immensely to show my little girl how the weak should end. I will tell her all about the father she never knew, and how he died, and she will fall to her knees and weep... but I tell you what she will *not* do: She will not embrace the Death Crone's rage. This is why my daughters will ever be poppets, made to serve my needs. The thought alone makes me happy—truly happy—for the first time since learning Elspeth ran away.

Ungrateful little bitch.

She could have had so much. She could have slept in the high priestess's bed. She could have cast her spells into the Witch Goddess's cauldron and she could have ruled Blackwood in my stead.

But nay! Oh, nay! She would prefer—what? A life on the run? With no safe harbor? Ever? Because some day, I tell you, England will, indeed, hand the crown to a lady... and that woman will be me, not Matilda. I have a hundred lifetimes to see it done... little... by little... by little.

One man across the room peers at me now—the one with the doublet—and I am drawn to him. I think about Blackwood. I think about Rhiannon and decide that she's the one who should inherit Blackwood anyway—for her father and for me—although my second eldest first requires a lesson in obeisance.

Annoyed now, I am compelled to retrieve my scrying stone... to look and be sure my will is being done. But I am equally *hungry* for something else... and the night is no longer quite so young.

The other occupant of the room is a kitchen boy, taking

his supper. The innkeeper hired the boy to keep him about as a second choice, but it is my experience that boys like that are never good to keep after a letting. They run their mouths. They run away.

Unfortunately, the other choice seems antsy. Apparently, he's a deserter, who, rather than meet his fate at the end of a sword blade, fled the battle. Luckily for me, the innkeeper has a reputation for helping *unfortunates* find a way across the narrow sea.

Calais. Calais. The sanctuary of the hapless.

Considering the deserter now, I fiddle with my ring, wondering over the spell I've been meaning to try... and thinking, down in my bones, now could be the time.

Daw is his name.

Daw.

In my native tongue, it means beloved one.

Come here, my beloved, I say without moving my lips.

Blinking, the lad peers up from his tankard, glancing in my direction—fair-haired with bright blue eyes, like a Viking. He'll do, I decide, and push my hood back, allowing him to see me for the first time. But, of course, he cannot resist, for I am a siren. I am a Goddess. I am lust incarnate.

I meet his gaze, and revel in the bright red aura of desire that ignites about him like a glorious flame. He arises from his bench and the youth in him warms my blood. My nipples pucker, and my hand falls beneath the table, sliding beneath my robe; I am famished.

"Hail," he says.

"Halloo, Daw."

In my peripheral, I see the innkeeper comes out from behind the bar and taps the kitchen boy on the shoulder to draw him into the back room as Daw seats himself in the facing bench before me. His cheeks are flushed, and his brow is moist with sweat, but his eyes are filled with lust while mine are filled with bloodlust. My aura draws his in, black swirling tendrils furling about the bright red desire, and sucking it hungrily inside the black.

"May I buy you an ale?" he says, but I know all he has in his purse is a single coin he was given by the innkeeper for cleaning the stable.

"What a dear, dear man," I say with a warm smile.

I shed my cloak now, revealing myself to his lustful gaze. "I am Morwen," I say silkily, and the Crone in me revels behind my shy Maiden's smile.

15

Despite the gritty wine, Malcom was half soused when the knock sounded on his door—a soft, tentative rap he may not have heard if he were not already painfully awake.

Wearied of attempting to finagle a comfortable position in the wooden chair, he rose to answer the door and found a young maid by the name of Alyss shrinking behind it.

He remembered the lass from his last visit. Not daring to look him in the eyes, she deposited a number of items into his arms, begged his pardon for the intrusion, then turned to flee as quickly as her legs could carry her.

Malcom was accustomed to such treatment from the fairer sex. He wasn't the most agreeable sort, nor, in truth, entirely pleasing to look at. He fingered the scar at the upper right corner of his forehead. Although he'd managed to save his face, for the most part, his body was a testament to the violence he'd engaged in over the past eleven years of his life.

He closed the door again, and supposing the gifts must

be for Elspeth, he carried them into the room, placing them at the foot of the bed where she slept so peacefully.

Somehow, the knock on the door hadn't disturbed her, and he marveled over the trust she'd placed in him to sleep so soundly, even despite the fright she must have taken over Beauchamp.

A blind man couldn't have missed the look of fear on her face when she'd laid her eyes on the man—or the stiffness in her body when they'd ridden into the bailey.

Skirting around the bed to the side where Elspeth lay, he stood scrutinizing her a long moment, trying to make sense over the protective feelings he was experiencing.

He understood intuitively what his Da must have felt when he'd taken Page into his keeping—enduring even her fury in order to save her feelings. Her father had cast her away, crowing to his Da that he could "keep her or kill her, he cared not which." In fact, those were his precise words, Malcom remembered. And lest he should wound her more than it seemed she must be already, his father had traveled all the way back to Scotia without ever telling Page the truth, even when his own men questioned his judgment and his sanity. In the end, his father had been prepared to do battle for her honor and defied even their king.

Was Malcom prepared to defy his?

The answer to that question niggled him because it made him question his own moral boundaries—and, of course, his motives as well. Was it a man's duty to keep his oaths at all cost? Or should he be compelled to break them for the ones he loved?

He didn't even wish to examine the point that he couldn't possibly love Elspeth. He didn't even know her. At any rate, back in those days when his father championed Page, his Da had never truly considered David his king, nor had he given David any oath, so the decision for him had been much simpler. And yet, could he imagine a world or circumstances where his father would not have defended him, or Page, no matter who he must defy?

Remembering that day before the Battle of the Standard, when he'd faced his father across a battlefield, he felt sick to his gut anew...

There stood a man who'd loved his kinsmen well, and his son no less. Yet, compelled by his own honor, Malcom had been forced to call him enemy.

His father's broken heart had been evident in those stark blue eyes, and Malcom had turned away with a sting in his own, lifting his sword regardless.

It hadn't mattered that he didn't trade blows with his father that day. What mattered was that he'd turned his back to the man who'd raised him, raising his sword against men he'd once considered compatriots, and his own sire could have easily died that day.

All these years later, it still gave him a turn of the gut.

So, then, would he now defy his king for a woman he barely knew, when he so readily had turned his back on his father? And what was this burden he felt—this undeniable sense of responsibility for the woman lying in that bed?

It was a conundrum for certain—one he didn't care to think about overmuch.

In the end, he must do what he was compelled to do, and damned be the consequences. Damned be everyone. Damned be himself.

Raking a hand through the growing stubble of his beard, he considered returning to the chair... but it was past time to seek Beauchamp. There would be time aplenty to sleep later... after he was dead.

He'd wake Elspeth once it was time for repast. As pleased as he was that she'd eaten a bit of the cheese and bread, he hoped she might be a good bit hungrier when she awoke. Certainly, Beauchamp would offer them a heartier meal belowstairs and the journey to Aldergh was bound to be long. He wanted to leave on the morrow with a belly full. Considering the situation with his father, he daren't stop again at Drakewich, or anywhere else on the journey north. Already, he'd tarried long enough—and to that end, if indeed she meant to accompany him all the way to Aldergh, he should impress upon Beauchamp to sell him another horse. That way, she could ride more befitting a lady. And neither did he prefer forcing Merry Bells to carry the weight of two.

Sighing again, Malcom rubbed the back of his neck to relieve a bit of tension, thinking about Cael d'Lucy. Elspeth might have been well served by an alliance with that man, but Malcom found himself inexplicably pleased she did not aspire to be his wife. Admittedly, she was a woman he could covet for himself—if he allowed it—and for an instant, just an instant, as he stood watching Elspeth sleep, he imagined again this could be their bedchamber... at Aldergh... And he remembered the waking dream he'd had, and his body sprang to life.

Oh, how he longed to crawl into that bed beside her. But far more than simply igniting his ardor, the images accosting him again gave him an intense longing for more than mere pleasures of the flesh. He longed for sleepy embraces and good night kisses... wee bairns clinging to his knees.

Ach, but God, it had been far too long since he'd enjoyed any such familial sounds, and right now, he craved them with a part of his soul too long denied.

So, then, was this why that impossible proclamation burst from his lips?

Did he covet Elspeth to be his bride?

The answer to that was: *aye*. He did.

Inexplicably, Malcom found himself bonded with the girl. But he would not have her unless she desired him as well—and for that matter, despite the morning's considerations, he would *never* hand her over to a man she did not wish to wed, no matter what Stephen decreed, and no matter whether she returned Malcom's ardor or not. He was Stephen's man in all things military, but he would no more hand this woman over against her will than he would betray his own mother... or a wee boy... as someone he'd once trusted had done to him.

No matter how old he might grow, Malcom would never forget that intense sense of betrayal and loss. And he would never forget the day when he'd found himself standing before Aldergh's gates, knees trembling and tears pricking at his eyes over merely the anticipation of being reunited with his father. Six years old he'd been that day—a wee lad torn from the bosom of his kin.

So, then, unless Elspeth herself should decree it, he could never allow her to be used against her will. But now that the notion had wormed its way into his head, he wondered... would she welcome an alliance with a Scots born man from the hinterlands... whose station was little different from the lord of Blackwood's? And even if she would agree to such a proposal... would Malcom, indeed, be willing to break his oath to keep her?

Crossing his arms, studying her face in slumber, he wondered... what was it about Elspeth that seemed so oddly familiar... could it be that he knew her mother?

Her father was dead, so she'd said; who was he?

At last, realizing there could be no better time to tend to his wound than now, whilst she slept, he removed his *gambeson*, tossing it onto the bed, grateful that Beauchamp had not yet asked what he was doing in the vicinity. He lifted the hem of his *sherte*, shrugging it off as well.

Opting for lighter accoutrements, he'd packed the hauberk and coif into his saddlebag, knowing full well that they were riding into allied lands and he wouldn't need them—not today.

It was only belatedly, as he tossed the *sherte* onto the bed that he realized his wound did not pain him. Surprised by the revelation, Malcom twisted to see what he could find... and found himself befuddled as he stared at the spot on his shoulder where his wound should have been... but wasn't. *It was gone.*

Gone as in *gone*—not simply healed. There was no trace of blood, not even a scab, or a long-healed scar. By all that was holy, it was as though there had never been any wound at all. At least not on his shoulder. Right there, in that very spot, his skin remained entirely unblemished, with nary a scratch. But... it couldn't be. Shaking his head in bewilderment, he retrieved his *sherte,* if only to inspect the integrity of the material, and sure enough, he found a rent as big as his fist.

The *gambeson*, as well, bore a telltale rip.

Only his shoulder had evidence to the contrary:

Slowly, he turned to Elspeth, blinking down at the girl. He knew instinctively—inexplicably—that it must have been her. Only what had she done? Naught that he could remember.

Mentally, Malcom retraced their steps since last evening. She'd washed his wound with his rag. Then later, after supping, she'd rubbed a salve on him that she'd made from herbs she'd foraged. Already annoyed, and unwilling to suffer the scent of his own burning flesh, he'd denied her the opportunity to cauterize the wound, thinking it far too soon anyway, and hoping it would heal on its own, because, God knew, he already had too many hideous scars and didn't relish another.

Of course, she had argued with him, only briefly, before setting about to making her salve, crushing herbs on the back of his shield with the hilt of his dagger. And then she'd also made him a strange tea, and whatever she'd given him put him straight to sleep...

Confused, he pressed his fingers into the flesh at his shoulder. But there was no soreness. Very simply, and mysteriously, the wound had... vanished.

Dumbfounded, Malcom tossed the *sherte* back down on the bed and went to retrieve a clean tunic from his bag—one last time, checking the ruined hauberk. Like the *sherte* and *gambeson*, the damage there remained. And now, again, he turned to study the girl sleeping on the bed...

Who the hell are you, Elspeth of Llanthony?

16

Stifling a yawn, Elspeth opened her eyes, slightly disoriented.

Having slept so soundly for the first time in two days, it took a moment to register where she lay. The curtains were still drawn, and it was impossible to say what the hour might be.

"My lady?"

Startled by the whispered voice, Elspeth bolted upright as a torch swept into the room.

Malcom was gone. Two women approached the bed—a lovely fair-haired woman with a sweet face and kindly brown eyes, joined by another with hair much the same color as Elspeth's—only curlier—and eyes the color of a bright blue flame. Both women were young, or at least younger than Elspeth, and their auras were not threatening—shades of pink, green, orange and silver.

Seeing that she was awake, the second woman, the one holding the torch, proceeded across the chamber to set her flame to each of the cressets, before putting the torch—the one she held—into a brace by the door. Afterward, she returned to stand behind her mistress, her hands crossed before her submissively.

"Art awake?" asked the girl with the fiery hair and disarming smile.

"Aye," Elspeth said. "Where is Malcom?"

"Your lord husband?"

Elspeth hedged, furrowing her brow. But then she nodded, blushing, surmising that one of these women must be Beauchamp's sister. The lady that addressed her smiled wider. "He's belowstairs, in the hall, speaking to my brother. As it has been many hours since you laid down to rest, my lord was concerned."

Malcom was concerned? Elspeth scooted to the edge of the bed, casting her feet over the side. "I... I am fine," she reassured the ladies. "I am but wearied from travel." And, it was true, although she didn't know why, though she was far more tired than she had ever been in her life—as though, body and soul she'd suffered some great ordeal, and perhaps she had.

"I thought as much," the girl said, smiling still. "But you should be up now, or you'll miss the feast we've provided in your honor."

"Feast?"

"Aye, my lady. Alyss and I have come to help you dress."

Realizing belatedly that she was still wearing the Llanthony tunic and breeches, Elspeth laid a hand atop her breast and gasped. "Oh," she said in consternation.

"You need have no cause for worry, Lady Aldergh."

The epithet startled Elspeth so much that she blinked.

"Your lord husband already explained... you lost your gown in the burn when you stopped to wash." But she hid a shy smile as she peered at her lady's maid, and their private exchange left very little doubt as to what they truly believed she and Malcom had been doing by the burn. Just to make it clearer, both their cheeks flushed so darkly that Elspeth thought they looked like poppets with painted cheeks.

"I am Dominique," said the girl with the flame-blue eyes, and she came forward to rummage through a pile of garments laying at the foot of the bed. She lifted up one of the pieces, unfurling it to show Elspeth what it was. It appeared to be wool, but a wool so fine that it could have been silk, with tiny gold threads woven into the material around the sleeves, neck and hem.

"If this one suits you, I will be pleased to gift it. 'Tis made of scarlet, dyed crimson, fully done by my lady Alyss." She turned to address the woman standing behind her, and the woman smiled diffidently, bowing her head. "She has a fine skill for such things, and I count my blessings to have her." Elspeth stared at the red gown, stunned over the generosity of the gift. She blinked again. Not since she'd spent time in her father's court had she ever seen wool so fine, and certainly none of its caliber had ever been wasted on her. The closest she'd ever come to owning something so lovely was the *tiretaine* wool she'd worn as a child. Alas, she'd long since outgrown that dress, and not in all the years she'd spent at Llanthony had she worn anything else so fine —neither had her sisters.

Like a moth to a flame, she found herself drawn to the dress, lured from the bed, if only to play her fingers along the length of it... so, so soft. And the color... it was as rich as any dye Elspeth had ever encountered. "Scarlet?" she asked.

Dominique nodded. "Dyed with the grain of the kermes." Without any reservation, she handed the sumptuous gown over to Elspeth with both hands, then reached out for the white *chainse* that had lain folded beneath it. "That surcoat is scarlet, but the *chainse* is sendal. I trust it will flatter you well." And then, once again, she looked to her lady's maid with such a fierce look of pride that it warmed Elspeth to her cockles. "I was told you had my coloring, and dear Alyss has perfected her crimson. It shows well with my color and I thought you might like it, too."

Indeed, it did, thought Elspeth. The color was rich and dark, with no yellow in the pigment at all—perhaps, blue.

Smiling still, Dominique handed Elspeth the sendal as well, and Elspeth didn't know what to say... so she said nothing... merely stood agape.

Dominique's face fell. "Oh, no! You do not like them?" she asked. "I beg your pardon," she rushed to say. "I thought to give you something finer, but I hoped the wool would serve you best for travel. It's soft and malleable."

"Oh, nay!" Elspeth said, realizing the girl must have mistaken her silence for displeasure. "In truth, Lady Dominique, I have never seen *anything* so fine."

Amazed, Elspeth ran her hand over the material again, beguiled by the texture. The sendal too was exquisite and so sheer it made her blush over the thought of wearing it.

Dominique's entire countenance brightened. If it were possible, she stood a little taller. Her eyes lit, and her aura brightened, but the maid's remained dim, Elspeth noticed.

"Did you spin the wool yourself?" she asked the shy lady.

Alyss didn't answer, so Dominique answered for her. "Alas, nay. Neither of us could ever produce a wool so fine. Fortunately, my brother is very generous. He ordered many, many ells for me to do as I wish. I fashioned a tunic for William and a dress or two for me because I like it far better than I do the samite." She leaned forward to whisper, "I cannot abide the sound it makes when I walk." But then she put a finger into the air, as though remembering something else. "Oh, but here... I made... this..." And she leaned forward again, grasping yet another garment. This one was a richly sewn tunic—also made with scarlet but fashioned for a man. There was a sigil on the front that Elspeth had come to recognize only too well—a golden two-headed falcon with a maxim that read *Altium, citius, fortius*. "For my lord Aldergh," she said, touching the embroidery reverently, a wistful smile lingering at the corners of her lovely lips, though without a trace of rancor.

"Oh... I'm so, so sorry." Elspeth said at once, realizing she must have sewn the garment as a gift for her betrothed. "I did not know."

"Are you not pleased?"

"Yes, of course. But—"

Dominique gave her a sympathetic look and waved a hand in dismissal. "Speak no more, my darling friend! 'Tis a woman's lot to serve her house," she said, interrupting. "You need not ever be sorry. Indeed, I have long admired the King's Enforcer, and I would have welcomed our union. But, alas, I could never begrudge the joy I saw so plainly in your lord's eyes when he spoke of his lady."

Elspeth blinked, lifting her gaze to meet Dominique's.

Malcom was the *King's Enforcer*?

Sweet fates! Cael d'Lucy shared this distinction. Enforcer was simply another name for assassin. So, then, Malcom was a member of the Rex Militum? She blinked again, realizing what it portended. *What was he doing near Llanthony?*

Oblivious to Elspeth's thoughts, Dominque's expression was filled with marvel, her eyes glistening with joy. "What a wonderful boon to be offered a love match—how fortunate you are!"

Love match?

But nay, nay... they barely knew one another.

"Come," demanded Dominique, beckoning Elspeth. "Let us help you dress. I cannot wait to see your lord's eyes when they feast upon you this evening." She chattered on and on, buoyant and happy. "I warrant, no matter the state of his belly, he'll have no more hunger for his meal." And then she giggled, and before Elspeth could protest, the maid Alyss rushed forward to help Elspeth remove her dirty Llanthony tunic.

Together, they worked like a maelstrom, arms aflutter, tugging, lifting, removing, tossing garments aside, before helping Elspeth wash and dress. In all this time, Elspeth had little choice but to allow the ministrations, because neither gave her any choice. She did, however, very discreetly stuff the Llanthony tunic aside, hiding it from their scrutiny.

And even abashed though she might be over so much ado, she found herself enjoying the unexpected attention. It indulged a yearning she had for her sisters, even though she and her siblings had fended for themselves from the day they were born, sharing the same scratchy undyed wool gowns for years and years before earning the right to ask for another.

At home, Elspeth's gowns had all been stained by earth and flora, and despite all their knowledge of simples, betimes they could not eradicate the stains from their clothes.

Far too easily, the scarlet wool slid over Elspeth's bare skin like a lover's caress, giving her gooseflesh. And once they were done dressing her, she wore the finest gown she'd ever beheld—finer yet than any Matilda had ever worn in her presence—with long flowing sleeves and a surcoat as rich as the color of blood. In contrast, the sendal *chainse* was whiter than the palest shade of a new moon. And if that were not well enough alone, they brushed her hair, plaiting her tresses into braids that fell to either side of her face, with silver ribbons threading through.

At long last, when their work was completed, Alyss handed Elspeth a small handheld mirror, withdrawing it from the pocket of her apron, and Elspeth peered into the polished silver with gasp.

The girl who peered back at her now was hardly the same girl she'd faced in the gurgling brook this morn... or the one who'd fled the priory. This lady was freshly washed and pink-faced, with hair that reminded Elspeth of Matilda herself whenever she'd returned from Germany as a widowed wife of the Emperor, with all her fine clothes and hair aglow with threads of gold.

"You are so beautiful," said Alyss, reticently.

Dominique agreed, but so much more enthusiastically. "Twill not only be your lord husband whose eyes will turn this eve." She laughed and clapped her hands. "My brother will think you lovely as a queen!"

The maid behind her flinched, and Dominique only belatedly seemed to realize what she'd said, and she flinched, leaving Elspeth to wonder over the exchange as Dominique put a hand to the maid's shoulder, stroking gently, while still addressing Elspeth.

"Now, shall we see you belowstairs for the feast? Tonight we have called a troubadour and a jongleur, as well, and my brother has butchered a sow for the occasion. In truth, 'tis been some time since we've enjoyed a meal so grand—in honor of you, my lady, and your lord husband."

A feast? In Elspeth's behalf?

Suddenly, all coherent thought fled from her head. Gone was her momentary curiosity over Alyss's discomfiture, vanished were any awkward questions over Malcom's betrothal to Dominique, or his appointment to the king's justice. Forgotten as well was the truth of why she'd come here after all... and just for the moment, or perhaps just the evening, she dared to *be* the Lady of Aldergh.

Tomorrow would be soon enough to face the truth... that she was but a runaway daughter of a long dead king, whose own mother would rather see her suffer than be happy.

And Malcom... he wasn't only the devoted servant of the man who'd stolen her sister's crown; he was the King's Enforcer—a mercenary, indeed, not so different from Cael d'Lucy, the man to whom her mother would have seen her betrothed.

So, it seemed, she'd leapt from the pot into the flames... and even so she found herself counting seconds before she could see Malcom again.

THE WINE WAS as poor as Malcom remembered it was, still he reached for it all too easily, sipping as he watched the harpist seduce her strings. But at least the music was sweet.

It was inordinately clear that Beauchamp was pleased over the proposal he'd made to wed his sister to the lord of Drakewich. His mood was high, and his mouth hadn't stopped yapping for nearly an hour, expounding on subjects that Malcom didn't feel comfortable discussing. And yet, very clearly, the man had gone above and beyond, for the last meal Malcom had here was hardly so fine. "So, my lord, tell me... do you anticipate this will be the end of Matilda?"

Malcom shrugged. "The lady is stubborn," he said distractedly. "I cannot see as she will stop until she has what she considers to be hers. But I ken she no longer has the resources to persevere. Robert is dead." He considered what news was public knowledge, and added, "Word is that Wallingford has grown ill as well."

Beauchamp nodded. "Brian Fitz Count?" He made a flourish with his hand, jostling his wine over the top of his cup. "Or rather should I say Fitz Cunt?" He smiled deviously, self-amused. "I cannot abide that fool. If anyone believes he isn't beard-splitting Matilda, I'd have a thing or two to say about that."

Bored with such utter nonsense, but allowing Beauchamp to carry on, Malcom lost himself amidst half-drunken reverie, thinking about his recent commission in Wales.

As far as he saw it, if the taking of a single life could save a thousand more, this was the *raison d'état* for the Rex Militum. The death of one culpable man was a far lesser tragedy than to have an entire countryside showered in the blood of innocents. As it was, he couldn't stomach the sweeping loss of life after thirteen years of warfare. For someone like Wallingford, who was complicit in the instigations of this war, and who'd been planning insurgency from the beginning, Malcom saw his demise no differently than he did facing his enemy on a battlefield. Whilst there was a lot he might be conflicted over, he was *not* conflicted over that. They'd received word that Wallingford intended to visit Llanthony to award the priory yet another grant for the sake of his soul. It was Malcom's assignment to intercept the man, attempt negotiations and dispose of him if necessary. But their intelligence had proven faulty, and it had cost him a squire. Still, he couldn't regret having gone, elsewise he'd never have encountered Elspeth... whose absence from this hall was beginning to turn his last nerve. Glancing at the stairwell, he took another sip of his nasty wine.

"Pious bitch," Beauchamp was saying of the Empress.

But, of course, Malcom would never use such words, though Matilda was, indeed, haughty and betimes mean and quick to anger, like her father—not to mention, more pious than was necessary.

But then, again, that brought to mind a point that had long been festering: There were still a number of the old tribes about Wales—as there were in Scotia—men and women who'd never relish being told to bend the knee to a God they did not know. It seemed to Malcom that if Stephen so much wished to gain Welsh support, rather than murdering his enemies, he should be looking for gentler ways to join their houses. But, of course, d'Lucy was no *eegit*: He could well have proposed such a thing already... which would explain Elspeth.

"Haughty as you please," Beauchamp persisted, perseverating like a mad dog with a bone. "But I tell you, no man enjoys being told what to do by *any* woman, no matter what her station."

"Oh, I don't know," Malcom replied absently, careful to keep the brogue from his words now that he was lighter on his toes. "I can think of a few occasions to prostrate myself before a lady."

Beauchamp guffawed loudly. He gave Malcom a thump of his elbow, highly amused. "Ah, you Scots are ever randy bastards," he said, and he took a hefty swig from his tankard. "As for me..." He set the tankard down with a hard thud. "I've not yet found a proper lady who could wet my whistle as well as my sister could."

Startled by the proclamation, Malcom straightened in his chair.

Beauchamp must have anticipated an objection, because he said very quickly. "Not that I have *ever* or would ever, mind you." He swiped his hand through the air. "My sister's as chaste as the Virgin herself."

By God. The wine must be getting to him, Malcom decided, because he suddenly had unspeakable images cavorting through his head, and it was quite a bit more distasteful than Beauchamp's dirty wine. God help him. If he didn't know better—know Beauchamp was too greedy to compromise his only sister—an asset—he would have to worry for the poor lass.

As it was, the erection that had begun to slowly tease him over the thought of Elspeth lying abovestairs in that bed, grew perfectly flaccid, and he was inordinately relieved when Beauchamp returned the conversation to Henry's women. "So, what's this I hear about Adeliza still scheming to put her stepdaughter on the throne? Meddling cow."

Malcom tried harder to eradicate the distasteful images from his head. "I would put little credence in any such rumor. D'Aubigny would not stand for it. He's Stephen's loyal man."

Eyeing the harpist, Beauchamp leaned backward in his chair. "Pah!" he said, throwing up a hand. "D'Aubigny is besotted by Henry's widow. Did you not hear say he's granted a shit pile of land at Wymondham to build the lady a leper hospital?

"And," he continued, dredging up old news, "what of Matilda? At his lady's behest, he allowed that nasty shrew to shelter at Arundel, and then he then let her go when Stephen bade him not to."

"So he did," Malcom said, growing impatient, though not merely with the conversation. It had been a long, long night and day, and he'd yet to get a good rest, and more and more he reconsidered the wisdom in hanging about. He had a father who could be dying, and he owed the man more than *this*, no matter what quarrels lay between them.

"I would have thought Stephen would charge him for that."

"What would you have had him do?" Malcom asked, arching a brow, casting Beauchamp a pointed glance. "Stephen, himself, released his cousin twice. 'Tis why I serve the man. I admire the respect he bears his kin, and particularly his lady kin. Why would he then punish D'Aubigny when D'Aubigny is more loyal than most?"

Feeling judged, perhaps, Beauchamp grumbled. "Betimes our king is as flaccid as an old cock. But thankfully, he's got that Welsh witch to see to him."

Welsh witch...

Morwen.

Something teased at Malcom's subconscious, though he couldn't bring it to light—mostly because he was preoccupied with Elspeth. Every so oft, his eyes were drawn to the stairwell at the back of the hall, only hoping for a glimpse of the woman he'd so boldly claimed to be his bride.

Would she tell Dominique?

Would she confess all?

If, indeed, she did so, Malcom would have more explanations to make, because so far as Beauchamp knew, he'd wed her by leave of their king, and there was no one here but Elspeth who could possibly deny it. At long last, he spotted a flutter of movement at the back of the hall.

And there she was...

Dominique was the first to appear, leading the way, her smile beatific, as ever. Yes, indeed, the girl was quite lovely, with a kindly demeanor. She would make some man a fine, fine wife. And only for the briefest instant, he wondered how he could have rebuffed her... particularly if she, herself, needed saving, for even now, her brother's jest sat like a pile of rot in Malcom's gut.

But then Elspeth arrived behind her, and Dominique was forgotten. Setting down his cup as Elspeth descended the stairwell, he stood.

Her crimson dress was generously laced with silver threads. Her pale-red hair fell into two rich copper plaits at either side of her lovely face, interwoven with glittering ribbons that caught the torchlight. Her long red sleeves flowed gracefully behind her, like the wind catching at a flame, and the white of her *chainse* contrasted like purest snow against the blood-red of her surcoat.

Whatever Malcom might have anticipated... she'd surpassed his expectations by degrees, and he could but stare... mouth agape... blinking at the sight she presented.

"Elspeth," he whispered with awe.

Only remembering himself belatedly—and the simple fact that he should not be so much surprised, considering she was meant to be his wife—he rushed across the dais to greet his *bride*, like a man, indeed, besotted.

17

Even at this distance Elspeth recognized the look of approval on Malcom's face, and it took her breath away. "You see my lady," Dominique said, leaning close to whisper. "I have *never, ever* seen *any* man look at his lady that way. I only hope I can be so fortunate someday."

Malcom stood tall on the dais—taller than any—looking very noble, standing beside the lord's table, with his long sun-kissed hair unbound and curling about his swarthy face. He smiled with those full lips, and she blushed and gave her new friend a timid glance. "I hope so, as well," she said for Dominque's sake, and then she was suddenly overly pleased with herself, though she hadn't any true reason why. Everything about this evening was false, including her place at Malcom's side.

And yet, for the first time in Elspeth's life, she felt like a princess, in truth, and all her troubles were swept aside. Never in her life had she been treated as a guest of honor.

In her father's home, children were not to be seen. They took their meals altogether, apart from the rest of the household. And then, at the priory, no one ever had any special treatment—not even the monks. For their part, she and her sisters had been relegated to a single table, but they were not to take their repast until the men were all finished and left the hall.

At the moment, she felt like her sister Matilda, all bedecked in finery, and she wanted to run to the dais and hug Malcom—for what, she hadn't any clue.

Alyss took her leave of them as she had a seat reserved among the lower tables. But there remained two places available at the lord's table, one on either side of the seat of honor.

Dominique would be seated to the right of her lord brother; Elspeth would be to his left, sharing a trencher with Malcom... her *husband*.

For the moment, even the simple fact that she must be seated beside William Beauchamp did very little to dampen her mood. Tonight, with so much reverie, it was easier to hope that she had been mistaken about the lord of Amdel. Here in this room alone, the colors were like the dazzling lights of Caer Arianrhod—the Moon Goddess, who shone her night rainbow from her palace up on high. It was only after seeing that Malcom stood to greet them that Amdel's lord rose as well. However, whilst he sat again very quickly, Malcom skirted around him, never taking his eyes off Elspeth, and came to procure her hand, kissing her sweetly, before leading her to her seat.

Elspeth's heart beat so fiercely that she feared he would hear. The blood rushed through her temples like the swoosh of a waterfall.

"As ever, my... love... you are stunning," he murmured so smoothly and silkily, and Elspeth's breast filled with a halting breath. She swallowed as he turned to Lady

Dominique, "Demoiselle," he said pleasantly. "Art lovely this evening."

"My Lord Aldergh," Dominique returned with a smile, and her eyes gleamed with excitement as she turned to meet Elspeth's gaze, winking—as though to say: *I told you so.*

Feeling flushed, Elspeth sat, but only after Dominique did, and Malcom remained standing until both women were seated, before assuming his place beside her.

That small courtesy was entirely lost to William, who then turned to Elspeth in his seat before greeting his sister and said, "I trust you slept well, Lady Aldergh?"

"Quite," Elspeth said with a nod.

"My sister's gown appears to have been fashioned especially for you," he said, with undisguised admiration. In fact, he lifted his chin to peer down Elspeth's gown, at the curve of her bosom, and she shrank back, leaning into Malcom, taking comfort in his proximity.

"Thank you," she said.

The lady Dominique seemed to have no inkling about her brother's rudeness. She smiled brightly. "I, too, have never seen a lady so fine!" she announced, with such genuine sincerity that Elspeth flushed to her toes. And from that moment on, the night passed like a dream.

If the vittles provided to them upstairs had seemed lean, the table before them was laden. There was, as Dominique claimed, a great big sow, and a fat pheasant, as yet untouched, with a great many plates surrounding it—including nuts, cheese, olives and bread. In truth, Elspeth had never seen so many elaborate dishes, with so many sauces, and she barely recognized most.

Also, the trenchers at the lord's table were not made of bread, but wood and Elspeth complimented the setting and the meal, assuming the responsibility for its planning had fallen to Lady Dominique as the provisional chatelaine of this house.

Of course, Lady Dominique was delightful, and there was little she did or said that left Elspeth to wonder over her sincerity or generosity. And, for the most part, her brother comported himself well enough, if not a true gentleman.

Beside her, Malcom remained quiet and brooding—and may the fates forgive her, but whereas Elspeth shrank back from Beauchamp's gaze, she found herself puffing her breast whenever she caught Malcom's gaze, hoping he would glance. It gave her a singly perverse pleasure to tempt him— and why shouldn't she? He was the one who'd claimed they were already wed, and of course, Beauchamp would expect a wife to be coy with her husband.

At any rate, Elspeth's people were not prudes. She was a maiden still, but not because she feared coupling. She had been taught to revel in all that made her a woman. In fact, her ancestors were pagans, who, rather than be ashamed of the act of creating life, had been taught the act was sacred. The greatest gift to bestow upon the world itself was a child of her womb.

Of course, at the priory, they'd been forced to cover themselves in shame, but neither she nor her sisters had ever forgotten her grandmamau's words: *We are not placed on this earth to ask forgiveness for our sins, we are here to honor the Goddess with our gifts.*

Right now, Elspeth felt a hunger in her womb, and she dared to revel in it... if only for the evening. She dared to love the way Malcom's gaze lingered... and found herself breathless as they shared the meal.

Aside from the trencher, they also shared a goblet, and on one particular occasion they both reached for the glass at the same time. Elspeth gasped softly as his hand covered hers, and she held her breath as his fingers lingered, entwining with hers, caressing her...

She swallowed as gooseflesh erupted on her arms—and her breasts—then he withdrew with a knowing smile, allowing Elspeth to drink from the cup whilst he watched. She did so quickly, her lips and throat suddenly parched, then set the cup aside, and once again held her breath as Malcom lifted up the goblet in turn and spun the glass so that his lips fell upon the very spot where Elspeth's lips had touched... He smiled at her.

Her heart leapt inside her breast, hurling itself against her ribs like a child with a tantrum, and only belatedly did she realize the folly of her actions. Sweet, sweet fates, but what seduction was she playing at? Would he later anticipate... *more*?

Swallowing convulsively, Elspeth turned away, overhearing Lady Dominique say to her brother that she wasn't in the mood to play. And it was only then that Elspeth realized the music in the hall had stopped. She had been so attuned to Malcom that she hadn't realized the entire room was staring expectantly at the lord's table.

"Lady Aldergh, do you play?" William Beauchamp asked, again.

Elspeth blinked. "Play?"

"The harp, My Lady. The harpist has requested a song from my sister, but Lady Dominique claims the mood does not strike her and she bids you to play in her stead."

Elspeth's hand fluttered to her breast. "Me?" she asked. And, well, she did know how to play the harp, but it had been ages since she'd had the means to—not since her days at court. She couldn't even be sure that her fingers knew how to span the chords.

"I would so dearly love to hear you play," Dominque

begged. "You are so lovely tonight and you deserve all the attention."

Elspeth cast a beleaguered glance at Malcom, but Malcom only smiled. And thinking, perhaps, that she was begging his permission, he waved a hand toward the harp that lay waiting at the center of the hall. "Well," she said. "I do know a song or two."

Beauchamp also waved her toward the harp, urging her to play for them. "By all means," he said, and still Elspeth hesitated, never having played for so many people all at once.

Finally, she stood, acutely aware of the hush that had fallen over the room as she moved across the dais and down the stairs. She heard whispers and murmurs as she passed.

One man said with a chuckle to his mate, "If she plays as beautifully as she looks, I myself will swoon like a lady at her feet."

Forsooth! Her music skills were not so fine as her sister Seren's. But then, everything Seren did was better than Elspeth—a fact that had never aggrieved her for a single day... until now.

As she moved across the room, she was very painfully aware of so many pairs of eyes upon her—and one more than all the rest. Malcom watched her intently as she took her seat behind the harp, and Elspeth lifted her gaze to him only once.

Goddess, help me... please.

After so, so long, she was afraid of what would come from her efforts. Very tentatively, she pressed her fingers to the strings, testing the sound. And, then, she closed her eyes, remembering the lessons of her youth, and simply let the music come forth...

She didn't know many songs—only a few. Most were not

suitable for good Christian ears. But everybody loved a faerie's tale with adventure, so she sang a song about Cerridwen, the great priestess of Avalon, who some would claim was herself the Mother Goddess. She was not, of course, but she was still the greatest *dewine* the world had ever known.

To begin with, the story was clever and sweet... inspired by love. For want of a lover Cerridwen lured Tegid Foel onto her Isle of Avalon, and for a short time, they lived together in love and harmony and had a precious daughter they called Creirwy. Creirwy soon came to be known as the loveliest maiden in all the world. Alas, as the newness of their love passed, Cerridwen began to resent that Tegid longed for a life away from her precious Avalon. She soon became embittered, and her bitterness manifested itself in her son. They called this new child Morfran, for his countenance was hideous. And realizing she was the cause of her son's misery, Cerridwen longed to gift her boy with something more precious than could be born of flesh and blood. She meant to *inspire* him with such artistry that it would make him even more beloved than his sister Creirwy. So... she prepared an Arwen potion for a year and a day, until, one sad, sad day, a boy called Gwion was busy stirring her pot, and out leapt a drop of the Arwen potion. Consequently, the wrong boy became enlightened, and foreseeing that the witch Goddess would attempt to destroy him for taking what should rightfully be due her son, he transformed himself into a hare. Cerridwen then became a greyhound to pursue him. Gwion became a fish. Elspeth's fingers moved over the strings more urgently, to symbolize his flight. Cerridwen became an otter, and the boy became a bird. Cerridwen pursued him as a hawk, and finally, at last... She slowed her fingers, to a sad, sad melody, because Gwion, thinking himself too wise to be bested by an old Crone, turned himself into a grain of corn in a field and was thence devoured by Cerridwen in the form of a hen.

But the story was far from done, and in looking about the room, Elspeth saw that the hall was enraptured, so she continued... her eyes filling with tears—less for the story and more for the memories it brought... of herself seated by her grandmother's skirts, watching her grandmamau play the harp. Flames ignited behind her lids, and she heard her grandmother's screams, but she pushed away those memories and continued to sing...

In swallowing Gwion, Cerridwen came to be with child. She bore the boy nine months in her womb, all the while swearing she would kill him after he was born. But, then, once that day came, she realized she could not kill her lovely child, so she wrapped the boy in swaddling and cast him out to sea, where he was found by good king Elfin. Under Elfin's tutelage, Gwion became a great, great bard known as Taliesin, whose radiant beauty was his curse, and whose progeny would forever share his burden. Some people knew him as Merlin.

But, of course, a beautiful man should be offered a beautiful lady to wife, and he was given to wed the loveliest lady in all the land, which happened to be Creirwy—Cerridwen's own daughter. Alas, for the Witch Goddess, she and the Island of Avalon were swallowed by the sea, gone with the sweep of the Goddess Mother's hand.

No one in the hall could have any notion that the tale Elspeth sang about was true, and thus she dared to sing all the rest, about how Taliesin built himself a fortress high in the Black Mountains, where he'd cherished his lovely bride.

But this is what Elspeth could never say: That fortress she sang about was Blackwood, and it was supposed to have been her legacy.

Alas, in surrendering to her hate and her need for retribution, Cerridwen forsook her Mother's love and mercy, and became an outcast of both worlds. *Poof* went the Isle of Avalon, just the same as would happen to Blackwood... just the same as could happen to England...

To the Welsh, her grandmamau had borne another name. She was the White Witch of *Bannau Brycheiniog*, whose castel was raised so high that she was given vigil over the Endless Sea, and her signal fires were meant to warn Wales of approaching invaders. She was the guardian of all their land. When Elspeth had finished her story, there were tears streaming from her own eyes and down her cheeks. But her fingers remained on the strings, playing of their own accord.

Gentle, blurring, drifting, rushing, clear and brilliant, glittery and flowy, dull, and then mellow and sharp, splashing, cascading, reverberating...

After a while, she opened her eyes to find that the fiber of the room began to vibrate along with the strings of the harp. Startled, Elspeth plucked them again, but with trepidation, blinking as the fabric of the aether gave way to reveal her first true vision... a darkened room... *pluck*... a blood-stained bath... *pluck*... a body discarded on the floor... *pluck*... Morwen... in a blood-soaked tub. *Pluck*. And one final image appeared to her now—one of Rhiannon locked in an iron-barred tumbril...

"Morwen," she whispered, and her fingers ceased to play all at once. The sound they made as they fell across the harp strings was as hideous as Morfran's face.

Elspeth stood, feeling heady, and then suddenly she was afraid as the room began to spin away...

. . .

MALCOM LISTENED CONTENTEDLY to the music. The hall fell silent as Elspeth played, and he'd never heard a sound so sweet as her voice. He sat with bated breath, enchanted by every word.

Beside him, even Beauchamp hushed—at last leaving off with talk of politics.

When Elspeth stopped playing, he stood and made ready to applaud—as did most of the audience—but then she cocked her head as though she were looking at something strange, and her fingers returned to the strings... playing again... only this time without her song.

For an instant, he could well imagine that it could be the most beautiful music he'd ever heard—even more lovely than her song—serene, beguiling, haunting... like songbirds at the end of a long, hard winter... or the gush of a mountain waterfall... or a mournful reed on the still of a summer night. It was so easy to imagine that the sound of her music was as timeless as the land itself... a gift from god on high. And then suddenly, the melody ended in discord, and the sound was a cacophony. Elspeth stood, looking as pale as the sendal she wore, and Malcom recognized that look on her face, because she'd looked that way once before. He bounded from his seat, rushing around the table, and leaping over the edge of the dais.

18

The vision of Rhiannon lingered, folding itself in and out of Elspeth's consciousness and space. Her sister's rueful amber eyes peered out between metal bars...

The piercing scent of *sal ammoniac* wafted into Elspeth's dream and she stirred, opening heavy lidded eyes, only to shut them yet again, and once again, the scent of *sal ammoniac* swept beneath her nostrils, removing the veil of slumber once and for all. She sat upright, crying out. "Rhiannon!"

"Nay, lass, 'tis but Alyss," Malcom said, urging her to lie back down, and then he told the anxious maid, "That will be all for now, Alyss. Thank you."

"I will be near should you need me, lord," Alyss said, and pinching her vial of *sal ammoniac* between her fingertips, she rushed away, casting Elspeth a worried glance.

Alas, Elspeth was far too unsettled to put the girl at ease. The door closed, and her hand grasped Malcom by the arm, pleading. "I *must* go back," she said, and suddenly, per force, she inhaled a calming breath and closed her eyes, shutting out the fear.

No, no, no, she thought.

Why did you do this to me, Rhiannon?

She was ensorcelled—rendered helpless. Every time she even thought about returning to Llanthony, she wanted only to sleep—and sleep some more.

And yet... it was a strange lethargy that crept over her body, not her mind. She was very much aware of every sound and scent surrounding her... the flickering of the torch in its brace, Malcom's unique male scent... He touched her hand, folding it neatly into his own, and Elspeth tried to squeeze it. "Elspeth?" he whispered, shaking her awake.

Elspeth's eyes fluttered open, focusing on the man whose glittering gaze she was coming to know so well—and then suddenly, she understood: *Look to your champion,* Rhiannon had said.

Malcom was the only one who could help her now. Thanks to her sister, Elspeth *couldn't* go back to Llanthony, and, if she tried, she would make the journey like a sack of grain, useless to everyone. But *he* could.

Malcom could go there. She reached out, grabbing him by the tunic, clutching him desperately. And yet, frustrated and frightened over the consequences of telling anyone her deepest secret, Elspeth pressed her head back into the pillow, released him, and tried not to weep. Unbidden, she remembered the day her mother had abandoned them at the priory. Elspeth was eleven, Rhiannon was nine, Seren was only seven and the twins were six.

"See you do not reveal yourself, or you will endanger everything I've worked for."

"Aye mamau."

"Someday I will reward you, but only if you are good."

Elspeth had wondered then what terrible thing had she and her sisters done to be ushered out of their beds in the middle of night and hurried to some remote place where no one could ever find them. But, of course, her grandmother had been a kindhearted lady. If she could be punished so horrendously in front of so many gleeful people, what chance had Elspeth and her sisters?

Betimes, Elspeth could be wicked, so her mother said. She did things she wasn't supposed to do—like sneak into the kitchen for bits of food for her sisters and fire the torches in the nursery because Seren was afraid of the dark.

"You are the eldest. 'Tis your responsibility. I have assured one and all that my mother's wickedness has not spread to me or my daughters. Do not be tempted, Elspeth. Be certain your sisters are never tempted."

"Aye mamau."

And still she persisted. *"Remember what happened to your grandmamau? This, too, will be your fate, and my fate, should you ever dare to defy me."*

"Aye mamau."

"You will burn," she'd continued angrily. *"They will tie you to a wooden stake in front of all those laughing people, and no matter how you weep, they will burn you till your skin turns black and blisters off your bones."*

"Aye mamau."

She squeezed Elspeth's hand very cruelly. *"Do you mean to bring your sisters harm?"*

"Nay, mamau.

"Do you want to burn?" Elspeth didn't answer quickly enough, and she squeezed her hand tighter and harder. *"Do you?"*

Elspeth swallowed, remembering her grandmother's screams.

Nay Mamau!"

And all this while, as Elspeth was so diligent about keeping her sisters from indulging in the Craft, her mother was practicing the worst of the *hud du*.

Morwen was no White Witch. She was a child of the Death Crone whose beauty was only a glamour. She was a monster—a heartless, greedy beast. And this was an untenable position to be in—to have glimpsed such terror, and to know that a pythoness held her sisters' destinies in her hand. *Sweet, sweet fates!* How could she ever have abandoned them? She was the eldest, and as the eldest she was responsible for them. She should have never allowed Rhiannon to convince her to leave. And now she wondered how much Rhiannon had known of their mother's crimes. Her sister had been so desperate for Elspeth to go, but she must have believed she had it all in hand—or at least that's what Elspeth hoped. Only now she wondered: Was it her intention all along to save them, and face Morwen alone?

Swallowing her grief, Elspeth understood now that their mother would stop at nothing to see her will done—including invoking the most hideous *hud du*. She had seen that clearly enough, and since none of her sisters would ever dare pay any such a price for the use of dark *magik*, none of them had any true recourse to fight Morwen alone.

Now Elspeth was at a loss as to what to do. And it wasn't enough to simply warn them. She *must* find a way to remove them from the priory before Morwen arrived to claim them, and to do so, she must trust in Malcom's good will—a man she had never set eyes upon before two days past.

Look to your champion...

CLEARLY, she was tormented, Malcom realized as he

watched the play of emotions cross Elspeth's features. *But why? What could he do to help?* More than any other time in his life, he felt driven to serve. Anything—literally *anything* he could do, he would, and he must.

But hadn't he proven as much?

Inexplicably, his own father could be dying, and, yet, he was here, with her...

Nay, it wasn't merely that he was enamored of her look, even though he was. And what a vision she was lying in that cloud of scarlet, her crimson dress pillowing beneath her.

"Elspeth," he said gently. "Do you know what ails you?"

She nodded, and Malcom suffered a moment of dread as he recalled her sleepy demeanor over the past few days. It was as though she'd suffered some sleeping sickness.

He had taken her brusque manner as a matter of consequence of their meeting, but, in truth, he was no less ill-mannered when he awoke in the mornings. And now it seemed to him that she was perpetually waking, and she was either ill, and she knew it... or... maybe... breeding...

Carrying d'Lucy's bairn?

Christ, no, please!

Of course, neither option appealed to him, and if the latter were true, he would be forced to reconsider his position. For all he knew, d'Lucy was an honorable man—as honorable as he could possibly be as a commander of the Rex Militum. He was more honorable than Malcom, in truth, because Malcom was certain the man had never murdered his own grandfather.

And regardless of who might be the better man, far be it from Malcom to keep any man from his own bairn—not even if the mother should be Elspeth... not unless she had a very good reason.

And then another thought occurred to him: What if the

child wasn't d'Lucy's? Betimes women were cloistered when a child was conceived without benefit of marriage. Was this even possible? He'd heard so many tales of ladies who'd been cast away by their families or kept hidden until the unwanted child could be born.

But none of that made sense, because all five sisters were sequestered together, not only Elspeth. They couldn't *all* be breeding. And yet, as much as he loathed to ask, he felt he must. "Is it possible you could be with child?" he asked, holding his breath for her answer.

"Nay!" she cried, and Malcom was instantly relieved to see her color. "I am not," she said, with such consternation and surety that he felt reassured.

But something *was* wrong. He could see it in the depths of her bonny eyes and sense it in her demeanor. "You can trust me, Elspeth. I have pledged myself to aid you."

He spoke his next words from the depths of his heart. "I will be your champion," he said, and then again, to be sure she knew he meant it. "I will be your champion, Elspeth."

For all the sins he'd ever committed, Malcom was determined to do right by this woman. Leaving her to fend for herself was simply not an option, nor did he trust Beauchamp with her welfare. And still she seemed unwilling to speak.

"Elspeth?" he pleaded.

She turned watery eyes to his shoulder, avoiding his gaze. "I'm afraid," she said, and then swallowed. "What ails me... is naught so simple as a babe."

And her gaze lingered over the spot where Malcom's wound had once been... and it struck him then... the impossible truth.

Elspeth healed him. How was that possible? It was as though she'd done so by witchery.

And the answer entered his head, unbidden. Because that was the answer: *witchery*.

He'd met a woman in Scotia once; her name was Una. Much like Elspeth, there had been something surreal about her—nothing he could put a finger to name, but if you were around her for any length of time, strange things occurred: rising mists, objects appearing in one place when you left them in another, and generally small things that defied explanation but were too mundane to worry over. Ever since meeting Elspeth, there had been a number of unusual occurrences—like the clearing of that fog in the woods, and the simple fact that she had predicted it so easily—as though she had known... or perhaps even conjured it.

But, of course, those things could easily be explained away as luck or coincidence... except the wound on his shoulder... and if wished to pretend it didn't happen, he had the damaged *hauberk* and *sherte* to prove otherwise.

She seemed so reluctant to continue, so Malcom reached out to clasp her hand. "Tell me what ails you, Elspeth..."

You would not believe me.

Malcom blinked, hearing *that* voice again... that strange voice he'd heard that morning in the woods—a soft murmur that sounded more as though it were a memory of a whisper at his ear. He did not avert his gaze. "I would," he said, responding, as though she'd spoken.

Surprised, her gaze snapped up to meet his. Her pupils widened, then darkened, and for a long, long instant, the silence in the room was deafening.

At long last, she turned away from him, and said, "Morwen... she's my mother. She's—"

Malcom sat straight, daunted though he hadn't anticipated it. "I know who she is," he said. And still, as stunning as her disclosure might have been, he never expected what she revealed next.

"My father is King Henry."

Malcom blinked. "*Dead* King Henry?"

Elspeth nodded, furrowing her brow, her lips thinning with displeasure. "My sisters and I have been sequestered for thirteen years, forgotten, until now that my mother has use of me."

Henry, Henry?

Not that Malcom meant to give her pause, but he allowed his hand to fall away from hers, only considering the king who'd once abducted him from his home as a wee boy of six. Henry Beauclerc was the reason Malcom agreed to fight Matilda. He could not in good conscience back a king—or queen—who would stoop to such an ignoble deed as to wrest a child from his home and use him for *politikal* means. It was also why he'd never felt any compunction over not serving David. The two kings—brothers by law—had schemed to put Malcom into Henry's court so they could barter with Malcom's father. Say what they would about Stephen, the man had a far nobler sense of justice, even if his virtue might, in fact, be responsible for prolonging this untenable war. But, least he didn't have the blood of women and children on his hands.

Elspeth's confession explained so much: her betrothal to d'Lucy, as well as her aversion to Stephen... and now he recalled what she'd said that morning he'd met her in the woods: *My fath—Henry would turn in his grave to hear you say such a thing.* She had evidently meant to say *my father*. Malcom had been too dull-witted to catch her slip. But, of course. Why else would five girls be ensconced in a well-endowed priory in Wales—a monastery run by King Henry's old chaplain?

"And your sisters?"

She nodded again, though now she would not face him, perhaps afraid to meet his gaze. "We are all daughters of Henry," she confessed. "Daughters of Morwen. Daughters of Avalon as well." And then she buried her face in her hands and wept.

19

Elspeth sobbed quietly.

For better or worse, now the truth was spent. She had confessed herself to this man—this stranger who'd been placed in her path—her champion so Rhiannon had claimed.

After all, she'd placed herself—and her sisters—at risk, and for all their differences, she should *not* be trusting this man, or any man.

She couldn't look at him now for fear of the repulsion she'd spy in his eyes, for Elspeth was truly someone to be reviled according to the faith of this land.

And what was more, she was kin to a king whose daughter Malcom fought so vehemently to oppose—in favor of a blackguard who'd stolen her father's throne.

For that matter, despite his pretty title, he was a Scots-born mercenary, who'd sworn his allegiance to her cousin. If he should decide to forsake her here and now, there would be naught she could do. For all that was said and done, theirs was an impossible bond.

Once again, Malcom placed a hand on hers, reassuring

her, and Elspeth dared to lift her gaze to his, tears glistening in her eyes. Only, by the look on his face, she realized that, somehow, he had already gleaned so much of what she'd yet to say.

Could it be that he would not revile her? Could it be that despite their differences, he would stand for her? *Look to your champion,* Rhiannon had said. *Look to your champion.*

Daring to trust him, Elspeth willed Malcom to open his heart to the truth, because she understood now that if she didn't place herself at his mercy, she would remain powerless to do aught to help her sisters. For better, or worse, he was her champion in truth.

"You healed my wound," he said, acknowledging his suspicions, and it wasn't a question, Elspeth realized.

She nodded soberly. "Whilst you slept."

He studied her a long moment, shaking his head. "I would not believe it had I not witnessed it with my own two eyes. Witchery, I presume?"

Elspeth winced. She didn't like that word, but mostly because of what it meant to others. She was a *dewine*, a child of the Earth Mother—a Maiden pledged to the *hud*. But for all he knew of the Craft, witchery was as good as any word she might use.

Taking a deep, deep breath, she confessed it all. All the while, Malcom listened... with a hand to his shoulder, rubbing idly at the spot where his wound had been, as though requiring proof.

But of course he would! It was not something he could swiftly embrace.

Only fearing she would lose her nerve if she stopped to consider what she was doing, she rushed on to tell him the rest—*everything, everything,* including the vision she'd had about her mother and her sister. Alas, some things were greater than the sum of one, she realized—or even five—and now she understood that Morwen was building herself a dynasty unlike any that Cerridwen had ever aspired to, and unless she and her sisters prevented it, Morwen, herself, would someday rule Britain. Her poppets would be kings.

To all her revelations, Malcom merely listened, and if he believed she could be tetched in the head, he didn't say so. To the contrary, he seemed to be taking her seriously, and when Elspeth told him about her vision, the color drained from his face. "Do you know where she could be?"

"En route to the priory, I presume."

He made a gesture toward his head, then tapped a finger at his temple and twirled them. "Can't you warn your sisters, somehow? Speak to their minds, as you did with me?"

Elspeth shook her head, frowning. "It doesn't work that way, Malcom. Though I am quite certain they already know. Even if Rhiannon has not seen it, Morwen was bound to hie there as soon as she learned. We knew the very day I left that she was bound to go."

He rubbed at his chin, considering all that she'd said. "I have heard much tittle-tattle about your mother, though I never believed it."

"Aye, well, you *must* believe it," Elspeth told him. "She is treacherous and there is much more I could say, but I would not have you look at me the same way you would look at her."

"I see," he said, raking a hand through his hair.

"I am not some evil sorceress, Malcom... I am a *dewine*," she explained. "Born of the blood of Avalon. I cannot turn anyone into a toad, nor can I create something from nothing."

His brow furrowed. "What *can* you do?"

Elspeth shrugged. "Not as much as my sister, more than you."

"That tells me naught, spinner of words." He smiled. And yet despite the smile, his blue eyes were full of turmoil—believing her, not believing her. But, thankfully, he did not seem to be afraid of her, because it was fear that was ultimately responsible for all the atrocities men had committed against her people. But he *was* conflicted, she realized, and his eyes needed to see to believe.

Resigning herself to the fact that most men were not born to comprehend this long-buried part of their beings, Elspeth prepared to show him. But there was only so much she could do without a proper ritual. Still, determined to win him, she held his gaze, willing him to believe, and without any movement on her part, she cast out the torches—all of them—bathing the room in shadows.

"Did you do that?"

"Aye."

In the darkness, she heard him swallow, and then and only then did she return the flames to the torch, but only to one—the one closest to the door.

And just to be sure, she fed the remaining torch her force, until the flames rose high enough to lick the ceiling, brightening the room so it looked like the inside of a kiln. Only after she was satisfied that he understood it was her doing, she returned the flame to its natural state, and revived the cressets. With a furrowed brow, Malcom peered up at the ceiling, at the black soot she'd left behind and stared in wonder. But, lest he mistake the truth, she said, "I am little different from you, Malcom. We are both children of the Goddess, save that you and your people have forgotten her, and she has forsaken you. You must believe in *magik*, or it cannot exist."

"And your song?"

"All true, though men will doubt it—as you must doubt me."

He rubbed his brow. "I cannot say I am clear on the particulars," he confessed. "But I do not doubt you, Elspeth. Only tell me what you need of me, and I have said I would help."

Tears of gratitude sprang to her eyes. "Thanks to my sister, I cannot return to Wales," she confessed. "So I must ask it of you in my stead."

He dropped his hand into his lap. "You want me to go back to Wales?"

Elspeth nodded. "To Llanthony," she explained, and, with a dull ache in her heart, she reached out, brushing a hand over Malcom's forehead, over his scar, begging him, despite knowing full well that this one bit of guile was the one charm no woman should ever abuse. And yet she was desperate, and she would give anything—including her body—if Malcom would but champion her sisters as well. "I would have you bring them north," she said.

He was quiet a long moment, and then his lips curved ever so slightly. "How far north? he asked, and Elspeth dared to grin, realizing he was jesting with her.

"As far north as you mean to go," she said, withdrawing her hand, but he placed his hand over hers, pressing her palm to his face, and sliding it to his cheek. Despite his moment of good humor, he said very soberly, "You would have me interfere in my king's affairs?"

Elspeth begged with her eyes. "I cannot abandon my sisters," she said. "If you will not go, I *must* try." And then, rising to her knees on the bed, she looked Malcom straight in the eyes.

She didn't know what it was she meant to say... or do...

but she would do or say anything to sway him. "Please, Malcom..."

LIKE AN ANGEL'S TOUCH, the hand on Malcom's cheek compelled him—and even more irresistible was the way she regarded him, with those watery violet eyes.

God's truth, he didn't know how or why, but he was bound to this woman, for better or worse, and he was beginning to fear it would be for the worst. Cael d'Lucy. King Stephen. Morwen. The list of his potential enemies was growing by the second.

A maelstrom of thoughts whirred through his brain—confusing thoughts he daren't give credence or voice to... but one thing he was not confused about was the way he felt about Elspeth.

She sat before him, as bewitching as any siren, her crimson gown spilling behind her, and her golden-red curls catching the torchlight like copper threads.

When she leaned forward so unexpectedly to press her lips to his, Malcom discovered he couldn't deny her—or himself—and no matter that he suspected her motives, he pulled her into his embrace, like a man starved. If she were some pagan goddess, bent on seducing him to her will, he would no more refuse her than he could have abandoned her in Wales.

At the touch of her lips, every part of him shuddered. Her kiss aroused a hunger inside him he didn't wish to deny. Heat suffused his loins as desire consumed him, and by all that was holy, if she had bewitched him, Malcom didn't bloody care. In that instant, he would have walked through the very fires of hell for her, and he would do anything she asked—*anything*, including betray his king. After all, if a man was not fighting for his home and his people... who the hell should he fight for?

Kissing her deeply, tasting the depths of her sweet, sweet mouth, Malcom prayed she would not tease him, and, then, somehow, sanity returned, and he managed to get hold of himself and push her gently away, fighting his desire to take her here and now.

Never in his life had he taken advantage of any lass in need and he didn't intend to begin now.

Suddenly, he didn't know if he was angrier over the fact that she would tempt him, or that he so desperately wanted to engage her. But more importantly, he would do exactly as she bade him. "You need not pay me in such a manner, Elspeth. I will go," he said, rising from the bed, abandoning her with arms wide.

Her luminous eyes were glassy with passion, and some part of him wondered how well-versed she was in the art of seduction—certainly she knew her part well enough to seduce him. The evidence of his lust could hardly be missed. He was hard as stone, and not even his tight breeches could hide it. He longed to free himself and feel her sweet lips in places too wicked to say.

His eyes glittered fiercely, but not with malice. And regardless, his words were far from affectionate. "I will do all you ask of me and more," he promised. "But on the day you lie beneath me, Elspeth, that day you'll be mine. Heed me well, I'll not turn you away next time, so think on that whilst I am gone." He swiped a hand across his mouth, to erase the taste of her lips, afraid that if he could taste her he might refuse to go.

ELSPETH SAT, reeling.

If she'd meant only to persuade him, their kiss affected her more deeply than she could have possibly foreseen. Through the haze of her passion, she felt his withdrawal acutely like the severing of a limb. And then she realized what he'd said, and her eyes grew round. "You will go?"

"Aye," he said. "I will go."

"What will you tell Beauchamp?"

"I will say you are with child—*my* child," he said vehemently. "And having only discovered this fact, I am returning now to fetch your sisters, before we travel too far north. You will have need of them in your confinement."

Stunned, Elspeth stared at him, her fingers drifting to her mouth. Already, her lips were swelling over the fervor of their kiss, and her body ached for him in ways she could not comprehend. And yet, far more than she craved Malcom's kisses, she coveted her sisters' safety.

He took a dagger from his boot and set it on the table. "For you," he said. "I have no cause to believe you will have need for it, or I'd never leave you, but here you are, just in case."

And then he went after his saddlebag and searched for and found a few silver and gold coins, discarding them, too, atop the table. In all, six coins fell from his fingertips. "Again, should you have need of them."

Elspeth sank from her knees, watching with wide eyes.

20

Driven by something he could not explain, Malcom returned to the bed, putting a hand to Elspeth's cheek as he asked, "Could you see me as your lord husband, Elspeth?"

"What are you asking, Malcom?"

Of course, he was asking her precisely what it sounded as though he were asking. He would protect her in truth. He would give her his name. If, for whatever reason he did not return from Wales, he wanted Elspeth to have somewhere to go.

He stared at the girl he'd known for so short a time, suspecting that nothing that had transpired since the morning he'd met her was an accident. He was meant to be with her, and if he did not believe this, he would not have claimed her as his wife. Those words had slipped from his tongue as easily as soap from wet fingers. So, yes, he wanted her to be his wife. On a whim, listening to his gut, he got up and pulled the ruined *sherte* from his saddlebag. He tore the hem into one long strip, then ripped that strip in half. Then, with both ribbons in his hand, he moved to the bed and sat so that he faced Elspeth. "I would give you the protection of my name," he said.

"What—"

He put a hand to her lips to hush her. "Listen to me, Elspeth. Only hear me out. I am a man unwed and now unbetrothed. I have spent the past ten years denying every bride's name put before me, and I have found fault with every lady with no just cause. When I so easily claimed you were my bride, those words came unbidden from my tongue, and I can only think 'tis because it is meant to be so." She stared at him, blinking, and he asked her again. "Could you see me as your lord husband?"

Wide eyed, Elspeth shook her head, but he sensed it was her confusion, not a denial, so he reached out to take her hand. "Be my wife. Wed me here and now."

"Malcom... I don't understand."

Malcom laid one of his ribbons over her wrist, leaving it unbound as he explained. "It is my people's custom to handfast. Whilst these vows must never be spoken lightly, they are lawful and true, and they are recognized by king and Church, so long as both husband and wife acknowledge they are bound." He handed her the other ribbon, entreating her to take it, and she did so, her eyes round and bright as heather.

"It was the same with my people in the old days," she confessed, holding her part of the ribbon before her, and neither did she shrug the one from her wrist. Malcom found himself desperate to convince her. "Men and women have been bound this way since long before there were priests in our land."

· · ·

ELSPETH HELD HER BREATH.

Somewhere, deep down, a tiny bubble of joy formed—relief, but joy as well, though not merely because she would have a true protector. She did, indeed, feel bonded to this man—in ways she couldn't explain. But... what if this was all Rhiannon's enchantment, and he would come to regret it later? And yet, for her part, she could never regret doing aught to help her sisters. She would lay herself prostrate before king and country and readily sacrifice herself to save their lives.

But... this... this was hardly any sacrifice. Malcom was a man any woman would be pleased to wed—even Dominique had said so. And despite that Lady Dominique had accepted their news so easily, it was clear to Elspeth that the girl had very much relished the thought of a marriage to Malcom. She'd hoped so much that she'd gone so far as to sew him a tunic as a wedding gift... and then she so selflessly gave it to Elspeth to give to him.

Perhaps he mistook her silence for reluctance because he endeavored to convince her. He held up his ribbon. "This would bind us as man and wife for one year and one day. If you find yourself regretting the marriage, I will release you from your vows without question."

Married. Here? Now?

In the unlikeliest of places?

The notion was unthinkable. How could she have ever aspired to such a thing? Had Rhiannon known this would happen? Swallowing, Elspeth asked, "Are you not worried your king will be angry?"

"Are you?"

Elspeth shook her head quickly, for nay, she was not. She had no concern at all for what her cousin might or might not think of her. But that Malcom would do such a selfless thing for her—bind himself to her as a husband when it served him not at all. It made so little sense—no sense for him, but it solved so much for her.

And, of course, she was not a very good liar; if he would leave her in this place with Beauchamp, it would help to know they were truly wed. "Art certain?"

He smiled darkly. "As certain as any man could be who would wed a witch, though we haven't time to debate this, have we?"

Elspeth's face fell, so did her hopes. He'd said it as a jest, but it wasn't particularly amusing—not to her, not when the very notion of a witch brought out the worst in others.

Malcom reached out, lifting her chin. "In one year's time, we'll each have the means to end this, should we wish to," he promised. "But in the meantime, if aught should happen to me whilst I am gone, you should take this..." He removed the signet ring from his finger and handed it to Elspeth. "Take it to my kinsmen in *Chreagach Mhor* and they will know what to do to help you claim what is rightfully your due as my lawful bride."

Stunned, Elspeth took the sigil ring from his fingers, displacing the ribbon from her wrist. But Malcom lifted it up, handing it back to her, leaving the onus on her.

"If tis what you truly wish, I am grateful," Elspeth said gently. "I, too, promise to release you if it be your wish."

He smiled again. "Unless you have beguiled me, Lady Elspeth, I cannot see it will be so."

But that, in truth, made Elspeth long to cry. He *was* beguiled, though not by her. And yet, she could not turn him away when she needed his help so desperately. She nodded, knowing that once the time arrived, she would set him free.

He started to bind her wrist and Elspeth shook herself free. "Oh! Wait! Wait!"

If, indeed, this was meant to be, she would have him remember this moment as fondly as he was able. Remembering the tunic Dominique sewed for him, she scrambled from the bed to retrieve it from the chair where she'd placed it. And, as strange as it felt to be giving him a bridal gift from the woman he was supposed to have wed, she unfurled it to show him.

"A gift for you... from Lady Dominique." A match to the dress Elspeth had worn tonight, and it was only now that she saw them together that she realized they were meant to be a pair. She was wearing Dominique's wedding gown. "It seems oddly fitting you should wear it now."

Malcom lifted both brows but took the garment from her hands. He considered it briefly before setting it back down on the bed, and for a long moment, Elspeth feared he would rescind his offer, in favor of the woman who'd fashioned such a generous gift.

But then, he removed the tunic he wore, and traded his plain one for Dominique's finely sewn regalia. Once he had it on, he smoothed a palm over the embroidered front and said with a sheepish grin, "If I did not know better, I would think this preordained."

Aye, that, or her sister's spell had robbed him and Lady Dominique of their future together, but Elspeth dared not speak those thoughts out loud, lest he change his mind. He offered her his wrist and she accepted his offer, lifting up her ribbon to bind it around his wrist.

"Do you enter this union freely, bringing truth, love and trust?"

There was nothing in those words that gave Elspeth a moment's pause. "I do," she said, as she then wrapped her ribbon about his wrist, binding it with a knot. And then afterward, she offered up her own wrist, and asked, "Do you enter this union freely, bringing truth, love and trust?"

Malcom lifted up his ribbon from the bed, wrapping it gently about her wrist and then tying it firmly with a binding knot. "I do," he said.

Fear makes the wolf bigger than he is.
—German Proverb

"Bury him deep so he cannot claw his way out," I say, sensing Bran's presence. The raven is watching from his perch nearby, cocking his sleek black head at the gathering in this copse. "Not so deep you'll crush his bones, please." But I wonder: *Will he suffocate?* Fresh from my bath, the cool night air teases the still-damp wisps at my nape as I consider this possibility.

Mordecai suggests, "We can put him in a box?"

The innkeeper peers back at me in question, shovel poised in midair. "I've still the one ye asked me to build," he says timidly, and I smile, because it is his casket, made by his own hands—a task I set before him some years past to make a salient point.

"It'll do," I say, and add very sweetly, "You'll have plenty of time to build another."

"Aye, m'lady. Should I go get it?"

"Nay, my dear. I'll send Mordecai."

But I have no need to speak the command. Without a

word, Mordecai turns and heads toward the stable, his gait unhurried. He knows the digging will be slow with only two men. It is not as though this is his first time.

"Aye, m'lady," says the gravedigger, and without another word, recommences shoveling. Following his lead, the kitchen boy lifts his shovel as well, and the two men fall into a rhythm as ancient and titillating as a Beltane song.

Whoosht. Thwack. Crunch. Whoosht. Thwack. Crunch. Whoosht.

Their shovels, both in cadence, glimmer where the metal is worn to a shine—costly tools, used too oft to settle for cheap wood.

By now, the gravedigger has grown accustomed to this task, but tonight will be different. I want this man to remain alive, and more; I want him to be so very grateful for the gift of his life that he will serve me in perpetuity. I think of him rolled in his shroud, laying in a box, beneath the dark, cold ground, and I smile, reveling in the fear I know he will feel as heap after heap of soil is tossed upon his grave. Darker, and darker. Darker and darker.

Whoosht. Thwack. Crunch. Whoosht. Thwack. Crunch. Whoosht.

I fan myself over the thought, realizing that he must think himself dead already, because his muscles have been paralyzed to the point his lungs will not soon fill, and his heartbeat is so timid that his extremities are growing cold as the ground surrounding him.

I fiddle with my ring, thinking it past time to hunt more newts and moon snails. If this works, I will, indeed, have succeeded in creating the first of my *meirw byw*—my living dead. Men whose lives will be indebted to me and only to me. Men who will remember the utter and overwhelming terror of their own deaths and remember... *always remember...*

It is I who will resurrect him.

It is I who will return him to the cold, dark ground if he should defy me.

Of course, he'll never know 'tis a ruse. He will remain in that state of suspended animation until I return for him, aware of every lengthening second down in that deep, dank hole.

Whoosht. Thwack. Crunch. Whoosht. Thwack. Crunch. Whoosht.

I will be his delivering angel. I will be the one who returns him to the light, gently brushing the worms from his shroud. And he will love me, even as he fears me.

I shall be his Maker.

I spy fear in the eyes of the kitchen boy and realize he's seen too much. *What a terrible pity.* Alas, he refuses to look at me even though I stand half-clad, with my breasts high beneath my gossamer gown and my dark hair shining beneath the pale halfmoon. I sigh loudly. And soon enough, when Mordecai returns, wheeling over the casket, I wave him forward, and whisper quietly into his ear. "Let the boy finish, then dispose of him. I shall have no need of him, after all."

"Won't you be returning to your room for a bath, m'dame?"

"Nay," I say. "There isn't time. I would fetch my daughters and return before the poison fades."

"Very well, m'dame," he says. "I will see it done." And then he turns to leave as I hear a squawk from the nearby trees.

"Oh, and Mordecai... please see that Bran is fed."

As though he anticipates the feast to come, a shadow passes over the moon as my familiar, my sweet raven, Bran, soars overhead, wings outstretched.

Blooded biscuits are his favorite and there will be plenty to share.

21

All that night, Malcom held Elspeth until she slept. When she awoke in the wee hours of the morn, she knew before opening her eyes... he was gone.

The bed beside her was cold as she slid her palm across the unsullied sheets. But, of course, no one should have expected to find virgin's blood in their bed. As far as everyone knew, they were already wed. And, even so, it surprised Elspeth that Malcom had not expected her to consummate their union. Though she was grateful for the courtesy, she remained confounded by the fact that he would risk so much without any expectations. Naturally, it reinforced her fear that Rhiannon's spell was responsible for his actions. He was beguiled—there was no other explanation for it.

Lifting her wrist to examine the ribbon he'd bound there, she reverently fingered the tattered cloth. It was simple—not silk, or sendal or any such fabric. It was but *camlet*, soft and worn with age, and yet it smelled like Malcom.

She brought her wrist to her nostrils to inhale deeply of

his scent, wondering where he would be now. On the journey from Wales, it had taken them most of the day to arrive here from Llanthony, so it stood to reason that he wouldn't arrive there till late this evening.

Be swift and strong, she called to Merry Bells.
Carry him safely there and back...
To me.

Closing her eyes, she thought about the kiss they'd shared... so impassioned... so hungry... so painfully real. Dare she hope?

It was just that... it didn't seem possible Rhiannon could change Elspeth's heart—or his—so completely from so far away. And yet, as with her mother, she clearly didn't know what her sister was capable of. And by the same token, there was a lot she didn't know about her own abilities, much less what was possible with the *hud*. For example: Why had she suddenly been granted visions when she'd never had any before? Could it be that she had been lazy in Rhiannon's presence? Taking for granted that her sister was the stronger one? Or mayhap it was a matter of self-preservation. Like her native tongue, Elspeth had trained herself to forget these things, not so much in order to belong, but more to hide. If no one noticed her and her sisters, no one could harm them.

During that first year after their arrival at the priory, they had taken such great pains to shed all trace of their *dewine* heritage. Elspeth particularly, but they'd tried so hard to belong, attending prayers all day long, in hopes that Ersinius might advise their mother to bring them home.

Very soon it became apparent that this would never happen, and still Elspeth had cautioned her sisters against any behavior that could be construed as aberrant. She had been diligent in keeping her sisters safe, and to be safe meant that they must do precisely as Morwen had advised.

Do not be tempted, Elspeth... be certain your sisters are never tempted.

Only later, once it became clear that she and her sisters were never leaving the priory—not until their mother found a good use for them, they grew lax, sometimes practicing spells alone in their cottage. But even then, they had been careful to hide the Craft.

Only Rhiannon had ever dared test the boundaries, defying their mother's mandate, and practicing whenever she could: a wiggled finger to move a pile of dirt in the garden, a loving glance to urge a seedling to burrow deeper, an explosion of flames in the hearth, a garden snake compelled to curl itself around Ersinius' shoes, an unexpected breeze on a hot day—very small things.

She and her sisters each had their predominant powers: For Elspeth this was her reading of auras and her affinity with animals. For Seren it was her talent for healing and all things apothecary. For Rose it was her affinity for elementals. She could turn a mist into freezing rain and cover a windowpane with frost in the middle of summer, bring a dew to puddle in the crook of a leaf without the first drop of rain. For Arwyn's part, her mastery was her charm. She could look a man in the eyes and entreat him to believe whatever she willed him to. But Rhiannon... Rhiannon could do all this and more.

Without having possession of their *grimoire* it was impossible to say what else they might do, and there was no way to practice. The recipes were ancient and hidden to anyone but those who bore the blood of a *dewine*. Unlike the grimoire they had begun to make at Llanthony, the Book of Secrets was bound by blood magic, and to anyone who opened it without right, it looked to be no more than ruined scripture, faded with age and stained by watermarks. Elspeth herself had only had the opportunity to open it once in her lifetime, under her grandmother's supervision. She would never forget the beauty of those pages, or the spell to open the pages.

> A drop of my blood to open or close,
> Speak now the song of ancient prose.
> Shadows be gone, words reveal
> The mysteries of life my book conceals.

Elspeth used to chant those words like prayer, and despite that she never again caressed the soft leather binding, or never did try to prick her own finger to join her blood to the dark-stained cover like so many of her ancestors, she often imagined herself doing so.

But now... the *grimoire* was in Morwen's possession, and one thing was certain: Not in a thousand years would she have guessed at her mother's perfidy.

So then, could it be possible that Elspeth simply hadn't wished to *know* the things Rhiannon knew? And regardless, whatever blinders she'd worn before last evening, they no longer served her, and she had a terrifying sense that something dreadful was looming—something dark and vile... something her mother had unleashed the day she'd embraced the *hud du*.

But much to her dismay, Elspeth didn't know how to prevent it, or how to warn folks, whose hearts and minds had already turned against them.

Speaking out as a *dewine* was not an option. She would find herself locked away as Rhiannon might well be or bound to a stake with flames dancing about her feet.

Her thoughts returned to Malcom.

As surely as Rhiannon had summoned him, Elspeth was equally certain she had also beguiled him, but she didn't know how, because as far as she knew most such spells were not castable outside proximity. However, her sister was proving to be quite gifted. While a charm spell was not so powerful it could make someone love where he would loathe, it was certainly possible to heighten the senses and sweeten his ardor, so that he believed he had deeper feelings than he actually did. And if this was true, it was equally possible that once the spell was broken, Malcom would sorely regret having bound himself to Elspeth. And once he came to his senses, he could well repudiate her.

And more, he could regret having repudiated Lady Dominique as well. Those two could never be wed now, because of Elspeth. And despite that Elspeth was grateful for Malcom's protection, what now if Lady Dominique should find herself bound to a man who meant to harm her? Any ill that befell that sweet girl because of their interference, the fault would lie squarely on Elspeth's shoulders and the Law of Three would not be kind.

Alas, what was done was done. No good could come of her brooding.

She arose from the bed and tied back the drapes to let in the sun. Then, she bathed herself in the cold water left in their basin. It was as sour as the wine they'd drunk last evening, and she smelled like *vin aigre* when she was finished, but at least she was clean.

She dressed herself in the beautiful gown Dominique gave her and hid the remainder of their garments under the bed, along with the *hauberk* Malcom removed from his bag, so that Merry Bells could travel unencumbered. It was either that or leave the heavy cloak, and he'd taken the cloak, instead, so he could use it by night for warmth. Precisely as he said he would, he left her his grandfather's ring—just in case. But how could she ever dare arrive on his kinsmen's doorstep and demand they help her secure Malcom's demesne?

Please, Goddess, don't let anything happen to him, she begged as she examined the ring he'd left her.

Regrettably, it didn't fit any of her fingers, and she didn't wish to lose it, so she tore a few more shreds of Malcom's ruined *sherte* and made herself a thin, tight braid, long enough to hang around her neck. That done, she threaded the ring through the braided necklace, then tied it securely about her neck so that it hung low enough to conceal between her breasts.

And simply because the *sherte* was already ruined, she took another patch to fashion herself a small purse to keep for her herbs, tying it with one of the silver ribbons Dominique gave her.

Once she was finished, she straightened the room a bit, and after a while, both Lady Dominique and Alyss came calling. Luckily for Elspeth she had no need to explain Malcom's absence. They already knew. "My dear, you gave us such a scare," Dominique said, as she entered the room, clasping Elspeth's cold hands. "But how exciting to know you are with child!"

"I... I am sorry," Elspeth said, her brows slanting. And, in truth, she was, not the least for which: She was lying. She was not breeding!

MUCH TO MALCOM'S RELIEF, Merry Bells seemed spry and eager to travel, almost as though Elspeth herself had inspired the animal. Driven by a growing sense of peril, he stopped only when he must and made the eight-hour journey in little more than five hours, reaching the Vale of Ewyas as the Llanthony bells tolled the sixth hour.

His head reeled with all that he'd learned, but if he needed proof of the events of the past days, the tunic he wore reassured him: It was not just a fevered dream, inspired by a wound he'd taken to his shoulder.

He *did* believe her, he reassured himself. Though, of course, he must harbor a doubt. Any sane man would question the things he'd seen and heard.

And nevertheless, there *must* be mysteries men could never conceive for what was faith in God, after all, but a belief in things unseen?

Wearing the tunic emblazoned with his sigil—chagrined over such a generous gift from a woman he'd rebuffed—he approached the priory gates and found the inner courtyard bustling with activity. The dispensation he had from Stephen gave him plausible cause to be in the area, so he decided his best recourse was to speak directly to the chaplain.

Entering behind him through the gates, a procession of men carried buckets of thrashing fish. To one side of the courtyard stood a swarthy-skinned clothier with a wagon laden with brightly colored cloth spilling over one side—crimson and emerald, sapphire blue, some woven with glimmering threads of silver, copper and gold. The material caught the afternoon sun with a hard, probing glint. It would seem a priory should be the last place for such a merchant. And nevertheless, there he was, and along with him there appeared to be many other merchants, either coming or going. And despite the number of visitants, there were no women to be found amongst them—certainly none that would appear to be Elspeth's sisters.

Awaiting the chaplain, he stared down at the finger, where he normally wore his mother's ring, considering how easily he had parted with the heirloom. In complete juxtaposition, he'd spent three years poring over his intentions toward Dominque, and never found himself anything less than reluctant. Obviously, she'd been anticipating a proposal. But having known her a good five years or more—since she was twelve—Malcom could never think of her as aught more than a child. Certainly, he didn't feel for her what he felt for Elspeth after just three short days.

He didn't have to wait long. Within minutes, Ersinius himself emerged to greet him, bidding him enter and rest awhile—there was plenty of ale to be had, so he said.

If, in truth, Malcom had expected the man to be taciturn and secretive, he was anything but. Bumbling and old, perhaps, but his mood was jovial, and if he'd found himself embroiled in some conspiracy, you'd never have guessed so by his temperament.

"Come, along, come along!" he bade Malcom, pulling at his long, white beard. "'Tis been overlong since we've been graced by such an esteemed guest."

Wanting nothing more than to inquire about Elspeth's sisters and be gone, Malcom nevertheless appeased the old man, following him into his hall, biding his time. If he must search the entire premise, he would do so, in due time.

"So my Lord Aldergh, do tell... what brings you to Llanthony," asked the priest once Malcom was comfortably seated at his table. But then he clapped his hands to order a servant to fetch vittles and wine. "Dear boy, you must pardon me," he said. "We've not had much cause of late to remember our manners." Malcom blinked. It had been overlong since anyone had called Malcom a *boy*, but he let it pass, thinking Ersinius too old to rebuke. God knew, the man must be one-hundred if he were a single day, and if Malcom recalled aright, he was the one who'd come to Aldergh all those years ago to prepare him for his journey to court. He must have been sixty, even then.

Malcom sat back, studying the man's demeanor, considering the wisdom in reminding Ersinius of their previous encounter. "You seem well enough called upon today," he said, instead.

Ersinius swished a silk-robed hand. "Fish today, alesmen on Wednesdays. No one of any import." But then he peered down at his long flowing sleeve, sweeping it about like a banner. "Do you like this?" he inquired. "A gift from... a dear, dear friend. Of course, you must know I am summoned now and again to call upon the king and I'd not show myself wearing rags."

Malcom nodded. "Impressive," he said, looking closer at the white on white pattern on the fabric as he wondered what "friend" had gifted such a rich cloth to a clergyman. "Is that dyaspin?"

The old man's lips formed a lopsided grin. "Why, yes! Yes, it is," he said, and he pointed to Malcom's scarlet tunic. "I can see you're a man well versed in his finery." He tsked loudly. "Not all men are so discerning." He studied the embroidery on Malcom's tunic a long moment, then launched into a diatribe about the merits of good cloth, and more importantly, the critical matter of meticulous tailoring. "I do swear, some men believe they can appear before the highest court dressed in tatters. But, I say to you, how can any man ever be taken seriously who will not distinguish himself by his dress?"

Malcom nodded, considering the way his father had

dressed. Ian MacKinnon had never concerned himself overmuch with the manner of his dress. Betimes he was grime-filled from head to toe after toiling long days in the fields with his clansmen. No man on this earth had ever distinguished himself more in Malcom's eyes. He was as honorable as they came, and Malcom had cast him away without looking back, in favor of men wearing silk robes who would sooner put a knife in your back if they could. He'd learned a lot through his years of service and worldly dealings, but rather than finding himself enriched, he felt poorer for the knowledge. As for regrets, he had more than a few.

"'Tis much the same with God, dear boy. He sees everything we do. If we cannot honor him in all things, how can we ever hope to be taken to heart?"

"Aye," Malcom said, though he thought it all a load of shite. The God he knew was gracious to poor and rich alike. But considering that he wanted something from this man, he was not quite prepared to put him on his toes.

He waited patiently, listening to Ersinius ramble on about how women were not the only ones who could sew a fine, straight seam, and he named an entire entourage of male seamsters all by name—none of which Malcom recognized. So this is how the chaplain spent his hours of prayers, memorizing the names and merits of seamsters? The very notion left Malcom bored and ready to rise. However, he listened patiently until the wine and vittles were placed before him, before inquiring.

"Speaking of women... I am told...." He ate a slice of cheese, leaving the chaplain to hang on his words. "I'm told I may find five lovely ladies in your keeping?" And he watched the man out of the corner of one eye.

The chaplain frowned. "Ladies?" he said, aghast.

Suddenly discomposed, he lifted up the flagon and sloshed wine into Malcom's goblet, then filled one for himself.

Malcom hitched his chin.

"Here?"

"Aye."

And to be sure, the chaplain asked again, raising his goblet and pausing with the glass in midair, his white brows furrowing dubiously. "At Llanthony?" he asked, his voice rising, and breaking with the pitch.

Malcom shrugged, as though the answer couldn't possibly matter. "'Tis what I'm told, father."

Shaking his head, Ersinius swallowed the entire contents of his glass. "Ah, well... no, no, no!" he said, sounding perfectly horrified by the prospect. He sat back now, a bit less jovial and set his glass down, turning it around and around and around on the wooden table. "And, tell me, have you any business with these... *ladies*?"

Malcom picked up a slice of mutton and put it into his mouth—well flavored and tender. "Aside from a mild curiosity? Nay, father."

The man seemed to relax before Malcom's eyes. "Alas, but nay. We are ill prepared to cater to aught but the needs of our men—good men, every one. I assure you."

Malcom nodded.

"Did you know that I once counseled King Henry's first wife? A very pious lady. Very pious." Without any segue, he carried on. "No girls here," he said, "No girls anywhere at all on these premises—although we did have an emissary from Matilda once, a Brian Fitz Count. Do you know that man?"

He watched Malcom then, very shrewdly, as though to gauge his reaction.

"I do," Malcom said, reassuring himself that the chaplain could have no inkling of Stephen's intentions toward Wallingford. *Or did he, perhaps?*

Licensed by the king to enforce his law and guard against insurrection, the Rex Militum was a secret league, known to but a few. But he realized that some of the priories were used to breed select pigeons and ravens for communications... and he wondered if somehow Ersinius might have been able to intercept one...

Ersinius gave him a thin-lipped smile. "Well, yes, I'm certain you do," he said. "But, of course, I cannot say why he has come, though I assure you it had little to do with the Empress herself. He was here one day, gone the next." He poured himself another tall glass of *vin* and Malcom had the impression that if he left the man to drink and gab, he would prattle on about everything he knew.

So, then, Fitz Count had come, after all. Evidently, Malcom had missed him—fortunately for Wallingford—and more so now that Malcom was otherwise occupied, because the price on Wallingford's head was the last thing on his mind.

Malcom took his time and ate what he had been served before asking, offhandedly, "So you have no women on these premises at all?"

"Of course not!" exclaimed Ersinius. And then he chortled and added, "Even the most pious of us would be hard-pressed to focus on our ministries—if you know what I mean?" He winked at Malcom in an exaggerated fashion, his cheeks growing fiery red, like two plump red apples.

"Indeed, I do," Malcom said with an answering grin. And the chaplain seemed so sincere that seeds of doubt once again began to creep into Malcom's head. Lifting a hand to his shoulder, he sought the evidence again, thinking Ersinius too old—and too arrogant—to be shrewd.

What was more, the man had no qualms over revealing all the names of his notable guests, or showing Malcom all his frivolous expenditures—even recounting those Malcom couldn't see.

"Have you seen our new windows, dear boy?" he asked gleefully. "Waldglas, 'tis called. Made in Deutschland." He fluttered his fingers. "But, of course, Stephen could equip an entire army for the cost—more's the pity, we've now had to replace the large one in the vestibule twice." He arched a brow and gave Malcom a discerning nod. "Perhaps this, after all, is the true reason you've come? I sent a bitter complaint to His Grace. One of my men saw some wretched brat scurry into those woods. But you can be sure he did not act alone. These damned Welsh, to send a boy to do what a man would not dare."

Malcom seized the opportunity. "Aye, father," he said. "I am well aware of your troubles here."

Malcom had long suspected the skirmishes were in protest over the appropriation of Welsh land used for the priory's construction. Its proprietors had lost sacks full of gold repairing the chapel, and the constant harrowing was undermining Stephen's efforts with the Marcher lords—particularly now with Matilda's allies creeping around begging for support.

Chugging the contents of his glass, he set down the cup. "Would you mind if I had a look about? I hope to locate your vandals and be away, so I may report to the King."

The frown lines eased from the chaplain's brow. "But, of course not, my dear boy! You must do what you must. I would love to find and flog that little heathen who dared desecrate God's house."

Malcom smiled thinly, remembering again the chaplain who'd sat before him at Aldergh, his smile cruel. *Your father does not want you, dear boy, but your God and your king surely do.* He'd shut his mouth after that, and spoke not another word.

"I don't know, father. I would suppose God himself would have you sooner forgive—would he not?"

The man blinked. His face flushed, until it turned purple, and then he recomposed himself. "Well... perhaps. However... according to Holy Scripture, 'He that spareth the rod hateth the son: but he that loveth the son chasteneth him betimes.' I consider it my greatest duty to love sinners the same as I do the devout."

Equal opportunity punishment, Malcom thought. "Of course," he said, eager to be away. He stood now, and the chaplain stood after him, looking for the first time ill at ease.

Malcom said, proffering his hand, "Thank you, good father, for nourishing this sinner at your table. I hope you will pardon my haste."

"So soon?" the old man asked. He grasped Malcom's forefinger, shaking it feebly with trembling hands. "But I hoped you might linger awhile, give news of court?"

"Another time," Malcom said as he made for the door. The chaplain followed, his rickety old legs hard-pressed to keep up. He was already out of breath even before they crossed the threshold. Once outside, Malcom bade him, "Would you care to join me, father?"

The open invitation seemed to put the man completely at ease. "Oh, nay!" he said, waving Malcom on. "I have too much to do today." He gestured toward the merchants lolling about. "Look at them all! However, you must feel free to wander as you please."

"Thank you," Malcom said, bowing. He started in the direction of the hatchery.

"Oh, but wait!" said the chaplain, waving after him. He

sounded hard of breath now, after only a few steps. "If it may be of any help, and you mean to search the surrounding area as well, you will find the Rhiw Pyscod well enough traveled," he said quickly, cutting his hand in a straight line, as though to forbid it. "I'd not bother with that route."

"Thank you," Malcom said, and continued on his way.

"Bless you, son!" exclaimed the chaplain, following part way down the trail, his pristine white silk robe dragging the black dirt behind him. He called out again. "Oh, and when you are done, please, please, be certain to thank His Grace for seeing to the needs of the humblest of his servants."

A rueful smile turned one corner of Malcom's lips. "Don't worry; I shall," he said, and with that, Malcom took off down the path, leaving Ersinius to peer after him.

22

Trying not to think about Malcom—or Rhiannon, for that matter—Elspeth spent the entire afternoon in the garden with Lady Dominique and Alyss.

Out here, with the sun shining so brightly, it was easier to ignore the dark aura looming overhead. And nevertheless, it wasn't quite so easy to keep her mind off her sisters, since this was how she and her siblings had spent so much of their day—cultivating plants, harvesting, sharing knowledge and experimenting. Even when they had not dared to practice the Craft, they had reveled in their garden.

Alas, having been allotted so little space, Amdel's garden was not so well stocked as their own. In this one thing, Ersinius had been generous—but of course, he'd benefited greatly from their toil. And nevertheless, Alyss appeared to be quite a skilled simpler.

Using herbs one at a time was the very best way to ascertain what a plant's optimum use was, and it was only after learning the basics that one might consider how best to combine them. But apothecary *magik* was not to be practiced lightly. Betimes it could be confusing, and even risky. There were quite a few dangerous plants, including witch's berry or deadly nightshade. But deadly nightshade was not at all the same as black nightshade, which was edible, so long as it wasn't raised in certain soil conditions. Deadly nightshade, on the other hand, was so powerfully perilous that it could cause madness even by simply touching it. This was the primary reason to keep a *grimoire,* and theirs at the priory had been fashioned from scraps of undyed wool and bound with simple thread. Every time they'd added a new page, they'd anchored it to the previous page and eventually meant to bind it.

Of course, the minute Alyss learned that Elspeth knew her way about a garden, she entreated upon Elspeth to teach her everything she knew. Now, Elspeth poked around the soil, with Alyss hanging over her shoulder, and if perchance the maid seemed reticent before, she blossomed here, like a beautiful flower beguiled by the sun.

"See this," Elspeth prompted, pointing to a bed of sprouts.

"Lady's bedstraw?"

"Aye," said Elspeth, nodding. "The roots will make a lovely dye—red, though not so rich as your scarlet. 'Tis much too small to pull right now, or I would show you the roots." She looked up at Alyss. "It seems as though you've recently harvested these, so give them a chance to proliferate—and, then, when you harvest them next time, examine the roots. You will see they are quite dark. I have seen many tints made from these, including one very, very close to the color of a daylily."

"Oh!" said Dominique. "We *must* try that! We pulled them recently to fill the guest-room mattress, and I would say 'tis a very good thing, considering your glad occasion. Does the bed sleep well?" she asked, smiling, perhaps much as her own sisters might have done were they fishing for information.

But, of course, Elspeth had nothing to disclose.

She had no proper knowledge of the marriage bed—none at all. And even if she did have some inkling, it would not be appropriate to share with two young ladies. Over the course of their conversation, she'd learned both Alyss and Dominique were merely seventeen—a full seven years younger than Elspeth and two years younger than her sisters Arwyn and Rose. "The bed slept quite well," she said, blushing. "The scent is lovely." It was a cross between vanilla and freshly cut hay. But that was all she had to say, and she didn't wish to linger on the topic, lest their conversation invite more inquiry.

"We were told that lady's bedstraw repels fleas," explained Dominique.

Elspeth pulled a few odd weeds that were in danger of strangling the sprouts. "It does," she said, "and did you know... it was used by druids to line their graves near Glastonbury?"

Alyss giggled. "I wonder if they worried their dead would suffer fleas?"

"Perhaps," said Elspeth, smiling, glad to hear the maid laughing. "And here's another use: The milk helps to curdle cheese. We raised goats at—home—and often used it instead of rennet."

"Truly?"

"What a marvelous herb," said Dominique, clapping her hands. "We shall have to plant more."

"Alas, be careful if you're foraging," advised Elspeth. "Do not mistake it for goosegrass, or you'll never grow anything else in these beds. My sister used to use it to stop a blooded nose." She made a face. "Don't ask me how I know such a thing."

"Goosegrass or Lady's Bedstraw?"

Elspeth smiled. "Lady's Bedstraw."

Rhiannon had endured a phase as a toddler where she used to smack her head on door frames—not a happy memory for any of them. On top of her crossed eyes, she'd run about black and blue, looking like a walking bruise.

"And this," she said, tugging on a sprig of meadowsweet.

"Mead wort?"

Elspeth snipped a piece and brought the cutting to her nose to smell. "Some would call it by that name. It works wonderfully for pain."

"We use it to flavor our wine," explained Alyss.

Elspeth smiled, enlightened now as to how and why she'd slept so heavily after she and Malcom traded vows. They'd left a full flagon of the flavored wine in their room.

Where was he now? she wondered.

Wistfully, she peered down at the ribbon that was tied about her wrist. The white cloth was dragging in the dirt, so she plucked up the ends, and tucked them quickly into the band beneath her sleeve.

Thankfully, if either of the ladies wondered over the ribbon, or recognized what it was, neither asked. Just for good measure, she slid a small sprig of meadowsweet into the band, and said with a smile, "An old Welsh legend claims that all women are divined by druid wizards from these blossoms, so, betimes they are placed in garlands for brides, to ensure peace and harmony in the home."

"Oh! I will be sure to do that for mine," said Lady Dominique. "Your wedding must have been so lovely. Will you tell us about it?"

"It was beautiful," Elspeth said, averting her gaze. She

pulled another small weed, tossing it aside, uncomfortable with the topic. And yet, in fact, for all that it had been a simple affair, she thought it was beautiful even so—that Malcom would sacrifice so much, just for her.

Thankfully, Dominique's girlish buoyance saved her from having to say aught more. She gushed, "You'll be a wonderful lady mother. I can see you with wee ones running about your skirts whilst you tend your beautiful garden."

Elspeth smiled, though, in truth, she couldn't envision any such a thing. She herself had never been much of a child to run about skirts, laughing or carrying on. Per force, she had been the one to care for all four of her sisters, and more than likely, it was her skirts they'd carried on about. And yet, she hadn't any regrets—not about that.

"You must be so pleased to be breeding so soon. Quite certainly, 'tis a sign that God himself has blessed your union."

"Aye," said Elspeth, smiling. But the quickening in her belly wasn't a babe; it was only the consequence of yet another lie.

"I am so pleased to meet you, Elspeth. If I had a sister I would wish her to be you."

"Thank you," Elspeth said, smiling, missing her own sisters so much. *Would Malcom reach them in time?* She prayed it would be so. "I would have been blessed to have you as a sister," Elspeth told her. She peered up at Alyss, smiling. "In truth, we are all sisters in the eyes of God."

"Oh! I think so too." Dominique reached out to grasp Alyss by the hand. "My dear Alyss is as close to a sister as I will ever know and now I have two."

Elspeth smiled again. And despite that the compliments left her ill at ease, she realized Dominique meant them sincerely. There was no guile in her words—no trace of malice in her aura. In fact, both girls had such a bright air about them that Elspeth sensed the pall cast over them even before the sun revealed the incoming shadow.

"Demoiselles," said Beauchamp.

Elspeth gasped aloud as the lord of Amdel appeared. Wearing black from head to toe, it was difficult to say where his shadow ended and the man himself began.

It took a long moment to grow accustomed to the glint of sun in her eyes, in order for Elspeth to see that he was wearing the vestments of a falconer, with a falconer's gauntlet on his right hand and a white-necked raven perched upon his glove, and seeing that bird, Elspeth swallowed convulsively, for these were not common, and she knew them only too well. They were precisely the sort of birds they raised at Llanthony —suited to only one purpose, to convey messages to her mother. The realization sent a cold shiver down her spine, even despite the heat of the sun.

"My lord," she said, forcing a smile. But her gaze settled on the bird and did not leave it.

"I trust you are enjoying the day." Giving lie to his aura, his tone was ebullient—not the least bit ominous. "I myself could not bring myself to remain indoors when the sun shines so beauteously."

With great effort, Elspeth shifted her gaze to Beauchamp's face, only to find that, once again, he was staring at her bosom—or perhaps the necklace she'd fashioned for her ring. "I... am..." Instinctively, she adjusted the braid and tugged on her décolletage, lifting it to hide her natural gifts from prying eyes. Seeing that she had nothing else, Dominque had very generously loaned her a simple, pale-blue woolen dress so she wouldn't soil her new finery whilst toiling in the garden, but perhaps it revealed more than Elspeth would have liked.

Dominique's voice was full of delight. "Elspeth is teaching us about simples!"

"Is she now?"

"Aye," Elspeth said, without looking at the man.

"Are you so well versed, Lady Aldergh?"

"Oh, yes, she is!" answered Dominque. And then she turned to Elspeth. "William has the most wonderful aviary—later, I will show you. He has quite the way with birds, and they are such good hunters. I am quite certain there is not another aviary in all of England to match it."

Try as she might, Elspeth couldn't take her eyes off the bird. But, indeed, there was. There was at least one more that she knew of, and probably more. Thanks to her mother's efforts, those babbling birds were housed in every loyal house across Britain.

Beauchamp must have mistaken Elspeth's interest in the bird, for he extended his hand to her, and he asked, "Would you care to hold him?"

"Hold him!" squealed the raven, and Elspeth gasped.

Dominique laughed. "He won't harm you, I promise." Dominique seemed genuinely amused by her reaction, laughing so hard that Elspeth felt resentment for the first time since meeting the girl.

Elspeth's hand splayed across her breast. "Just the same, no thank you," she said.

"All his ravens talk," said Dominique. And then she blushed. "You should hear them when they're hungry. They curse like pagans, don't they, Alyss?"

Whatever blossoming Alyss had done over the morning, her demeanor now wilted before Elspeth's eyes. "Yes, m'lady."

And when she lifted her gaze to William, he said. "When you have a moment, Alyss, I would have a word with you. Alone."

"Yes, m'lord."

He inclined his head toward the donjon, urging her to leave.

"Now, m'lord?"

"Aye," he said gruffly. And then to Dominque and Elspeth he said, "You ladies must stay and enjoy the garden. Alyss will rejoin you anon." But then he stood for a moment longer, scrutinizing Elspeth one last time, as poor Alyss hurried ahead. "Tis a pity you'll be so paunchy soon though I expect you'll regain your form in no time once the babe is born. You are young yet," he said.

Elspeth's cheeks burned hot.

And he persisted. "How old?"

Elspeth averted her gaze. "Four and twenty, my lord."

"Not so young as my sister, but I do understand why your lord husband espoused you so quickly."

Elspeth's cheeks burned hotter. Her throat felt too thick to speak—and that bird. She felt it staring at her... as though it *knew*.

"William," protested Dominique, and for the first time since meeting her, the girl's voice sounded dispirited. "Elspeth, what my brother means to say is that we are both quite pleased for you and my Lord Aldergh."

Elspeth had the sense that she'd cast her brother a rebuke, because he left without another word, and walked away, with his snorting bird in hand.

"Don't mind him," Dominque said once he was gone. "He means well, though betimes he can be so rude."

"I understand."

"Oh, but, nay, you do not," Lady Dominque persisted. "I

am beyond pleased for you, and so is William. He tells me now that he anticipates a wonderful, new match for me—one that should please him immensely. But, of course, you know how men can be. Betimes they are sore to lose."

"I am sorry," Elspeth felt compelled to say again.

"Oh, nay! Do not be." Dominique fluttered her fingers, dismissing her brother once and for all. "He will be in a *much* better mood tonight," she said, casting a glance after her brother and Alyss. And then she beamed. "Those two are meant to be wed someday, did you know?"

"William and Alyss?"

Dominique nodded. "Tis why she's here, after all. As much as I would like to say otherwise, we are not a great house. Her lord father would never have sent her but for the promise of an alliance."

"I see," said Elspeth, and she cast another glance at the donjon door, through which Alyss disappeared, and where William now stood, handing over his raven to the master falconer. With some trepidation, Elspeth watched the falconer take the black bird, and then observed as William Beauchamp climbed the steps into his keep.

She wasn't at all sure which gave her the most dread.

There was only one reason he would keep those birds... *and* only one reason Alyss should shrivel in his presence. Both portended something vile.

MALCOM SEARCHED THE ENTIRE GROUNDS.

He didn't happen upon Elspeth's sisters, but he did discover a well-tended garden, settled inside a stone-walled courtyard, complete with a gardener's hut. But the hut itself was vacant, save for a few necessities: a bed—perhaps large enough to sleep five girls; a table; four crude chairs; one broken—as though it had been smashed for tinder; a box full of gardening tools; and a small cauldron nestled in the stone and mortar hearth.

Stooping to examine the ashes, he found them cold now. He also discovered a half-burnt chair leg in the pit. But when he set a hand to the iron cauldron, he found a bit of lingering heat, so he plucked up the chair leg from the ashes and stirred the coals.

Beneath the white ash glowed red.

Whoever was here couldn't have been gone long, he surmised. And nevertheless, they were gone, and he wished he'd come sooner—although, in truth, he couldn't have done so without raising suspicions. As it was, Rufford, Beauchamp's longtime steward, had looked him askance and would have shot back a dozen inquiries but for the simple fact that he must have sensed Malcom would never welcome the intrusion.

Malcom didn't answer in such a fashion to his own steward; he would never tolerate it from Beauchamp's. He was an Earl of the realm, a respected member of the King's Guard and the Rex Militum. There was no one in Beauchamp's demesne he should be answering to. Not today. Not any day.

He stood now, studying the room a long while, then walked out of the cottage, and stood looking over the garden before shifting his focus over the Vale of Ewyas...

He could see the entirety of the grounds from this vantage, and in the distance, he watched a falconer set loose a dark-feathered bird—perhaps a peregrine.

It was unfathomable how much money had been poured into this remote priory—a brand-new hatchery, an aviary—quite substantial by the looks of it—a well-vested chapel, plus that doddering old priest who probably knew more than he claimed. He wondered idly: Whose money was invested here? Stephen's? Henry's? Matilda's? All three, and then some? More importantly, to whom did the priory answer? Not to God, because Malcom didn't sense his presence here at all.

In fact, as well visited as the priory appeared to be, and as much hustle and bustle as there was today, he felt a dark underbelly to this institution... an oppression that made him wonder how Elspeth and her sisters could possibly have lived in such a place for so long.

And yet, there was no proof she ever did.

The cottage, save for the abundance of chairs in such a small hovel, seemed to be little more than a gardener's hut. If, in fact, five young ladies had ever resided there, someone must have swept through the house and removed all traces of their existence.

Why?

Contemplating all the possible answers, Malcom took to his horse without speaking to the chaplain, eager to be away. And just because the chaplain bothered to mention the Rhiw Pyscod, he took the well-worn footpath west to Llangorse—a fortuitous choice, because about an hour down the road he discovered what he was searching for. It was an old prison tumbril. One of the wheels had broken and the vehicle rested precariously on the old Roman path.

Malcom approached cautiously, though he needn't have; dressed in his finery, the men all hailed him—three in total, only one a swordsman.

The swordsman was the one who greeted Malcom, but he scratched his head, looking askance as though he were hoping for something more. "Art come from the priory, m'lord?"

The prisoner behind the bars met Malcom's gaze—a

woman, dark haired, amber eyes—and he believed he detected a hint of a smile. Malcom daren't allow his gaze to linger. He nodded to the swordsman. "The good father said you'd found some trouble."

"I'd say. Damned old paddy. I'll warrant 'tis seen more bodies dragged to the gallows than any other. If I had my druthers, I'd slay the witch and set the wagon afire. Better yet, I'd fix her a stake, and burn her right here, use the wood for kindling."

Frowning, Malcom dismounted, positioning Merry Bells precisely where the path diverted, sloping downward, fully expecting to have to make a run for it. He removed his sword from the saddle scabbard, sliding it into his sword belt as though it were a matter of habit. He patted Merry Bells, then casually walked over to examine the wreck, paying little attention to its passenger.

The spokes on one wheel had somehow split—all of them. Simply put, the wagon needed a new wheel. "There's no repairing this," he said. "You'll need a new trundle."

"Aye, m'lord, but I already knew that, and so I said." And once again, he peered down the footpath, scowling. "Where's Randel?"

Malcom forced a smile, patting his belly. "Lingering to fill his gut with fish, I suppose. He'll be along soon," he said, realizing it must be true and that he must have missed Randel at Llanthony. The messenger must have been coming as Malcom was going.

Satisfied for the instant, the swordsman nodded, and then explained how the accident occurred. They were moving along nicely, without much trouble. Suddenly they struck a stone that wasn't there before. The damned thing appeared out of nowhere. He was sure the witch had placed it there because Randel swore it wasn't in their path before. Every week, carts and horses and people filed down this road, and clearly this had never happened before. They heard the crack and the wagon nearly tumbled down the hill. They should have let it go, he groused. The passenger was naught but a filthy witch, best left to the lord's judgment.

Malcom met the prisoner's gaze and found her eyes twinkled with barely concealed mirth.

Do not address me, Malcom Ceann Ràs.

Startled, Malcom looked away, surprised by her use of a name he'd been given by his kinsmen—a name he hadn't heard in far too long.

He turned to look at the man beside him, to be sure no one else had heard. But nay, the man was prattling on and on. Malcom cast another glance at the girl in the tumbril. Beneath the dirt, she was pretty, and he could detect a resemblance to Elspeth, but her color was darker, and her eyes, when she looked at him, seemed to cross unnaturally. She shook her head slowly and Malcom averted his gaze, pretending to examine the broken wheel. He stooped to wiggle a spoke.

Do not linger, Lord Aldergh. You haven't time. Randel will return anon.

Startling him again, the girl suddenly squawked an ungodly sound, hurling a cloth object at him, smacking him so hard that Malcom's head popped to one side and he stabbed himself with a wheel spoke. "Be damned!" he said, with genuine annoyance.

"Never mind that stupid bitch," the swordsman said. "She'll get what she deserves."

Frowning, Malcom drew a hand across his cheek, where the spoke had stabbed him and came away with a trace of blood. God's bones, by the time he returned to Aldergh, he would bear a whole new round of scars.

Take that book to Elspeth. By it she will know you speak true. Tell her this for me: I merely called you. I did not beguile you.

Quite unused to this manner of speaking, and uncomfortable with the scrutiny of these men, particularly under the circumstances, Malcom peered down at the small bound volume that lay discarded on the ground.

It appeared to be naught more than a lump of dirty cloth. But he hesitated a moment too long.

"What is that?" asked the swordsman, bending to lift it up.

Malcom swept it up before he could touch it. "Whatever it is, 'tis mine now," he said, lifting his gaze to the man. "Bloody she-wolf."

"Indeed," said the swordsman. "Bitch bites like a wolf as well. You should take that to Ersinius and be done with it. Everything she touches is evil."

Malcom's gaze scanned the faces of the other two men, and did, indeed, spy one whose cheek bore the mark of a full set of teeth.

He deserved it.

Malcom concentrated on speaking to her the way he had with Elspeth. *I don't doubt it.*

There you are, she said, her tone smug.

Take the grimoire to my sister, Malcom Ceann Ràs. Tell her our mother came sooner than we anticipated. She has our sisters, but worry not. So long as she believes them to be compliant she won't harm them. Rather, you must return quickly to Elspeth, hasten her north. Amdel is no place to keep her.

Malcom had no need to ask how she knew where he'd left her sister—or even how she'd known his name. If, indeed, Elspeth's abilities unnerved him, her sister's unnerved him all the more. The very air here was filled with her presence, as though her spirit loomed larger than life.

You must go... now... Beauchamp is sworn to my mother.

Morwen?

Aye.

Stunned, Malcom remained stooped by the broken wagon wheel, bemused. He examined the book in his hand, and then, as though it were an afterthought, slid it into his tunic, letting it fall to his waist, catching on his sword belt. Only now he realized how stupid it was that he'd left Elspeth alone, with naught more than a dirk for protection. Indeed, he must go. But, he couldn't abandon Rhiannon.

I go where I need to go, she said.

Inconceivably, Malcom argued with her—in his head. *These men are no match for me...* He realized he didn't know her name.

Rhiannon, she said. *They are no match for me either, Lord Aldergh. Who do you think broke their wheel?*

Of course, Malcom didn't answer. And if the men wondered why he remained stooped so quietly, staring at a broken wheel, they said nothing, and he knew instinctively that Rhiannon was telling the truth. Only fearing Elspeth would never forgive him if he abandoned her to these lackeys, he couldn't bring himself to leave her. He examined his surroundings, considering how best to engage these three men. Only one of them was armed.

He waited so long, a procession of monks, all bearing buckets with dying burdens came up over the rise, marching past. Pretending to consider the tumbril, Malcom waited for them to pass, all the while fiddling with the broken wheel.

"Afternoon," said the swordsman to the monks.

"God bless," said the monks.

"More fish?"

"Aye, sir. Carp and pike."

"Pity they're still flailing or I'd steal a bite."

The monks all chortled and walked on by. The swordsman returned his attention to Malcom. "As you say, m'lord... there's naught to be done with that. I've no idea why you were sent when I specifically told Randel to tell them we needed a replacement and a wheelwright."

Malcom raked a hand through his hair. "If you give me the prisoner, I will take her off your hands, save you the delivery."

"Nay, m'lord. Where would you put her? I'd not have you lose an ear to the filthy bitch, and then have it said I did not do my job."

Malcom nodded, considering that if he took out the swordsman, the other two would prostrate themselves easily. The tumbril was another matter entirely. As old as it appeared, the bars were each at least a centimeter wide, and as corroded as they might appear, he was fairly certain that the most he would get by wrestling with the rusted metal was a case of Holy Fire.

I know what you are doing, Lord Aldergh. I will not allow it. If you release me, they will arrest you. If you kill them, they will know it was you, and what recourse will you have when you face my cousin in defense of my sister? This game will be long, my friend. There will be time enough for heroics before all is said and done. Go now, she demanded. *Before the chance has fled.*

No sooner had she finished speaking, when she shrieked insanely, kicking a leg out between the bars, narrowly missing Malcom's jaw. "Away, fool! Or I'll put a turd in your teeth and turd in your bride's teeth too!"

Startled, Malcom cast the girl a beleaguered glance. He stood, confused though he oughtn't be by now. The past two days had borne more things than ever could be explained. Still, it took him a moment to regain his bearings and then he said to the swordsman, "Regrettably, you are right." Rubbing the back of his neck, he cast a weary glance at Rhiannon, and then back to the swordsman. "If only I'd realized, I would have brought you lads a bit of ale to pass the time."

"No worries, m'lord. God will provide his own rewards."

Malcom nodded, then, reluctantly, went after his horse. He mounted, then peered at the girl one last time. *Art certain, Rhiannon?*

I go where I need to go, she said again. *I go where I will best contend with my mother.*

And nevertheless, he hesitated, knowing full well that Elspeth would demand to know why he'd left her.

Tell her what I said. She will not like it, but she will understand. Please tell her for me... when she fears most what to do, she must raise her hand... and believe.

"Very well," he said, scratching his head. "Hold tight, lads." He gave them a nod. "Help'll be along soon."

"Thank you, m'lord. Don't worry about us. We're on to Blackwood soon enough."

"Very well," Malcom said, once again, ruefully, then snapped Merry Bells' reins. And the last thing Rhiannon said to him filled his heart with relief, then dread.

Your father is not ill. But hie thee north. Call your banners. War is nigh.

23

Elspeth awoke before the cock's crow.

She dressed again in the pale-blue gown Dominque had loaned her because she felt overdressed in the scarlet. Had the sendal not been so diaphanous, she would have made do with that alone, because, in truth, even the blue gown was more luxurious than any dress she'd ever owned. Made of linsey-woolsey, its design was simple enough, but the seams were delicately sewn, with exquisite appliqué about the sleeves, hem and bodice. Although Elspeth didn't care much for the cut of the bodice itself, it was little more revealing than the scarlet she'd worn. And regardless, it was better than the Llanthony tunic she'd arrived in.

However, it seemed to Elspeth that Dominique's brother shouldn't encourage such immodesty in a young woman. If, in truth, this was now the style, it would be difficult for Elspeth to grow accustomed to it, having lived so long in a priory. Especially now, having been in William's presence and noted his lechery, as far as she was concerned, it was ill-advised to tempt a man she did not intend to wed, and for Elspeth, there was only one man she ever cared to entice.

Malcom.

Where are you?

This was a first for her: pining over the company of a man—and, nay, it hadn't nary as much to do with her sordid predicament as it did a simple, but overwhelming desire to see him—to see with her own two eyes that he was unharmed.

Somehow, over such a short time, she had swiftly grown accustomed to Malcom's company, and the precious moments they'd shared the night before he'd left were sweet enough that she could have languished in his arms.

He'd snuggled himself behind her, holding her close, and she'd fallen asleep with his hand clasping hers. As little as she'd ever trusted anyone except her sisters, she knew the disparity of trust even more acutely now, with the shadow of the lord of Amdel hanging over her shoulder—that man, she did not trust at all.

Intending to make her way into the garden to pass her time, Elspeth didn't wait to be called upon by Dominique or Alyss. She hung her makeshift purse on her belt and tied a single ribbon about her thick hair to keep it from her face whilst she toiled in the garden.

Anyway, she was annoyed. Those two silly chits had imbibed too much the night before and both had stumbled away from the hall, giggling like little girls, leaving Elspeth alone to entertain Dominique's strange brother.

All those presentiments she'd had upon arriving at Amdel had come crashing down, leaving her ill at ease the entire evening, and hardly in any mood for drink or banter. If anything, she'd found herself growing more and more vexed at Dominique for her unwavering naiveté, despite that she realized it was a function of her age. But, of course, she must think everything beautiful, everything magical, and everyone honorable—including her lord brother.

Fie on that man!

Just as soon as William had become preoccupied with a serving woman—so much for his attachment to Alyss—Elspeth slipped away, none the wiser, and ran to hide in her chamber, wishing Malcom would hurry back—and more, that when she opened her eyes, he would be there already, lying beside her.

Not for the first time, she tugged at the ribbon tied around her wrist, pulling it between her fingers, before tucking it away inside her sleeve.

Last night, for some odd reason, she'd been compelled to hide it, despite that she doubted the lord of Amdel would even comprehend what it meant. Handfasting had never been much of an English custom. And regardless, even if he could perceive it, there was no one to say they'd not handfasted long before arriving at Amdel. Even so, she was embarrassed that he so obviously believed Malcom had married her only because he'd "put a babe in her belly." Clearly, he thought her unchaste, and ready to try another man's favor. The very thought of it sickened her belly.

If only he knew: Elspeth had offered herself up for Malcom's pleasure and he'd put her aside without so much as a thought—it was only now that this simple truth began to gnaw at her.

Did she not appeal to him? Was he perhaps struggling with whatever feelings her sister had imbued in him—or did he somehow realize that, without the enchantment, he'd no more embroil himself in this mess than he would have kissed Matilda's feet?

Rhiannon, she said, furiously. *Oh, Rhiannon!*

Of course, she expected no response, and neither did she receive one.

Still, she was vexed with her sister for having beguiled a man—a good man.

And regardless, had she not taken the chance to do so, where would Elspeth be now? Stranded in the woods in Wales, or caught and returned to the priory to face her mother's wrath?

Ambivalence was her constant companion—but where were her sisters *right now*?

With every minute that passed, she worried all the more. Had Malcom arrived at Llanthony in time? Did he have any opportunity to speak to them? Would he be successful in saving them? Had Ersinius somehow discovered Malcom's intent and had him arrested? Could Malcom, even now, be caught in shackles? And what about her sisters? The questions were as endless as her worries.

She thought about the dream she'd had of Rhiannon in the tumbril and shuddered.

But perhaps that was only a dream, for Elspeth had never, ever had much of the sight, and there was nothing to say this vision had been aught more than a terrible fantasy wrought by her tired and anxious mind.

And nonetheless, Ersinius was no man to be trifled with. He had friends in very high places, and if he'd found himself headmaster of a priory, not an abbey, it was precisely as he'd intended. There was no doubt he would never wish to have more scrutiny from the Church than he had already. Nor would he care to answer directly to the Pope. As it was, Llanthony was an Augustinian priory answerable to an abbot many, many leagues away, and even the newly appointed Abbey Dore, with its Cistercian allegiance, was of little concern to him.

In truth, Elspeth had long wondered over his true mission in Ewyas, and found herself contemplating, precisely, who it was that Ersinius answered to... perhaps not to Stephen, after all? Or to Matilda, for in spite of the fact that he was quick to take her grants, the *only* person he seemed to fear was... Morwen.

Don't think of her. Don't give her more power than she already has.

The hour must be near *Terce*, she thought. By now, the villein would have been up since *Prime* or *Lauds*, stoking the kitchen fires and seeing to their chores.

Dominique wouldn't rise until it was time to break her fast. The schedule here was nothing like the priory, and neither did her lord brother seem overly pious. There would be no prayers at the chapel. If Alyss seemed a bit more devout, that was lost on her "guardian." As if she didn't have enough on her plate, Elspeth worried for that girl—and no less for herself.

Those birds Beauchamp kept were inauspicious. They were bred only in one place that she knew of: *Llanthony*. Brought there from distant lands. If Beauchamp owned one, it was because Morwen had given it to him.

It was with great relief that she heard the horn blow and she ran to the curtained window to look below. A single rider approached, on a shining black mare.

Malcom.

THE MORE HE considered his encounter with Rhiannon, the

more Malcom feared, and it was a gut-wrenching fright he couldn't shake.

He rode faster, pushing Merry Bells harder, even knowing it wasn't in the animal's best interest. Thank God he'd trained her for endurance. But if he didn't drive her to death this day, he swore he'd keep an easier pace once he reclaimed Elspeth—*only, please, God, keep her safe.*

"Stay with me, lass," he begged the mare, leaning close to her withers. He stroked her lovingly, even as he set his spurs to her flanks.

Naturally, he wanted to deny everything. Malcom wasn't an overly pious man, and neither did he believe in faerie's tales. And yet, it wasn't possible for Rhiannon to have known the name his kinsmen gave him in his youth—hot head. *Ceann Ràs.* None of his English peers had ever known his Gael name because he'd cast it away like a dirty robe the instant he'd risen as lord of Aldergh. So determined he was to be his own man, and to shed the trappings of his youth, he'd made himself a new man, styling himself Malcom Scott.

Malcom Scott.

Not Malcom Ceann Ràs.

If his peers ever knew him else wise it was only as the Mad Scot—a nickname he'd earned not through the angst-filled fury of his youth, but because he'd fearlessly embraced every challenge set before him by his king. And yet, until now, he'd never known what it was to be afraid because he'd never once feared for himself. This terrible new feeling deep in the pit of his gut—it was not for himself, but for Elspeth, and the further he rode, the harder he rode, the more he sensed the advent of something worse than the war Rhiannon had portended.

Hie thee north.

Call your banners.

War is nigh.

Was Matilda returning with a new army? Was Scotia bound to join the fight? Were the northern barons even now renouncing their oaths?

If only Elspeth hadn't spoken to him in the same fashion, he might have thought himself gone mad as a sack of ferrets. And now, if he believed all that he'd encountered with Rhiannon, he must also wonder how much of his thoughts Elspeth could glean as well.

No matter, he told himself; whatever secrets should be known to her, that unsettling discovery took a low grade to the one he harbored deep in his gut: Somehow, this mistress of Stephen's was far more than she appeared to be. Morwen was a danger to the realm.

God's truth, he had never believed in witches—or *dewines*, or druids or whatever name they should like to be called—but they appeared to be as real as the sweat on his brow.

When finally he spotted Amdel's turrets looming on the horizon, he felt a rush of relief—though not nearly the rush he would feel once he had Elspeth back in his keeping.

Relieved to find that Beauchamp's men did not hurry out in droves to place him in shackles, he rode straight into the lord's bailey, half expecting to have to draw his sword from his scabbard. He swung his leg over Merry Bells, riding on one stirrup.

When only a groomsman came to greet him, he ushered the lad away, commanding him to leave the horse where she stood because he intended to ride within the hour. The boy bolted away, but not to the stables; he ran quickly to the donjon as fast as his skinny legs could carry him.

Cursing beneath his breath, he left Merry Bells drinking

at the trough, loosely hobbled to a post, with the express purpose of going inside long enough to rouse Elspeth from her slumber. He was more than relieved to find her rushing out the door, tripping down the steps in her haste to greet him. She passed by the groomsman and Malcom bolted after her, overjoyed when she embraced him as vigorously as he did her. "Malcom! Oh, Malcom!"

He swept her into his arms, holding her close.

"You're back!" she cried, and for the first time in his life, he was beside himself with glee to hold a woman—this woman. He allowed himself an instant to drink her in, to revel in the feel of her soft, warm body and her familiar scent.

He splayed his fingers through her unbound hair, turning her face up to his scrutiny. The words, 'I love you' teased his tongue, parting his lips... alas, they were not words he'd ever said. "We're leaving," he told her, instead.

"Now?"

"Aye, now." Far too aware of the need to be away, he released Elspeth from his embrace and took her firmly by the hand.

"What's wrong, Malcom?"

Peering back at the donjon, Malcom pulled Elspeth toward Merry Bells, rueful that he would be putting his faithful horse back on the run. "I'll explain when we're away."

"Malcom! You are frightening me!"

"I'll explain everything when we're gone," he said again.

She tried to free her hand from his. "My dress!" she protested. "It was a gift."

"There's a coffer full of rich gowns at home that belonged to my grandmother. You may do with them what you will, and if they do not please you, I will buy you a hundred more."

Still, she struggled to free herself. "But your silver, your *hauberk*, your blade?"

"I have plenty of silver," Malcom reassured, refusing to release her. "My armorer will fashion me another. And it was an old dirk; I'll get myself another."

"It was *not* an old dirk," she argued. "Tis shiny and new and bears the sigil of your house!"

"*Our* house," he reminded her. "What is mine is also yours."

"Wait!" She gasped, sounding alarmed. "My Llanthony tunic, Malcom! We cannot leave it here, or he'll know."

They reached Merry Bells and even before he lifted her up to put her on the horse, he untied Merry Bells from the post. Then he grasped Elspeth about the waist and set her atop his saddle, praying Merry Bells was up to the challenge.

"'Tis like he already knows," he told her. "You must trust me," he demanded. "As I trusted you." As he'd trusted her sister, though he wasn't ready to say that yet, lest she wish to dally longer to hear more.

She opened her mouth to speak, but said not another word, and Malcom mounted behind her, drawing up Merry Bell's reins. "Hie, lass!" he called. "Hie!"

OUTSIDE THE CHAMBER room where Elspeth slept, Alyss knocked gently.

"M'lady?"

There was no answer, so she pushed open the door, calling again for the lady of Aldergh. Only after she entered, she found the room empty—save for the scarlet dress that lay folded on one chair.

Could she have gone to break her fast? *But nay.* Alyss had come straight from there, having gone to fetch Dominique a slice of bread to settle her belly. After all, that's why she was here now: to explain to Elspeth that her mistress would see her later once the ill effects of their festive evening had passed. The bed was still mussed. The drapes were left open. She went to the window to pull them closed, but first peered down below, and saw that the Lord Aldergh had returned. Confused, she watched as he put Elspeth atop his black horse, then mounted behind her.

Were they leaving? Now? With no good-bye? But how rude.

Evidently, she hadn't liked her gown—the one that Dominique had been saving for her own wedding and so graciously gifted it. Instead, she'd stolen the gown Dominique let her borrow.

"Hmph!" she said and turned about, once again examining the room with the morning sun.

Spotting a glint of silver at the foot of the bed, she bent to pick up the coin, and then spied the gleam of a blade under the bed. She stooped lower to find a pile of garments hidden there. Frowning, she reached under to pull out the pile, examining the garments one by one.

On top lay a costly hauberk, probably worth more than Alyss's entire dowry. The blade itself was expertly fashioned, and she recognized Lord Aldergh's sigil. There were also a few more coins tucked into the folds of an old ruined *sherte*, but the tunic and breeches were a shock. The breeches were leather, like those a soldier might wear, and the tunic was done in coarse *blanchet*. It was nicely embroidered with the sigil of the Church, a red cross extending across the front, with four small, identical crosses beneath each arm of the crucifix.

She screwed her face. *Had Elspeth come from a nunnery? But why hadn't she said so?* Could it be that Lord Aldergh impregnated a nun? *How very, very gauche!*

Somehow, she sensed William would be pleased to know these things—and perhaps he would reward her well? More than anything in this world, she craved her lord's approval, and so often it seemed she displeased him. Taking the garments and folding them all neatly into a pile, she set the blade on top, but slipped the silver into the pocket of her skirt.

Unfortunately, the pile was too heavy to bear whilst rising from her knees, so she stood up, then lifted up the hauberk, which must weigh no less than a full stone. She folded it neatly on the bed, then bent to pick up the remaining garments and placed them all on top of the *hauberk*, and then she lifted them all up together, heading toward the door with her arms laden.

First, she would stop by her own chamber to hide the pieces of gold and silver, then she would take the garments to William. If later Elspeth should return for her belongings, she would gladly return the silver, but if she gave them to William they would never be seen again. She knew her betrothed very well. Moving into the hall, she closed the door behind her, intending to return later to clean the room.

THEY COULDN'T HAVE TRAVELED MORE than a few miles when Elspeth turned to see if they were being followed. The sight that greeted her made her stomach plummet.

A conspiracy of ravens flew from a smoke damaged

tower at Amdel, a fluttering of wings so dense it looked like more smoke unfurling. Her breath caught as the mass swelled, lifting and diving in sync then separated after a macabre dance across the dusky morning sky.

Swallowing, she turned to peer into Malcom's taut-jawed face. "Malcom?" she said. "Whatever it is you need to say, I beg you tell me now."

24

By the look on his face, Elspeth didn't need to hear him say so to know that her mother had swept into the priory in the middle of the night, taking Seren, Rose and Arwyn. What she wished she hadn't foreseen was that she'd sent Rhiannon by tumbril to Blackwood.

Obviously, they had been wrong about d'Lucy. He must have agreed to accept Rhiannon as a bride, but, if so, why the tumbril? Perhaps Morwen meant to make a point and humble Rhiannon in the process: that, for all the Goddess' favor, Rhiannon was still subject to her mother's whims.

But if d'Lucy knew of this and approved, he was more of a monster than Elspeth ever supposed. She had abandoned her sister to this man!

It didn't matter that Rhiannon was more accomplished than she was; Elspeth was the eldest, and as the eldest, it was her duty to protect her sisters—a task she'd failed at, quite miserably.

If there was any comfort to be found it was that Rhiannon had been very clear with Malcom: She was going precisely where she wished to go.

And now, apparently, so was Elspeth, for Rhiannon had charged her "champion" with spiriting her north to Aldergh. And though Aldergh was also where Elspeth wished to go, she didn't appreciate being used as a pawn in a game of Queen's Chess.

Nevertheless, none of this was Malcom's fault. He was but answering a call from the Goddess, and perhaps after all was said and done, he would be equally as horrified as Elspeth.

Only after they were far enough away from Amdel, with no sign of pursuit, did he finally slow their pace and produce the *grimoire* she and her sisters had begun putting together. Small as it was, Rhiannon must have found a way to hide it in on her person. And if Elspeth weren't so appalled over the entirety of the situation, she might have laughed over the manner of Rhiannon's delivery. It was just like her sister to be so theatrical—a small trait she and Morwen shared, along with her temper. Thankfully, that was all they had in common, and the world was a safer place for the disparity.

I'll put a turd in your teeth and turd in your bride's teeth too! she'd screamed. But where in the name of the Goddess had Rhiannon ever learned to speak such blasphemy?

Evidently, there was a lot Elspeth was beginning to realize she didn't know about her sister—perhaps not all of it good.

As for the book... there was little wonder no one suspected it. There weren't many men who could read or write, and fewer women. But, of course, they would think it no more than a heap of filthy rags.

And, it *was* dirty—stained with so much soil from their garden and all the tints and tinctures they'd created whilst crushing herbs. Malcom had hesitated to put it into his saddlebag after she was through with it, but Elspeth reminded him that he'd ridden halfway from Wales with the book nestled against his bare chest. He laughed, but it was rueful.

Along the way, he slowly confessed everything: He told Elspeth about finding the empty hut where she'd lived with her sisters, scrubbed free of every trace of its occupants; the strange conversation he'd shared with Ersinius; the broken wheel on the tumbril; the unsettling conversation he'd had with Rhiannon—*everything*.

And if he, too, seemed quiet thereafter, Elspeth well understood why: It was not every day a man was asked to believe the impossible.

How she longed to explain everything she knew about the Craft, but she wouldn't do so, unless he asked. It was not her custom to speak openly about such things—not when her whole life she'd been warned against it and her grandmamau had suffered deadly consequences.

And aye—perhaps Morwen did betray their grandmother, but it was Elspeth who'd told the Scots king's son about her grandmamau's skills. At scarcely five years of age, she had boasted to that wicked little boy that her grandmamau would cast a spell on him if he didn't stop teasing her, and the wretch had gone to tattle to his father, who then told the Bishop, who then approached Morwen for confirmation. For the price of Blackwood, Morwen then handed her mother over to the Church to be burned alive, swearing her own innocence and devotion to the Church.

But Morwen was no Christian. She was a disciple of the Crone, the witch Goddess whose dabbling in the *hud du* had been the downfall of Avalon.

Fortunately, her sister was right about this much: So long as Seren, Rose and Arwyn did not challenge Morwen, her mother would no more harm them than she would toss a pot of gold into the Endless Sea. They were but a means to whatever end she'd imagined, and Elspeth suspected Morwen meant to place them all strategically, as she did her gruesome little ravens, each daughter in the house of a lord she could manipulate to her will.

Her mother was naught if not patient and she had been planning this ill-conceived scheme for some thirteen years or more—most likely from the day she'd beguiled their father.

Poor, poor Henry.

But he was not alone; there weren't many men who could resist Morwen's wiles, and those who could, had little chance against her sorcery—dark *magik* Elspeth had no knowledge of, and therefore little recourse against.

They rode much of the afternoon in silence, and over the course of the following two days, they traveled by day, staying clear of the king's roads, and sleeping by night on pallets, snuggling for warmth.

Malcom didn't try to kiss her again, and neither did Elspeth tempt him—even if she did long to see if she could feel again what she'd felt that night of their vows. But it bedeviled her to know that even ensorcelled, he hadn't wished to bed her.

Breeding, humph! She was not breeding, and quite likely she would never know the joys of children. Come one year and one day, Malcom would cast her away like that turd Rhiannon promised to cast between her teeth.

In fact, some part of her worried that he knew, deep down, that whatever he felt for her, it wasn't real, but the problem was... Elspeth was coming to love him, as surely as her bones ached from so many hours in the saddle.

What was love, after all, but a higher form of *magik* born of faith, trust and affection?

In retrospect, she realized Rhiannon must be right: Whatever care Robert had had for them was perfunctory—as it was with Matilda.

For all that he'd rebuffed her, Malcom was the only man who'd ever truly supported her, in spite of their differences, and despite his fealty to Stephen—even despite the way she'd treated him on the day she'd first met him.

All this time, he'd fed her, cared for her, worried for her, and he'd offered her the ultimate sacrifice of all... he'd wed her. He'd put his entire life on hold, trusting her when she'd claimed that her sisters were in trouble, and without any proof that he could see, he'd ridden to aid them.

Once the spell faded, would he come to regret it?
Don't think about that, Elspeth.
Don't think about Rhiannon, or Seren, or Gwen or Arwyn.
Put your best face forward, and do what you must.
Of course, it was sage advice, but whence had it come?
Is it you, Rhiannon?
Silence.
Rhiannon!

With a shudder, she recalled the ravens that were released at Amdel. By now, they would have probably reached her mother. But she tried not to think about that either, lest she summon her mother's *hud du* without intention.

Only considering the *grimoire* in his saddlebag, Elspeth peered down at the white ribbon that slipped from her sleeve. Yesterday, she'd attempted to return his ring, but he'd bade her keep it, and remembering it now, she felt for the cold knob between her breast.

What is mine is yours, he'd said—did he mean it?

Regardless... until such time as he should cast her away, Elspeth swore she would make him a good, loyal wife. Somehow, she would repay him for all he had done for her.

You are the lady of Aldergh, she told herself. *Raise your chin high.*

But this was difficult to remember, hour after hour, mile after mile, as Merry Bells ambled ever northward.

The closer they came to their destination the more anxious Elspeth became. Would they accept her as their lady? Would they come to look at her askance for all her beliefs and her kinship? Would they cross themselves in her presence—or gnash their teeth behind her back?

Malcom's brooding silence worried her more.

Swallowing her questions, Elspeth watched as the countryside shifted from lowlands to midlands and then into the rugged uplands of the north. "How long before we arrive?" she dared ask when her backside grew numb.

"Four, perhaps five days. I'm reluctant to push Merry Bells more than I have."

Her bottom ached, but, of course, it must be as it must be, Elspeth told herself. So long as she was with Malcom, she had no complaints over the pace, and she was far less concerned over the journey north than she was over the prospect of leaving her sisters so far behind.

But Malcom's persistent silence was killing her, because in that silence she imagined all the worst possibilities.

Once again, she tried to engage him. "Why do you call her Merry Bells?"

No answer.

"My father called his horse 'horse.'"

There was a strange quality to his tone—not quite bitterness, though not affection either. "Your father, the king, do you mean?"

"Aye," Elspeth said, noting the condescension. But she didn't believe it was directed at her. It seemed more that he didn't like Henry. "Did you ever meet my father?"

"Nay," he said curtly, and Elspeth wanted to ask him why he loathed a man he'd never met. But now wasn't the time, and she didn't wish to take any chance to lose the only champion she had left in this mad, mad world. After a while, he said, softening perhaps, "If you must know, I named her after a dog. What is a horse, after all, but a big loyal dog?"

"Hmm," Elspeth said. "I suppose 'tis true." And she wanted to tell him that this, too, was a form of magic—the imbuing of a trait from one beast to another, although Malcom didn't encourage any more conversation, so she resigned herself to his brooding silence.

Later in the day, when they stopped to water the horse at a small burn and Elspeth stretched her legs, she tried not to think about the bear growling in her belly or the bruises forming on her bottom.

It was too early to stop for the day, so they were again on the road after doing the necessary, and Malcom traded places with her, letting her ride behind him, so that she was forced to put her arms about his chest. She didn't mind this; she rather liked laying her head on his back and listening to the calming *thump thump* of his heart.

"I have a question," he said very soberly after they were well on the way, and Elspeth's stomach roiled at his tone.

"What question?"

It took him a long, long while to respond again, and it seemed to Elspeth as though he were searching for the proper words—or perhaps preparing to say something she might not wish to hear. The muscles in her shoulders tightened as she waited. Had the time finally arrived for regrets? She held her breath, waiting...

"How much of my thoughts can you read, Elspeth?"

Elspeth blinked in surprise. "Me?"

"Aye, lass, I wasn't talking about Rhiannon. I *know* what she can do."

And now, at last, Elspeth understood his long hours of brooding silence. "Not so much as Rhiannon," she reassured him.

"How much?" he persisted.

Elspeth was forced to think about the question a long moment. "In truth, I have never been able to do *that* with any person save Rhiannon. I always assumed it was her, not me. The most I've ever been able to do is commune with animals, and, of course, they cannot answer me, save by their actions."

"Not with your other sisters?"

Elspeth shook her head, even though he couldn't see her. "Nay," she said. "And neither have they done any such thing with me. It was only Rhiannon who could ever do it—and in, truth, not even Morwen ever pervaded my thoughts."

"Never?"

"Nay. Never," she said, only now realizing the truth of the matter. She couldn't remember a single time her mother had ever spoken through thoughts, and she would have known it because she would have *felt* her prying.

Elspeth considered this revelation curiously, wondering why it should be so. Her grandmother had had the ability as far as she could remember. With all the tools of their Craft at her disposal—the family *grimoire* and the scrying stone—it would seem that Morwen should have so much more inherent power. And yet it was only Rhiannon who could do so much without rites. In fact, so far as Elspeth knew, Rhiannon herself had never even cracked the spine of the grimoire. To do so meant pricking a finger for a drop of *dewine* blood, and all of her sisters had been too young to subject them to such a ritual. Elspeth was the only one her grandmother ever taught to open the Book of Secrets.

"Interesting," he said. "Though it doesn't answer my question, Elspeth. How much?"

Elspeth resisted the urge to reach up and fiddle with the small curls at the back of his nape. She tilted her head, and asked playfully, "Have you been keeping secrets from me, Malcom?"

He was silent a long moment, and Elspeth feared she'd angered him, but he finally said. "Did you not hear me?"

Elspeth frowned, perhaps not understanding. "Well, I did. You asked how much I could glean of your thoughts, and I answered you. Then I asked if you had been keeping secrets from me—and you did not answer."

"I see," he said, seemingly satisfied.

But, of course, he must be worried that she could read everything that passed through his head, so now she explained more soberly. "I can only hear what you wish me to hear, Malcom, the same as with you. If I will it to be so, and you have a reception to me, this is how it goes."

He remained silent, listening.

"In this world, we are bound to one another—all of us. Simple beasts have far less guile and are not so different now from the day they were created. Have you never wondered why during a forest fire, animals flee together, even when the fire is miles away?"

Still, he listened without responding.

"Or, perhaps how birds will fly together seeming to know where their fellows will fly?"

"Messenger pigeons are drawn to whatever place they were born," he argued.

"Of course. But I do not mean them. Rather, I mean, have you never seen them fly in formation? Altogether suddenly they will turn and fly in a different direction? Or even how Merry Bells may seem to know your intentions without your command?"

Still he said nothing, and Elspeth continued. "My grandmamau explained to me that long, long ago—many thousands of years, perhaps—people were far more accustomed to conversing with their minds. Not merely *dewines*, but everyone. You can imagine the cacophony they must have endured. A constant barrage of words, not merely their own, everyone's all at once.

Still, he listened.

"Well, she claimed folks went mad, rising up against one another. And whether the Goddess decided to save them from their tumult, or whether they eventually learned to block this ability is not known. Perhaps in self-defense, it simply went away?"

Still, he said nothing.

"The only reason *I* still have the ability is because my people learned to control the skills our Great Mother gave us. But even amongst my own kind, all these many years gone, we are not equally skilled, and some of us are more open to the *hud* than others."

For such a simple concept, Elspeth realized that the *hud* was not so simple for others to comprehend. She laid her head on Malcom's back, letting him ponder what she'd already told him. And though he remained silent, he was calmer now; she could tell by the slowing of his heartbeat.

The sun was lowering on the horizon, filling the sky with a warm, dusky light, heralding the approaching Golden Hour—a time she and her sisters had once cherished. Depending upon the nature of a man's heart, it was either the most peaceful hour of the day... or the most treacherous.

"What about Rhiannon?"

Elspeth lifted her head, encouraged by his question. "Rhiannon is one whose skills surpass all others, though in truth, I do not believe Rhiannon knows all she is capable of. And now that I am gone from the priory, I am discovering I, too, have skills I did not realize I possessed."

"Such as?"

"Well... as I said... I have always been able to influence animals, but I suppose the ability to speak without voice is a surprise to me. And, of course, you know I have the ability to heal. I can sometimes manipulate elements as well, but, most gifts are bestowed by the Goddess, and I must speak rites to summon her divinity."

"Rites?"

"Sacred words known to my people. I spoke them the night I healed you."

"But I do not remember you speaking any words when you roused the torches at Amdel?"

Never having really considered why she needed rites for some spells, but not others, Elspeth considered his question a long moment. For most of her life she had simply accepted her abilities in much the same way that one accepted that some folks could croon like songbirds and others croaked like frogs. But though she didn't have any plausible answers, she supposed. "For some reason the kindling of a flame comes easier than most spells. I suppose that some spells require more of the *hud* than I can summon on my own."

She wanted to tell him about the aether spell, but didn't want to think over the consequences she might still face over that, much less explain how it worked—especially when she didn't know anything with certainty.

But he seemed pensive now, ready to hear more, so she tried to help him understand. "Only think of it this way, Malcom: All spells come from my own inner light. Harnessing it is like focusing sunlight through a glass."

"And your visions?"

"Much the same, but different. Most who are sensitive still use a scrying stone—or fire, or water. Some might descry by touching an object and focusing on something connected to it. Yet others might do so in dreams. But, in truth, I did not know I could have any visions. That night, in the hall was my first, and before then, I had not known it was possible for me to see without rites."

Again, only Rhiannon had the ability for this, and she seemed to need nothing but her mind and her desire to do so. But, in truth, there was little of the *hud* that existed beyond the natural world, and in theory, anyone should be able to do so. A dream was a dream was a dream, and it was not so difficult to summon, but rather it was the interpretation one attached to the occurrence. Most people simply took such things for granted.

"I don't think it was your first," he suggested.

"Nay?"

"Nay."

And before Elspeth could ask precisely what he meant, she remembered the waking vision they'd shared, and her cheeks burned over the memory.

But then, the more she thought about it, the warmer she

grew, and after a while, she felt a stirring in her womb that was exacerbated by the trot of his horse. She wiggled in the saddle, and much to her dismay, it only made matters worse.

"Sweet fates," she said, aloud.

"What?"

"I remember," she said. "I do remember." And, thereafter, she was acutely aware of the heat of Malcom's skin, even through the layers of her clothing. Her nipples ached, and she pressed her breasts against her *husband*, wanting to command him to stop. But stop what? He wasn't doing anything—she was!

Elspeth groaned, wiggling again, leaning her weight on Malcom, trying to make it stop, praying he wouldn't guess at her troubles.

The horse kept right on trotting—*trot, trot, trot.*

"Oh, my," she said breathlessly.

"What?"

Without warning, her eyes rolled back in her head, and she clutched at Malcom's arms, gasping softly as tiny tremors rushed through her body. Once they'd passed she swallowed, blinking, startled. Never in her life had she experienced such a keen surge of pleasure, and now her body was... entirely too sensitive, and she didn't know what to say. "Tis naught," she said, in a small voice, embarrassed.

It felt like an eternity passed before he spoke again, and then he said, "Oh!" as though he hadn't any inkling that she'd experienced some miraculous awakening. "I nearly forgot."

Elspeth was almost too dazed to follow.

"Your sister bade me tell you something: She said, 'I merely called you, I did not beguile you.' Do you know what she meant by that?"

Elspeth blinked.

She did not beguile Malcom?

"Nay," she lied, swallowing as she laid her head back down, closing her eyes, her heart flowering with joy.

All he was doing... all he had done... it was by his own free will and knowing this pleased Elspeth immensely. And sweet fates, her body suddenly felt sated in a way she hadn't ever known before. "I'm sleepy," she whispered, smiling.

"Not that wretched sleeping spell, I hope?"

Elspeth laughed, nuzzling her cheek against his scarlet tunic, only a wee bit regretful now that she'd lost her matching gown. And she dared to jest with him. "Evidently, we are traveling in the right direction."

There was a hint of smile in his voice, but rather than annoy her, it pleased her immensely. "We are going home," he told her, and if, indeed, he was coming to rue the day he'd met her, it wasn't obvious in his tone.

Elspeth dared to hope.

HOURS LATER, she couldn't stop thinking about... *that thing*... that delicious thing that happened in the saddle. It was like *magik* and she wanted to do it again—and again, and again.

Even now, with merely the memory, her body seemed to be on the verge of something spectacular, and it was Malcom's presence that evoked it. She was warm, despite the cool evening, and wished she were lying in his arms.

What, in the name of the Goddess, came over her?

Instinctively, she knew her aura must be burning a bright red, and she was grateful Malcom could not see it. For his part, he sat striking together flint to steel, trying to catch a flame whilst she sat watching, longing to help, but reluctant to do anything unless he asked.

They had spoken more, at length, about the Craft and *dewines* and the *hud*, but it seemed to Elspeth that he held this particular task rather sacred—as though his ability to rouse a flame were somehow integral to his manhood. If he only realized what other flame he had kindled—perhaps then he wouldn't be so concerned with the one beneath his flint.

Alas, the onetime she'd attempted to start it for him, he'd cast her a warning glare and said, "I need no *magik* to feed my belly or yours."

Five days now they'd been traveling, and they'd stopped early this evening to camp in a boggy woodland. Everything felt grey and dewy, as though it had been raining for years. She longed to bring out the sun and burn off the haze, but she knew better than to go about willy-nilly, casting aether spells. Even if it wouldn't revile Malcom, it wasn't in anyone's best interest to thwart the will of the gods. As yet, she still had no inkling what fate would demand for that spell she and her sisters cast in Wales. And so far, she'd not told Malcom about that—or about the auras she could read. It didn't seem to behoove her, considering his concerns.

If he realized she could read his desires, and his fears, and his joys in the air surrounding him, even before a thought ever reached his head, what then would he say?

So, then, she let him strike away at his flint, saying nothing, looking askance, and trying not to notice the deep red hue surrounding him—deeper yet by the second, and she knew very well it wasn't anger.

Well, so he might be annoyed by the lack of fire, but that was only frustration. With her, he had been nothing if not kind and gentle, and the closer they came to arriving "home," the sweeter he became.

He desires me, she realized, with a clarity borne of her sister's message. *He truly desires me.*

Tonight the evidence was plain to see—a vivid cloud of red that enveloped him wholly. And if she wasn't quite so famished, she would show him exactly how she felt about him. Alas, her stomach growled.

"Art hungry?" he asked.

"Quite," Elspeth said, and she curled up her knees, wrapping her hands about her legs, trying not to think about the butterflies flitting in her belly.

Ever since leaving Amdel, they hadn't had much to eat but chickweed and sorrel and berries, eggs and mushrooms. Malcom hadn't wished to hunt, for fear of borrowing anymore trouble.

Thankfully, he, too, was quite well versed in foraging, but Elspeth could do it better. She knew precisely which plants were edible, and by now, she was beginning to fill her purse.

Evidently, now that they were closer to Aldergh, he felt more at ease to hunt, but no matter how hard he tried to make it work, the sparks would not fly, and Elspeth feared it was because everything was so wet. She herself felt damp to her bones, and she was eager for the coming fire—if only he'd allow her to light it for him.

At last, looking furious—more at himself—he turned to look at her, and said, "Go on. Do it. I know you're dying to."

"Art sure?"

"As sure as I am that I will begin gnawing at Merry Bells herself if I dinna put something substantial in my belly."

Elspeth laughed, sending Merry Bells a thought of reassurance. She closed her eyes, imagining the flash of light before her lids, and whispered:

Fire burn, light bestow, I conjure you, high and low.

She felt a burst of heat, and then opened her eyes to see that Malcom was looking at her, scowling. "You had to speak words this time? I thought you didn't have to do that? Did you do it just for show?"

Elspeth tried not to laugh. "Everything is wet," she explained.

To that, he gave her a dubious nod, arching a brow. "You can't wave your hand and conjure a cony while you're at it, can you?"

Elspeth shook her head, though, in fact, she could.

Well… she couldn't produce one from thin air, but she could certainly lure one to her hands. And nevertheless, she would no more summon some poor beast from its sanctuary, urging it to trust her, only to fill her belly. That would be a grievous sin. There was more than enough to be found foraging, and a few hunger pangs never put anyone at risk of starvation.

With the fire now lit, Malcom grabbed his bow, annoyed, and set out to hunt. "I'll stay close," he reassured, and Elspeth nodded.

Sighing, she got up from the blanket to go after the blackberries she'd saved for later. Of course, she would try whatever Malcom brought back as well, if only to soothe his injured pride, but she would leave most of it for him. She didn't mind a bit of flesh, but preferred not to make it a habit. And while she was looking for the berries, she remembered the book down in Malcom's saddlebag, and fished it out, bringing it back to the blanket and sitting down to peruse it.

With her hand full of berries, trying not to squash them,

and the juice seeping from her palm, she laid the berries down, glad for the tartan in case she might stain it. And once she was settled, she opened the *grimoire*.

A small slip of parchment slipped out from the pages. It was a drawing—a golden two-headed falcon with a maxim that read *Altium, citius, fortius.*

25

There was no mistaking her sister's artwork.

Rhiannon's drawings were done with a practiced hand. It was her work that graced the pages of their *grimoire* —all the sketches of flora and fauna, detailed to the smallest degree.

If Elspeth needed more proof than the words with which Malcom had returned from Wales, she had it now in the sketch done by her sister's hand, scribbled in ash and sealed with wax.

How long had she known?

Obviously, her sister had had a vision of Elspeth's future, and now that Elspeth realized, she, too, could see more clearly...

Their bond was irrefutable by the simple fact that Malcom could *hear* her, and that he so easily had championed her. He was her soul mate bonded to her by the Goddess—and she understood now that he must feel it as well, or else he would never have wed her so swiftly, without dispensation from the Church, or consent from his king. Without any hesitation, they had bound themselves together as man and wife in the oldest imaginable ceremony, practiced by lovers since time immemorial.

But, now, Elspeth wondered: Could Malcom also be the key to *all* their futures? Was it possible Rhiannon had seen this, as well, and this was why her sister had insisted so vehemently that Elspeth must leave the priory?

All things were connected, Elspeth realized.

Where a butterfly fluttered its wings, that's where the mighty gale was spawned. Consequently, it was the angry flap of a mean hen's wings after swallowing a seed that birthed a sea swell tremendous enough to sink the entire Island of Avalon.

Thinking about that, later that evening, she lay next to Malcom, facing his back in the darkness, listening to him breathe, remembering the delightful feelings she had experienced whilst riding behind him in the saddle. Her cheeks burned over the memory, but if she could experience *that* with nothing but his proximity, spurred by the sound of his voice and the warmth of his body, what more could she feel? Even now, her skin warmed as she considered what to do...

Up in the sky, the moon was but a sliver.

Do it, Elspeth.

Tomorrow they would arrive at Aldergh, and, if Malcom would accept her, in truth, she wanted to give herself to him, body and soul. She would like to arrive as the lady he'd raised her to be. With little innocence in her intentions—she draped her arm about him, wiggling closer...

"Malcom," she whispered, and dared to slip a knee into the warmth between his thighs.

He stirred, but did not immediately respond, and Elspeth knew instinctively there would be no better time than now, whilst the breeze smelled so achingly sweet and the crackling of the flames reminded her of Beltane fires.

She wasn't a child any longer. She was four and twenty. She understood what passed between men and women. It was impossible to sleep within hearing distance of Morwen and not glean these things, even as a child. But the more Elspeth thought about it, the more she wanted to *know* Malcom... as a woman should *know* a man... as a wife should *know* a husband. And someday, she wanted to carry his babe in truth.

Pressing closer, reveling in the warmth of his skin, desire roused in her body, warming her to her womb. She felt an ache deep down, imagining him pressing her down into the blanket, flesh to flesh, mouth to mouth, body to body... soul to soul.

"Malcom?"

Dare she wake him?

But what if he denied her?

Again.

At the moment, she didn't care. Her body felt as though it were afire, her breasts aching for his touch.

Intuitively, she needed a deeper bond with this man lying so close beside her. "Malcom," she whispered insistently, and this time he opened his eyes, turning to face her on the pallet.

"What is it, lass?"

They were face to face now... breath to breath... and Elspeth's heart beat so fiercely that she thought it might burst from her breast. Her mouth felt parched, her lips too dry to speak. Her arms ached to hold him...

"Malcom... if you will have me... I would be your wife, in truth..."

"Elspeth?" he said hoarsely, and her name seemed to be a question. Inhaling a breath for courage, Elspeth slid closer, and then, emboldened, she covered his body with hers, not entirely certain what to do, listening to the siren's voice all women possessed. Short of breath, needing something she knew only Malcom could give her, she lifted a hand to her breast...

MALCOM WATCHED her with hooded eyes, the veil of sleep vanished. Bold and unashamed, she loomed over him, her body arching for his touch, looking like a goddess incarnate.

"I would be your wife in truth," she said again, and it was as though she beguiled him with her soft, sweet words, because Malcom's cock rose to nestle greedily between her thighs, like a poppet-master with a marionette.

Somehow, he managed to clear the fog from his brain. "Elspeth," he said. "I warned you once... I would not turn you away next time."

"I do not want you to turn me away," she said silkily, bending to cover his mouth with her soft, sweet lips. And giving truth to her words, her fingers slid from her breast, down to his belly, teasing him like a woman who knew what she wanted.

Somehow—by his own hand or hers—the laces fell away from Malcom's breeches. He shrugged them off, heat simmering through his loins, and seized her hand, wanting her to understand beyond a shadow of doubt what it was he would have of her. He slid their joined hands down to the part of him that most needed her caresses, pressing it firmly against his shaft, begging her to understand.

To his surprise, and delight, she closed her hand about him, and the feel of her warm fist racked him with shivers.

Ach, God... it had been so long since he'd lain with a woman—and Elspeth... she was his wife.

Night after night, he'd lain beside her, exercising incredible will not to touch her. Tonight his efforts would come to naught.

Any mind he had to release her flew out of his head as he lifted her skirt, sliding his hand beneath her gown, caressing her warm, soft thigh. And before he could think to prepare her, she settled herself over him and Malcom cried out with pleasure as her warm, sweet body embraced him like glove meant only for him.

"Elspeth," he said again, with a guttural moan, but gone now was the shy, retiring lass. Now she was in control.

And then he felt it and knew... She was a virgin. Her maidenhead was intact.

With some effort, he stilled her hips, searching her lovely face, painted amber by the light of the fire. He brushed a thumb across the soft hairs of her mons, teasing her soft wet flesh, even as his fogged brain commanded him to stop.

She was his wife, he reminded himself and this was naught he should deny himself. But he wanted her to understand that what came next was binding. But even as he tried to warn her, her gaze filled with unbridled desire, and her body came alive with a purpose all its own, tempting him to lose his mind.

Rolling instinctively to regain control, Malcom carried her with him, so that she lay beneath him. He peered down into her beautiful violet eyes, willing her to understand all that was in his heart. "Elspeth," he said gruffly. "If you stay with me, I will promise you my heart and soul."

"I wish to be your wife, in truth," she said again, insistently, and Malcom's heart flowered with joy. Eager to lose himself in the promise of her arms, he thrust her gown aside, regretting the time and place and slowly pushed himself inside her. Groaning with pent up desire, he swallowed her soft cries with his mouth. And then, all thought was banished as she moved beneath him like a siren, taunting, teasing...

She reached for him, wrapping her arms and legs about his middle greedily and Malcom abandoned himself to her.

By the light of a Bright Moon, they made love by the fire, binding themselves together.

"You are mine," he said sweetly, and promised, "I am yours..."

THE FOLLOWING MORNING, it surprised Elspeth to learn how close they were to Aldergh. Perhaps intending to surprise her, Malcom hadn't said a word. They arrived midmorning to much hustle and bustle.

The castel itself reminded Elspeth of the rough and rubble Roman fortresses so predominant throughout the country of her birth. Only the landscape here was different —flat-topped hills in the wake of the Pennines, covered with cottongrass, purple moor grass and heath rush.

Along the journey north, they had skirted about the mountains. However, now they found themselves nestled along the foothills generously peppered with oak and maple groves.

With its soaring corner towers and a massive curtain wall, the castel itself seemed impervious to intruders, and with bulwarks like these under his rule, it was no wonder Stephen managed to hold onto his throne. Whatever ground Matilda might gain, there would always be strongholds like these to prevent her from seizing the rest, and unless she turned the hearts of these men, her cause would be lost. Merely gazing upon her new home gave lie to any hope she had for her sister's triumph. But now, how could she dare hope for Matilda's victory when winning meant a defeat for Malcom?

Reining in Merry Bells, Malcom sat for a moment, perhaps to allow Elspeth time to take in the remarkable sight of her new abode.

Merry Bells seemed to scent where she was, because the horse danced beneath them like a child filled with excitement. Elspeth herself took in a lungful of air, scenting the heath rush.

Malcom said after a moment, "God's truth... I never grow tired of seeing it from this vantage. 'Tis hardly a thing I ever dreamt I would do as a boy." And the look in his eyes held a certain wistfulness.

Of course, she could see why he would be proud; even Blackwood wasn't so sizable. If there was aught about her family's ancestral home that surpassed this stronghold, it was merely its position so high atop the Black Mountains. Also like Blackwood, this was no upstart castel; it was built for the ages, added upon little by little, until it seemed particularly... monstrous—a miscellany of construction, with red stone and yellow. A band of red brick in the Roman fashion wove itself along the entire edifice, continuing from the wall into the two multangular towers that stood on either side of the fort. The rough and rubble wall itself had putlog holes to provide for the platformed floor inside and she knew this because it mirrored the construction at Blackwood—even down to the arched entryways.

"My grandfather added the moat," he said, pointing it out. "I expanded it and constructed the new bridge. The corner towers were two; I built the third and fourth."

"Tis..." Elspeth nodded, uncertain what to say. It

certainly wasn't beautiful by any means, but it wasn't poor. "Tis..."

Malcom laughed. "Tis ours," he said, finishing for her at last, as he tightened the arm about her waist, reassuring her. "It seems formidable from this vantage, but I can assure you that you will have every comfort within."

That was *not* what Elspeth was concerned about at all. She had lived crudely for most of her life. Whatever creature comforts she would enjoy inside her new home, she would appreciate beyond measure. But whilst it didn't have precisely the aura Amdel had, it was still... unnerving.

For the most part, she couldn't quite tell whether she had this strange hesitancy because of the castel itself, or whether it was her terror over being judged by its people.

Early this morning, they had awakened together, arms and legs entwined, and Malcom had kissed her firmly upon the lips, then as though he were a practiced lady's maid, he'd helped Elspeth dress. And if that were not enough, he'd combed the mess of her tangles with his fingertips, and then plaited her hair in much the same fashion she'd had done the night of their vows. For all that anyone could tell, she was a proper lady arrived at her new home—a lady dressed in fine linsey-woolsey, and once again, she bemoaned the fact that she'd left the scarlet at Amdel. How striking it would have been to arrive home dressed as the lord and lady in matching finery.

In the distance, Elspeth heard the creaking and groaning of metal as the heavy portcullis rose. Even without banners, they knew their lord and were prepared to welcome him.

"The portcullis itself is rather ingenious, he said. "Normally, in times of war, you would cut ropes to close it quickly. But my grandfather employed engineers to design a clasp that would release with the turn of a latch. As far as I have seen, it is not a well-used design." He leaned his chin on her shoulder, pointing to the left of the castel. "There's a postern gate as well, but I keep it sealed."

Elspeth nodded. "So, did your grandsire inherit the estate?"

"Nay," he said. "He did not. Though I cannot glean more than that it was once a Roman bastion, built around the same time as York. But, unlike York, this fortress was destroyed before the Roman's departed. It was my grandsire who seized upon its potential and with your father's blessings, he created this monstrosity."

Aye, so that was the word Elspeth might have used: *Monstrosity*.

Instinctively, her fingers moved to her braided necklace and she drew it out of her gown, clasping the signet ring. "He must have been a great man," she said, for lack of a better thing to say. If his grandsire had answered to her father, it was because Henry had considered him worthy.

"Hardly," Malcom replied. "But he made up for it in the end."

"How so?"

"By dying," he said, and snapped Merry Bells reins.

Elspeth frowned. It wasn't the first time he'd suggested his grandsire's disfavor, but Elspeth held her tongue, leaving this discussion for another day. Now was not the time to broach unhappy memories. They were home now, at last. Sweet fates, but she was nervous.

The gates opened wide to greet them. But, unlike at Amdel, there were smiles aplenty for them once they crossed the bridge.

"Welcome home, my lord!"

"Welcome!"

"Malcom! Malcom!" they shouted.

Hues and cries sounded from every direction, and by the time they reached the inner bailey, Elspeth could hear them already lowering the portcullis. The villein—not just the soldiers—filtered in to greet their newly returned lord, accompanied by women and children.

Malcom dismounted, patting Elspeth's thigh, bidding her to wait, and if she sensed curiosity in the sundry faces that surrounded her, it was momentarily overshadowed by their hearty welcome for the lord himself. Clearly, they cherished Malcom.

"Di' ye bring me a Welsh bow—like ye said, Mal?" It was a small boy dressed like a page with flaxen hair, and bright green eyes who'd elbowed his way through the crowd, and Elspeth knew a moment of surprise, because he looked to be the spitting image of Malcom.

Malcom grinned. "I did, Wee Davey, but you'll have to wait to get it." He patted the boy on the head as the lad clapped his hands gleefully.

Another man came forward. "Tis a bloody good thing ye've returned, my lord. There's an envoy from Carlisle."

"Envoy?"

"Cameron, with news," explained the man.

"You gave us a scare, m'lord," complained a well-rounded woman. "We worried when Daw came crawling' home w'oot ye!"

Malcom started. "Daw returned?"

"Aye, my lord, evening past. But he seems worse for the wear. Bertie is tending him."

Malcom nodded. "Good, I suppose," he said. And then he raised a hand to hush everybody all at once. He peered up at Elspeth, winking at her, then reached up to bear her down from the saddle and set her down so she stood beside him. "I have news of my own," he announced, taking

Elspeth by the hand, and raising their joined hands for all to see. "I am returned a man wed. I present to you your lady of Aldergh!"

There was a moment of stunned silence, and then slowly, very slowly, one by one, as though realizing it wasn't a jest, the crowd began to clap. And if their initial quietude was anything at all, it seemed to be a case of genuine shock because the smiles that ensued appeared to be genuine.

"You will heed her *every* word," he said, "and you will come to love her as I do."

Elspeth blinked in surprise, having never heard him speak those words. He looked at her, and smiled, and the boyish curve of his lips, like the sparkle in his green eyes, nearly buckled her knees.

"All hail my lady of Aldergh!" shouted Wee Davie, with such unbridled joy that Elspeth burst out with a giggle, and the crowd followed the boy's lead. "All hail my lady of Aldergh!"

26

Hours later, Malcom's sweet words still sang through Elspeth's heart like a gleeful song. But of course, she didn't have the chance to tell him so because he was ushered away the instant he finished his announcement.

With apologies, he kissed Elspeth on the forehead and left her in the care of an older woman by the name of Cora. He bent to whisper something into the maid's ear, then winked at Elspeth one last time before taking his leave, and like a wee child being deprived of a parent, Elspeth longed to leap at him and beg him not to go.

And nevertheless, whatever anxiety she'd felt over his departure soon diminished because she found herself surrounded by ladies, all vying for her attention, each one more nervous than she.

She met Cora, whose husband was the steward in Malcom's absence, her daughters Ellyn, Mary and Agnes, and then she also met the ladies who worked in the kitchen —Margery, Ava, Meggie and Rhoslyn. Of course, there were more, but it would take time to learn everyone's names.

Enduring the nervous giggles from the young girls, Cora

gave Elspeth a quick tour of the premise and then led the cluster of women into the separate kitchens, where the maid then relinquished the chatelaine's keys to Elspeth, and ordered her ladies to get back to work in preparation of the evening's meal. But, of course, they had guests in house, and the lord himself was newly returned—with a bride no less!

Listening to Cora go on and on about the customs of their house, Elspeth clutched the chatelaine's keys, praying she would rise to the occasion, because she'd never been taught any of the particulars of managing a household, great or small. There was so much to learn—what food to serve, which supplies to buy, which crops to plant or harvest, what clothes to make and mend, which areas of the house to clean first and last, which supplies to make, and how. Fortunately, she knew well enough how to read and write; the rest she would investigate.

But she soon realized she hadn't much to worry over, because despite the lord's absence, she found the castel to be in wonderful keeping. Fresh rushes were already strewn about the floors, the tapestries were clean and well-tended, and there were no cobwebs in the corners.

The kitchens, too, were well kept, and the garden was large, if lacking. And this was the one place Elspeth excelled.

Once the tour was over, Cora sent her giggling daughters away and led Elspeth up the stairwell to the lord's chamber. There, she proceeded to show Elspeth the coffers Malcom had told her about, each one filled to bursting with garments and jewelry that had once belonged to Malcom's grandmother.

"All these are Lady Eleanore's," Cora said, opening the largest of the chests and removing a beautiful silver chatelaine's belt, meant to be worn about the waist.

Attached to the belt was a small silver coin purse, and a silver clasp for her keys. Elspeth gasped, for she had never seen anything so fine. Nor had she ever had any coins to put in any such purse. She tried to imagine herself entertaining merchants and opening up her lovely little purse, but couldn't quite picture it. Perhaps she would use it for herbs? It was so much finer than the one she'd fashioned of Malcom's *sherte*. But lord, there were so many keys! Brushing a finger across the filigree, she said, "Art certain I should be wearing this?"

The woman's head cocked back, like a hen's. "Why ever not, m'lady? The lord himself bade me give it to you."

Elspeth lifted her chin, realizing that must be what Malcom had been whispering into her ear.

She nodded, accepting the belt from Cora and tried it at her waist. Cora immediately jumped up to help her clasp it around the back. Once done, she sat back down, and left Elspeth to admire her new possession.

"So lovely," Elspeth murmured, entirely preoccupied with the shining belt, but then she peered up and gasped aloud at the gown Cora removed from the coffer—a ruby-red brocade trimmed with ermine, followed by a companion cloak to the one Malcom wore. And thereafter, it seemed every dress unveiled was finer than the one before. By the blessed cauldron, it was too rich a bestowal for a girl who'd knelt so short a time ago on dirt floors in order to kindle a fire in her hearth. Rather than wear all these fine gowns herself, it would be so much more rewarding to share a few with her sisters. The very thought of them made her heart sore.

Where were they now? In London, simpering before the king?

Lord, but it galled Elspeth to think such things. But she tried not to think about that, or the reason she was here...

because of the sacrifices her sisters had made in her behalf —and in particular Rhiannon, who'd so adamantly insisted Elspeth leave. And regardless, seated before such a plethora of riches, she felt acutely the guilt she'd felt over leaving her sisters behind. By all rights, they should be here with her now, sharing in her good fortune. Saddened by the thought, she nevertheless sat, poring through coffers, putting dresses aside to be fitted and altered, thinking how beautiful Seren might look in this one or that one, and all the while she listened to Cora, eager to know more about the man she'd wed.

"This, too, was Lady Eleanore's," Cora explained, handing over a small ring—once again, a match to the one Malcom wore—to the one she now wore about her neck. And she wondered if Malcom knew it existed.

Taking the small ring from Cora, she slid it onto her finger and found the fit to be perfect. It was a more delicate version than the lord's ring, still it bore the same golden two-headed falcon.

"O' course, *he* took it away from *her* when he sent *her* away," Cora said.

"He?"

The old maid smoothed a liver-spotted hand across her graying hair. "The auld lord," she lamented. "If'n ye ask me, the Lady Eleanore was far too good for the likes of him." She smiled ruefully at Elspeth.

"He wanted a boy, loathed the child he was given. Certain as he was he could never sire himself a lass, he accused the Lady of infidelity and sent her to live and die in a nunnery, leaving his daughter to roam his halls in tatters —for shame."

Malcom's stepmother, Elspeth presumed. The girl without a name. She fiddled with her new ring, longing to hear more and Cora must have sensed her interest, because she continued with a wistful smile.

"She was the Lady's spitting image. Poor little thing, hair so matted ye caudna push a comb through it. I always feared to find birds nesting in that mess."

Elspeth drew a lovely rose-colored gown out of the coffer, rolling it across the floor, listening to Cora go on about the birds nesting in Page's tangles. And then, just to be sure, she found herself asking, "So... you keep birds here?"

"O'course, lass! Hens, cocks. The lord himself keeps an aviary with peregrines for hunting."

Elspeth looked askance at the maid. "Only peregrines?"

"Mayhap a pigeon or two," she said, shrugging, casting Elspeth a curious glance. And then her stomach growled, and she said with a bark of laughter, "Most birds we tend here are sitting on trenchers."

Elspeth giggled. So, too, did Cora.

She marveled over the magnificent toiletries, thinking how strange luck should be. Little less than two weeks ago, she'd been worrying over marrying Cael d'Lucy and today she had a wonderful new home to tend to—and incredible gifts to enjoy. But, of course, Cora must assume it was no more than Elspeth's due as the wife of an earl, but she had no clue how mean Elspeth's life had been before now. And she wondered idly if Cora would have preferred to have seen all this finery awarded to Lady Eleanore's daughter. But why hadn't Malcom given them to her before now? Curiosity got the best of her. "I take it you knew Page well?"

"Well enough... she was my friend," the maid said.

Friend, Elspeth marveled. How curious. Not for an instant could she ever imagine Dominique considering her reticent maid to be her friend. She had called her sister, perhaps, but she'd treated her more like a servant. And yet, not unkindly, for though she clearly had been brought up to consider her station, she hadn't had a mean bone in her body.

Elspeth regretted having left so quickly, if only for Dominique's sake. She'd been so very kind—but forsooth, as generous as Dominique had been, and as lovely as her gifts were, she felt lost now amidst a sea of shining gold and silver and beautiful gowns. She was like a child with awe. "My lord is a generous man," Elspeth said, surrounded by the proof of it. The old lord might not have cherished or trusted his poor wife, but he had lavished riches upon her whilst she was here.

The woman smiled fondly. "Aye, lass, but lest ye've known him so long I have, ye'll never know the truth of it."

Elspeth lifted her chin, dangling a silver girdle from her fingertips. "How long?"

Cora gave her a single nod. "Eleven years since he rode through those gates, my dear, but I knew that boy when he was six, brought here by treachery."

"Treachery?"

"Mean old Henry meant to steal him south to court."

Startled, Elspeth opened her mouth to speak against the accusation, but closed it again. She pulled out one last gown from the coffer—a sapphire blue with silver appliqué about the bodice—and pretended an interest in the embroidery, running her fingers across the design.

Her father brought Malcom to Aldergh? At six? Why? And why hadn't Malcom told her?

Cora grinned. "His Da came riding up to these gates, bold as you please, demanding the return of his boy."

Elspeth fiddled with the sleeve of the gown, pressing out

a wrinkle. "But... Henry must have intended him to be his cherished ward?"

"Pah!" said the maid. "He meant to use that boy to bend the father to his will. But you see how that turned out." She gave Elspeth a vengeful nod. "Little wonder he met his end the way he did—and no wonder at all my darling Page had no love for the house she was born in." Reliving the memory perhaps, Cora brushed a finger under one eye.

Only now Elspeth remembered another conversation...
Aldergh belonged to my grandsire, Malcom had said. *It passed to me after he died.*

Elspeth had been so focused on the grievous injustice that a woman should be passed over for a man—yet again— that she'd not even considered asking why.

How did he die? she'd asked.

How do most dishonorable men meet their end?

Elspeth folded the sapphire blue gown, setting it aside. "And how, precisely, did the old lord meet his end?"

The woman was busy refolding gowns and putting them into piles—some to be laundered, some to be fitted, and some to put back in storage. "Ah, well, ye know, I wasn't there. But I did hear the tale. My lord slew him, put a sword through his cauld heart."

Elspeth screwed her face. "Malcom?"

"Yes, m'lady. He did."

Stunned. Elspeth sat back.

Malcom murdered his grandsire?

I am quite certain you won your title by honorable means, she'd said so sourly. Only now she understood why he'd been so furious with her, and her heart despaired for him.

No wonder he now supported Stephen and forswore her father! She loathed to think what he must have endured— with the death of his birth mother, and his abduction by her father—but as much as the discovery aggrieved her, she was glad, at least, to know and understand his past, and she vowed again to be the best wife she could be—no matter his *politikal* affiliations. If her father's widow, Adeliza of Louvain, who'd wed Stephen's ally, could love two men, both with different *politiks*, so could Elspeth.

Only now, for the first time in her life Elspeth understood how it might be possible for different minds to ally. Insofar as Elspeth was concerned, it didn't matter to her who Malcom served. She would find a way to treat him with honor and still find a way to serve her sister as well.

Sensing the importance of his war council—for what else could it be called?—Elspeth had deferred the evening's festivities for tomorrow, sending the kitchen's efforts into Malcom's council room instead.

That he wasn't with her on their first evening returned to Aldergh sorely aggrieved him, but there was little doubt; his heart wasn't in the mood for a celebration tonight.

As Rhiannon had claimed, war was, indeed, nigh. It came to him from all sides now, and no doubt there would be hell to pay for absconding with and marrying Elspeth.

Only now, that was the least of his troubles; as he'd long suspected, the summons north was but a ruse to get him to the table and David of Scotia was now mounting a campaign from Carlisle. He'd sent Malcom's cousin Cameron along with Caden Mac Swein to persuade Malcom to join his fight.

It was his intention to bring the entirety of the kingdom of Northumbria under his dominion, and at the instant, he had his sights set on York. Like so many, he feared Stephen meant to abdicate his throne in favor of his son, and he'd made himself clear: He would never ally with Eustace.

If the father was ineffectual, the son was a miscreant.

Malcom raked a hand wearily through his hair, because, in truth, though he could be right, so long as Stephen wore the English crown, Malcom swore him an oath of fealty. "So my father is with David at Carlisle?"

Cameron nodded.

"Why did he not come himself?"

Cameron lifted a shoulder. "He's proud, Mal. As he must see it, 'tis your duty as his firstborn to come to heel."

Malcom lifted a brow. "Come to heel?"

"Tis a matter of speech, Mal. You know what I mean."

"Nay. I *do not* know what you mean," snapped Malcom. "And it angers me that he had so little compunction over allowing his name to be used to summon me north." Malcom slammed his fist against the table, and the sound of it reverberated through the hall, like thunder. "How dare he leave me to believe he could be dying!"

Cameron lifted his shoulder yet again. "If it makes ye feel better, Mal, it wasn't your father's idea. It was mine."

"Nay! That most assuredly does *not* make me feel better."

Stretching his neck, Cameron poured the last of the *vin* from the flagon into his own cup. "So then... you'll keep your vows if Stephen abdicates?"

Considering the question, Malcom tipped his own glass to peer inside, wishing now that he'd not ordered the last of the serving girls out of the hall. His tongue was parched, and they'd yet to come to any sort of agreement.

By now, Elspeth must be long abed, and to his mind, this was no way to welcome his bride to her new home. "I am certain it will never come to pass," he said finally, annoyed, tired, ready to be abed.

Cameron was clearly not of the same mind. "'Tis blind faith ye gi' a man who's already claimed he would do so, and if he manages to convince Theobald to confirm him, he will do it."

Malcom shook his head. "The Archbishop will not agree to it so long as the Pope disagrees, and I am certain he is through with the matter. We've all seen what his meddling begot him—exile."

Cameron gulped down his drink and smacked down his cup. "I disagree. Whatever disagreement lies between him and Stephen, 'tis but this small matter that prevents him from returning to England, and Stephen tempts him. Eventually, he will succumb."

Caden agreed. "Eventually, Stephen must forgive and allow the man tae return. One way or another, he's the only one who can crown Eustace, and I promise ye he'll never allow Duke Henry to come anywhere near his throne."

He was referring to recent whispers that had been circulating—that Matilda would allow Stephen to keep the crown, so long as he might appoint her son as his successor instead of Eustace. But, in this, Malcom was forced to agree. "I warrant his wife would like that less than him. She would cut out his tongue before she ever allowed him to bargain with Matilda."

"Ach, cousin, dinna doubt it. She allows that witch leman to warm his cock because she knows Morwen would sooner see her own son crowned. She's as greedy as her boy. And speaking of that witch," Cameron continued. "What's this I hear o' ye wedding Morwen's daughter?"

Malcom narrowed his eyes. "How did you learn so quickly?"

Cameron tilted his cup, eyeing Malcom with an arched brow. "A wee birdie may have told me," he confessed.

Malcom frowned.

"Christ! Not *those* birds. Stephen sent pigeons as far north as Edinburgh in search of that girl. Ye'd think her made of gold by the tone of his inquiries. I warrant if ye dinna join David's fight, ye'll be answering to *your king* over this matter afore long."

Malcom sighed heavily, wearied over talk of *politiks*.

What he would like to say now was that David had never been his king—never—and he would be damned if he'd be made to feel indebted to a man who'd colluded with Henry in his abduction. David of Scotia was no less guilty over that crime, and it was something Malcom was tired of repeating to his sire. Loyalty was not preordained. Simply because he was born in the north did not mean he owed his allegiance to David—or to Scotia for that matter. Right now, he owed his allegiance to Stephen because he'd bent his knee to Stephen, and because he'd sworn an oath to that man's face.

"Elspeth is Henry's daughter too," Malcom confessed.

His cousin's eyes widened. "*Dead* King Henry?"

"Aye mon. *Dead* King Henry."

Cameron scratched his head, looking from Malcom to Caden, and then back again. "Ach, Mal. When your Da says ye dinna mess aboot, ye dinna mess aboot, cousin. Not only is her connection to Henry a means to settle his barons, her mother is—"

"I know. She's a witch—you can say it, Cameron. She's a bluidy witch."

"And ye believe it?"

"What?"

"That she's a witch."

Malcom nodded. "She's a witch alright."

Caden asked, "And what's it mean for ye if ye dinna join us? Won't Stephen demand her return?"

"Plow her well and get yourself a babe before then," Cameron advised, laughing mirthlessly.

Malcom narrowed his eyes. He and Cameron had never had an easy relationship, and there was a good deal Malcom would never forgive the man for. "Never speak that way of my wife. Cousin or nay, I'll see you drawn and quartered for the offense."

Cameron whistled low and sat back. "So ye love her?"

Malcom nodded. "I do. And what's it to ye?"

Cameron and Caden both shared a glance, and then a grin, and Malcom wasn't sure whether it was a genuine show of pleasure for Malcom's good fortune, or if he thought it propitious for other reasons. "So tell me about York."

Cameron held his gaze. "So you can run and tell your king?"

"What would stop me from telling him now? What difference will a few details make?

Cameron gave Malcom an assessing glance, then said, "While you're at it, tell him Earl Maddadsson sent men from Orkney and Caithness."

"What about Sutherland?"

"Him too."

"And what of my father? Suddenly, he's decided that David is his rightful sovereign and he willingly bends his knee?"

"Aye." Cameron nodded affirmatively. "And so comes Broc Ceannfhionn and Aidan dún Scoti. The Brodies, too, are prepared to fight, along with the MacLeans, Montgomerie and McNaught."

"And de Moray?"

Cameron nodded smugly. "Him too, despite his quarrel with Keane dún Scoti."

"Well, then, seems to me you have it all covered and what need have you for me? Simply so David might put another Northumbrian castel under his rule? No, thank you, cousin."

Malcom rose from the table, finished with talk of treason. "You may tell David—and my father—my answer is nay. I intend to keep my vows until such time as I can no longer do so. And now, *my friends,* I will retire to my bed and will advise you to do the same. Before you leave on the morrow, you must do me a boon by breaking your fast with my wife, lest she take your sudden departure as an insult."

Cameron lifted up his cup, banging it twice on the table, as though he regretted what he was forced to say. "Very well, Malcom," he said, looking grim. "But... now I regret to inform you that I must be taking my boy when I go."

"I ken," Malcom said, expecting as much. His jaw tautened—more with regret than with anger. "Before you go, I have a gift to give Wee Davie, but I will see that his belongings are packed, and he is ready to leave by the morn."

"I would not see him embroiled—"

"I ken," Malcom said again, cutting him off, and he quit the hall, knowing full well what his cousin meant to say: Aldergh itself was in David's sights. The implication couldn't be clearer. He didn't want his own son in harm's way.

But keeping in mind treacherous messengers, he couldn't help but remember another role his cousin had played so long ago. Malcom was naught more than six or seven when the original Merry Bells died, and Cameron himself was the cause of her death. FitzSimon broke the sweet dog's neck with his own two fists and tossed her at

Cameron's feet over a bargain gone sour. Cameron had colluded with the enemy—a man who'd stolen Malcom from his father. And this, after all, was the *true* reason he'd named his Merry Bells after that sweet dog—to remind himself that the enemy sometimes appeared like a wolf in sheep's clothing.

And now, he would have to part with a child he'd grown to cherish as though he were his own—and why? Because, as Rhiannon said, war was nigh.

Bloody tired over the long, long day—half a morning in the saddle and a long day in his council, Malcom, climbed the tower stairs, only belatedly remembering Daw.

With all the bustle of the day, he'd forgotten about the squire. In truth, he didn't know precisely how to deal with the man, but he would sleep on it, and perhaps by morning light, he'd be granted an epiphany. Alas, for the moment, all he truly wanted was to see his wife and forget his troubles between her sweet thighs.

PACING the lord's chamber after her bath, Elspeth waited for Malcom. It had been a long, long day and she'd accomplished so much. She'd made many new friends. But there was something bothering her she couldn't point a finger to.

It wasn't that she was left wanting. To the contrary, she had a plethora of new gowns to choose from, and tonight she would sleep on a plump, feathered mattress.

The lord's chamber itself was very well furnished. There was a curtained bed in the center of the room, facing a lovely arched window with glass—put there so Malcom could awake to greet the day.

Unlike at Amdel, there were no curtains to be found

here, but there were beautiful, polished wood shutters that could be closed by night. And there was a brazier on both sides of the bed, lit even during summer because Malcom apparently did not relish cold feet. That discovery amused Elspeth, because he didn't strike her as someone who complained overmuch. But she supposed every man had preferences in his own home—particularly in the privacy of his chamber.

And this was something that pleased her: She would keep an entire solar at her disposal, with a great big hearth and plenty of room for a cauldron—if she should ever dare to use one. But for that matter, there was absolutely no reason she couldn't use the brazier here in her chamber. Malcom already knew what she was.

Resolved to find out what was plaguing her, she went after the purse she'd begun to fill with herbs, ferreting out the dried bits of coltsfoot.

She took out a pinch, putting it to her tongue to be sure. It was sweet, like honey. And this was something else she could grow because the flowers could also be used to flavor wine or make a tea. She rewrapped the cloth, then tied it again with the ribbon, leaving the pouch on the bed as she carried the pinch to the fire. And, then, for the very first time in her life, without any concern of being discovered, she tossed the herbs into the brazier, and said:

> Blazing fires as you dance,
> Give me but a fleeting glance.

A puff of smoke lifted from the brazier, the scent like burnt honey. The wisps and curls took shape, forming above the fire, and to Elspeth's surprise, it was Merry Bells who appeared.

Merry Bells?

For all she knew Malcom's horse was down in the stables, being pampered.

But, then, when she lowered her gaze into the dancing flames, she saw blood trickle from the mare's black eyes, creeping down over her face. Slowly, as Elspeth watched, transfixed, her black coat turned blood red.

And then just as quickly as it appeared, the image faded, replaced by another... a man dressed in armor... holding a longbow... seated atop a pure-white stallion. He stood gazing upon a white-necked raven that was perched atop Aldergh's tower—unmistakable for the red line of brick.

As Elspeth watched, entranced, the man loosed an arrow, putting the missile through the raven's breast. And then the image suddenly vanished as Malcom opened the door, breaking her concentration.

Tired, but smiling, her husband sauntered into the room.

MALCOM FROZE ONCE he saw her.

"Dear God, you are beautiful."

Whatever he had expected, it wasn't this. Elspeth was standing near the brazier, wearing a scandalously diaphanous *chainse* that left little to the imagination. The room was misty, perhaps from her bath, and the firelight played off the shadows in her gown, revealing the darkened valley of her breast and the hollow between her thighs. Her red-gold hair was still damp and braided into one full plait that fell over one shoulder. God help him, even as tired as he was, the sight of her hardened him fully.

"I was..."

"Waiting for me?" he said with a slow grin, and now that

they were home, preparing to spend their first night together... alone... in their bed... he felt the rightness of this union down to his bones—and in one bone in particular.

He swept across the room and took her into his arms, kissing her soundly. "You're here," she said with a gasp once their lips parted. And then she reached up, caressing his cheek, smiling sweetly. "Tis no dream."

"If it is," he said, "would that I never awaken." And then he drew her slowly toward the bed, kissing her shoulder, letting his hands roam over the treasure of her body, inordinately pleased to find that she had discovered her own treasures in the depths of his grandmother's coffers.

"Malcom," she protested. "There's something I should tell you..."

He reached up, covering her lips with a finger, having heard more than enough for one evening. He kissed her again, laying her down on the bed, flicking her pouch aside as he said, "Save it for tomorrow, my love. Tonight there is only you... and me." He kissed her again. "Husband and wife." He kissed her again, even more slowly, with far greater purpose. He untied the ribbons at her throat with incredible relish, and finally, she slid her hands into his hair, pulling him closer.

"I love you," he said. "Did I fail to say so?"

She smiled at him, a smile he was coming to know and love, and said, "I love you, Malcom." And with those words, he was lost. All strife was forgotten. All that mattered was here and now, and the woman so pliant in his arms.

27

As the bells rang Prime, Elspeth awoke to find herself alone in the bed she'd shared with her husband.

Her bed.

His bed.

She was the lady of Aldergh.

For a long moment, she lay contentedly, until she remembered and rolled out of bed with a gasp.

It wouldn't do for her ladies to think her a lie-abed, and she wanted to make a good impression. After nearly a *sennight* in the saddle, she was certain her blue dress needed a good cleaning. In a hurry, plucking up the rose-colored gown she'd set aside, she dressed quickly, with the intent of attending morning prayers before breaking fast.

More than anything she wanted to show these good folks that there was naught for them to worry over merely because she possessed talents they did not understand—of course, neither did she intend to broadcast her affiliations or her Craft. Malcom would prefer it that way. In good time, they would come to know her, and in the meantime, Elspeth wanted them to know beyond a shadow of doubt that their lady supported their love for the Church.

She realized, of course, this was not Llanthony, but she still wanted to be sure the souls of her people were well cared for. It was such a great responsibility that Malcom had given her and she would rise to the task with joy.

Hurrying so she wouldn't be late, she left the pale-blue gown to be laundered, rushing down the stairs.

Later, when she had the opportunity she would teach her ladies the wonders of simples. She would take stock of what she had in her garden and plant what was necessary—tansy, perhaps, and lavender and pennyroyal to rid the house of flies, moths and fleas; cloves and sandalwood for all their bed linens; sweet bags filled with orris root, red rose petals, marjoram and sweet basil to sweeten the coffers; sage, basil and rosemary for hand-washing at the table; and mint and vinegar to sweeten the breath—which, by the way, she wished desperately that she had right now.

Testing her breath discreetly behind a hand, she rushed down the stairs, more than prepared to greet the day as the lady of her house. In fact, she was beside herself with joy, even despite her lingering malaise, and she was mired in thought, trying to interpret her vision of Merry Bells when she was set upon by Cora at the bottom of the stairs.

"There you are, m'lady!"

Quite pleased to see the maid, Elspeth gave the woman a smile and a hug, then smoothed her skirts, and bent to put a finger inside the back of her slipper to straighten the fold that was gnawing at her heel.

For the first time in her life, she had shoes—fine shoes—soft and plush and pressed with silk. "Good morning, Cora! Have you need of me?"

"Yes, m'lady."

Elspeth's cheeks warmed. "I fear I slept too late, but you must realize, you are always welcome to call at my chamber."

Cora smiled warmly. "Thank ye, m'lady. Alas, m'lord bade us not to wake ye. He said ye were too weary and to leave you abed sleeping."

"Ah, well, I must thank him for that," Elspeth said, smiling. "But, next time, if you have need of me, I must insist you come to me at once—never mind what my lord says. After all, I am now your lady, and you are my kinsmen and I will never put my sleep over your needs. How thoughtless would that be?"

The maid's smile brightened all the more. "Bless you, lady! You have my word; I will do so if I must. Alas, but now, you must hurry to the hall. M'lord's kinsman will be departing anon and he's taking Wee Davie wi' him. M'lord wishes you've had a moment to greet them."

"Oh," said Elspeth, with a bit of surprise. "He did not tell me." She had no idea at all that he had a kinsman in the house, or who in the name of the Goddess Wee Davie was! Rather, she'd thought he had an emissary from Scotia's king.

But, of course, with all her own problems, they'd spoken so little about his household, and she now, faced with her lateness to break her fast, she felt guilty about that.

"I am quite certain he did not wish to trouble you, m'lady. I dinna believe his council went very well." She gave Elspeth a twisted, worried face. "My girls were talking all about it this morn, and for that, I beg your pardon. I gave them a good speakin' to and they know better than to gossip aboot the things they hear in our lord's council."

"I see," Elspeth said, wondering why Malcom did not speak to her of any of this last night.

But, of course, she knew why. She had sorely tempted

him with that *chainse* she'd worn, and no doubt it was her fault he'd been distracted. The very thought of it made her blush. "And where are they now?"

"In the hall, breaking fast, m'lady. M'lord will be expectin' ye."

"Thank you, Cora."

Nervous, but curious nonetheless, Elspeth left the maid and hurried down into the hall, finding the morning meal sparsely attended. But, of course, the morning prayers were not yet over. Thankfully, she didn't have to look far to find her husband. He was seated upon the dais, at the lord's table. He spied her at once, waving her in, having saved her the seat of honor beside him.

Elspeth hurried over, smiling and nodding to all who greeted her. "Good morn," she said to a servant girl. And to Rhoslyn as she passed, "Good morning."

"Good morning, my lady," said Rhoslyn.

And even before she'd sat her bottom in the chair beside Malcom, Cora's daughter Ellyn swept a plate full of sop in *vin* down before her—toasted bread with wine—and Elspeth noticed with some surprise that there was also a child at the table.

"Hallooo," said the boy she remembered from yesterday. He waved at Elspeth and Elspeth waved back. "I'm Davie."

"Halloo, Davie. I am Elspeth."

He shoved a fat slice of toast into his mouth and said with a full gob, "Yah, I ken. I'da been pleased to know ye better, lady, but my Da says we gots important business to attend at Carlisle and we'll be leaving now, I suppose."

His father—or at least the man she assumed to be his father—tipped Elspeth a nod. "My lady," he said. "Ye're as bonny as my cousin said, and I've never seen that fellow so besotted. You must have bewitched him."

Elspeth blinked. She opened her mouth to speak as Malcom's arm slid around her waist, and she inhaled a breath, grateful for his presence, although the reference to *witchery* befuddled her. She turned a wary smile to Malcom.

He squeezed her waist reassuringly, answering his cousin. "Of course she's bewitched me, ye oaf. But no less than your Cailin did, and ye pined like a puppy far too long. At least I knew what I wanted and seized the opportunity when it presented itself."

And then he turned to the wee boy, without giving his cousin a chance to respond. "I'm sure your mother's eager to see you, Wee Davie. Dinna forget the bow I gae ye, and I'll be expecting a big fat cony when I come visit. D' ye remember what I taught you?"

The boy nodded excitedly. "Practice close-range with eyes closed."

"There ye go," Malcom said. "Dinna forget."

"Ye'll ha'e the boy clipping the king's arse with that advice," said the other man seated to the cousin's left. All three men laughed, and Elspeth chuckled.

"Uncle Mal... when will ye come visit?" said Wee Davie, though his gaze lingered on Elspeth.

"Soon," Malcom said.

The boy's father scratched the back of his head. "We'll be hoping you mean that," he said, and then he turned to Elspeth, saying, "My Lady, clearly, ye're husband has the manners of a boor. I am Cameron MacKinnon and I've known this rude fellow since he was a boy fresh off his father's knee." And then he turned to the man beside him, introducing him as well. "Caden Mac Swein," he said. "From Inverness."

"Inverness?" Elspeth said.

Caden nodded. "An' ye're welcome tae visit any time, my

lady. I've three lassies of my own, and a wee boy the same age as Davie here. My wife would welcome the company."

Elspeth turned to her husband and said, "It would please me to know them."

"We'll see," said Malcom curtly, and he cast both men a narrow-eyed glance. Elspeth sensed the underlying tension.

Caden Mac Swein forced a smile. "The offer stands," he said, and for the remainder of the meal, they shared a lively enough conversation—lively enough that one might never have known these men were at odds. But Elspeth felt the strain. It was subtle but certain. It prickled the hairs at the back of her nape, though she didn't have a feeling of danger... not precisely.

"So, then, how's that filly o' yours?" Cameron asked, and her husband stiffened, giving his cousin an odd glance.

"She fares well enough... so long as you stay clear of her. I've already lost two without any help."

"Aye well, mayhap if ye'd stop naming them sae morbidly ye'd better keep one." And the look that passed between them after that was... unpleasant. It didn't take a witch to sense the ill will between them, but Elspeth didn't comprehend any of the undercurrents of their conversation.

Wee Davie said, looking straight at Elspeth, "Uncle Mal ga'e me a bow."

"Very good," she said.

"It's a Welsh bow. He brought it all the way from Wales. Said he nicked it from some Welshman."

"Oh," said Elspeth, frowning. Sometimes it was too easy to forget who Malcom was—a mercenary for his king. And now she wondered who it was that had died in Wales to give up that bow his nephew so innocently exulted over. It was a gentle reminder that, no, all was not precisely well. No matter how she felt about Malcom, there were troubles yet to come. And... there was that vision she'd of Merry Bells that made her fear trouble was closer than it seemed.

Elspeth blinked as last night's imagery flashed before her eyes. Merry Bells... her coat turning red... but then she remembered something else about her vision... something that hadn't stood out to her last night, because she'd not known Cameron then. It was his livery... or more precisely the sigil emblazoned on the front... a red lion, rampant on a yellow field with a maxim that read: *Nimo Me Impune Lacessit*. If she remembered correctly, that was the sigil of the Scot's king. So, if David or Cameron could be the man holding the longbow... could the raven be her mother?

Really, she was ill-practiced at interpretation. And she really hadn't a clue about Merry Bells, or what the blood in her vision portended—or even what Cameron's part in this should be... but she suddenly had a sense down in her bones that Morwen was coming to Aldergh. And, when she considered that, she realized that, somehow, Malcom's cousin was the means to defeat her. *But how?* What did it all mean?

Disheartened, and heavy-hearted, she leaned back, letting the men talk amongst themselves.

So much for putting her attention into her household. Evidently, until the matter with Morwen was settled, there would be no starting over.

The men were still conversing, but Elspeth was no longer listening. She only wished her visions could be more specific, instead of leaving her with a puzzle to decipher.

She knew that Merry Bells was named after a dog... could the cousins' strife somehow be connected?

Malcom had said he'd lost two already—did he mean he'd lost two horses both bearing the same name?

Cameron said he must stop naming animals so

morbidly. What did that have to do with the man on horseback with the longbow? Anything?

Meeting the little boy's gaze, watching him chew his meal with his mouth open, while he watched her curiously, Elspeth picked at a fingernail.

The two visions didn't necessarily have to be connected, but if Morwen was the raven perched on Aldergh's tower... mayhap the man with the longbow was equally symbolic—King David, perhaps?

So, obviously, her mother was a threat to Aldergh... but the raven wasn't flying in... it was *already* there... which meant... the threat was not imminent but immediate. Suddenly, her heart thumped with fear. *Was Morwen already here?*

It was entirely possible. They had not precisely traveled at great speed. Malcom had taken his time, reluctant to push Merry Bells after the trek to Wales and back...

Elspeth frowned suddenly. Malcom believed he could protect her, but Elspeth knew better. There was no way any one person alone could defeat her mother—save possibly Rhiannon—and there *must* be a reason Rhiannon had insisted Elspeth ride north. *Why?* What could Elspeth do differently here than she might do elsewhere?

The key must be Malcom and his connection to—and then it occurred to her... it *was* David. Despite all his waffling, she was quite certain David supported Matilda. But Malcom had long ago broken faith with his kinsmen. As the lord of Aldergh, he served Stephen faithfully—unless...

"Isn't that right, Lady Aldergh?"

Elspeth looked up from her musing, confused. "What?"

Malcom's look was one of concern, and Elspeth wondered if perhaps he'd recognized the fact that she'd had another premonition. A very disconcerting notion was suddenly closing in all about her, dark and oppressive, like storm clouds descending. "Art well, Elspeth?"

"Oh, yes," she said, turning to address Cameron as calmly as she was able. "So... are you returning to Carlisle?"

"Aye, my lady. We leave within the hour."

"And the king... is... there?"

Cameron smiled, a boyish grin he shared with Malcom. "Which king?" he asked pleasantly. "Yours or mine?"

Humor escaped her this morning. "David," Elspeth said.

Caden Mac Swein looked guardedly at Cameron, then cockeyed at Malcom. Malcom arched a brow in answer.

"My king is, indeed, in residence at Carlisle," Cameron replied.

There was a feeling Elspeth got when the pieces of her intuition began to meld together. She had that feeling now. And equally as intuitively she knew that even if she could convince Malcom to understand her vision, she wasn't at all certain he would agree with her interpretation—or, more importantly, put aside his pride long enough to seek help from someone who was not his sovereign.

With a clarity unlike any she'd ever known before, Elspeth realized what her role must be in her crusade for Matilda—and to save her husband.

In helping Elspeth, Malcom had lain down a gauntlet before Morwen, and Morwen would stop at naught until she crushed him, no matter where his loyalties lay. It didn't matter how well-intended he'd been or to whom he swore his allegiance. Like it or not, Malcom had already made a choice, and lest he embrace it now, his cause would be lost. Even now, her mother could be out there.

Right now.

Elspeth didn't have time to explain her suspicions. Nor did she intend to allow Malcom to prevent her from doing what she must—particularly if it meant she must commit treason. It was better he didn't know.

With gooseflesh prickling at her limbs, she rose from her seat at the table, and said with a forced smile, "Pardon me, lords." And she hurried away before anyone could stop her. She ran all the way up the stairs, taking the narrow steps two at a time, and rushed into the solar, where she'd discovered a desk yesterday. She hurried to the desk, taking up the quill she found there, then looked about for a slip of parchment—anything. She found one beneath a paper weight, dipped the quill into the ink pot, and, hoping her husband would find it in his heart to forgive her for what she was about to do, she wrote, with bold firm lines:

To David mac Maíl Choluim, King of Scots

If your conscience be true, I am certain you'll not soon forget me. I swear by the love we both bear my sister Matilda, you have impugned the wrong woman. Morwen le Fae is the realm's true enemy and she arrives here forthwith. You must come to our defense.

Subscribed and sealed this thirtieth day of May... by me...

Elspeth swallowed her pride, but not her self-worth. She knew full well David would come after receiving her letter and warning. He was a very pious man, and he wanted to reveal Morwen no less than Matilda did—no less than Elspeth did. Alas, she could never forgive him for his part in the death of her grandmother, and she wanted him to know precisely where her heart lay. She signed her letter:

Elspeth, lady of Aldergh, loving daughter of your beloved Henry and granddaughter of the late Morgan Pendragon, lady of Blackwood, daughter of Avalon.

Once she was done, Elspeth rolled the parchment, untied her handfasting ribbon and tied the parchment with her ribbon, then she hurried down the stairs, to the stables, realizing time was of the essence.

28

With a skip in her step, Cora rushed out of the lord's chamber, humming as she carried Elspeth's dirty gown over her arm. What a sweet, sweet lass! Already, she approved of her lord's choice of lady, and she wanted to surprise the girl with a clean gown. How refreshing she was! How plainly spoken! How delightful and lovely!

But she was so distracted, and in such a hurry, she started at the sight that greeted her as she hurried out of the lord's chamber—a man, sweat-soaked and feverish, clawing his way down the corridor—and she froze, realizing only belatedly who it was. "Daw! Good heavens. What're ye doing oot of bed?"

There was a febrile gleam in the man's gaze that Cora had never seen before. "I'm looking for the lady of Aldergh."

"Odsbodikins, lad! Ye ought to be keeping your bed. Ye look like the devil! And, anyhoo, what would ye be wanting with our lady?" She waved him away impatiently. "Off wi' ye, and get well. There'll be plenty o' time for everything later." He took a step toward her, with bloodshot eyes and it made Cora nervous just to see him. She took a wary step backward.

"Don't matter any to ye," he barked. "I need to speak w' the lady, so tell me where's she gone."

There was something about him Cora didn't like. He wasn't acting like his old self. Ever since he'd returned two nights past, burning up with fever, he'd been raving like a lunatic about things she didn't understand. "I-I don't know," she said, and he took another threatening step toward her. Cora frowned. "Last I seen her, boy... she was running to the stables." In a far less sure tone of voice, she chastised, "But you'd best not be bothering her now. She's too busy and—"

Like a rabid wolf, Daw lunged at her, shoving her back against the wall. She heard the sound of her own head cracking as she fell.

CONFUSED by Elspeth's actions in the hall, Malcom had let her go. He said goodbye to his cousin and gave Wee Davie a bear hug, sorry to see the boy go. And then, once the trio departed the hall, he climbed the stairs to search for his wife, saddened by the turn of events.

He had a long history of conflict with the boy's father, but he had grown to love Wee Davie, and he wasn't all that certain he'd be seeing the child again—not any time soon.

God's truth, life had grown so very complicated, and if, in fact, David advanced upon York, Stephen would call Malcom to war yet again. And this time, he was certain to face *all* his kinsmen, not merely his father. That realization soured his stomach, even more than the wine they'd used for his toast this morning, and the news sat rancid in his belly.

How had things grown so complicated in a matter of such a short time?

Not that he regretted it, but from the instant he'd made the decision to intervene with Elspeth, he'd possibly sealed his fate with Stephen. Now, to make matters worse, hostilities gnawed at him from all directions.

If Stephen didn't demand Elspeth's return, Malcom would be honor-bound to face his kinsmen across a battlefield.

If he did demand her return and Malcom refused, he should be prepared to stand alone. Already, in so many ways, he was a man without a country. But he didn't regret it, and given the same circumstances again, he'd doubtless make the same decisions. As he'd known the day he'd spirited Elspeth away from Wales, he would die to protect her, and knew down in his gut that he possibly might well do that.

Step by step, shouldering his burdens, he climbed the tower to his chamber, feeling a certain calm before the storm.

Alas, whatever resignation or composure he'd mustered over the inevitability of his decisions, it vanished the instant he spied Cora sprawled over the floor, her arm twisted impossibly and tangled over Elspeth's blue dress. His gut turned violently.

"Elspeth!" he shouted, as he rushed to Cora's aid, straightening the woman gently, and pulling Elspeth's dress out from beneath her. It was stained with blood—but whose? "Elspeth!" he shouted again, but there wasn't any answer, and he knew intuitively she wasn't in their bower. "Alwin!" he roared, calling for his steward. "Alwin!"

Cameron, Wee Davie and Caden were mounted and ready to depart when Elspeth found her way to the stable. With his son seated before him in the saddle, Malcom's cousin lifted the reins.

"Wait!" Elspeth cried, and with no small amount of guilt, she rushed over to hand her letter to Cameron, begging him to deliver the missive to David. "Please," she begged.

Cameron crushed his brows together. "Ach, lass, does your husband ken what ye've asked me to do?"

Elspeth shook her head, and for a terrifying instant, she feared he might refuse it.

He glanced at Caden and the two men shared a discerning glance, though perhaps his loyalty to his king overruled his loyalty to his kin. With some hesitation, he took Elspeth's letter, and said, "I trust whatever is written herein serves both my cousin and my king?"

Elspeth nodded, praying that her husband would see it so as well. She understood very well that she was undermining him, scheming behind his back.

He smiled ruefully. "Very well," he said, reaching back to drop the letter into his saddlebag. "Alas, my Lady Elspeth, I cannot say we'll meet again, so I must leave you with confidence that you will honor my cousin as I know he will honor you."

Elspeth's eyes watered as she clasped her hands together. "With all my heart," she promised, noting the strength of their family resemblance—the strong jaw and flaxen hair, shared by the son as well.

If there was one notable difference between them it was simply this: Cameron was older than Malcom, with deeper crow's feet clawing at the corners of his eyes. The elder man nodded sadly. "Would that we could have met under different circumstances," he said.

"Would that we could have," Elspeth agreed, hot tears stinging her eyes.

One last time, he nodded, looking as though he had something more to say, but in the end, he said nothing, and he gave his companion the command to ride.

The two men left, with Wee Davie holding his bow, peering over his shoulder.

Elspeth waved them away, watching as they made short work of the bailey, ambling out the open gate, with her letter to David in their safekeeping. Reassuring herself it was for the best, she restrained herself from going after them, and then, at last, the decision was irreversible. The gates closed with a woeful groan, and the portcullis lowered, settling at last with a definitive thud. And that was that, she decided. Whatever should come of her meddling, she would very soon know.

But what if she was wrong? What if Morwen wasn't coming after all? What if David arrived without any good reason and she forced those two men into opposition?

Or worse, what if Morwen had arrived, but David refused to come? What if he didn't remember that sad little girl who'd watched from the shadows as her grandmother was sentenced by his testimony? What if he didn't care? Or —far worse—what if her mother lay in wait close by and her message was thwarted?

And regardless, after everything was said and done, what if Malcom never forgave her?

I hope you are right, Rhiannon.

Elspeth stared at the closed gate, lost in thought, and then, remembering Merry Bells, she wandered back into the stable to check on the mare before returning to her chamber.

As surely as she loved Malcom, she had come to love

that animal, as well, and it would please her immensely to be sure that Merry Bells was safe.

Much to her relief, she found her fears unfounded. Like the castel itself, the stable was well stocked, with at least twenty or thirty stalls, and most of them filled.

She found Merry Bells sequestered in the largest stall of all—as, of course, it should be, according to her station as the lord's favored mare. Pleased to see her, Elspeth opened the stall door and stepped inside, sighing contentedly to see gaze into her familiar black eyes.

"There you are," she said, smiling. "My beautiful, beautiful lady." And then she stood, petting the long black mane, thinking about the rest of her vision and what it could possibly mean. She never even heard the approaching footsteps; she was so lost in thought.

If Cora knew Elspeth's whereabouts, she was in no condition to say. Malcom had a deep sense of foreboding that only intensified as he untangled Elspeth's blue gown from about the maid's arms and he felt a rush of relief when her husband finally arrived. He slid Cora into Alwin's arms, and directed him, "Put her in my bed. I'll send for the physician."

"Aye, my lord," the man said gratefully, lifting up his injured wife. He bore the maid into the lord's chamber, as Malcom rushed away, with the intent of locating his wife. He bolted down the steps, taking them two at a time, and stopped cold as an image arose in his mind—Merry Bells in the stables, her face spattered with blood. And there was Elspeth.

A sense of portent overwhelmed him—a sense so powerful he couldn't ignore it.

There were times in his life that he'd had moments of this ilk. So often he'd denied them, as most people would. It was only after meeting Elspeth that he realized these were not to be ignored. He felt it now, like a summons... and he knew it as surely as he knew... Elspeth was in danger.

She was in the stable.

With a growing knot of apprehension in his gut, he hurled himself down the tower stairs, his heart pounding like hammer and steel against his ribs. He raced through the hall, ordering one of Cora's daughters to see to the physician. He rushed from the keep, and when he burst into the stables, the sight that greeted him buckled his knees—blood, everywhere.

So much blood. Blood on the stall, blood on Merry Bells. Blood on Elspeth.

29

Blood-spattered though she was, his wife was unharmed. She stood, looking as dumbfounded as Malcom, staring at Merry Bells, whose black coat was dappled with blood.

Daw—or what remained of Daw—lay on the ground between them, trampled to death.

Elspeth turned to face him, her eyes round and filling with tears as Malcom rushed to embrace her. "You came," she said woodenly, still in shock.

"Elspeth." He hugged her, then brushed a hand across her forehead, smearing blood from her face. "What in God's name happened?"

Her gaze was filled with confusion. "I... I don't know... He—" She looked down at Daw. "He... attacked me. And he said... He told me that Morwen had sent him and..." Her gaze lifted to Merry Bells. "Merry Bells saved me."

The mare stood placidly, and if there had once been blood lust in her gaze, it was gone. She blinked serenely, staring at Malcom with calm, ebony eyes.

Once again, Malcom peered down at the barely recognizable body, misshapen in the hay at his feet. But no sooner had Elspeth finished her explanation when they heard the blast of a horn—three short wails.

Malcom's first thought was that his cousin must have returned—but nay, for that alone, his men would never have presumed a call to arms.

ONE BY ONE, crimson tents arose on Aldergh's parklands, mottling the landscape, like blood-spray across their fields.

Recognizing the obvious signs of a siege—troops in formation, supply wagons incoming, and the sound of hammering wood—Malcom watched the event unfold with no small degree of trepidation.

He had been a part of too many sieges not to know what they looked like and sounded like. But this strike had come so swiftly that Stephen must have ordered it the minute he heard news of Malcom's intervention, all without ever having heard Malcom's explanations, or bothering with an attempt at negotiation. Considering these truths, perhaps Malcom shouldn't have been so surprised to find it was Eustace's banner that flew in tandem with the royal standard.

The King's son was not an admirer of Malcom's, and it was no secret to anyone that Malcom believed Stephen afforded his son too much power. Of course Eustace would seize any opportunity to oppose him. But what did surprise him was that Stephen would forsake him so easily, giving leave to his miscreant son to campaign against him, when only three weeks ago, he had stood in his presence, and assigned him the most sensitive task in all the land—the assassination of Brian Fitz Count, the lord of Wallingford.

So, then, was this what eleven years of loyalty had earned him?

By late afternoon, a good thousand men had already gathered over Aldergh's parklands, with hundreds more filtering in by the hour. For the time being, they remained outside missile range.

At the first sign of hostilities, most of his *villein* had rushed for the gates. The fortress was now locked and sealed—front and postern gates. Anyone remaining outside would be forced to take their chances. He knew there were a few old folks who would stay with their homesteads and livestock, particularly since, in truth, this was not the enemy that descended upon them. It was their king, and with a simple word, Malcom himself had become an enemy to the crown.

Thankfully, if there was one thing Malcom trusted about the man he'd served more than ten years: This siege would be long and slow, with every attempt made to come to terms.

Alas, if Stephen should insist upon Elspeth's return, Malcom would never release her without a fight, and if that should be the case, Stephen would find him well prepared.

It wouldn't be the first time his king gave up on a siege, and Malcom had taken an example from Wallingford, himself, hoarding supplies for years in the event of an advance by Matilda. After all, she was her uncle's favored candidate for the throne and Malcom's demesne lay far, far to the north. So far, in fact, that it should have taken weeks for Stephen to gather his men and march north. While it was certainly possible for a small number of riders to reach Aldergh, he would have had to draw forces from surrounding lordships—men that Malcom had once called compatriots.

How swiftly the tides turned.

Whatever the case, the sight before them was proof of two things: Morwen's ravens were inordinately efficient communicators; and Stephen was, indeed, far too easily influenced by his son.

Shivering beside him, Elspeth rubbed her arms, whispering for Malcom's ears alone, "She's out there. I *feel* her."

"Aye well, unless she can walk through walls," he said, "she'll remain out there. We have supplies enough to outlast them."

That didn't seem to ease the frown from Elspeth's face, but, in fact, the fortress was as impenetrable as she was unsightly, and Malcom had never cared much for aesthetics over advantage. Thirteen long years of warfare had never given him much leave to consider anything but the protection of his people, and, besides, Aldergh was the manifestation of a paranoid man, whose sole purpose in life had been the defense of his lands. Hugh FitzSimon had cared more for Aldergh than he had for his own flesh and blood.

Elspeth hugged herself. "Please, please do not discount her, Malcom. I do not know what she is capable of."

Hearing the note of fear in his wife's voice, he spun her about so that she could look into his eyes, and he asked her firmly but gently, "Would you have me return you to your mother?"

"Like so much chattel?"

"Precisely," he said. "And lest ye tell me you would leave me, I would never willingly let you go." He offered a sore attempt at a smile. "I did warn you, did I not?"

Her lips quivered in a sore attempt at a smile, and her eyes filled with tears as she shook her head, then nodded, clearly confused. "But if it would keep you and your people safe from harm..."

"*Our* people," Malcom reminded as he brushed a finger

across the bruise that was forming on her cheek—God's truth, he wished that Daw were alive, so he could beat him to a pulp. "You are my wife, Elspeth. We took vows." He showed her the white slip at his wrist—trimmed and tucked, but still there. "I intend to keep them."

Already, he'd come too damned close to losing her, and he shuddered to think what might have happened had Merry Bells not been so ready to defend her. He smiled. "*You* are the lady of Aldergh and there is not a man or beast behind these walls who would not die to protect you, as you would no doubt do for them. Would you not?"

Elspeth nodded, a single tear slipping through her lashes, and Malcom pulled her close and turned about to watch the siege unfold. "I am your champion," he reminded her. "Remember?"

"I remember," she said softly, and he crushed her against him, praying to God that he would rise to the occasion.

For all her husband's bold, sweet words, he still did not realize what she had done.

After two days without word from David, Elspeth began to fear the possibility of Cameron's and Wee Davie's capture. It seemed to her that no more than thirty minutes could have passed between his leaving Aldergh and Stephen's arrival, but she prayed with all her heart that Cameron had spied the approaching army and that the three of them had taken shelter without Stephen any wiser.

When three days later there came no messenger, no demands and there seemed to be no sign of Cameron's presence anywhere near the siege camp, Elspeth began to take heart. *Sweet fates, please, please,* she prayed.

Alas, after her meddling was discovered, Malcom might wish to return her to her mother, after all, though in the meantime, she fully intended to do her part to keep his household as best she could.

By now, Cora had awakened, but she remained indisposed. Until such time as she could return to the household chores, Elspeth took it upon herself to lead. All day long, she flitted between Cora's sickroom, tending the maid's wound and then marching through the keep, with Cora's daughters en tow. "Art certain mother will be alright?" each girl asked in turn.

"I promise," Elspeth reassured, but she daren't explain how and why she knew it would be so: Of course, she had performed a bit of *magik* to speed the maid's recovery—not so much as to raise suspicion, just enough to ensure their mother would be on her feet before too long.

It wasn't entirely a selfless act. As much as Elspeth loathed to confess it, she needed Cora desperately. She was completely ignorant about the running of a household—and lost.

She started with the things that made sense to her: The feast for her nuptials was postponed again. They would need all the supplies they could get for the siege to come.

Of course, Malcom had reassured her: There was plenty enough for everyone and Elspeth need not worry. Even without the livestock from their fields or the season's yield, they had food enough for more than a year.

Malcom also kept a fair share of cattle, goats and hens safely within the castel walls. At the moment, the entire premise was a living crush—animals and people sleeping all about—in the hall, in the bailey, on the ramparts, in the corridors. The only place that was free of bodies at night happened to be the stairs.

During the day, children rushed about, chasing chickens and goats, not entirely aware that this was not a celebration. Elspeth supposed that until the first casualties were lost, they would think it no more than an adventure.

Unfortunately, with so many tasks to manage, she needed every woman she could get. All the men were expected to bear arms in shifts, including the butcher, the barber and the blacksmith.

Elspeth gathered up the children and took them to her solar leaving them in Ellyn's care while Agnes continued to follow her about. And despite their constant barrage of questions, Elspeth was grateful for the help, because, in truth, when she excelled at one thing, she failed miserably at another.

At night, Malcom tiptoed over sleeping people en route to their bed, and he was gone by morning light, without so much as a complaint, but Elspeth missed him desperately. So, tonight, with her keys jangling on her new chatelaine's belt, she swept through the kitchen, making certain that supper was progressing, and then, once the stew was complete, she poured a trencher full for her husband, and thinking that once they used up the last of the meat they'd butchered for the feast, she would see to it that they kept the remainder of the livestock for milk, cheese and eggs. It wouldn't do to be killing their best means for supplies. And anyway, they didn't need meat; she knew a hundred ways to flavor a good porridge to please the palate.

She made her way across the Bailey, with the trencher in hand, careful not to spill it. It wasn't until she was near the stairs that she noticed the stench that filled the air, and her heart wrenched. Dropping the trencher, she ran toward the parapets.

. . .

FOR NEARLY AN HOUR, Malcom watched as fields were set ablaze, surrounding the castel with burning crops and black smoke that puffed into an ever-darkening sky. But, then, rather than dissipate, those clouds seem to be gathering on the horizon, tumbling and turning.

All this time he'd been preparing for a good, long siege, but now he realized an attack must be imminent—all without ever having sent a single messenger, or any attempt at negotiation.

Furious now, incensed by the betrayal, he ordered pitch vats to be established at intervals along the wall. These would be used for men scaling their walls or battering with rams. Fortunately, they had more than enough missiles to launch a sustained attack. Armload after armload, his men brought and stacked supplies between machicolations. He'd slept little more than an hour or two at intervals, and the stress was beginning to darken his mood until it was black as the clouds gathering in the distance.

It was near dusk, when a messenger finally arrived—a boy, no older than Wee Davie. For a terrifying instant, that's who Malcom thought it must be as the boy ran stumbling across a fallow field. He stood below the gates, and Malcom had a sudden vision of himself at six, watching from the bailey side as FitzSimon bargained with his father. Only this time, it was Malcom on the parapet as the boy—a fair-haired child Malcom recognized from one of the farms—shouted up at him, puffing his chest with pride.

"My lord Aldergh," he announced, between breaths. "In the name of our king... you must surrender."

That was it. No opportunity for Malcom's side to be heard. No recommendation for a meeting. Eleven years of service gone in a blaze of smoke.

Black, hot fury shot through Malcom's veins—anger unlike anything he'd experienced in his life.

At the instant, he sorely regretted sending his cousin away. At least then, he might have had the backing of his kinsmen. Now, he was alone, floundering in a sea of cottongrass and heather. But come what may, he would never give up his bride. By God, *she'd* sent one of Malcom's own men into his home to harm Elspeth—her own flesh and blood.

Malcom had little comprehension over what that woman must have done to mild-mannered Daw, or how she'd forced his hand, but if she wanted an answer, Malcom knew precisely what to give her.

He ordered one of his men forward, whispering into the man's ear. The man rushed away to do Malcom's bidding. Only then did he step forward to address the child.

"I'll gi' ye my answer, lad—as a gift for the lady Morwen."

The boy nodded eagerly, awaiting his charge—and this too, infuriated Malcom. It was inconceivable that any man should use a boy so rudely. Thankfully, he took comfort in that no honorable man would ever harm an innocent child. The rules of engagement commanded a messenger's safe passage.

ONCE UP ON THE RAMPARTS, Elspeth approached her husband with trepidation. Making herself as invisible as possible so as not to distract him.

The gates creaked open, and the portcullis rose barely high enough to push a box outside. Elspeth watched as the child came forward to take his burden, then, very innocently, peered up and waved before hurrying away.

No doubt, he felt important today—a messenger for his king and his lord.

Along with the rest of the men at arms, Elspeth watched with bated breath as the boy ran the long distance to the king's camp—about four hundred meters—during which time the silence on the ramparts grew thick enough to cut with a blade. What must have been minutes felt like an eternity.

And then, suddenly, before anyone could wonder over the king's response, the child came rushing back, only this time, there was terror in his gait. Whatever they'd said to him must have frightened him because he ran fast and faster, all the while those smoke clouds on the horizon began to roil, moving closer, swirling, closing in. Elspeth watched the advance with a growing sense of trepidation...

Only once the child was halfway across the field, the cloud formation dove on him, and suddenly Elspeth knew—too late for the boy. He dove to the ground, throwing up his hands to cover his ears and head. Alas, they could hear his screams of agony from whence they stood.

"What in God's name is that?" asked one of the men at arms.

"Ravens," whispered Elspeth.

By the thousands, they came swooping in, the sound of their rushing black wings like a raging wind, and their squawks inspiring terror.

Something terrible awakened inside her, as Elspeth realized that even if they loosed every arrow in their possession, they would still be lacking.

Sprawled out in the field, the child no longer struggled. His body lay as still as Daw had been after Merry Bells was through with him. All together now, the dense cloud of birds swooped up and moved closer, closer... closer...

If only she could stop them. If only she had some means to prevent them from coming inside the castel walls... if only...

Tell her... she must raise her hand... and believe.

Elspeth blinked, suddenly understanding.

Believe, she thought she heard Rhiannon say. *Believe.*

Only fearing the consequences of revealing herself, Elspeth hesitated, looking first at Malcom, begging with her eyes, and somehow, somehow, he must have sensed her regard and he slowly turned and gave her a nod.

Believe.

Elspeth had never considered attempting such a feat. She had never imagined any time when she should have to try. But if she did this... if she did this... there could be no doubt about *what* or *who* she was after she was done. She was a witch. A *dewine*. A sorceress.

So be it.

Come what may—if they should hang her from the ramparts for this spell, it still must be done. She felt a surge of power rise up from parts unknown, tingling her skin, rising, rising, until she was a burst of energy, ready to ignite. And then suddenly, she had a terrifying sense of blinding white as she splayed a hand and whispered over the incoming roar.

> *By the power of earth, fire, air and water, my*
> *Goddess, I beg thee protection.*
> *By the power of earth, fire, air and water, my*
> *Goddess, I beg thee protection.*
> *By the power of earth, fire, air and water, my*
> *Goddess, I beg thee protection. By all on high*
> *and law of three, it is my will, so may it be.*

The King's Favorite

The onslaught stopped.

A hush fell over the demesne.

Some of the birds slid from the sky, as though they'd encountered an invisible, immovable force. Not a single one came closer than Elspeth bade them. They dropped from the sky to the ground, forming a perfect line of black about the castel.

With a shuddering breath, Elspeth met her husband's gaze, and the look in his eyes was full of—not admiration, but horror. Lowering her hand before anyone could see what she'd done, she stood, as everyone else stood, stupefied, watching the remaining ravens swoop up and retreat.

30

"Elspeth, love... I swear to you... I am but grateful."

Elspeth sat despondently at the lord's table, stabbing at her trencher with her jeweled poniard—another gift from Malcom's grandmother's coffers. She wasn't hungry.

No matter how hard he tried to convince her, she would never forget that look of terror in her husband's eyes.

"I care not what you think you saw," he persuaded her. "It was naught but awe for what I witnessed with my own two eyes."

"You, and everyone else," Elspeth said ruefully, knowing only too well that once the danger was past, she would become subject to their fears. Visions of her grandmamau's burning tormented her and no matter that she was astounded by her own power to fight Morwen's *magik*, she feared the price yet to be paid. Gratitude only went so far. Today *magik* was evoked against *magik*. It was impossible not to know this instinctively, even if these people didn't immediately comprehend from whence it had come.

It had come from her.

She had summoned it—a shield to keep the birds at bay,

and the evidence of her intervention surrounded the castel. Thousands of black birds lay piled like dry-stacked stone no more than ten feet from the castel walls.

She tried to find the will to eat, to regain her strength, because her body felt limp with exhaustion, and she doubted she had any strength to climb the stairs to bed, much less fend off another of her mother's attacks. The spell she'd cast—nay, not a spell, but a plea to the Goddess—had sapped every bit of energy from her body, and now, she felt like a dirty, limp rag... waiting to be discarded.

Malcom pushed her hair out of her face. "No one saw anything, Elspeth. They were too busy fearing for their lives."

Finally, with a plea in her eyes, she peered up at her husband, daring to hope.

"Tis true," he swore. He tipped up her chin, forcing her to meet his gaze. "I have not heard not one word spoken against you, my love, and if anyone saw what I saw, I will make certain they understand... their lady works wonders in the name of love."

Elspeth flung her arms around him and said, "I love you so much, Malcom. I am so blessed to be your wife and no matter what happens know that I count myself blessed for having known you." Alas, there was a niggling sense of terror still growing deep inside her, for she had betrayed Malcom, and would he still feel the same about her once he knew?

"I love you, too," he said, kissing Elspeth on the head.

Elspeth held him tight, so afraid to let go, lest he change his mind and send her home.

Finally, he peeled himself away. "Why don't you go see to Cora... and then, if you must, join me on the ramparts."

Elspeth nodded and dried her eyes.

. . .

It was near dawn when she joined Malcom on the parapets. From her vantage between machicolations, she could see the child's prostrate body still lying in the field, and the sight of it made her long to run out and clasp him to her breast.

Poor, poor child.

It was a grim reminder that her mother would dare anything, and they waited with bated breath to see what more would come.

As for Stephen, there was no word from their *King*, but his camp remained. All those bright red tents remained squatting at the foot of their hill, the once billowing cloths as still as stone. It was almost as though there was no life in that quarter, but it was an illusion, Elspeth realized—a glamour placed by her mother to hide the scurry of movement between tents, and the night-long councils. There was little doubt in Elspeth's mind that if she was so surprised by the power of the spell she had conjured, her mother was equally startled, and would certainly be taking measures to veil her plans from prying eyes—Elspeth's eyes.

This morning, it seemed death had prevailed. The stench of it was overpowering.

By the first rays of the morning sun, they could bear it no longer and men lit pitch-soaked arrows and aimed them into the carnage of shining black wings, lighting a bonfire that was slow to ignite, but once it caught flame, it sent dirty, stinking flames into a grey morning.

Half the fields were scorched. The other half lay fallow. The roads in and out of the parklands were blocked. The colors of the morning were gray, brown and black—the colors of the land and sky and the aura surrounding Stephen's camp.

Fortunately, Morwen did not repeat her attack, and no doubt, that unexpected feat of *magik*, fueled by her rage, had depleted her precious birds. It would take her years to breed so many.

When he saw her, Malcom took Elspeth by the hand, tugging her close, and drawing her under his arm. She could feel his exhaustion in the weight of the arm he'd placed about her shoulders. "Go to bed, love. You should sleep," he said, and then he frowned, realizing only now that her handfasting ribbon was gone. He lifted her hand, examining her wrist. "You took it off?"

Elspeth nodded, thinking perhaps now would be a good time to explain what she had done. At least then, if he was going to be angry, she could bear the worst all at once—or then, finally, perhaps, he might prefer to be rid of her, and send her back to her mother in tears.

She opened her mouth to speak but then he shushed her and said, "Go to bed. We'll talk when you're rested."

"I would go if you go," she entreated, brushing a hand across the small cleft in his chin. Her heart broke for the turmoil she spied in his eyes. "What good will you be to your men without sleep, my love. I feel certain my mother has exhausted her efforts for the time being." Certainly she had, if Elspeth's exhaustion was any indication. She was weary to her bones. A bit of sleep would do them both good, and this siege promised to last long enough to warrant keeping them on their toes.

He sighed, drawing her into his arms, holding her tight. Elspeth laid her head on his chest, and said, "We go together, or I stay. But you know they would summon you at once should they need you."

It was a long, long moment, before Malcom said, "Very

well. Go. I'll follow. I need only let my men know where I'll be."

Elspeth nodded. She kissed him on the cheek, and then turned and made her way down the ladder. She was halfway down when there was a sudden horn blast...

She heard Malcom's cursing. "For the love of—"

"What is it?" Elspeth demanded, her heart filling with dread as she scrambled back up. *Goddess, please, no more birds!* Her legs trembled as she re-ascended the ladder, and, she tried to summon the last of her reserves as she climbed.

Wide eyed, Malcom turned to take her by the hand and drew her up and back onto the ramparts.

Elspeth's heart leapt against her ribs at the sight that greeted her...

Beyond the burning mass of dry-stacked birds, beyond the blackened fields, beyond Stephen's encampment, thousands of armed men approached in formation, flying banners of every color—many, many unrecognizable to Elspeth. They approached from the north, west and east.

David.

He'd come... and despite that she knew she would have to answer for her meddling, Elspeth nearly swooned in relief.

David had come!

Within moments, tents began to collapse, deflating one by one, and the siege army began to disperse, like ants scurrying at the poke of a stick. Malcom turned to look at her, and said with an unmistakable note of relief, "Elspeth... by chance, have you something to do with this?"

Eyes wide and stinging, Elspeth nodded.

And rather frown, Malcom grinned at her. "God's truth, 'tis the second most welcome sight I have spied in all my life."

Elspeth felt a rush of relief. "What would be the first?"

If possible, his grin widened until she could see all his straight, white teeth. "Any day I set eyes upon my beautiful wife," he said, and pulled her into his arms, kissing her soundly.

Let them be hunted soundly. At this hour Lies at my mercy all mine enemies. —*Shakespeare*

"Let's go!" snaps Eustace. "Or better yet, stay," he says rudely. "But if you do, you will find yourself in David's hands and I warrant he is no disciple of witches. Need I remind you how he persecuted your mother?"

Despite the command, I linger, furious over the turn of events. So, they say, "Never kill the messenger." And 'tis an unspoken diplomacy of war. But I say, "If the messenger be my own, I should do what I will."

Somewhere out in that field lies a little boy, eyes plucked out of his skull...

No one thwarts me.

No one.

And yet, for the love of my own daughter, this north man has dared. After all is said and done, I will crush his bones like dried leaves beneath a pestle, and my daughter will weep tears of blood.

As men rush to heed Eustace's commands to abandon this ill-planned siege, I bide my time, once more opening my "gift," if only to remind myself.

A severed head, barely recognizable with death-glazed

eyes peers back at me. *Daw. Well played, I think. Well played, my Lord Aldergh. And Elspeth, too, well played.*

"My father will be furious," worries Eustace.

"Perhaps," I say, with a shrug, and now I rise, knowing full well that, for the time being, we are done. The battle is lost. The war is not.

And yet... and yet... a mother's pride wars with rage, because I had no idea my eldest bore such unbridled power. And what must this say for Rhiannon? So, now, I must ponder the answer to this question, even as I prepare for the next encounter, because this is not over.

It is far from over.

31

As evening fell on Aldergh's parklands, one by one new tents arose on the horizon, replacing the king's red with bright gold, white and blue. From the midst of these new tents came a modest cavalcade, sporting familiar colors, banners and cloaks flying at their backs.

"Open the gates!" shouted Malcom. "Now! Open the gates!"

He was downstairs even before the portcullis's first groan. The heavy metal rose, and Malcom himself pushed open the gates, ordering a path to be cleared. Kicking ash and bone out of the way, their men swept aside the debris, leaving the way clear.

Elspeth rushed over to join him, and together they watched from the bailey as his father's older, wiser face came into view, followed by Angus, Dougal and Kerwyn—all faces he recognized from his youth.

Angus, the auld sot, was still alive and wielding a sword, old as he was. Dougal looked worse for wear.

Riding tall and proud before them all, Ian MacKinnon rode straight into his bailey for the first time in eleven years.

Malcom awaited him with a little boy's glee, telltale tears stinging his eyes, but he told himself it was the sting of the wind.

His father took his measure for a long moment, then dismounted without a word. But whatever he didn't say with words, he said with his eyes as he came to embrace Malcom, clapping him hard on the back.

At fifty-four and thirty, father and son's embrace was equally as emotional as it was during their reunion two score and four years ago. And though some might deny it, there wasn't a dry eye in the house for anyone who understood the momentousness of the occasion.

Father and son, reunited. At last.

His jaw taut and chest straining with emotion, it occurred to Malcom that he was now precisely the age his father had been that day when they'd stood together embracing outside Aldergh's gates when Malcom was but six. But though his father hadn't changed much over the past ten years, his hair was as silver as his sword and his golden eyes were bracketed by crow's feet. Once again, he clapped Malcom on the back, and Malcom gulped back the lump in his throat.

"Aren't ye too auld to be wielding a sword, Da?" he teased.

The MacKinnon's amber eyes were glassy with emotion. "God's truth. I'd face the devil himself tae see ye, son, and naught but death could keep me from ye."

True to his words, he seemed unable to unhand Malcom, and Malcom endured the embrace with honest tears stinging his eyes. Finally, the elder man released him, stepping back once more to appraise him. "'Tis guid tae see ye," Malcom said, and his father nodded, pulling him back again for one more hug. This time, Malcom complained, his words muffled by his father's leather tunic. "If ye dinna unhand me, ye'll have my men teasing me like a stripling."

His father laughed hoarsely, releasing him at long last, and then wiped his face on the sleeve of his tunic.

It took him yet another moment to compose himself before he could speak, but then he said, "Where's your manners, boy? Ere ye going to let an auld mon freeze to death standing in this drafty palace, or will ye take me somewhere tae warm my bones and fill my belly?"

Malcom laughed at the complaint. It wasn't the least bit cold outside, but he well understood: His father needed a reason to mask his quivering face and hands. He smiled fondly, and said, falling easily into his Scots brogue. "What's the matter, Da? Yer auld bones getting saft in yer auld age?"

His old man laughed. "Betimes," he confessed. "Betimes." And he nodded and patted Malcom's shoulder, just a wee bit less enthusiastically as he said, "Your mother sends love, my son, bids ye come meet your brother and see your sister. Ye'd nae even recognize Liana. She's bonny as her ma. And you're brother, Alex is anxious to know ye."

Malcom's eyes crinkled with joy. In truth, he'd love to take Elspeth home to Chreagach Mhor. And remembering suddenly that she was here with him in the bailey, he turned to give his wife a smile and wave her forward, eager to introduce his father to the woman he loved.

ELSPETH STARED, knowing intuitively who it was.

No two men had ever looked more alike—barring the silver in the elder's hair, and the subtle difference in the color of their eyes. She hesitated when Malcom called her, loathe to intrude on their heartfelt moment, but he insisted, and she rushed forward, only to be enveloped into a bear hug by his father.

She choked back laughter, pinned between his arms.

"My wife," Malcom said, only after his father presumed as much.

"Ach, my boy, ye think I dinna ken? I see the way ye look at her."

Elspeth could barely breathe, much less speak, swallowed as she was by enormous arms—strong, burly arms, nearly as strong as his son's. At long last, the MacKinnon released her, and stepped back, bowing to greet her. "Tis glad I am tae meet ye, Lady Aldergh." He winked, his amber eyes glinting, with unfailing good humor, very much like his son's. "I prayed my son would get himself a good lady to warm his bones and cool his hot head. I ha'e never known a lad so cross."

MALCOM CHUCKLED, though his wife was quick to argue.

"Nay, my lord, I have never known your son to be aught but full of mirth. In truth, he has the same twinkle in his eyes as you do."

His father laughed again and peered at Malcom, winking. "'Tis guid to hear," he said. "'Tis guid to hear." And then he gave Malcom his back, wooed by Elspeth's smile and demeanor. Taking Elspeth by the hand, he bade her tell him her story, from beginning to end, promising to be only ears and Malcom watched as she led them toward the keep, enjoying the sight of his father and bride walking hand in hand. Half-drunk with joy alone, he overheard his father say, "Ye'll visit for the Yule, daughter, and I'll be hearing nae argument over the matter."

Elspeth peered back at Malcom, smiling beautifully, and he gave her a nod.

"That would be so lovely," she said, leading the burly man into their hall, and Malcom stopped, if only for a moment, to watch the two conversing as though they'd known each other an eternity. The sight of them made his heart glad, even as he realized their tribulations were far from over.

Morwen Pendragon was still out there, scheming.

Elspeth's sisters still needed saving.

And even now, the northern barons were being rallied, and the Scots clans were gathering under David's banner.

Malcom had no doubt that David of Scotia would ask him to bend the knee. But right now, for the moment, he was a man unfettered, save for the loyalty he bore his kin.

Eleven years ago, he'd wanted naught more than to leave his father's home. Today, he would be pleased enough to return. He called his steward over, asking, "How is Cora?"

"Well, m'lord. She is well. I am only grateful ye asked."

Much like his father had done, Malcom clapped the man on the back. "Do me a favor and see that our tables are laden this evening. Make certain our wine flows freely and bring up the Spanish wine. Everyone is welcome. Have the poor lad in the field returned to his parents and see he is given a proper burial. Then, after you have seen to these matters, see to your wife as I will to mine."

"Aye, m'lord," the man said, with gratitude.

"Go, then," Malcom said, and then he hurried to catch his wife, who was even now regaling his father with some overwrought tale of Malcom's heroics.

"And when did you realize you loved the fool?" his father asked jovially, sliding an arm about Elspeth's waist.

"But, of course," she said with a giggle that Malcom had

never heard before—girlish laughter that, for the instant, was free of strife. "Once I learned the name of his horse."

"Oh? And what might this be?" his father inquired.

"Merry Bells," Elspeth replied, laughing. "To this day, I cannot imagine such a name for a warrior's horse."

His father peered over his shoulder, blinking, meeting Malcom's gaze, his old amber eyes filled with some unnamed emotion. His jaw was taut, his lips in danger of quivering. But so was Malcom's. *Ach, Da, I never really left ye,* he said, never moving his lips. *My heart remains in Chreagach Mhor*

His father pulled Elspeth closer, and something about his gaze said, *I know, my son. I know.*

But perhaps it was only Malcom's imagination—a contrivance of the moment because the MacKinnon spoke not a word to him. He turned about, following his wife into the hall, laughing joyfully as he went with her hand in hand. "Yule," he said again, with great meaning.

"You can be sure I will insist," Elspeth promised.

But she wouldn't have to. So long as Malcom had breath in his body, and war did not keep him, he would move heaven and earth to be in Chreagach Mhor on the Yuletide.

NEXT IN THE DAUGHTERS OF AVALON SERIES...

A WINTER'S ROSE

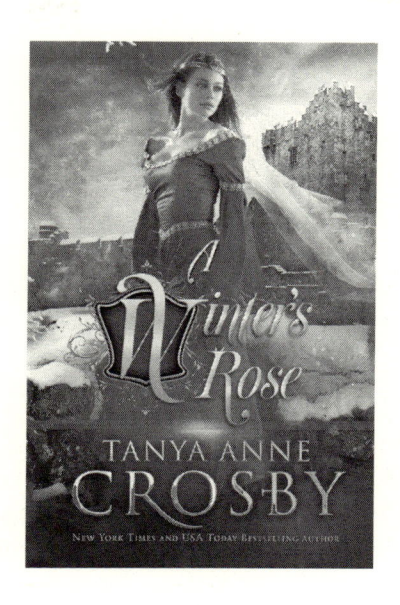

Don't miss the next installment in the exciting new Daughters of Avalon series by Tanya Anne Crosby. A Winter's Rose is now available for preorder.

Buy A Winter's Rose

CONNECTED SERIES
SERIES BIBLIOGRAPHY

Have you also read the Highland Brides and the Guardians of the Stone? While it's not necessary to read these past series to enjoy Daughters of Avalon, all three series are related with shared characters.

These books are ALSO AVAILABLE AS AUDIOBOOKS

START WITH THE MACKINNON'S BRIDE FREE

THE HIGHLAND BRIDES

The MacKinnon's Bride

Lyon's Gift

On Bended Knee

Lion Heart

Highland Song

MacKinnon's Hope

GUARDIANS OF THE STONE

Once Upon a Highland Legend

Highland Fire

Highland Steel

Highland Storm

Maiden of the Mist

ALSO CONNECTED...

Once Upon a Kiss

Angel of Fire

DAUGHTERS OF AVALON

The King's Favorite

The Holly & the Ivy

A Winter's Rose

Fire Song

Rhiannon

ALSO BY TANYA ANNE CROSBY

Daughters of Avalon
The King's Favorite

The Holly & the Ivy

A Winter's Rose

Fire Song

Rhiannon

The Highland Brides
The MacKinnon's Bride

Lyon's Gift

On Bended Knee

Lion Heart

Highland Song

MacKinnon's Hope

Guardians of the Stone
Once Upon a Highland Legend

Highland Fire

Highland Steel

Highland Storm

Maiden of the Mist

The Medievals Heroes
Once Upon a Kiss

Angel of Fire

Viking's Prize

THE IMPOSTOR SERIES
The Impostor's Kiss
The Impostor Prince

REDEEMABLE ROGUES
Happily Ever After
Perfect In My Sight
McKenzie's Bride
Kissed by a Rogue
Mischief & Mistletoe
A Perfectly Scandalous Proposal

ANTHOLOGIES & NOVELLAS
Lady's Man
Married at Midnight
The Winter Stone

ROMANTIC SUSPENSE
Speak No Evil
Tell No Lies
Leave No Trace

MAINSTREAM FICTION
The Girl Who Stayed
The Things We Leave Behind
Redemption Song
Everyday Lies

ABOUT THE AUTHOR

Tanya Anne Crosby is the New York Times and USA Today bestselling author of thirty novels. She has been featured in magazines, such as People, Romantic Times and Publisher's Weekly, and her books have been translated into eight languages. Her first novel was published in 1992 by Avon Books, where Tanya was hailed as "one of Avon's fastest rising stars." Her fourth book was chosen to launch the company's Avon Romantic Treasure imprint.

Known for stories charged with emotion and humor and filled with flawed characters Tanya is an award-winning author, journalist, and editor, and her novels have garnered reader praise and glowing critical reviews. She and her writer husband split their time between Charleston, SC, where she was raised, and northern Michigan, where the couple make their home.

For more information
Website
Email
Newsletter

Made in the USA
Middletown, DE
21 January 2023